Air Mogadishu

Gabriel Timar

A Wings ePress, Inc.
Historical Novel

Wings ePress, Inc.

Edited by: Jeanne Smith
Copy Edited by: Joan C. Powell
Executive Editor: Jeanne Smith
Cover Artist: Richard Stroud

All rights reserved

Wings ePress Books
www.wingsepress.com

Copyright © 2018 by Gabriel Timar
ISBN-13: 978-1-61309-638-3
ISBN-10: 1-61309-638-0

Published In the United States Of America

Wings ePress Inc.
3000 N. Rock Road
Newton, KS 67114

What They Are Saying About
Air Mogadishu

This is a rollicking great adventure of back in the days when Britain ruled the world and men were men and women were women and you could still tell the difference. The author obviously knows his stuff and the aviation sequences hark back to a time when flying was still an adventure that mass tourism had not discovered. Timar keeps the story moving and every page makes you want to meet Laura, sooner rather than later. What I want to know is: when will the movie be made? The story would be perfect for the silver screen.

5 Stars
—Alan Harmon - Nostalgia

Dedication

To Ilona, my love and inspiration

* * *

One

Hot, humid air hung over the harbor of Mogadishu. Even the seagulls did not bother to fly in the hundred degree heat. The white coral buildings reflected the blinding African sun. The few white shirted individuals chewing *khatt* sitting in the shadow melted into the background. In the midday heat, the colonial civil servants wearing dark suits and ties by executive order did not dare to venture onto the steaming streets of the city.

In the early nineteen thirties, Somalia, an Italian colony, acquired the Mediterranean look, although in the heart of the city the market remained vibrant and distinctly African.

The *S.S. Oleandris* tied up for two days, and the passengers landed to do some sightseeing and shopping. The twenty-one year old Laura Blake-Stanton enjoyed the scenery very much. As she had grown up in India, the heat did not bother her. She felt at home on the steaming sidewalks in the midst of the exploding kaleidoscope of color. In addition to Arabs, Asians and Chinese, most East African tribes were represented at the market.

Laura's stepfather sat at a quaint sidewalk café while she waded into the melee of the Somali businessmen.

On the middle of the square, the temporary shelves of the sidewalk vendors displayed items manufactured in the distant corners of the world. Opium, herbs, gold, Persian rugs, Burmese aphrodisiacs, Chinese ivory carvings, Russian icons, Dutch electric razors, and fake Schaffhausen watches competed for the scarce shelf space.

Laura suspected most of the merchandise was smuggled or stolen, but this was par for the course in the colonial market places. After much haggling, she bought a red silk headscarf, a *hijab*, usually worn by the willowy Somali women, allegedly the most beautiful, most desirable females of the Dark Continent.

From the middle of the square, she fought her way to the sidewalk where the better stores stood embedded in stone or coral buildings, and stepped into a silversmith's shop. First, the smiling owner started speaking Italian, but since Laura did not seem to understand, he switched to English.

"What can I sell you today, Missy?"

"I heard about a silver broche called the Mogadishu star. Have you any in stock?"

"I have many. What size do you desire?"

"Well, I don't really know. Let me see them."

From the shelf, the man took a large tray full of beautiful brooches shaped like ornate, eight-pointed stars.

"All sterling silver," the man said. "I give you good price."

Laura looked at the jewelry, touching and picking them up. Finally, she took one, about two inches in diameter.

"How much?" she asked.

"For you, Missy, but only for you, I let it go for an English pound."

Laura put it down as if the brooch burned her fingers.

"I didn't know this piece of junk was made of gold," Laura said. "I want a silver Mogadishu star."

"This is silver," said the man. "Special price, sixteen shillings, not a penny less..."

Laura had learned to bargain in India.

"I give you five," she retorted.

"I am a poor man, Missy. Silver is very expensive these days. I cannot possibly sell it for less than twelve shillings."

"Look," Laura replied, "you seem to be an honest man. Therefore, I'll offer you eight shillings for the star, but I know I am overpaying you."

"Have heart, Missy. I have two wives, many children, and a sick mother. Ten shillings is my very last price."

Laura took a deep breath, shook her head, and remarked, "It is contrary to good judgment, but since I have to return to my ship and have no time to find another silversmith, I am going to accept your ridiculous price."

She took a ten-shilling note from her purse and put it on the counter.

"It was a pleasure doing business with you, Missy. The Mogadishu star always brings good luck."

Laura pinned the brooch on the lapel of her blouse, and holding on to her purse, stepped out onto the sidewalk.

The scent of oriental spices mingled with the smell of sweating bodies. The excited cacophony of the many languages dazed her a little. Her stepfather sat at the same table with two Somali men, and engaged in animated conversation.

She waved to him, and he signaled to her. Edward Blake stood and walked to Laura.

"Did you buy everything, darling?"

"I want to buy your birthday present. Do you think I can wait until we tie up in Mombasa?"

"You should buy it here, Laura. I have an old friend in Mombasa and when we get there, we should visit him. You won't have time to go shopping. Besides, I heard that Mogadishu was much cheaper. We still have plenty of time to return to the ship."

"Okay, I will look around."

"Very well, I am going to have another cup of tea. I'll meet you here at the café in about an hour," he said.

"See you later," said Laura.

Her stepfather disappeared in the colorful crowd. She thought of buying silver cufflinks from the same silversmith who had just sold her the star. He was still sitting behind his counter, and stood, greeting her as an old friend. The bargaining was less intense, but in the end, she managed to buy exactly what she wanted.

Leaving the shop, she stopped on the sidewalk looking in the direction of the café. Her stepfather was sitting alone.

It is just like Chittagong, she thought. *The heat is oppressive, but I love the energy of the place. I think I am going to like it in East Africa.*

Laura started toward the café, but before reaching it, someone came out of nowhere and pushed her into a narrow laneway between two buildings. Strong arms grabbed her and a dirty hand clamped on her mouth.

"If you scream, I kill you," whispered the man holding her.

Although fear almost paralyzed her, she did not lose her head. She nodded, and as soon as the man's grip loosened a little, she kicked him in the shin as hard as she could, and with the heel of her shoe stomped on the man's bare foot.

The attacker roared like a wounded lion, and for a moment, his grip loosened. Laura started screaming, but somebody hit her on the head. Her knees buckled, and she could not make a sound. Someone hit her again.

~ * ~

When she regained consciousness, she felt most uncomfortable, could not breathe or move, and had a king size headache. It took some time to realize that someone had tied her hands together, and surgical tape covered her mouth. She did not see anything, but in a few minutes, her eyes adjusted to the semidarkness. Faint rays of light came in through the cracks in the heavy wooden shutters on the window.

She lay on the earthen floor of an empty room. The interior was not finished, so she noted that the walls were made of coarse white coral

I hope nobody raped me, she thought, and wiggled her hips. She felt her panties still in place, and the thought calmed her. She knew if someone had done anything to her, he would not have bothered to put the underwear back on her unconscious body.

The ship must be gone, she thought, and hopelessness started overtaking her. It took some time to begin thinking clearly. *If my grandmother at the age of ten could escape the rebellious sepoys in 1857, I could get out of this place as well. I am sure my stepfather and the police are already looking for me. I must free my hands and get out of this prison.* Slowly Laura rolled to the wall and tried to stand. As she got to her feet, the sharp coral of the wall cut into her naked arm.

I should have worn long sleeves, she thought, but the sharpness of the coral gave her an idea. *If the damned thing can slice into my skin, it could also cut the rope.*

She put the twine holding her hands together on the sharp edge of the windowsill and begun rubbing. The rope did not resist the coral very long. In a minute or so, Laura's hands were free. She removed the tape from her mouth and took a deep breath of the musty air.

How in hell do I get out of here, she asked herself, stepping to the door. It was solid and barred. *The only way out is through the window*, she thought and moved to investigate.

Surprisingly, her captors had not barred the shutters; therefore, she could open the latch. She realized the sun had already set, but she could see the ground. Figuring the window about six feet off the ground, she climbed through and jumped.

Although she landed hard, the fall did not hurt her legs. She quickly stood, dusted herself, and started walking uncertainly away from the building downhill, because she knew that it was the direction toward the sea, the harbor, and perceived safety. The streets were deserted.

At the end of the lane, she reached a road resembling a main street, but did not see any people. She took a deep breath to clear her head. Her balance improved a great deal, but the headache persisted.

"Where am I going to find a bloody policeman?" she asked herself. Looking at the building on the corner, she spied the street sign saying "Via Lido." She remembered seeing the name coming out of the fenced harbor area on their way to the market square.

At first, she did not know which way to turn. On her left in a distance, she saw some lights on a building.

It must be a hotel or a restaurant. They might direct me to a cop or the British Consulate, Laura thought and she headed for the light.

Before reaching the entrance of Hotel Lido, she noticed a motorcycle with a sidecar standing by the curb. Even though she was about fifty feet from the vehicle, she immediately recognized the machine as a Norton, identical to the bike her father owned when she was a little girl. On her vacations, Laura learned to ride it with or without the sidecar. To the horror of her mother, she occasionally took the powerful motorbike for long rides. The Norton looked like an old friend, something familiar in the sea of unknown.

An old white man with a flock of gray hair, wearing a safari suit, left the hotel carrying a cardboard box. He stepped to the bike and wanted to place the parcel into the sidecar, but lost his balance and fell forward. For a few seconds he did not move.

I wonder if he's drunk? Laura thought, but since the guy was white, according to the norms of the British expatriate society, she hurried to his aid. By the time she reached him, the man had rolled onto his back propping his upper body against the sidecar.

"May I help you?" Laura asked.

Realizing the man was semi-conscious, she knelt and tried to make him sit upright. The fellow slowly opened his eyes, looked at Laura, and said in a weak voice: "Please, give me my smelling salts. They're in a small metal container in one of my side pockets."

Laura tapped his jackets and felt the box. She took it out, flipped the lid, and held it under the man's nose.

The smelling salt had the desired effect. The man's eyes cleared, and he took a deep breath.

"Thank you," he said, trying to stand, but didn't quite make it. He staggered a few paces backward, and leaned against the stone wall of the hotel. While Laura caught him, she had a chance to look him over. He was big, lean, and muscular. Above his left breast pocket, he wore a pair of gold wings and a nametag saying *Captain Ray Madison*, and underneath a strange crest.

"May I take you home?" he asked.

"You are not in shape to drive. I'd better drive you to your house. Where do you live?" Laura asked.

"Two fifty-six Lido," he said weakly, as his knees started to buckle again.

"Lean on me," Laura said, offering her arm. Madison took it and started for the motorbike.

She noticed the pleasant, masculine scent of Madison's cologne, and did not smell alcohol on his breath. He made a valiant effort to stay upright, but without Laura's support, he did not have a chance.

"Get into the sidecar," said Laura and using all her strength, helped the man to take his place.

Apparently, he wanted to say something, but the words stuck in his throat, and he passed out again.

Fortunately, the keys were in the ignition, and Laura could turn it on. She pumped some gas into the carburetor and kick-started the motor. The engine caught at the first attempt, and started with a healthy roar. Sitting on the bike, her skirt slipped all the way up, exposing her ivory-colored, well-shaped legs and muscular thighs.

I hope the locals are not going to see me like this, she thought while putting the bike into gear and slowly releasing the clutch. The powerful machine rolled forward.

Laura held the speed down because she had to keep checking the house numbers. The Via Lido appeared to be an exclusive residential area; some buildings had several hundred feet of frontage. The number 256 was almost the last building. Laura turned onto the driveway, revved the engine and pressed the horn.

The heavy wooden gate opened slowly, and a young Somali wearing a white uniform stood there.

"Get Memsahib," Laura shouted as she drove the bike to the courtyard and brought it to a halt at the stairs leading to the patio. She stopped the engine, jumped off the bike, and went over to the unconscious man. He was alive, but the next whiff of the vile smelling concoction in the small metal box had negligible effect on him.

A big fat Somali woman appeared from the servants' quarters. Among the three of them, they managed to take Madison from the sidecar, carry him into the bedroom, and unceremoniously dump him on the bed.

The woman took a little gauze package from the drawer of the nightstand, hit it with the bottom of a thick glass, and held it under the nose of the man. He convulsed.

"He is going to be all right," she said. "Ali is going to stay with him and give him his medicine. Come to the patio, Missy, and I'll brew a cuppa for you."

"Thank you," Laura said, and followed the woman.

"Thanks for bringing the captain home. I keep telling him not to go anywhere alone without his medicine, but he doesn't listen. I'll get your tea in a minute. Do you want some biscuits?"

"Yes, thank you very much," Laura replied, realizing she had not had anything to eat or drink since the morning.

The housekeeper lumbered away in the direction of the kitchen at the other end of the building.

The strength left Laura's body. The tea arrived with three small, buttered English tea biscuits. Contrary to her expectation, she had plenty of strength to lift the cup and wolf down the biscuits. The hot tea relaxed her a little, and she started feeling alive again.

Suddenly, the bedroom door opened, and the captain appeared. He did not walk steadily, but seemed conscious.

"I am most grateful to you for picking me up from the gutter. It was stupid of me to forget my medicine. I am Ray Madison."

"I am Laura Blake," she replied. "It was no trouble at all. I enjoyed driving a Norton again."

He sat and poured himself a cup of tea.

"Tell me, Laura, where do you live? I am going to send Ali to inform your father or husband where you are and they could send a car for you. Unfortunately, I am not in good enough shape to drive."

At that point, Laura's self-control suddenly vanished. She burst out crying, but quickly forced herself to calm down.

"I am not from Mogadishu, sir. We were traveling on board the *S.S. Oleandris*, and the ship left without me. My stepfather must be worried sick."

"How in the name of God did you miss the ship?"

"Local thugs kidnapped me, but I managed to escape. I wanted to find a policeman."

"They are never around when you need them," interrupted Madison. "I am sure they are already looking for you. Let me call the central police station."

"I am most grateful, Mr. Madison."

"Please call me Ray. It makes me feel younger."

Madison went into the house. Laura heard him talking on the telephone: "This is Ray Madison. May I speak to the desk sergeant? ...Yes, thank you ...Very well, Sergeant...I would like to report finding a missing person ... She is Miss Laura Blake...It is impossible. Please check again...Can you check with the harbor police and the other precincts?...Yes, of course, call me when you find out anything. My number is seven-two-oh...Thank you, Sergeant, thank you very much."

He hung up, came to the patio again, sat and declared: "Policemen are stupid. Can you imagine the desk sergeant trying to tell me that your stepfather never reported you missing? I told him to check with the harbor police and the other precincts. He'll call when he learns anything. Don't worry, Laura, we'll find your stepfather."

"I am most grateful," she said.

"Let me call the Croce," Ray said and stood.

"What is that?"

"Hotel Croce Del Sud, it is the best hotel in Mogadishu. All expatriates stay there. What is the name of your stepfather?"

"Edward, Edward Blake," Laura replied.

Ray went inside again, but this time Laura did not hear the conversation because she fell asleep. The noise of Ray closing the door woke her.

"I do not understand. He is not registered in the Croce."

"How about the British Consulate?"

"We do not have one in Mogadishu," Ray replied. "We had an honorary consul for a while, but he quit and returned to England."

"What am I going to do?" Laura asked with desperation in her voice.

"You are going to move into my wife's room until we sort this mess out."

"Won't she mind?"

"I am sure she won't. You see she died a year ago, and I just could not force myself to change anything in her room, or give away her things. I still expect Ellen to walk in and tell me her death was just a big joke," said Ray with a teardrop appearing in the corner of his eye.

"You loved her very much, did you?"

"Yes, even though we were married for only six years."

"Have you any children?"

"Not anymore. My son died when he was two years old."

"I am sorry."

"I am a Jonah," Madison said sadly. "I lose everybody I love. Now it is better if we both go to bed and get a good rest. We'll have a hard day coming up."

"Thank you very much."

"I am the one to be grateful. Without you I may have died. Make yourself at home, and use Ellen's clothes as your own. She was about the same height, but a little heavier than you."

"I appreciate it very much, Ray. I wish I could somehow—"

"Hush," he interrupted. "Tomorrow morning, you are going to get up at six, and put one of my wife's flight suits on. After breakfast get the motorbike and drive me to the harbor."

"Why?"

"If your stepfather does not turn up by the morning, I must assume he boarded the ship without you. We are going to send a radio message to the *Oleandris* letting him know you are all right."

"Thank you very much."

"Don't thank me, young lady, you are going to work for it. From now on, as long as you are here, I am going to make you earn your keep. If I have to go somewhere, you are going to drive the bike."

"Are you serious? I love driving the Norton."

"You could even come with me on the regular mail run."

"Are you a postman?"

Ray laughed.

"In the strictest sense of the word, I am. I fly the mail to all the major centers in Somalia. You see, there are no roads in this godforsaken colony. On the way back, I pick up whatever they want to send to Mogadishu."

"Could I really go up in an aircraft with you?"

"Of course, but you have to make sure to have my medicine and smelling salts ready if I start feeling ill."

"Why do you keep flying if your health does not permit it?"

"I'll tell you about it tomorrow. You had a full day. I think you should go to bed and rest up. As I was saying, we'll have a hard day coming up," said Ray. "Let me show you the room."

He stood and invited Laura into the house.

The inside was cool and very pleasant.

"This is an old stone building," Ray explained. "The colonial administration built it many years ago."

"It is almost the same as the one I grew up in India."

"It could be a colonial office standard," Ray said and opened the door of his wife's bedroom.

The sight stunned Laura. It appeared to be a carbon copy of her mother's sleeping quarters in India. She just stood there motionless.

"Anything wrong?" Ray asked.

"No, this room is just like my mother's was. I bet I know the layout of the bathroom as well."

"Feel yourself at home. Good night, Laura," said Ray, and walking rather uncertainly, he left.

Testing her memory, Laura opened the closet. It looked just like her mother's. Even the low wattage electric bulb burning on the ceiling to keep the fungi and the molds away was the same.

She undressed and took the one-pound note out of her left shoe. The money reminded her of Granny. Laura could still hear her voice: "A girl must be always careful. If you haven't any money, you are at the mercy of others. Always carry a pound in your shoe."

Good old Granny, Laura thought. She also suggested carrying a dagger, but it would have been taking independence too far. Come to think of it, a weapon would have come in handy this morning."

She instinctively knew where Mrs. Madison kept her lingerie and took out a nightgown.

"It is just like mother's," she said with a heavy sigh.

Laura undressed and entered the bathroom. Standing under the shower, she let the lukewarm water run down on her ivory colored body. Small rivulets ran between her breasts causing a tingling sensation.

If I were a couple of inches taller and my breasts two sizes larger, I would be a really beautiful woman, she thought, stepping out from under the shower and looking at the mirror. She put some iodine on the scars on her arm and went to bed.

Ever since she had been a little girl, she always said an unusual evening prayer. She picked up the habit at the age of ten when she arrived in England from India and spent a few days with her grandmother before going to the boarding school. On the first evening at eight o'clock sharp, she said to Granny, "Mommy always makes me go to bed at eight-thirty. First, I brush my teeth, comb my hair, and then say my Hail Marys. It takes twenty-five minutes. May I retire?"

"Most certainly," Granny replied. "I haven't said any Hail Marys since the sepoy rebellion in 1857."

"Why?" Laura asked, rather perturbed.

"Well, I was ten years old and hid in the most unlikely places. I had to stay quiet."

"Did you forget your evening prayer?"

"No, I just talked to the Lord, telling him what I did during the day and thanked him for helping me staying alive. He hears too many Hail Marys."

From that day on, Laura suspended the Hail Marys and when she went to bed, had a chat with the Almighty. This day was no different.

Thanks for seeing me through this day, Lord. I don't know what I did to deserve being kidnapped, but it is all right. I'm sure you have a plan. Perhaps you needed someone to save Ray's life, and I happened to be in the vicinity. I don't know, but I accept your decision, whatever your reasons might have been. Good night, my Lord.

She closed her eyes and fell asleep in a matter of seconds.

Two

Laura woke up on her own. As the kidnappers had taken her watch, she just guessed the time. She got out of the bed, threw off the sweat soaked nightgown, and stepped to the window. Pulling the curtain, she saw the dark, well-kept garden and the slim orange line of the rising sun on the horizon. As a sun worshipper, she wanted to go to the garden and greet the rising sun naked. However, in the colonies of the British Empire, suntanned women were frowned upon.

By the time Amina, the housekeeper, got around to knock on her door, she was wide-awake. As Laura stepped to the closet, she wondered whether Ray had gone to his wife's bedroom, or she visited him for their lovemaking sessions. *However, as he is ill, I do not want him dying in my arms I'd visit him, even though he is as old as my stepfather*, she thought. Looking at Mrs. Madison's wardrobe hanging in the closet, she found identical, lightweight, white cotton coveralls with red zippers in the front and over the pockets. *They are ideal for riding a motorbike in the tropics*, she thought.

After having a bath and combing her long auburn hair, she tied it up with a white ribbon, brushed her teeth with a brand new toothbrush found in the cabinet, put on a flight suit with a pair of thick white socks, pinned on her Mogadishu star for luck, and slipped on a pair of white tennis shoes.

She ventured onto the patio. "Good morning, Missy," said the Somali woman setting the table for breakfast. "How do you like your eggs?"

"Scrambled please, without salt," Laura replied.

"Two or three eggs?"

"Three if you don't mind."

"Please sit down, the captain is coming in a minute."

Taking her place at the table, she felt like she was at home in India. Even the smells were the same.

Ray appeared, walking steadily and in good spirits. He wore a khaki flight suit similar to Laura's, had the gold wings pinned on his chest, looking healthy, strong, and sure of himself. The signs of yesterday's malady had disappeared. His musk cologne aroused Laura. She wondered if he put it on to impress her, or he always wore the cologne.

"Good morning, Laura," he said.

"Good morning, Ray. I hope you had a good night's sleep."

"I did. It is nice to have company at breakfast. I hate eating alone." He rang the little bell at the table, and Amina appeared with a tray carrying the first course.

"I always have fruit salad with every meal," Ray said. "I hope you don't mind."

"Not at all. I'm sure it is going to be delicious."

The fruit salad tasted very good. She considered asking for a second helping, but Ray read her mind.

"You'd better have another plateful, young lady," he said. "We are going to have a long day and only a couple of sandwiches to keep us from starving to death."

After breakfast, Ray returned to his bedroom and came back carrying a black leather satchel.

"Let's go," he said.

"Not until I have made sure I have your smelling salts and medicine in my pocket," Laura said.

"You're right, of course. How silly of me," replied Ray. He returned to the bedroom to pick up the medications, came out, and handed them to Laura.

"That's better," she said, and put the bottles in her pocket. "Where are we going?"

"First, we go to the harbor master's radio operator and then to the airfield."

"Were you serious yesterday when you said I might get a chance to fly with you?"

"I was dead serious," Ray replied. "However, if you are afraid..."

"I am not afraid. In fact, I am dying to have a chance to ride in an aircraft."

"I am glad to hear that. Let us make a deal: you drive the Norton, and I fly the plane."

Laura looked over the bike while Ray took his place in the sidecar. The tires were okay, the chain tight, and the tank almost full. She charged the carburetor and kicked the starter. The engine caught at the first try.

"This is a well-maintained machine," she remarked.

"The most expensive mechanics in Mogadishu look after it."

"Which way do I go?" Laura asked.

"Turn right on Lido and go straight until you reach the harbor entrance. Don't go too fast and watch for the kids," Ray said.

The warning about the children surprised her, but after the first few hundred meters, Laura understood what Ray meant. The Somali children playing by the side of the road suddenly darted in front of the motorbike and crossed the road. Laura stood on the brakes and managed to clear one child by a couple of meters.

"The little fool," she remarked. "We could have killed him."

Ray just smiled. "You made him look bad in the eyes of his friends," he said.

"Why?"

"You slowed down. Their favorite game is to run across a motor vehicle as close to it as possible. The greatest feat is to touch the hood of a car. The drivers know it and never brake for a child," Ray explained.

"What happens if I hit one of them?"

"You won't. These kids are experts. They have the timing down pat. I have been driving here for quite a few years, but never heard of anybody hitting a child."

"There he goes," replied Laura as another boy darted in front of the bike. Although she throttled back, she did not hit the brake. The kid came awfully close to being trampled by the motorbike.

At the gate of the harbor, they turned in. The guards saluted Ray, and he waved to the uniformed harbor police officers.

"Park at the white building over there. We are going to see the radio operator," he said.

Laura killed the engine. She followed Ray into the building to the third floor, and entered a small room cluttered with radio equipment. A young Somali wearing headphones sat at the Morse key.

"Hello, skipper," he said with a big smile and took off the headset. "What can I do for you, Mr. Madison?"

"Can you contact the *S.S. Oleandris* for me?"

"Not right now," he said. "I have many messages ahead of yours, but I am sure I'll be able to reach her by ten."

"Please do and keep their reply for me. I am going to pick it up on my way home. I'd say it would be about five o'clock."

"Hassan will relieve me at three. I'll tell him to put the message in your box."

"Very kind of you," Ray said. "Please write out the message."

Ray looked at Laura and asked: "Do you want to write the message or should I?"

"I think you know better what to say." Ray nodded, picked up a telegram form, took a pencil from his pocket and composed the message. When he finished writing, he put the paper in front of Laura.

"I think this will be clear enough."

The message read: To the Master of the *S.S. Oleandris*. Kindly inform passenger Edward Blake that his stepdaughter Laura is safe in Mogadishu. Kindly advise how to reunite them. Signed Captain Raymond Madison, D.S.M., D.F.C. Director, Air Mogadishu.

Laura read the note and remarked: "I am sure it will serve the purpose."

"Please send this, my friend. The poor man must be worried sick about his stepdaughter," Ray said to the radio operator.

"I will send it as soon as I can, Mr. Madison."

"Thank you, Ali. I'll pick up his reply when we return from Kismayo. See you later." They left the radio room.

"Learning that you are okay should be a relief to your stepfather. I am sure of it."

"Thank you very much."

"Don't thank me. Any employer should do that for a new staff member," said Ray with a smile.

They got back onto the bike and headed further to the north. When they passed the last house, Laura noticed the red and white windsock hanging limply on a pole.

"That is the airfield," said Ray, pointing ahead. "Turn left here."

While riding on the narrow, sandy road, she passed the dunes and saw the airfield. She noticed a little shack, a hangar, and a shining, silver-colored airplane standing on the concrete apron.

"It is beautiful," said Laura with admiration in her voice. She had never seen anything more attractive than the plane. The aircraft did not strike her as a piece of machinery. It was a living, breathing, sensual being.

"It is one of my aircraft, a Junkers F13. This one we call *Cornwall*, named for my birthplace. We are taking this plane today."

They drove to the hangar. Looking inside Laura saw two other identical aircraft.

"The one on the left is *Calabrese* and the one on the right is *York*. Those were the birthplaces of my partners," Ray said.

"Do you have partners? Do they also fly?"

"No, I do not have partners anymore. We bought out Jim, the Yorkshire man. Aldo, the Italian, is on leave or disappeared. It is a long story. I'll tell you after we come back."

Two young Somali men came to meet them. Both wore blue flight suits and had different tools sticking out of their pockets.

"Laura, meet Deria and Abdullahi, the two highest paid Somali technicians. This is Miss Laura, fellows."

"It is a pleasure to meet you, Miss Laura," said Abdullahi. He had almost no accent.

"Laura is flying with me today," said Ray. "Did the posties bring the bags?"

"They are all on board, Captain. The *Cornwall* is fuelled and checked," reported Abdullahi.

"How are the others?"

"*York* is ready to fly, but the fuel pump on *Calabrese* is acting up."

"Very well, guys. Fill up the bike and check it over."

"I'll take care of it, Captain," said Deria.

"Okay, see you later." They walked to the plane, and Ray opened the door. The interior was spacious. Behind the cockpit bulkhead, the plane had four leather-covered seats. The mailbags were on the floor, kept in place by a light fishing net clipped to steel rings on the wall. Ray led the way to the cockpit.

"Laura, please make sure the nets are properly fastened. If we hit a little turbulence, I wouldn't like the mailbags walking all over the plane."

Laura checked the net. She found it in place, fastened, and followed Ray.

"You should sit on the right side. As long as you are in the cockpit, your seatbelt must be fastened," Ray said.

Squeezing by Ray, her left arm touched his shoulder. The contact sent an electrifying shockwave through Laura's body. She took her place, fixed the belt, and feasted her eyes on the many different dials, switches, and levers. However, when she concentrated on the control panel, she suddenly forgot about her momentary infatuation with Ray. She hardly noticed Deria walking up to the side of the plane, ahead of the cockpit, and fitting a crank-bar in place.

She noticed Ray looking at a small tab on the instrument panel reading whatever was on it. He looked up. "This is the pre-flight checklist. I must make sure everything is set before Deria starts cranking."

"I see." After a while, Ray stuck his hand out on the window and made a circling motion with his index finger. Almost instantly, the propeller started to turn. It accelerated, and when the engine caught, Ray immediately opened the throttle a little.

"Although the chocks will prevent the plane from moving, you must keep your feet on the brakes."

By this time, the engine purred like a kitten, and Ray slowly opened the throttle a little more.

"Are we waiting for something?" Laura asked innocently.

"We must warm up the engine properly. A cold engine conking out on you in the middle of the takeoff would be most embarrassing. Watch this one," he said, pointing at one of the dials. "This is the temperature gauge. When the needle reaches the green, we can start the takeoff."

Her eyes glued to the temperature gauge, Laura willed it to climb into the green.

"Here we go," said Ray and signaled to Deria.

"What was that signal?"

"I just told him to remove the chocks," Ray said and pushed the throttle forward. The plane started to move slowly. Laura's eyes jumped from dial to dial noting the readings while she watched what Ray was doing.

"Now we taxi to the end of the runway, turn into the wind and open the throttle."

"I can't wait for lift-off," she said.

"Patience, my dear, patience."

At the end of the runway, Ray turned the plane around.

"How did you do that?" Laura asked.

"I braked one of the wheels with these pedals," he replied. "It works like this: if you want to right, brake the right wheel."

"I see."

Ray opened the throttle, the engine roared, and the plane started its takeoff. Laura's eyes shifted rapidly from the dials to the horizon and back.

"Are you sure you have never flown?" Ray asked.

"What makes you think so? I have only seen aircraft in pictures," she replied.

"You are behaving like a pilot. Watching the gauges and trying to see where you are going, is the way pilots must behave."

Ray pushed the yoke forward a little. The plane lifted its tail and started accelerating further. He pulled back the yoke, and the *Cornwall* lifted off the runway.

"Fantastic," said Laura.

Ray throttled back, but the plane kept climbing.

"When we reach a thousand meters, we'll turn south and follow the coastline to Brava."

Laura kept watching Ray. Although the man's body infatuated her, she tried to memorize his movements. For a few moments, the teacher and master of his trade fascinated her. She could hardly take her eyes off the scenery. The countryside slipping by below, the sky above and the healthy roar of the engine gave her the feeling of being on the top of the world. She hardly noticed Ray turning the plane to the south. The sound of the engine changed a little, but it did not bother her.

"Brava is less than an hour from here," said Ray. "You can recognize it by its church steeple. It is the highest on the coast. When we come in, you'll see the fishermen on the beach."

They flew in silence for a while. Suddenly, Ray turned to Laura. "Do you want to drive?"

The question came as a shock. "Aren't you afraid that I will crash the plane?"

Ray smiled and remarked, "Not as long as I am here. Just put your hand on the wheel and your feet on the rudder. Just feel the way I move it."

Laura tried to absorb the movements made by Ray as much as possible. It was almost sensual. She felt becoming one with the aircraft, and since Ray held the controls, she united with him completely, body and soul.

"There is the church steeple," Ray said. "Now, we turn and line up the runway."

The gentle moves of the controls flowed through Laura's arms and legs. She did not know if the union with Ray made her remember every move he made, or her actions were governed by insatiable thirst for control. She felt she could copy manipulating the controls like Ray did, and guide the movements of the plane. Through the window, Laura clearly saw the runway, the windsock indicating the strength and the direction of the wind.

Ray pulled back the throttle, and the *Cornwall* started losing altitude. The surface came closer rapidly. When Ray pulled back on the yoke, the horizon seemed to rise, and the landscape suddenly closed in. The aircraft landed with a slight bump.

"Welcome to Brava," he said as the plane slowed. He turned the airplane slightly, and they rolled to a shack with the thatch roof. Although they halted, Ray let the propeller turn over slowly. "I never stop the engine in Brava," he said. "We have plenty of fuel to take us to Kismayo. We'll refuel there."

Someone opened the rear door of the plane, and a Somali man entered. He came to the cockpit and greeted Ray cordially.

"Nice to see you again, Captain. How are you?"

"I am well, Asif. How is the family?"

"Very well. May I have the bill of lading?"

"Of course," replied Ray, and he extracted a sheaf of papers from his satchel. "I have three bags for you."

"I see. Two of them go to Merca, and the third bag is for us."

"That's right, it says so on my summary sheet," Ray replied. "How many do you have for me?"

"Just one bag. It has to go to Mogadishu."

"Very well, Asif. See you next week."

"Bye, Captain," said the man and withdrew quietly. Ray turned his head to check if the nets were in place. "Okay, we are going to take off now."

"Are you going to read the pre-flight checklist again?" Laura asked.

"Yes, I must. I do not trust my memory."

The takeoff seemed no different from the one in Mogadishu. When they reached the altitude of a thousand meters, Ray kept the plane level, adjusted the throttle and a few other things on the control panel, making the sound of the engine change a little.

"We are going to hit the Merca low," he said. "The air is always choppy in this area."

As if to punctuate his words, the plane started bucking. First, the nose went down and the left wing dipped, but Ray quickly tamed the aircraft.

"Now we have clear sailing all the way to Kismayo. Do you want to drive?"

"Yes," said Laura with excitement in her voice.

"Okay, take it," rapped Ray. As soon as he saw Laura holding the wheel, he let go and took his feet off the rudder pedals. It was an exhilarating, sensual feeling to control the aircraft, the machine reacting to the slightest movement of the controls. *I am only a weak female, but I rule over a powerful brute like this plane,* Laura thought with satisfied pride as she experienced being the lord and master for the first time in her life.

"How do you like flying?"

"It is fantastic," replied Laura. "I'd love to learn."

"Most likely you would be an excellent pilot. However, the training would take at least six months. Apart from steering the aircraft, you must learn a lot of engineering, meteorology, and the navigation techniques before you could call yourself a pilot. It takes as much effort as a university degree, perhaps more, since flight technology is changing rapidly," explained Ray. "I have many books about aeronautical engineering."

"I don't know if there is an airport in Dar es Salaam and someone who could teach me flying," Laura said.

"Is that the place you were heading for?" Ray asked.

"Yes, the Colonial Office assigned my stepfather to Tanganyika as Chief Administrator. We were on our way to Dar es Salaam when I missed the boat."

"Was your mother on board too?"

"No. She died a couple of years ago."

"I'm sorry," said Ray.

Laura enjoyed keeping the plane flying straight and level. Occasionally she had to make minor adjustments to keep the altimeter needle exactly on the thousand-meter mark and the course set on the gyrocompass within one degree.

After about two hours of flying, a large town appeared on the coast.

"This is Kismayo," announced Ray. "Let me take control because we have to make a few turns to line up to the runway. It is well hidden by the vegetation."

Laura regretted having to give up control of the aircraft, but kept her hand on the yoke to feel the moves Ray made. She managed to maintain the union with him through the controls of the plane.

"Do you see the yellow house over there with the large silo?" Ray asked.

"Yes."

"Well, the runway starts about a kilometer beyond that. We should make our approach on the course of exactly oh-one at the altitude of five hundred meters. Over the silo, just cut the engine, and you'll line up correctly, hitting the end of the runway," Ray explained and started the landing procedure.

They were down to about two hundred meters when Laura saw the runway. It was much shorter than the one at Brava. The *Cornwall* landed with an almost imperceptible bump, rolled to a halt at the terminal building, somewhat larger and more elaborate than the one in Brava. Ray stopped the engine, but did not leave the cockpit. A man with a donkey cart appeared carrying two steel drums and came up to the plane.

'Hello," Ray said through the window. "How are you?"

"Very well, Captain," the man said and fitted the hose to the fueling port. He started working a hand pump and let the fuel flow into the tanks of the *Cornwall*. In a short while, he stopped pumping and came to the window. "Two hundred and twenty liters, Captain," Lupo said, handing a piece of paper to Ray.

He signed the receipt and put the copy into the black leather satchel wedged in between the two seats.

"See you next week, Lupo. Give my regards to Demona. I hope she'll get better."

"Who is Demona? His wife?" asked Laura.

"No. She is the regular donkey that pulls the fuelling cart. She had a foal and did not want to come back to work so soon. Donkeys can be stubborn, you know."

"Just like me," said Laura.

They had ten bags of mail for the town and loaded six for Mogadishu. Lupo cranked the engine and it started with a loud bang. Ray played a little with the throttle as one would do with a motorcycle, and started the takeoff. Including the refueling, the plane stayed on the ground only twenty minutes.

The takeoff differed from the one in Brava and Mogadishu, but Laura kept in touch with the pilot's moves, and thought she could copy Ray's movements. After they were airborne, Ray took the plane up to a thousand meters and following the coastline, headed for Mogadishu.

"You'd better have your tea and the sandwich," he suggested and took out a small lunchbox from his satchel. "There is one for you and one for me."

Laura took the sandwich, and from the thermos bottle, she poured a small cup of tea. The food and the hot drink revitalized her.

"Take the wheel while I have my snack," said Ray.

After another hour of letting Laura control the plane, Ray took it back just minutes before they hit the Merca low. After taming the aircraft, he handed the wheel to her and relaxed in his chair. They passed the church steeple of Brava, and Laura knew the end of their journey was near

"Mogadishu coming up, Ray."

He did not move. "Ray," she shouted. "Wake up!"

He stirred, opened his eyes, and asked, "What's the problem? Is the house on fire?"

"No. I was just too engrossed in flying and did not notice you dozing off. When you did not answer, I thought you passed out."

"Have no fear, Laura. I have quite a few miles left in me. However, since this is Mogadishu, why don't you try lining up the runway?"

"Do you mean I have to make the turns?"

"You have to start sometime. What's wrong with the present?"

"Yes, sir," she replied and started the turn. Somehow, she lined up the runway and looked at Ray.

"It wasn't perfect, but you did it. Now let me take over."

After landing, the mechanics unloaded the mailbags and placed them on the waiting post office truck.

"How did the plane behave, Captain?" asked Abdullahi after the truck left the airport.

"She was okay, but tomorrow I'll take the *York* for the inland run."

"We'll have her ready and fuelled for you by seven o'clock. We'll let the posties load the mailbags."

"Very well, fellows. See you tomorrow," said Ray, and with Laura headed for the motorbike.

"Here, you are the captain," he said as he climbed into the sidecar. They reached the radio room of the harbor office by four thirty. Hassan, the duty operator, stood and extended his hand:

"Nice to see you, Captain. Did you come for your message?" he asked, shaking the pilot's hand.

"That's the general idea."

"Well, the news is good," Hassan said and handed over the form to Ray. "I just got it a few minutes ago."

Ray looked at the paper, but didn't say anything, just stuffed it into his pocket.

"Thanks, Hassan. I might visit you guys tomorrow morning again. Let's go, Laura."

He stayed quiet until they reached the house. As they entered, Ray headed for the patio. He sat down and told Amina to bring him two whiskeys.

"Sit down, Laura, sit down," he said and patted the couch next to him. "I have bad news, my dear, and I want you to have a strong drink to restart your heart in case it stops."

"Why? What's the problem?"

"Read this," he said taking the message from his pocket. "I don't understand it."

The message read: To Captain Madison, Air Mogadishu, from the Master of the *Oleandris*.Miss Laura Blake-Stanton and her stepfather, Edward Blake are on board the *Oleandris*. Captain Winston Warren.

The world closed in on Laura. She did not know what to say, just looked at Ray. With tears filling her eyes she said: "Believe me, I am Laura Blake-Stanton. Someone is impersonating me. I don't understand what is happening."

Ray put his arms around Laura trying to console her, and it seemed he immediately succeeded. Safe in his strong arms, Laura pressed her body against his. She felt the desire swelling in Ray, but she knew he was not going to start anything.

"I think it is a misunderstanding," Ray said. "The radio operators make all kinds of strange mistakes. Look at this message. If Hassan just left three letters out, it might have an entirely different meaning. It should read like this: *Miss Laura Blake-Stanton and her stepfather, Edward Blake are NOT on board the* Oleandris," said Ray, as he put a little distance between himself and Laura.

"What am I going to do?" Laura asked.

"Nothing, my dear. Have a good rest, and tomorrow morning we will send another message before taking the inland run. When we come back, Hassan will let us know where your stepfather got off the ship."

"I hope you are right, Ray."

"Now, let us have a drink for the successful completion of the Kismayo run," said Ray reaching for the whiskey.

"I'll drink to that," replied Laura and had the first shot of whiskey in her life. Deep down she was concerned about the message, but her first experience of flying overshadowed the error in the message from the *Oleandris*. She had a shower and put on one of Mrs. Madison's dresses. She picked a dark blue, rather revealing outfit, accentuating her small waist.

I know it is unfair, but I hope he will realize that I am a different woman, she thought.

Although Ray did not comment on Laura's changed appearance, the look in his eyes betrayed that he appreciated her superb figure. Laura ate heartily, because the flying and the nerve-racking news had taken a lot out of her. They sat on the patio for a while. Laura asked many questions about the different instruments on Ray's aircraft.

He patiently explained everything to the satisfaction of her inquiring mind. Obviously, he treated Laura as a student pilot, but also noticed her being a woman.

"You'd better go to bed, Laura, because tomorrow will be another long day."

"You're right. Good night, Ray. And thanks for everything," she said.

In the safety of her own room, Laura undressed, put the dress on a hanger, discarded her nightgown, and went to bed naked. After turning out the lights, she prayed to the Almighty: *Thank you for the wonderful day, my Lord. Forgive my carnal desire for Ray, but you planted the craving in me. I do not think it would be sinful to go to bed with him, because any action motivated by love cannot be sinful. I thank you for letting me find my vocation. I want to be a pilot. Please help me, and don't punish the poor radio operator for making the mistake in taking down the message. Good night, my God."*

Three

Laura slept like a log. She awoke to Amina's thumping on the door. Although Laura could have slept some more, the chance of flying again perked her up. She dressed swiftly and went to the patio, beating Ray to the table only by a couple of minutes.

"Good morning, Laura. Did you sleep well?"

"Yes, I did. I was very tired."

"Flying does it to you all the time. Although it isn't physically tiring, the strain hits you when you get back to terra firma."

"I never thought a few hours of holding the yoke would wear me out so much," she said.

"Wait till we fly the northern run. It is too damn long."

After breakfast, they took the Norton to the airfield, but stopped at the harbor's radio room. This time Ray sent the following message:

To the Master of the S.S. Oleandris. Kindly confirm the presence of passenger Edward Blake and his stepdaughter on board of the Oleandris.

Captain Raymond Madison, D.S.M., D.F.C. Director, Air Mogadishu

"This should do it. I am sure Hassan made a mistake copying the message yesterday. My query does not cast a shadow on his ability as a radio operator," said Ray.

"Staying in the good graces of Hassan is a good idea. We never know when we need a favor of him," said Laura, starting the Norton.

"You should be a diplomat," remarked Ray.

The *York* was parked at the same place as the *Cornwall* had been the day before, and the mailbags were already on board. Abdullahi handed the bills of lading to Ray. After he stuffed the papers into his satchel, he asked, "Is there anything else?"

"Yes, sir. Postmaster Panetta was here yesterday after you left. He wants to talk to you before you take off to the north on Friday."

"I'll wait for him," Ray said. "Have you any idea of what he wants?"

"Not really. He was sniffing around the hangar wanting to know how many operational aircraft we had."

"What did you tell him?"

"I told him we had three, although one was being serviced."

"That reminds me: what is the status of the fuel pump on the *Calabrese*?"

"It is all right now. One of the gears wore out, but Deria made a new one and we replaced it. We tested the fuel pump last night, and it's as good as new. We'll install it this morning, and test the damn thing again."

"Okay. Just to make sure Mr. Panetta could not call you a liar, I'll take the *Calabrese* on Friday," Ray said and turned to Laura. "Let's go."

Being near to Ray and the scent of his cologne filled Laura with desire. She fought the feeling, realizing she had other important things to do and learn. Ray started the engine and ran through the pre-flight checklist.

"This is the worst route," he said. "It is much longer than the flight to Kismayo, and we have to land and take off several times. We stop the engine at Galcaio and refuel."

They turned into the wind, and Ray opened the throttle.

"Take the map from my bag and set the bearing to Bulo Burti on the gyrocompass," said Ray.

Reaching into the bag, Laura spread the chart over her knees. The old British Admiralty map showed their route drawn with pencil. Apparently, Ray wrote the course, the distance, and the approximate flying time on the line connecting the towns with colored pen.

Like a pro, Laura set the course on the gyrocompass.

Following the takeoff, they climbed to fifteen hundred meters under the clear blue skies of Africa. Ray made a small course correction, turning the plane in the right direction.

Laura checked the map. After Baidoa they planned to fly to Beled Uen and on to Galcaio. The flight plan called for another stop on the coast in Obbia. She quickly added up the distances, and found it almost twice as long as the flight they had taken yesterday.

"You said we'll refuel in Galcaio," said Laura.

"Yes. A guy named Amir is supplying the fuel. I am going to pay him today for the fuel he supplied last month. The highest expense in running an airline is the cost of fuel," Ray explained.

"How about the planes? Were they expensive?"

"Not really. We actually got them as gifts."

"The donor had to be very generous."

Ray laughed and said, "It was not so simple. After the war the Royal Flying Corps demobilized my squadron, and most of us were looking for some work flying."

"I thought you were a career officer."

"No. I graduated as a structural engineer a few years before the war broke out. I immediately volunteered for the army. When I got my officer's commission, on a friend's suggestion I volunteered for the Royal Flying Corps. I served in France, ending the war as a squadron leader with thirty-one confirmed kills. Anyway, when the R.A.F. demobilized me, I met a guy looking for mercenaries to fly for Kolchak, the White Russian admiral in Crimea. Jim Thorpe and I signed up, but getting to Russia turned out very difficult."

"Why?"

"We traveled on the Orient Express as far as Istanbul, but for a while we were stuck. After a couple of weeks, we took a Romanian tramp steamer to Odessa. By the time we got there, the admiral already had two pilots: a Russian and an Italian. For aircraft, they had five old German Albatross fighters. They were good planes, but we did not have mechanics and lacked parts. Nevertheless, we kept flying them, attacking the Reds on the ground. The enemy did not have any aircraft, but still managed to hit our planes often with their rifles and machine guns. Compared to the war in France, it was less dangerous. However, we knew if the Reds captured us, we would be shot on the spot."

"I heard they did not take prisoners."

"The whites did not treat them gently either. They executed every captured Red soldier. It was a brutal war. Anyway, one day a ship arrived and unloaded four brand new, dual control Junkers F13 aircraft. The admiral told us to use them as bombers and trainers. However, we had to assemble the planes first. It was a big job, but we managed somehow."

"Did you use the planes to bomb the enemy?" Laura asked.

"We tried it a few times, but the raids were rather inefficient. The Germans built the F13s to serve as airliners, not bombers. We had six seats behind the two pilots, but as we did not fly passengers often, I had two of them taken out, removed the door, had one of us sit on the floor, and throw hand grenades at the enemy. It was useless. By the time we got into the act, the Reds had already overwhelmed the admiral's troops. One morning, in early January of 1920, a colonel came to our billet and told us the war was over. He expected the Reds to capture the city in a matter of hours. He offered us the planes in exchange for flying them and some Russian aristocrats out of Odessa."

"Did you leave without telling the admiral?"

"I wanted to say farewell, but the colonel told me Kolchak had surrendered at Krasnoyarsk. Anyway, we took off with all four planes loaded with passengers and flew to Turkey. We registered the aircraft as our own."

"What were you planning to do with the planes?"

"Aldo, the Italian pilot, suggested flying to Italy and starting a small airline in Calabria, his home province. His father was an influential politician, and we hoped he could help us," Ray said.

"Why didn't you settle there? Italy would be a much better place than Somalia," Laura said.

"I suppose we could have tried, but the risks were enormous. We did not have enough money and couldn't get a steady job for the planes. However, the Italian Colonial Administration offered us the airmail delivery contract in Somalia. It seemed very lucrative and involved a lot of flying. We accepted."

"Did you fly here?"

"Yes, we did. Before leaving Italy, we loaded up with spare parts from Germany. Sergey, our Russian friend, did not come with us. He went to Norway and put floats on his plane. He is doing good business."

"Where are the other two?"

"I'll tell you after we take off from Bulo Burti. You'd better take over flying because I have to check the bills of lading," said Ray and handed the plane to Laura.

Taking over the controls, the energy emanating from the *York's* engine flowed through Laura's body. She felt strong and in charge.

This is total domination. A man must feel like this making love to a woman, she thought.

Ray opened his case and took out the papers. After looking them over, he leaned back on the seat.

"We could use a few passengers occasionally," Ray remarked. "The fares would improve our cash flow a great deal."

"Why? Are you losing money?"

"No, not really, but the interest payments are killing me."

He did not have time to explain anything else because a large village appeared on the horizon.

"That's Bulo Burti. You have to go around and come in from the north. Descend to a thousand meters," Ray instructed.

She reached for the throttle and pulled it back slightly. The sound of the engine changed a little, and the *York* started descending.

"Change course to two-seventy," Ray said.

She started turning the plane.

"Bank a little steeper, Laura, and watch the needle and the ball. That's better."

The compass read 270, and the needle of the altimeter settled at one thousand meters. Laura held the plane steady.

"Well done," Ray said. "Now let me take over."

It was hard giving up control of the plane. Ray landed as smooth as silk, and they spent only a few minutes on the ground.

"Beled Uen is about half an hour," said Ray after the takeoff. "Take over flying, set the course, and climb to five hundred meters only."

The plane being no more than a hundred meters above the desert made Laura nervous. Nevertheless, she made the right moves and started climbing.

"It is nice to have a copilot," remark Ray. "I could get used to have someone in the right seat."

"I wouldn't mind," mused Laura, thinking, flying with Ray every day would be fulfillment.

In twenty minutes, he took over and landed the plane at Beled Uen. They dumped the mailbags and were on their way.

After the takeoff, Ray kept control of the plane, and Laura set the gyrocompass for him. They flew in silence for a while. She broke the silence, "What happened after you arrived in Mogadishu?"

"We were very lucky. The Italian Colonial Army had built the hangar and a storage shack, but their planes never arrived. We bought the whole shebang, the buildings, the runway, and a lot of desert around us for one pound."

"Do you own the airfield?"

"Yes I do."

"Where did you find the mechanics?"

"As we needed some help to do the menial work, I hired six or seven people. Eventually, we trained Abdullahi and Deria as mechanics. Two years after starting the business, I ordered new engines for the planes. A technician came here from the Junkers factory to help install them, and he trained the guys further. Now they are second to none. I pay them the equivalent of three pounds a week, which is the same as an aircraft mechanic makes in Britain."

"You are very bighearted," remarked Laura with admiration in her voice.

"It is not generosity. I am running a business with skeleton personnel. I cannot afford underpaid mechanics, because they not only hold my life in their hands, but they control the future of the airline."

"What happened to your partners?"

"Well, Jim Thorpe developed some problems with his eyes and could not fly anymore. Aldo and I bought him out."

"With him gone, you had to work more," said Laura. "Did you mind?"

"No, not at all. In fact, we were glad to have a chance to fly more. However, we missed Jim. He is back in England running an automobile dealership. His wife was happy to go, because she did not like living in Somalia."

"How did your wife like it here?"

"When she arrived, I already had the house set up, and had everything working well. She enjoyed her stay in Mogadishu, but did not like the Italians."

"Was she British?"

"Yes, I met her eight years ago. Our planes needed parts and new engines. We drew lots, and I lost. I had to sail to Germany, visit the Junkers factory in Dessau, and place our order. As Jim was still with us, we were not short of pilots, and I did not have to hurry back. After finishing the business discussions with the Germans, I visited England to see the few relatives I have and to meet the sister of an old friend who went down in flames over the Somme. This was the first opportunity to see her and tell her about the way her brother fought and died. When we met, it was love at first sight. We were married in two weeks, and she came to Mogadishu with me."

"How romantic," said Laura, thinking enviously of Mrs. Madison.

"Actually, it was a very good marriage while it lasted. We had a boy in a year, but he died suddenly. He just did not wake up one morning. The doctor did not know why he died."

"I am sorry."

"We tried having another child, but Ellen never got pregnant again. Nevertheless, we were very happy. About a year ago, she died in two days. According to the doctor, she had congenital heart failure."

"I am sorry."

"I recovered from the shock and returned to flying. After a while, Aldo said we needed new engines again. I checked the flying hours of each plane and found that he was right. One of us had to visit Dessau, order the engines and spare parts. I suggested that Aldo should go and in the meanwhile look into the possibility of installing radios in our planes."

"It would be a good idea," Laura remarked. "If something happened to a plane, you wouldn't know where to start looking."

"We have a short-wave radio in the shack, and every town we visit has one. I could find out where we lost a plane and locate it rather easily."

"Did you get the radios for the planes?"

"I am afraid not. You see, Aldo sailed to Germany to buy the engines and the radios, taking all our money with him. A month ago, I got a letter saying he had quit the airline business and would keep the money. He signed over his shares in the business to me."

"Terrible. What did you do?"

"I had a choice. Shoot myself or try carrying on."

"I would not commit suicide. It is cowardly."

"I was on the brink of doing it. I had my revolver on the desk, but I realized there was nobody interested in reading my farewell note. Although the situation turned desperate, I changed my mind and decided to soldier on. The airline needed new engines and a mountain of spare parts, but I could not go to Germany, as I had nobody to share the flying with me. I borrowed money from the bank, wrote to Junkers, ordered the engines and the spare parts. They should be here soon. However, I am worried about the installation."

"Why? You said Abdullahi and Deria are competent mechanics. They could install them."

"They could, but I want to supervise them, just to be sure. The last time we replaced the engines, we had a German technician guiding them."

"I am sure they could do it on their own."

"I have no choice in the matter. I must trust them and keep flying."

"Could you hire pilots?"

"I am planning to do just that. I wrote Jim Thorpe asking him to find me a few pilots in England willing to come out here, but so far he has not replied," said Ray with a sad smile.

"You must be under tremendous strain," Laura remarked.

"Losing Ellen shocked me to the core. However, I've seen plenty of people close to me die. If my health held, I knew I would recover. A couple of weeks ago I had my first fainting spell. The doctor said I should stop flying, but it is impossible because I employ ten people. If I threw in the towel, they would lose their jobs. Most of have been with me for years. I owe them something."

"How about you? Aren't you concerned with your health?"

"Not since Ellen died. The only thing I care about are my people. If I can last until Jim finds me a couple of pilots, I'd be happy to retire."

"What would you do?"

"I'd sell Air Mogadishu. I could retire to my cottage in Cornwall or go to work as an engineer. Anyway, I'll cross that bridge when I come to it."

"I wish I could help," remarked Laura.

"You are already a great help, and you'd be even more help if you took over flying right now."

Laura took the yoke and declared: "I've got it."

Ray let the wheel go and leaned back.

"I am tired, very tired," he said closing his eyes.

She held the plane on course and occasionally checked the position of the villages or the prominent features of the land.

"We are on course," she concluded when she saw the unnamed oasis penciled onto the map half way to Galcaio. In another half hour, she woke Ray.

"Where are we?" he asked.

"We passed the oasis twenty minutes ago," she replied.

Ray checked his watch and said, "Fifteen minutes to Galcaio. Let me take over."

"You've got it," said Laura.

After landing, Ray stopped the engine, let the post office people unload the mailbags and place three sacks of mail on board, destined to Mogadishu. Galcaio, a large, sprawling village in the middle of the desert, built around a couple of stone-rimmed wells, looked to be a happy place. Throngs of smiling children came running and surrounded the plane. Ray left the aircraft first and offered his hand to Laura as she stepped out of the door. Touching him was like an electric shock again. She saw a strange little smile on Ray's face.

We are on the same wavelength, she thought as they sat at a rickety table in the shade adjacent to a shack built of sticks and palm fronds next to the runway.

"Believe it or not, this is the best restaurant in Galcaio," Ray said.

"Is it really?"

They did not have to wait long before a young Somali man came.

"Greetings, Captain. Do you want anything to eat or drink?"

"Just tea," Ray said.

"Pronto," the man said and disappeared.

"You shouldn't take milk in your tea," suggested Ray. "We don't know where it comes from."

"Did you ever eat here?"

"I never had the courage. Ellen tried it, though. She said the meat was tasty, but a little tough."

"Did she fly with you often?"

"No. She did not like the planes, but like you, she always drove the Norton. The ladies in the club were making nasty remarks about her riding the motorbike," Ray said with a smile.

"Did she mind?"

"No. She said they were only colonial Italians."

Laura did not reply, realizing that the late Mrs. Madison was a typical, early twentieth century upper-class Briton who thought civilized life ended at the cliffs of Dover. Some of the girls in the boarding school called Laura a "colonial" quite often and snubbed her for being born in India. Apparently, the attitude of the late Mrs. Madison was similar to her "high-caste" schoolmates.

Even though Laura despised the type of the late Mrs. Madison, she knew she had to fight the memory of her for Ray's affections. She did not know how, but her instinct suggested never to say anything derogatory about her.

How do you confront someone who is dead? she thought.

After finishing the tea, Ray stood up, stretched his muscular limbs and remarked, "Look, here comes Amir with our fuel," and he pointed at a Somali driving a donkey cart with two steel drums on it.

He paid for the tea, and signaled Laura to follow.

They met the donkey cart at the plane.

"Salaam, Captain Madison," said Amir. "How is the business?"

"Very well, Amir. How is the family?"

"Number two wife had a baby girl. Now I have to work much harder to make enough money to give her a decent dowry."

"Thinking of money, have you prepared my bill?" Ray asked.

"Yes, Captain. I have it right here," Amir replied. From underneath his *galabiah,* he took a sheet of paper and handed it to Ray.

He checked it carefully, took his wallet, and paid the man.

"Just sign here, Amir," Ray said.

"Thank you, Captain," Amir replied, signing the receipt. "It is nice to do business with you."

"Let us fill up the plane," said Ray and stepped to the *York.*

Amir knew exactly what to do. He fitted the hose to the fuelling port, and with a hand pump started filling the tanks. He emptied one barrel and started on the second.

"It is full now, Captain," said Amir. "Please check how much I have left in the barrel."

Ray took the piece of wire Amir used as a dipstick, and put it into the barrel. He read the mark and signed the receipt.

"Thank you, Amir. I'll see you next week. Now please start the engine for me."

"As you wish, Captain," the Somali replied and bowed.

Laura and Ray got into the cockpit and fastened their belts. She felt full of energy and desire. However, she did not immediately know what the target of her longing was...Ray or control over the aircraft.

"I think you should try the pre-flight check," Ray said, reading her mind and pointed at the list on the instrument panel.

Laura happily obliged. She read the list several times and knew what the switches were and how to set them. When she finished, she turned to Ray and declared, "We are ready to start the engine."

Ray nodded and signaled to Amir.

"You should handle the engine, Laura."

She just nodded and put her hand on the throttle.

"Just like I would have done it," remarked Ray after she started the engine.

They waited until Amir got out of the way, and Ray turned to Laura again. "You did everything so far. Why don't you get us off the ground?"

"Are you sure I can do it?" she asked, knowing she could take the *York* off the ground.

"I wouldn't ask you if I did not think so," replied Ray.

She set the course on the gyro and nudged the throttle forward. Lifting off terra firma gave Laura the sensation of a great accomplishment and fulfillment of her desire. Nevertheless, something was still missing.

Without instructions from Ray, she laid on the course for Obbia.

"Actually, I am not needed here," remarked Ray with a smile. "I'll be sorry to see you go."

Laura did not reply. She would have liked to remain in Mogadishu, take the place of Ellen and train as a pilot, but she did not think it was the proper thing to say.

They flew in silence until Obbia and the sea appeared on the horizon.

"I'll take it now," said Ray and took control of the aircraft.

He landed, exchanged the bags of mail, and took off from the seaside runway.

"That is not a pleasant place to land," he said when they reached cruising altitude and handed the plane over to Laura. There is always a nasty crosswind off the sea. You have to watch your landing. It might blow you off the runway."

They landed in Mogadishu near five o' clock in the evening.

Abdullahi and Deria were waiting. After the pilots debarked, the mechanics took care of the aircraft. Leaving the plane, Laura put her hand on the wing of the *York* and remarked, "We like each other."

Ray just stood there smiling. Before he took his place in the sidecar, he said, "You are the first student pilot who realized that all aircraft have a soul. You'd get along with them famously."

In the Harbor Authority compound, Ray told her to wait for him and ran up the stairs to the radio room.

In a few minutes he came back, appeared nervous, and jumped into the sidecar. "Let's go."

On the way to the house, three little boys ran across the path of the motorbike, but this time Laura respected their wishes and did not brake for them.

On the patio, Ray called Amina and asked her to bring them the whiskey.

"Why do you take a drink after landing?" Laura asked.

"It is a bad habit. In France, our fighter planes used ricinus oil for lubricant. As the fumes had a strong laxative effect, we had to take a drink to counteract it."

"Do we use ricinus oil in these planes?"

"Yes, but the cockpit is closed and it is doubtful the fumes could enter. I take the whiskey just to be on the safe side. Besides, I like it."

"I don't," said Laura.

"You should taste the stuff Aldo used to drink. I still have about ten bottles of it."

"What is it?"

"It's an ugly red liquid called Campari. He drank it with iced soda water."

"I am going to be adventurous," Laura replied. "It cannot be as bad as the whiskey. Let me have a shot of Campari mixed just like your friend used to drink it."

It was pleasantly bitter, and the alcohol did not burn her throat.

"I like it," she said.

"I am glad," Ray replied. "You'd better take another, because the message I got today will shock you."

"What do you mean?"

"Just look at the message I got from the *Oleandris*," he said handing the sheet of paper to Laura.

To Captain Raymond Madison, D.S.M., D.F.C.
Director, Air Mogadishu
This is to confirm Mr. Edward Blake and his stepdaughter, Miss Laura Blake-Stanton being on board of the Oleandris. Passport numbers are AX 129876 and DN 980012 respectively. Kindly let us know the purpose of your inquiry.
Signed Captain Winston Warren Master of the S.S. Oleandris

Laura burst out crying, but she did not feel as rejected as yesterday. Ray put his arms around her and held her tight. She snuggled up to him and slowly took control of her emotions.

"I don't understand. Honest, I don't. I am Laura Blake-Stanton. Someone is impersonating me, and I cannot guess who and why."

"I don't understand what is happening," Ray replied, "but I am not going to worry about it, and you should not bother either. We had a hard day, my mind is like mashed potatoes, and I am sure yours doesn't work at full efficiency. Let us have our dinner, and then go to bed early. Forget about the *Oleandris*, and tomorrow we'll figure out what to do."

Laura looked up at Ray. Through misty eyes, she saw the desire on the man's face, but he exercised tremendous control, kissed her gently on the forehead, and relaxed his hold on her.

"I guess you're right. I'd better dress for dinner," Laura said, peeling Ray's arms off her.

She returned to her room and put on the dress she had worn when she met Ray. It was clean and freshly ironed.

I'd better not wear Ellen's clothes because he might take me for her. I must establish myself as a different person than his late wife. I am now in his hands, and I do not want to create a false impression.

For dinner, they had an Italian dish, which was filling but not too heavy. As if nothing had happened, Laura asked many questions about flying and Ray answered patiently. It was nine thirty when Ray suggested going to bed.

In Ellen Madison's room, Laura took off her clothes. In the tropical heat, she did not bother with the nightgown. Her thoughts were in a turmoil switching rapidly from the control of the aircraft to the touch of Ray's hands and his body.

"I must go to him," Laura said to herself.

As if she were a sleepwalker, she picked up Ellen's silk robe, put it on, and started for Ray's room. The scent of the flowers from the garden hit her as soon as she stepped out onto the patio. At the door to his room, she stopped.

I am completely crazy, she thought. *If I entered his room wearing this robe, he would think I was the reincarnation of his wife. He would make love to me, and in his moment of high ecstasy, he'd call me Ellen.*

She threw off the robe and stood there naked. In a few seconds, she changed her mind.

I cannot enter his room naked, she thought, picking up Ellen's robe and quietly slipped it on.

She returned to her room, then after slamming the robe into a corner, threw herself on the bed.

For a while, she lay on her back staring at the ceiling. Her thoughts were in turmoil. *What is happening to me? What have I done, Lord? I don't know what I want, what would be right or wrong. I am sure you have the answers, but you just do not say.*

Amid such rebellious thoughts, Laura started to cry. *I am alone, so desperately alone.* And eventually she cried herself to sleep.

Four

In the morning, Amina did not thump on Laura's door at sunrise. As they did not fly on Wednesdays and Thursdays, she slept in, only waking by nine o'clock. She had a shower, put on a fresh flight suit, and went to the patio to have breakfast.

After she finished, Ray came out of his room fresh as a daisy.

"Morning, Laura. I bet you were very tired. I got up at seven, but did not have the heart to wake you."

"Indeed, I was really worn out."

Ray came to the table and sat down. He gave Laura a long look and asked, "Do you feel up to discuss the message from the *Oleandris*?"

"I have to face it sooner or later."

"I take it is a yes."

She nodded.

"Okay, I thought about it long and hard. I do not understand how your stepfather could leave you here."

"I've no idea."

"The fact of someone impersonating you is puzzling. Eventually, we'll figure out who she is and why she is doing it."

"I don't understand how Edward could let all this happen," said Laura. "We were such good friends."

"Perhaps someone is blackmailing your stepfather," Ray said.

"I don't know about that. Dad died four years ago while I was still at school in England. When I heard of my father's death, I expected Mother to come back to live in England, but it did not happen."

"Why?"

"She came to see me in school with Edward, and she said they were getting married and returning to India. I did not like it to happen so soon after Dad's death, but if my mother wanted to remarry, I'd have no say in the matter. Actually, Edward turned out a very nice person, adopting me to make sure that when he died, I would inherit his share of the Blake estates worth hundreds of thousands of pounds," Laura explained.

"Very considerate of him. Apparently, he loved your mother very much."

"It seemed so. I spent a summer in Dacca with them and found my mother very happy. During my vacation in East Bengal, Edward Blake and I became very good friends. After graduation from high school, I went to live with them until I figured out what to do with myself."

"Did you consider getting married?"

"I had many suitors in India, but I did not like the civil servant types. After six months, I decided to go to university in England and study medicine or science, but suddenly lost my mother. According to the doctor, she died of cholera."

"I am sorry."

"I'm afraid the disease was common among Britons working in the Indian Civil Service. If you visited the graves in the Dacca cemetery, you'd realize most expatriates died of cholera,"

"In the nineteenth century perhaps, but we live in the twentieth now. We know how to avoid the disease," said Ray.

"I know," she replied. "My mother was very careful about what she ate and drank, but somehow contracted the disease. After she died, apart from my grandmother I had no one else, just Edward. He was very considerate and treated me as well as my own father would. Shortly after Mother's death, Edward applied for the position of Chief Administrator of the Colony of Tanganyika, and he got the job. As Dar es Salaam had an accredited university, Edward suggested that I should go with him to Tanganyika, take a year or two in the university before going to England to finish my studies. We boarded the *Oleandris* in Calcutta, and you know what happened afterwards."

"That's quite a story," Ray said. "For the life of me, I do not understand him. I cannot figure out why he left you in Mogadishu and who is impersonating you."

"I've no idea."

"Is your family rich?"

"I don't really know. I think we are well off. My grandmother owns Stanton Manor in Kent near Folkestone and I am going to inherit it. Although Granny lives well on the income generated by the estate, I doubt it would be worth too much."

"Is there anything else?"

"I inherited a small trust from my maternal grandfather. He retired from the Navy as a commander, owned a small cottage and a schooner when he died. There is nobody alive on that side of the family. Barclay's in London has the trust, and I am going to take possession of it when I become twenty-four years old," Laura said.

"Did you try finding out how much the trust is worth?"

"No, I did not care. It cannot be more than a thousand pounds. Anyway, my father's death benefits would finance my university studies easily," she said.

"I have a nagging feeling about your stepfather knowing how much you are really worth. If your grandmother died, and you took possession of her estate and the trust account left to you by your grandfather, you could be very rich. As long as he is your father by adoption, in case you died without a will, he would automatically inherit your fortune. Perhaps he wanted to do away with you."

"Edward wouldn't dream of such things, I am sure of that," she said indignantly.

"Then how do you explain him leaving you in Mogadishu and having someone impersonate you?"

Laura stopped to think for a moment. She suddenly remembered seeing Edward walking by and actually looking at her lying on the ground just before she passed out in the alley. There had to be some truth in what Ray said.

"I'd suggest you write your grandmother, describe what happened, and ask her to help you."

"I am going to do that."

"Write the letter now, and we'll mail it this afternoon."

"Good idea," she agreed.

"What do you want to do after sending the letter?"

"Just wait. As soon as Granny sends me money for the fare, I should go to England, and retrieve my name and identity."

"You could not board a ship without a passport. There is no British Consul here to help you."

"That is a problem. What can I do?"

"Friday we take the northern run. It is much longer than the other two, and normally I sleep in Bossasso. This time, however, after the last stop we'll refuel and go on to Aden. An R.A.F. bomber squadron is stationed there, and I know them well. We can land at the military airfield since there is no passport control there. The guys will keep you entertained while I visit the consulate or the British Administrator. They'll tell us what to do."

"Would you do that for me?"

"I am your employer."

"Are you really?"

"Yes, I am. You are hired, young lady, as my loadmaster. The pay is not much. I can pay you a guinea a week plus board and room, including all the Campari you can drink."

Laura stood and kissed Ray on the cheek.

"I don't know if I can ever repay you."

"Just keep me alive until those pilots from England get here," Ray interrupted.

"I will. I promise, I will," said Laura.

"In addition, I will teach you piloting."

"You know, Ray, I am actually grateful to Edward and the woman impersonating me. Without them I would not have discovered my true vocation."

"Now, we have solved the principal problem. What do I tell the captain of the *Oleandris*?" Ray asked.

"It's a good question."

They sat side by side in silence. Finally, Ray stood, went to his room and took out a writing pad. He sat and started writing. In a few minutes he turned to Laura, pointing at the pad: "What do you think?"

The message was clear:

To Captain Winston Warren Master of the S.S. Oleandris
For your information: Someone on behalf of Miss Laura Blake-Stanton chartered one of our aircraft to fly her to Mombasa. The man claimed Miss Laura missed the Oleandris at her Mogadishu stopover. However, nobody showed up at the appointed time.
Signed
Captain Raymond Madison, D.S.M., D.F.C.
Director, Air Mogadishu

"Whatever Edward planned, this message would have him believe I am lost in Somalia somewhere," Laura remarked.

"Alternately, he might think you are on your way overland to Dar es Salaam," said Ray. "They would not expect you for a few weeks or months. If you didn't show, they'd believe you died or were sold to a camel herder."

The possibility made Laura cringe. Up to that point, she had not realized the danger she was in before she met Ray.

"We are going to send the letter to your grandmother today, and have lunch at the club. The food is not very good there, but I usually give Amina Wednesday and Sunday off. Nevertheless, the club's chef beats my cooking."

"Should I wear a flight suit?" Laura asked.

"No, just wear a dress. I am going to drive the Norton. If I don't, I'll forget how to ride a motorcycle."

The Italian Club was a new experience for Laura. It was noisy, the bearers were running around like chicken with their heads cut off, and the cleanliness of the tables left a great deal to be desired.

She was used to the quiet, well-organized clubs in India where the bearers wore all white with chrome buttons and turbans. In addition, the tablecloths were immaculate white. Nevertheless, in the Italian club somehow they got their food and didn't have to wait very long.

They met several people. Ray always introduced Laura as his niece. Although the Italians were pleasant, they did not invite Ray and Laura to sit with them.

"I am considered an outsider here," Ray explained. "My Italian is mediocre, I am a bad bridge player, and I gave up tennis years ago. I occasionally come here for lunch, and every Thursday I swim in the pool. In case you wanted to come here alone to meet people of your age, I'd get a card for you."

"I doubt I would come here alone. Although I do not play bridge, I am a good swimmer and better than average tennis player."

"Did you learn at school?"

"I did, but played a lot of tennis in Dacca. However, my number one sport was fencing. I even competed successfully at the county tournaments."

"You should meet Bob Carstairs, the squadron leader in Aden. He was a provincial fencing champion in England and has many trophies. It is too hot here to dress up and fence, but Bob manages to practice somehow. He wants to compete again in England when his tour of duty expires," said Ray. "You'll meet him on Friday."

After lunch, Laura tried on Mrs. Madison's swimsuits and found them too large for her. While wondering about the woman, she spent an hour adjusting the size of one. Obviously, Ellen was much heavier, although her waist was almost as small as Laura's.

Later in the afternoon, they went swimming and had an early dinner at the club. They were just finishing dessert when an elderly Italian stepped up to them.

"Captain Madison, let me introduce myself. I am Marco Orsini."

"Nice meeting you, sir. Would you care to sit down?"

"Thank you very much, Captain. I don't think I should. I just started my business, and I wanted to offer my services to your airline."

"What business are you in, Mr. Orsini?"

"I opened a photo studio in the Croce. I take passport and family photographs, but if you wanted to mount an advertising campaign, I could take pictures of your aircraft."

Ray thought for a moment and said, "We may as well visit your studio after dinner. My niece's passport will expire soon, and she'll need the photographs."

"I'll be in the shop until nine. See you later, Captain."

Following the meal, they visited the Orsini Studio. The assistant, a young girl about Laura's age, took the pictures, and disappeared into the darkroom, while Orsini chatted with Ray.

The pictures turned out quite well. Ray paid the photographer and put the pictures in his wallet.

As they left the studio, Ray remarked, "I am an optimist. I hope I can persuade the consul in Aden to issue a temporary passport for you."

"We shall see," Laura said as she took her place in the sidecar, and Ray kick-started the Norton.

Laura sat on the patio while Ray went to the kitchen and came back carrying a tray with two glasses, a bottle of whiskey, ice, the soda siphon, and the Campari.

"I thought we should have a nightcap," he said.

"It is an excellent idea."

Ray put the tray down, put some ice in Laura's glass, poured the Campari, and added the soda.

"Aldo liked it half and half," he said.

"I like it his way."

Ray poured himself two fingers of whiskey, and sat on the couch next to her. Their hands touched briefly, and the contact sent an electric current through Laura's body.

"Cheers," said Ray, raising his glass.

They drank silently.

"I was thinking," said Laura. "I managed to get over the chicanery of my stepfather. However, as long as Granny is alive, and I haven't passed my twenty-fourth birthday, Edward cannot get his clammy hands on the family assets."

"You're right. How old is your grandmother?"

"She is near ninety," Laura replied.

"In that case, my dear, you should go to England as soon as possible."

"Granny should get my letter in a couple of weeks. I am sure she'll send me enough money to go to England, and offer a practical suggestion about retrieving my passport. I'd be ready to travel in about a month."

"Although I'd hate to lose you, a month seems to be a reasonable assumption," Ray said.

"Would you really miss me?" Laura asked with a coquettish smile.

"Actually, I would. You are a great help, and you make me feel safe in the air," he said and took Laura's hand.

"You are my protector, my knight in shining armor," she replied and edged closer to the man. Their thighs touched. Through the thin skirt, Ray's hard muscles excited her.

He put his right arm over Laura's shoulder and pulled her closer. She did not resist, looked up at him, and offered her lips. The kiss came as a surprise. She sensed the hunger and the burning desire in the man, put her arm around him and buried her lips in his. It was like being in heaven.

Suddenly, Ray pulled away.

"This is all wrong," he said.

"Why?"

"Look, I am old enough to be your father, and I don't make a habit of seducing young virgins."

Laura laughed and replied, "To start with, I am already twenty-one, and I am not a virgin. Do you think I would flirt with you if I were?"

Ray looked at her, surprised and mesmerized. Without further ado, Laura gently kissed him on the lips.

"Well, what am I supposed to say?" Ray mumbled.

"Should I tell you?"

"No," replied Ray and took her into his arms.

His left hand slipped in under her blouse and caressed her breast. As it was one of her sensuality points, Laura pressed her body against his, feeling the desire swelling in Ray.

Suddenly, he released her and stood. With one fluid movement, he picked her up as if she were a doll, and started toward the door of his bedroom.

"Put me down," said Laura firmly as soon as they entered.

Ray looked at her surprised, but before he could say anything, Laura started shedding her clothes. By the time she reached Ray's bed, she was stark naked.

"I can do it faster than you fumbling with every button," she said with a smile and sat on the bed. Ray stepped up to her and again picked her up.

"I love you," he said quietly.

An hour later, following the mutually enjoyable and satisfying session of lovemaking, Ray still had Laura in his arms.

"It was hard to believe you were not a virgin. You looked like a fresh English rose."

"Since you know I am not, do I still look like one?" Laura asked.

"No, you are a whole garden of roses."

"Quite an improvement," she mused.

"Tell me, when did you..."

"It happened a long time ago in Stanton Manor. At the age of fifteen, I spent the summer vacation with Granny. The son of the vicar, Bert, an excellent horseman, actually a Sandhurst cadet, promised to marry me as soon as he graduated. He seduced me in the barn, had me in a haystack, the sacristy, and on the train to London. Needless to say, I enjoyed it immensely."

"What happened to him?"

"Nothing, really, he forgot his forever like most men do, and married the daughter of a banker. They live in Scotland somewhere."

"I am sorry I took advantage of you, Laura," said Ray. "I should not have done it."

"Come on, Ray. I almost came to your room last night. I stood at your door on the patio naked, but I thought it would be bad form."

"You are the most exciting woman I've ever had," Ray said and kissed Laura's breast.

She responded like a thoroughbred to the spur.

The orange line of the rising sun appeared on the horizon before Laura and Ray fell asleep in each other's arms.

~ * ~

On Thursday, they did not go to the club. Instead, they sat on the patio, and Ray lectured Laura at length about the mysteries of meteorology. She listened intently, asking the proper questions at the right time.

Nevertheless, after the sun set and Amina retired, she walked into Ray's room with him, but as they had to fly next day, she returned to her own bed by ten o'clock.

Laura did not cry this time when the lights were out. Although pleasantly tired, she never forgot her prayer. *"Thank you for letting me have Ray, my Lord. I made him happy, and he deserves every minute of happiness. Please, help my letter reach Granny,"* she said, and fell into a deep, exhausted sleep.

Friday at sunrise they went to the airfield. They had their overnight bags, as they planned to spend a night in Aden. The mechanics prepared the *Calabrese* for the trip, loaded the mailbags, but the post office truck still stood there. A small, dumpy fellow wearing an impeccable dark suit and a Pitt helmet stood there, apparently waiting for Ray.

"Mr. Panetta, what a pleasure to see you," Ray said and introduced Laura as his niece.

"Nice meeting you, Miss," the Italian said gruffly. "I have a very important matter to discuss with you, Captain. Is there a place where we can talk in private?"

"Come into my office," suggested Ray and invited the man into the small shack next to the hangar.

As they disappeared into the shack, according to the normal pre-flight routine, Laura walked around the plane and she discovered one of the tires was a little low.

She trotted over to the hangar and asked Abdullahi to come out and have a look. As they passed the shack, Laura could not help but overhear the heated discussion inside. She slowed down unintentionally, and eventually stopped to hear the gist of the conversation.

"I am warning you, Captain, for the last time. Your contract calls for at least two operational aircraft and two pilots. You have been in violation of the contract for quite some time. There is no second pilot. If you miss just one run, I'll have your contract lifted. No two ways about it, *capisce*?" Panetta said.

"I have two pilots coming from England," Ray said quietly. "I expect them any day. Meanwhile, if I miss a flight, you are welcome to the goddamned contract. In the last ten years, I have not missed a single run. Why should I start now?"

"You had your last warning, Captain," grunted Panetta and stormed out of the office.

Without saying anything to Laura, the Italian got into the truck and signaled the driver to start. They disappeared in a great cloud of dust.

Ray came out of the office seemingly upset, but as soon as he took his place in the cockpit, he became the picture of calm competence again.

"The first leg of our run to Garoe is the longest," Ray said. "Flying it alone is tiring. One could easily fall asleep."

Nevertheless, he did not hand the plane over to Laura. However, after the takeoff from the short, dusty strip of Garoe, he gave Laura a chance to fly the *Calabrese* all the way to Gardo. He landed the plane and let Laura look after the handling of the mailbags. When they took off, Laura took the wheel again. They flew in silence for a while, and then Laura asked, "Who is this guy, Panetta?"

"A greasy little bastard who doesn't like me."

"Why? What has he got against you?"

"Nothing, really. He is just bored to tears and likes being officious. Don't worry about him."

In Bossasso, Ray somehow misjudged the strip and overshot. The *Calabrese* was halfway down the landing strip when they touched. Ray promptly opened the throttle, took off again, and went around. The second time he nailed the runway perfectly.

"This shows you I am becoming overconfident," he said. "Don't let it happen to you ever. By the way, I am a little tired. Please, look after the refueling. Make sure they take all the mailbags off the plane and store it in the post office until tomorrow."

"I will," said Laura.

"I'll give you the money for Ahmed. He's the guy supplying our fuel," said Ray, rummaging in his black leather bag. He found the receipt book and the money due to Ahmed clipped to it.

Having to deal with a woman surprised the Somali, but he realized Laura being as thorough and precise as Ray would have been, and he accepted her.

"Is anything wrong with the captain?" Ahmed asked. "Why doesn't he get off the plane?"

"He is resting. We had a late night, and we still have a long way to fly today," replied Laura.

"Are you going to Aden?"

"Yes."

"In that case, you'll need fuel tomorrow. In the past, the captain always arrived by ten o'clock in the morning. I'll be here with your fuel."

The local postmaster had no objection to storing the mail and giving Laura a receipt for the bags.

"I'll have them here for you tomorrow," he said. "I also have about a hundred kilos of freight going to Mogadishu."

"What is it?"

"Four cartons of khatt."

"I'll ask the captain," replied Laura, and she climbed back into the plane.

"The postmaster wants to ship four cartons of khatt to Mogadishu."

"Charge him twenty pounds; that is the regular charge. Don't forget to give him a receipt and make out a bill of lading," explained Ray. "The blanks are in my bag. He might as well check it in now and store it with the bags."

Laura was learning the administration relevant to running an airline. It took about an hour to refuel and store the bags. Laura climbed back to her seat, fastened her belt, and looked up the course to Aden.

"Can you do the pre-flight and take us to Aden? I will take care of the landing, but I leave everything else in your capable hands," Ray said.

"Gladly," Laura replied and began the pre-flight checks.

The takeoff was uneventful. The *Calabrese*, under Laura's gentle control, climbed to fifteen hundred meters and set course to Aden.

It was still light when Ray landed the plane at the military airfield. He taxied off the runway and parked the *Calabrese* next to a row of biplanes. As he stopped the engine, an automobile drove up to them. At the sight of the young fliers, Ray perked up.

"I wish I were one of them," he remarked as he opened his safety belt.

The R.A.F. officers treated Ray with respect.

"Fellows, let me introduce my niece," he said.

"Laura, this is Squadron Leader Bob Carstairs, the man I was talking about," he pointed at one of the officers.

As she looked at him, her heart stopped. She had never laid eyes on a more attractive man than Carstairs.

"The pleasure is mine, Miss Laura," said the officer and offered to shake hands.

"Squadron Leader."

Perhaps that was the longest handshake in both their lives. They looked at each other, mesmerized.

"This guy is Flight Lieutenant Fred Hanley," intervened Ray, pointing at the other officer.

Finally, Bob let Laura's hand go, and she shook hands with Hanley.

"Let's go to the mess," suggested Bob, helping Laura into the car. He turned to Ray. "You should have sent us a radio message about the surprise guest. We could have prepared an exciting meal and organized the proper reception."

"I don't want to cause any trouble," Laura said.

"No trouble at all. Perhaps we should take you to one of the hotels."

"I am afraid it is not possible," Ray said. "As Laura lost her passport, she cannot leave the base. I am going to ask you to take me to the Consul, the Chief Secretary, or whomever you have here. I'll ask him to issue a temporary passport to her."

"I'm sure Fred would gladly drive you while I take care of your niece. We'll arrange the dinner for seven. You should be back by then," said Bob.

"That will be okay," Ray said.

"Well, just drop us at the bachelor officers' quarters, Fred. I'll set Miss Laura up in the guest room. Ray will bunk with me."

"Roger," said Fred and turned the car in the direction of the buildings not too far from the runway.

When they stopped, Bob jumped off the car and helped Laura out, again holding her just a little longer than was necessary. Although feeling guilty, she did not mind Bob's hand on her. In fact, she wanted the contact to last much longer.

"Follow me, Miss Laura."

"Just call me Laura," she interrupted.

"I am Bob. I'll show you to your room."

They entered the barracks, and Bob led Laura to the last room on the corridor. He opened the door, saying, "This is it. I'm afraid it is not much, but this is the best we have."

"It is perfect," she replied.

"Just freshen up. I'll wait for you and walk you to the mess."

"Thank you."

In the utilitarian room, Laura felt great. Her tiredness vanished. As she wanted to be near Bob, she hurriedly washed.

"Is it possible to want two men at the same time?" she asked herself as she left the room.

"By God, you are a fast dresser," Bob remarked. "Just like a soldier. Let's go."

They left the building. A few minutes after sunset, the desert temperature began dropping rapidly.

"It is going to be cold. Take it," Bob said, and took off his leather jacket.

Laura wasn't cold at all, but she accepted. The smell of the leather combined with the scent of Bob's aftershave excited her.

"I appreciate your kindness."

"Think nothing of it. The pleasure is mine."

They walked side by side, their hands occasionally touching. Laura looked at the man. He was almost as tall as Ray. His well-developed muscles showed through the thin shirt. Bob had wavy blond hair, blue eyes, and a mischievous smile lurking on his sensual lips. She could easily imagine herself in his arms.

"If you had come earlier, I would have invited you for a trip in one of our planes," he said.

"I'd like that. The only aircraft I've ever seen from close quarters was the Junkers F13," Laura said.

"It seems a nice machine, although it is getting old. I never flew in one of them."

"It is dark now, and I haven't yet learned how to turn on the cabin lights. However, if you get up before Ray tomorrow, I will show it to you."

"Are you planning to wake early?"

"For a chance to show off with our plane I would get up before sunrise," Laura said.

She did not add that for a chance to be with Bob she'd be willing to get up at midnight.

"It is a date," replied Bob. "I'll be at your door by five-thirty."

"Very well."

"How did you lose your passport?" Bob queried.

The thought of having to lie appalled Laura, but she had to do it.

"I was on my way to Dar es Salaam and the boat tied up at Mogadishu. Naturally, I got off to see Ray, but before returning to the ship, a couple of locals mugged me. I lost my passport and missed the ship. So, I am staying with Ray until I can get a new passport and arrange for passage to Tanganyika," Laura explained.

"I am sorry you had to go through such an ordeal, but I am also glad. If the locals had not mugged you, I'd never have met you."

Me too, thought Laura.

They reached the Officers' Mess and walked in. Only a few people were standing by the bar holding mugs of beer. Although Laura did not like the taste of the beer Bob ordered, she drank it anyway, not wishing to offend her host.

"Where did you meet Ray?" Laura asked.

"Right here. After his wife died, he came over one day, just to have some company. You see, Ray is an institution in the R.A.F. Everybody knows his name."

"What do you mean?"

"He flew bombers until late 1917, and suddenly transferred to command a fighter squadron. He had thirty-two confirmed kills in the matter of a few months. Imagine if he had flown fighters from the very beginning...he could have had more than a hundred kills easily. Everybody in the R.A.F. knows about him."

"I heard that," Laura lied. "Why did they demobilize him?"

"It was the stupidity of the War Office. For a change, they tried to be humane, demobilizing everybody who had some other means of making a living. As you know, Ray had an engineering degree and came from a rich Cornish family. Therefore, they demobilized him, even though he begged the Air Marshall not to," explained Bob. "Speak of the devil, here he comes."

Ray and Fred entered, came over to their table, and sat down.

"I can see you are guarding Laura very carefully," said Ray, and he ordered a beer.

"What did the consul say?" Laura asked.

"Not much," Ray replied. "He referred me to the chief administrator in Nairobi or Dar es Salaam. This guy has no authority to issue travel documents."

Somehow, the bad news did not disappoint Laura.

"You should visit us sometime, Bob. I am sure Ray would teach you to fly his planes," she said."

"You could even fly for Air Mogadishu," added Ray.

"It would be interesting," mused Bob. "I'll think about it."

They had dinner, and after the meal Bob offered to walk Laura to her room while Ray stayed in the Officers' Mess a little longer. Laura had a strange feeling about Ray. It seemed he wanted her to go with Bob.

"Where are your quarters?" Laura asked when they left the mess.

"In the same building," replied Bob. "We are practically neighbors."

As they walked in the dark, Laura stumbled, almost fell, and Bob caught her.

"You just as well hang on to me. This place is full of potholes, and I know them all."

"Thanks," she said and took Bob's arm.

To be near him was a strange but very pleasant sensation. His touch was as electrifying as Ray's. *I wonder if he will try to kiss me?* Laura thought as they reached the BOQ. At the door, Bob did not try to kiss her, but held her hand for a long time.

"Good night, Laura," he said. "See you tomorrow morning at sunrise."

"You bet," replied Laura, relinquishing the man's hand.

In her room she wondered what she would have done if Bob had tried to kiss her.

"I don't know, but I would not have fought him too hard," she concluded.

As the nighttime temperature was much cooler in Aden than in Mogadishu, Laura put on the nightgown and pulled the blanket up to her chin.

"What are you doing to me, my Lord?" she asked. *"Am I supposed to fall for two men at the same time? Should I choose? I don't know."*

With doubts in her mind, she could not fall asleep as fast as she normally did, but eventually she managed.

~ * ~

The next morning, Bob was waiting for Laura at sunrise, and they made a beeline for the Junkers.

Once inside, Laura sat in Ray's side of the plane and started rattling off the technical data relevant to the F13.

Bob listened intently, and in the end he remarked, "Are you sure you are not a pilot?"

"I've held the wheel a few times," she replied, blushing.

"Well, next time you come to Aden, I will take you up in my bomber. It is also an old plane, but sturdy and very reliable."

"What make is it?"

"It is a two-seater Hawker Hind. The old biplane can carry quite a bomb load."

"We can haul up to six people and about two hundred kilos of freight," she said, but was not sure about it. They talked about the performance of the old Junkers until the sun rose fully.

"Let's go back to the mess for breakfast," suggested Bob.

He again helped Laura off the plane, but this time he did not let her hand go until they reached the mess hall. It was quite all right with her.

After breakfast, they said farewell, and Ray took off at seven o'clock.

As soon as they were over the sea, he handed the responsibility of flying the *Calabrese* to Laura and relaxed.

"What did you do to Bob?" Ray asked.

"Nothing," she replied blushing. "Why?"

"He kept me up half the night asking and talking about you. He is falling for you. Made me swear to fly you over here before you take a ship to Dar es Salaam."

"Did you promise?" Laura said.

"Of course I did. He is a handsome devil, precisely your type, isn't he?" mused Ray and did not say anything until Bossasso appeared on the horizon.

They landed, refueled, and by ten o'clock, they were on their way to Mogadishu with Ray flying the *Calabrese.*

As they passed Galcaio, Ray suddenly handed over control to Laura saying, "I think I am going to faint."

Laura took the smelling salts and dug out one of Ray's tablets. The smelling salt had its effect, and Ray recovered sufficiently to swallow the capsule with some water from the bottle Laura kept under her seat.

"I am sorry," Ray said. "I have no idea when I am going to pass out. This is hell for a pilot. If you weren't here, we would have crashed for sure. Perhaps it would be a fitting end to a fighter pilot."

"You are not going to crash as long as I am here with you."

"You see how lucky I am," Ray said with a weak smile.

Mogadishu appeared on the horizon.

"I think it is time for you to try landing the plane. If I kick the bucket up there, you wouldn't know how to return to terra firma."

Laura concentrated on the landing. She came in a little too fast, a little too high, and hit the ground with a bone jarring thump, using most of the runway to slow the plane.

"That was an arrival," announced Ray. "You have to practice the landing a few times."

The postmen unloaded the mailbags and the freight, put it on their truck, and left the airfield.

They took the Norton with Laura driving. As they entered the house, Amina appeared with a tray bringing the whisky for Ray and the Campari with soda for Laura.

"I am at a loss what to do about your passport," Ray admitted.

"Let us wait for Granny's letter. She always knows what to do. She is a tough old lady. She survived the sepoy rebellion when she was only ten. Allegedly she killed one of the mutineers with her dagger."

"Let us hope she stays alive until you reach England."

"We shall see. Right now I am quite happy wherever I am," Laura said.

"I am sure the presence of Squadron Leader Carstairs would improve your state of well-being," Ray said with a smile.

Laura blushed. She stood up and declared, "I'd better have a long bath and change for dinner. I am a little tired."

"I am not in the pink either," replied Ray. "We'd better turn in early."

Five

After the excellent dinner, Laura had plenty of energy left. She went to her room by eight, took a long shower, and took Mrs. Madison's robe out of the closet. Bob's picture flashed in her mind. *I wonder how he would react to seeing me naked*, she thought, and put the robe on. She looked out on the door to the patio, and saw the light in Amina's room across the garden.

Laura slipped out onto the patio, walked to Ray's door, and knocked.

"Who is it?" came Ray's voice from the inside.

"Guess," she replied, and dropped the robe to the floor.

Ray appeared and pulled Laura into the room. Without further ado, he took her into his arms and kissed her gently on the lips.

"Tell me, darling, are you a mind-reader?" Ray asked when they came up for air.

"No, but our minds work on the same frequency," she replied and opened his robe.

"You are amazing, Laura, you always know what I want."

"I may desire the same things," she replied.

An hour later, Laura was back in her own room lying naked on her bed. She was pleasantly tired and satisfied. *Thank you, Lord, for letting me have Ray tonight. May I have Bob one of these days?* Although the Almighty did not answer her, Laura thought his reply would be affirmative. Almost immediately, she fell asleep and did not stir for ten hours.

They had breakfast together. When they finished eating, Ray handed Laura a pound and a shilling saying, "This is your pay for the first week. Although there is nothing to buy here, I thought I'd better give it you."

"Quite the contrary," Laura said. "I would like to buy a dagger and carry it strapped to my leg. Granny always told me never go anywhere unarmed."

"I have a better idea. If you are so determined about being armed, why don't you carry Ellen's gun? She had a little revolver with a silk holster she wore under her skirt. She was a bit paranoid."

"How about the flight suit?"

"She kept it in her left lower pocket. Nobody could see it. However, I must warn you, carrying a gun in public might be illegal."

"I'd rather go to jail than suffer an abduction again," Laura said seriously.

"I understand," Ray said. "We always have a gun on the plane. I have an old Webley revolver in my bag. That is legal. Even your little gun might be permissible when you are flying. By the way, can you handle a gun?"

"Sure. My father, the real one, taught me early because Granny insisted."

"Wait, I'll get the gun for you."

They went to the airfield and fired a few bullets into the sand dunes allowing Laura to get the feel of both weapons.

After dinner at the club, Laura and Ray were sitting on the patio talking about meteorology when suddenly Ray remarked, "It is exceptionally hot tonight."

Strange, Laura thought, because she felt the cool offshore winds, but she did not react.

"I think I am going to turn in early," Ray said. "I feel tired."

"I'll stay here for a while and perhaps have another Campari," replied Laura. "Good night, darling."

Laura let her imagination run wild. She fantasized having Ray and Bob in her bed at the same time. *That would be a problem*, she thought. *I wouldn't know which way to turn. Perhaps they would have some creative ideas.* She was immersed in her thoughts when she heard the bell ringing in Ray's room.

"Amina," she shouted. "The captain wants you."

"I'm coming," she replied and lumbered into the bedroom. In less than a minute, she came out visibly disturbed.

"The captain is very sick, Missy, you should get Doctor Bertoli."

Laura's heart missed a couple of beats. "Where can I find the doctor?"

"Ali, the gardener knows. He'll go with you and show the way."

"Can I telephone him first?"

"No, he does not have a telephone," Amina said. "Doctor Swanson has a phone, but he would not come here."

"Why?"

"Last time the captain threatened to shoot him. It has to be Doctor Bertoli."

"Let's go." Before going anywhere, Laura stepped into the bedroom. Ray was on the bed, his eyes closed, his face was very pale with cold sweat on his forehead.

"What's the problem?" she asked.

"Just a touch of malaria."

"Did you take your quinine?"

"I did, but it had no effect. I was coming down with it day before yesterday."

Ray passed out. Laura took his pulse. The man's heart was racing.

"Amina," she shouted, "come in here."

"Yes, Missy."

"Stay with him and do not let him get up. Put cold compresses on his forehead and keep him calm. I am getting the doctor."

Laura just slipped into a flight suit, started the Norton, and with Ali in the sidecar, took off. The doctor lived near the port. He had just finished his dinner and sat on the porch enjoying the cool evening breeze with his wife. When Laura told him about Ray, he immediately took his bag and jumped into his car.

"Please, follow me," said Laura and started the motorcycle.

Arriving at the house, they found Ray still out, unconscious. The doctor took his pulse, listened to Ray's heart, shook his head, and declared, "He is in a bad way."

"What can you do for him?"

"He is a strong man. I think he'll recover. I'll give him a shot now, which will keep him asleep for twelve hours. In the morning, before I open my clinic, I'll come back and give him another shot. You must keep him in bed for a few days. If he gets up, he's liable to die on you," the doctor explained.

"I might not be here tomorrow, sir. Please give the instructions to Amina, the housekeeper."

"That's all right."

"Good night, Doctor, thank you for coming."

"Good night, Miss."

After Bertoli left, Laura's conscience started bothering her. *Perhaps I was too aggressive last night. After all, he is over fifty and not a young stallion anymore,* she thought. Apart from worrying about Ray's health, the thought of him not being able to fly for a while struck her like a stonewall collapsing on her. That bastard, Panetta, is going to lift Ray's contract. If that happened, it would be curtains for Ray Madison, Air Mogadishu, and Laura Blake-Stanton. Where in hell am I going to find a pilot between now and tomorrow morning? *I could use Bob right now, in more ways than one,* she thought. Even though Laura knew it was ridiculous, she drove by the club, but found it closed. She opened the throttle and returned to the house. Amina was still with Ray. She took a deep breath, and stepped to Amina.

"I am afraid you must stay with the captain all night. As he cannot fly, I am taking the mail to Kismayo tomorrow. To do that, I need to rest. However, if his condition should worsen, wake me."

"Yes, Missy."

"Thank you, Amina," said Laura and went to her room. Getting onto her bed, she let a brief prayer go. "I don't know if I am doing the right thing, Lord, but even if it kills me, I must try flying the mail to Kismayo for Ray. Please help me." She calmed down, but could not fall asleep; kept tossing and turning for hours. Nevertheless, she got up by sunrise. Apparently, Amina heard Laura moving around in the room next to Ray's, because she came out to make breakfast. Laura felt strange sitting at the table alone. "One week can change a person's habits drastically," she mused. "I feel as if I've lived here for years, but in fact, it has been only eight days."

Laura had just finished breakfast when Doctor Bertoli arrived. He greeted her and went straight to the bedroom to examine Ray. He came out in a few minutes, sat down, wiped his forehead, and said to Laura, "He is much better now, sound asleep. When he wakes, give him some warm soup, but nothing else. I'll come by in the evening."

"You heard the doctor, Amina. You should look after him."

"Are you going somewhere, Miss?" the doctor asked.

"Yes, I am flying to Kismayo," replied Laura and went to Ray's room. She picked up the black leather bag, said farewell to the doctor, started the Norton to drove to the airfield.

Laura knew she was late. On the side road, she met the post office truck with Panetta sitting next to the driver. They slowed, apparently wanting to say something, but Laura just waved to the postmen and kept on going. The mechanics parked the *York* on the apron, fuelled, and loaded as they had the previous week. Abdullahi fussed with the starter bar, and looked up when Laura arrived.

"Where is the captain?" he asked.

"He is very sick and cannot fly. I am going to take the Kismayo run."

"Are you trained?"

"Sure, I had plenty of training in India," lied Laura. The mechanic shrugged and gave Laura the bills of lading.

"You have some freight to Kismayo today," Abdullahi said. "It is a small pump for their waterworks. I tied it down between the first and second row. You'll have to step over it."

"Very well. Thank you, Abdullahi," she said and got into the plane. Going through the cabin a morbid thought crossed Laura's mind. *Am I walking through my coffin?*

She took Ray's seat on the left side, fixed her seat belt, but before giving the signal to Abdullahi, she took a piece of paper out of Ray's bag and wrote on it: Dear Ray, I stole your aircraft. I love you. Laura Blake-Stanton. She put the paper in an envelope, closed it, and handing it to Abdullahi remarked, "If anything happens to me, give this to the captain. Otherwise, I want it back."

"As you wish, Missy," said the mechanic with a smile. When Laura gave him the signal to start, he did not move. He looked up at Laura and asked, "Are you sure you want to do this, Missy?"

"Yes, I am doing it for Ray, you, Deria, Amina and all of us. Start cranking."

Abdullahi shrugged and started the engine. On Laura's signal, he took the chocks and gave her the thumbs-up sign. She waved and slowly pushed the throttle forward. At the end of the runway, Laura turned the *York* into the wind. Suddenly, she was short of breath. *My goddamned bra is choking me,* she thought, pulled down the zipper of her flight suit, and practically tore off the useless garment. Immediately, she felt much better. She pulled the zipper up and opened the throttle. The takeoff was smooth. When the plane reached cruising altitude, Laura relaxed a little. I got up here without any complications. I am sure I can find Brava, but the landing will be a problem. *If I had at least two landings before tackling this one, I wouldn't worry*, she thought. Her eyes were always jumping from dial to dial, carefully monitoring the well-being of the engine. There was no sign of trouble.

An hour passed when the tall church steeple of Brava appeared in the distance. *Here I go, the moment of truth*, Laura thought as she lined up the runway and closed the throttle. As the plane slowly sank toward the ground, Laura noticed a darker shade of sand near the end of the runway. *That is the spot where I want to touch down,* she thought, and fought the plane a little because the *York* always wanted to lower its nose. In the end, Laura won, and the wheels gently bumped the runway at the exact spot she wanted. *I can get along with this plane,* she thought. *We like each other.*

She gently applied the brakes, and the *York* slowed to a crawl.

We arrived at Brava in one piece, she said to herself. Laura turned the plane toward the shack with the thatch roof, stood on the brakes, parking at the same place as Ray had last week. She did not stop the engine, but let the propeller turn over slowly. She heard someone opening the rear door.

"Is that you, Asif?" she asked. The man came through the cabin to the cockpit and greeted Laura.

"Good morning, Missy. It's nice to see you again. Where is the captain?"

"He is not well today. I am sure he will be all right next week."

"May I have the bills of lading?"

"I have them right here," replied Laura, and from the black satchel she extracted a sheaf of papers.

"We have three bags for you today."

"I see. This time it's one for Merca, and two for us."

"That's right, it checks with the summary," Laura replied. "How many bags do you have for me?"

"Two big ones for Mogadishu."

"Very well, Asif. Please, tie them down properly. See you next week."

"I always do, Missy. Have a nice trip," said the man and withdrew quietly. Laura leaned out of her seat to check if Asif had fastened the net.

"Okay, my Lord. Here I go again," she said with a heavy sigh, and opened the throttle. Like a racehorse out of the gate, the *York* accelerated. It was easy to lift her off the runway and start climbing. The successful takeoff from the long Brava strip gave Laura a sense of security. She kept climbing to a thousand meters, made the right turn, and parallel to the coastline, flew in the direction of Kismayo. A few wisps of clouds raced by the window looking like pieces of fine, white muslin in the wind, and disappeared behind the plane. Laura's mind wandered. *This is fun,* she thought. *I am in control of a beast much stronger than any motorbike or automobile on the surface, and it will do whatever I want. I am beginning to understand the people who risk their lives to rule over a country. This is the same feeling. Perhaps I am developing megalomania. Nevertheless, flying makes me feel like a queen sitting on a throne made of clouds.*

She was flying in calm air for about an hour when suddenly, without warning, the plane lifted its nose like a spooked horse, then dropped it, throwing Laura against her safety belt. The left wing went down, and the *York* started a steep left turn heading for the beach. Staring forward, Laura saw the waves of the sea below coming at her at an alarming rate.

"Oh no, you won't," Laura said to the rebellious plane, and she instinctively kicked the right rudder trying to stop the turn, and she attempted to level the wings with the aileron. To her surprise, the maneuver worked, and the plane recovered, although in a steep dive. She managed to pull it up and checked the altimeter. It showed only two hundred meters. As soon as the *York* began a slow climb, Laura realized her heart was pounding, her palms sweating, her flight suit being wet throughout, and the cold sweat running down her back.

Getting the *York* back on even keel gave Laura the feeling of a queen putting down a rebellion. As she needed the aircraft, she struck a more conciliatory tone talking to the plane.

"Now you know who the boss is. We are going to be best friends. I am going to treat you nice and gentle, hoping you won't let me down. Okay?"

She felt the plane was behaving like a rebellious male, but she knew if aircraft could talk, the *York* would have smiled, assuring Laura of his love and friendship while acknowledging the pilot's mastery over him. Laura realized she just conquered the Merca low, the most unpredictable wind shear in the vicinity.

"I have to do it once more today," she sighed, knowing the exercise would be just as dangerous on the way back.

An hour and twenty minutes, later the town of Kismayo crept up on the horizon. The yellow house with the silo appeared. Laura checked the altimeter. It read five hundred meters exactly. It took a little bit of twisting and turning to put the plane over the silo keeping the heading of 01 degrees, but she managed, and chopped the throttle.

When the runway appeared, it seemed frighteningly short. Remembering Ray lowering the flaps one quarter, keeping the plane on the verge of a stall all the way down, she tried to imitate his maneuvers. It was not easy. Laura had to fight the plane all the way to the edge of the runway because the *York*, again, wanted to drop its nose. When she hit the runway, the bump was harder than in Brava, but not as drastic as her first landing in Mogadishu.

Lupo appeared with the fuel and waved to Laura. When he finished fueling and gave Laura the receipt, she asked, "How is Demona?"

"Very well," Lupo declared. "Meet Demona, Missy," he pointed at the donkey pulling the fuel cart.

"Hi, Demona," said Laura as she handed the signed receipt to Lupo. As if the donkey understood the message, she softly brayed before turning around, and without Lupo telling her anything she started moving toward the terminal shack.

The postmen unloaded ten bags of mail, the pump, and put six heavy mailbags on the plane. The postmaster boarded the plane. Finding Laura in the pilot's seat instead of Ray surprised him.

"Where is the captain?"

"He has a touch of malaria. He should be all right next week," replied Laura.

"I wish him well," the man said. "I have a passenger for you."

Laura swallowed hard. The awesome responsibility for someone else's life weighed heavily on her mind, and she felt cornered.

My life is on the line too, she thought, and with bravado in her voice, she declared, "Let him come aboard."

"I'll load his baggage first," the postmaster said and brought three large suitcases into the cabin.

"Just tie them down because I hate walking suitcases in case we hit some turbulence," Laura said paraphrasing Ray.

"As you wish, Missy," the man said.

Finally, the passenger, an elderly Italian officer, appeared. He had many medals, plenty of gold on his epaulets, and gold chevrons on the sleeve of his jacket.

"Where do you want me to sit?" he asked.

"Right here, in the copilot's seat, sir," Laura replied. The man took his place and extended his hand.

"I am General Alessandro Ponti."

"My name is Laura."

From the corner of her eyes she studied the general. He was about Ray's age, not as tall as the Englishman, but built well, in the mold of an athlete. He looked at Laura, as a man who appreciates women. After feasting his eyes on her face, hair, and the clinging, damp flight suit, he quietly remarked, "I am glad to meet you. Perhaps you should write the ticket. Ray always does it prior to takeoff to make sure I would be insured if something went wrong," he suggested.

"There is nothing to worry about, sir," said Laura as she dug into the black bag and extracted the blank tickets. *The fare seems ridiculous*, she thought, *but it is Ray's business, his airline, and he sets the rules.* She wrote the name of the general in the appropriate place and rather nervously handed it over without saying a word.

The general reached into his pocket, and without much ado, gave Laura twenty pounds, the amount Ray specified for passengers.

"Thank you, sir," she said, stuffing the money in her pocket. "Please, fasten your safety belt."

"Why? Do you expect a rough ride?"

"No, sir, but in the airline business unexpected things could happen. If you fell out of your seat, you might interfere with the controls. I know we'll have to fly through the Merca wind shear, and it could be rough. In addition, my boss ordered me to have every passenger securely tied in."

The general smiled, fixed his seatbelt, and remarked, "You'd make an excellent military pilot."

Laura did not answer. She had to concentrate on the pre-flight checks. Lupo cranked the engine to life, and they were on their way. At the end of the runway, Laura turned the *York* into the wind, she looked down the runway, and a cold shiver ran down on her back: "We'll never make it. The damn thing is too short."

She stopped to think, but fortunately, the way Ray took off at Kismayo popped up in her mind. Laura thought she had the solution.

"Here we go," she said and stood on the brakes, pushing the throttle forward. Under full power, the *York* shook like a dry leaf in the wind. She took her feet off the brake, and indeed the plane accelerated a little better than it normally did.

It's better, but still not good enough, she thought. Half way down the runway, she managed to lift the plane's tail, but the speed was still not enough. *We are going to crash, unless I do something fast*, she thought as fear began to overtake her thoughts. Again, Ray's technique came back, and with a smooth move, she dropped the flaps. Just like hitting a pillow, the plane slowed a little, and somewhat reluctantly left the ground. With eyes glued to the airspeed indicator, she gradually pulled up the flaps, as the airspeed increased.

Thank you, York, she thought. *If you were a man, I would kiss you.* Although she wanted to let a sigh of relief go, she controlled herself and smiled at her passenger saying, "Sorry about the hairy maneuver, sir, but the Kismayo runway is a little short."

"I know," the general said. "The captain reminded me often. Our army fliers refused to come here after one of their planes crashed on takeoff. I promise you, I will have it extended after my return from Rome."

"We will appreciate it, sir."

They reached cruising altitude and headed for the north. Impulsively, Laura decided to climb five hundred meters higher to have some extra room to maneuver if the Merca low hit them hard.

"I am going to climb higher than usual, sir," she said, "because the wind shear at Merca was very bad this morning. Having a distinguished passenger on board, I want to have extra margin of safety."

"It is very professional of you. Where did you learn to fly?"

"In India," she lied.

"They taught you well," concluded the general.

When Merca appeared on the horizon, Laura tensed. The plane started buffeting, but she could counteract the irregular wind thrusts. The *York* wanted to raise its nose a couple of times, but Laura tamed the bucking aircraft. In a few minutes, they passed the danger zone, and the *York* flew in calm air again.

Brava crept up on the horizon. "That is the Brava Catholic Church, sir, the tallest steeple on the coast," Laura said, even though she was sure the general knew about it.

"We'll reach Mogadishu in an hour."

The General nodded, but kept quiet.

I think the poor fellow is scared stiff having to fly with a woman at the controls, Laura thought as Mogadishu appeared in the distance. *I hope I'll get the speed right this time*, she thought while lining up the runway. At the proper distance, she chopped the throttle, and the *York* began her slow descent. They landed surprisingly well. There was hardly a bump. Laura still had to control her desire for a sigh of relief.

"Thank you for the pleasant trip," the general said as they rolled to a stop on the apron.

"If they ever give me the aircraft I've been asking for, I will hire you as my personal pilot. You are the greatest. Even Ray could take lessons from you."

"I was just lucky," Laura said, blushing.

The posties put the general's suitcases on the post office truck and he stood on the running board waving good-bye to Laura, while disappearing in a great cloud of dust.

The time for the big sigh of relief arrived. Laura retrieved the envelope she had given to Abdullahi in the morning, climbed on the Norton, and headed for the house feeling tired but satisfied. Flying is definitely sensual. *One may even substitute it for sex*, she thought driving down on the Via Lido.

The children were active on the street. At least three young adventurers dashed in front of Laura's motorbike. Respecting their wishes, she did not brake for them, missing the kids by inches.

I hope Ray is better, she thought when Ali opened the gate.

Laura stopped the bike, got off, and climbed the stairs to the patio to find Ray reclining on the couch, wearing a sleeveless safari suit and sneakers instead of the riding boots he normally wore.

"I see you made it," he said. "Congratulations, but if you pull another stupid stunt like this, I'll cut you out of my will. What made you do such an idiotic thing? You could have been killed!"

Amina appeared with Laura's Campari. She sat down and took a sip.

"Yes, I knew very well I could have been killed, but it would not have mattered. I am nobody. I don't even have a name. You could have buried me and written on my gravestone: *Here lies an airplane thief without identity.* The insurance company would have paid for the plane, and Panetta could not have lifted your contract. The jobs of your people and Air Mogadishu would have been safe for another day. As I managed to fly the southern run for you, we have a new lease on life and a chance to survive," Laura finished her tirade, running out of breath.

"I am eternally grateful," Ray said. "You are the bravest, most generous person, I've ever met. If I were thirty years younger, I'd propose to you, but since I am not, I have no idea how to thank you."

"If we looked at the balance, I believe I still owe you big time," Laura said with a smile.

"What are you saying?"

"Look, Ray, without you I would be still the empty-headed little girl from the colonies without a goal in life, or perhaps the slave of a camel herder. I wouldn't know what I wanted out of life. Now I know."

"Without you I would be dead. You saved my life so far three times, and saved Air Mogadishu. How can I thank you?"

"Do you remember last Wednesday night? That was sufficient thanks for at least nine savings of your life," Laura said. "In fact, it is counterproductive to argue about the balance of payments. Let me kiss you and tell you about my day at the office."

She leaned over to Ray and kissed him passionately on the lips. However, when Ray put his arms around her, she gently peeled the muscular arms off her.

"No matter how much I would like it, darling, you are not supposed to indulge in stressful activities. Doctor's orders."

"Okay, tell me about the flight," Ray interrupted, and drew away from her.

"It was nothing special," she said. "Even my passenger enjoyed it. The man offered me a job, if the government gives him a plane. He wants me to be his personal pilot."

"My God, did you fly the governor to Mogadishu?"

"I don't know his position. Nevertheless, he behaved like a proper, brave gentleman. His name is General Alessandro Ponti."

"He is the supreme commander of the colonial army in Somalia. Not bad."

"He was nice and polite, but I bet he was scared stiff."

"Okay, young lady, we have a mission before you can take a rest," Ray said.

"The doctor said you must remain in bed."

"I expect him to say stupid things like that. I have work to do. Come on." He stood up, but he was not standing firm. Laura had to support him.

"It won't work, Ray."

"It has to," he replied and called in Ali. Laura and the gardener managed to help Ray into the sidecar and they headed downtown. By the market, they stopped at the lane where Laura had escaped from the kidnappers. Ray climbed out of the sidecar with difficulty, told Ali to help him, and lumbered into the lane. When Laura wanted to follow them, Ray bluntly remarked, "You stay with the bike." Laura looked up and recognized the window from where she had jumped. It was much higher than the six feet she thought when taking the plunge. Fear grabbed her. She stood next to the bike with her back to the wall of the building on the corner. Laura pulled the zipper on the lower left pocket of her flight suit and put her hand on the gun.

It was decidedly unpleasant standing there in the twilight, having the memories of the kidnap still fresh in her mind. Ray and Ali came back in about half an hour, and the captain got into the sidecar.

"Take us home, Laura, if you please," he said in a tired voice.

When they reached the house, she decided to handle her employer with an iron fist, ordering Ray into bed. Amina gave him chicken noodle soup, and Laura sat by the side of the bed. Ray did not look like the man she had held in her arms a couple of days ago. The strength seemed to have evaporated from his body, but the love and desire still burned in his eyes. He held Laura's hand as if she were his only link to life. She sat by the bed silently. Love and sorrow alternated in her soul.

She willed Ray to recover, and the possibility of losing him frightened her.

"Give me the satchel," Ray said.

Laura handed it to him and opened the cover.

Ray took an envelope out, tore it open, and read the single sheet inside. He picked up his fountain pen from the night table and wrote something on it.

"This is my last will," he said and put the envelope on his nightstand.

"I doubt you'll need it in the near future, darling," Laura said.

"One never knows," he said.

"Okay, Ray, now get some rest."

"Not until I've told you how to manage the crosswind landing at Obbia tomorrow," he interrupted.

Although Ray seemed tired, he gave detailed instructions to Laura. By nine o'clock, Ray finished.

"Don't worry about those maneuvers, darling, I can deal with the cross wind landing," Laura said. "You must rest."

She gave him the medicine the doctor had prescribed, kissed him gently on the lips, waited until he fell asleep, tucked him in, and went to the patio for a nightcap.

As Amina brought her Campari, Laura explained to her to keep the captain in bed no matter what.

Looking at the stars, Laura felt satisfied. She just realized how dangerous her flight had been. Her hand started shaking and she felt the taste of brass in her mouth.

I could have killed my passenger and myself. I took an awful chance, but someone had to do it, she thought. Looking at the cloudless African sky with its crooked moon, her thoughts wandered.

Strangely, her strong feelings for Ray started slowly eroding when she thought of Bob.

"This is how a married woman must feel when she meets the man of her dreams," she mused. *Thank you, my Lord, for being my copilot on the Kismayo run. May I count on you tomorrow?*

Laura sighed as she stood up and retired to her room for the night.

Six

Laura managed the inland routes easily. She had no problems anywhere except in Obbia. She had to abort the first attempt at landing, but on the second approach, she nailed the runway perfectly. Following the tiring day, Laura happily landed at Mogadishu. Abdullahi and Deria treated her with the respect due to a fully qualified pilot. Getting on the Norton and driving through the usual route to home was a relief. On the patio, just as the day before, Ray was reclining on the couch.

She dropped the satchel and kissed him gently on the lips.

"It is so good to be home. How do you feel?"

"Eighty-five percent," he replied.

"What did the doctor say?"

"A lot of crap. He warned me about taking it easy, stay away from women and aircraft, but how can I do that? The only things worth living for are you and the planes."

"As I wouldn't want to lose you, we should respect his orders. At least for a little while longer."

"As you wish. How was the trip?" Ray asked.

"Tiresome," she replied. "I had to abort the first attempt at landing in Obbia, but the second time I managed it."

"Next time, it will be much easier. You'll see," Ray said while Amina brought Laura her Campari.

"I am bushed," Laura said taking a sip of her drink.

"You should not change for dinner tonight," Ray interrupted. "You had a long, hard day. Amina found some lean ham, and the doctor permitted me to eat some of it on toast. Thus, if you have no objection, we are going to have ham sandwiches for dinner."

Amina served the food, and Laura dug in. After the meal, they were having tea when a car drove into the compound. An elderly Somali man wearing the traditional prayer suit got out and walked to the patio.

"Come on in, Mr. Abdi," shouted Ray. "Have a cup of tea with us."

"Don't mind if I do," the man replied and came in.

"This is my niece. Laura, meet Mr. Abdi."

"*Enchante, Mademoiselle,*" replied Abdi, but did not offer to shake hands.

He accepted the tea and seemed to enjoy it.

"Well, Captain, I have the papers I promised you," he said and handed an envelope to Ray.

"Thanks," Ray said and checked the content. "There is only one document here."

"Oh, yes, I meant to tell you about the other. The text of the other document says: *the candidate passed the necessary tests to qualify.* I must ask the young lady to take a flight test."

"Who would conduct the exam?"

"I would, of course."

"Do you know anything about flying?"

"No, but if she takes off with me and lands, I will know if she is qualified or not."

They are talking about me taking a flight test, Laura thought. *It is going to be interesting.*

"All right, Mr. Abdi, come to the airfield at ten o'clock tomorrow morning to test her flying abilities."

"Well, I'll see you tomorrow, Captain," he said and stood. "I must hurry to the mosque for prayers. Bye."

Abdi got into his car and drove away.

"What was this all about?" Laura asked.

"Well, it is a long story. Abdi is the Commissioner of Licensing for the Colony, and in part- time, he is the star forger of Somalia. Last night, I asked him to modify my wife's old passport."

"Why was it necessary?"

"You need some documents, Laura. A forged passport is better than nothing."

"What can I do with it?"

"You can enter England with it."

"Would it not be dangerous?"

"I don't think so. Anyway, here is a British passport issued to Laura Madison, born in 1913 with your picture in it. Take it," he said and handed Laura the passport. "If anything happens to me, I am leaving Air Mogadishu to you. You could take possession and sell it. With this passport, you could return to England anytime."

"Thank you, Ray, thank you very much," she said, stood up and kissed him on the lips. "Although I am a person again, I have no desire to leave you. At least not until you have proper pilots to take care of all the routes. It is great being a person again."

"You are not entirely legitimate yet. I asked Abdi to make a commercial pilot's license for you, but he refused. He said he is not going to forge one, but would arrange for a proper license if you're willing to take a flight test."

"What do you mean a proper license? Has he the authority to issue a pilot's license?"

"I don't know, but if anyone can issue one in Somalia, he is the man. You are taking a flight test with him tomorrow."

"That will be interesting."

"You can say that again."

"What else did the doctor tell you?" Laura asked.

"He permitted me to get up and engage in moderately stressful activities."

"What does it mean?"

"He cut me off airplanes."

"How about other sources of excitement?"

"If you are referring to a cute little redhead called Laura, he did not."

"Are you sure?"

"I specifically asked him about women, and he said that I can have them in moderation."

"That I want to see. How can you do that in moderation?"

"Let me show you," Ray replied, stood up, took Laura by the hand, and headed for his room.

~ * ~

"I would not call that moderation," mused Laura an hour later when following the most satisfying lovemaking, she got back to her room.

Despite the flight test hanging over her head like the sword of Damocles, Laura was calm. She took a shower and lay on the bed, staring at the ceiling: *"Thank you, my Lord, for making Ray healthy and giving me a chance to give him a few moments of happiness. Please, let him recover, and Jim find a few pilots for him. Then I could go back to England, recover my identity, and come back to Ray."*

Strangely, she did not think of Bob.

Laura slept like a log. In the morning, she got up earlier than Ray, and sat at the breakfast table admiring her passport. Abdi certainly had done a fine job. He just took Mrs. Madison's passport, exchanged the two photographs and put the indentations of the seal on her picture. He altered Mrs. Madison's first name and a couple of numerals in the year of birth. The forgery was perfect. The signs of somebody tampering with the document were undetectable.

Walking steadily, Ray came to the breakfast table.

"Are you coming to witness my test?" Laura asked.

"I wouldn't miss it for the world."

At ten o'clock, they arrived at the airfield. Deria had the *Calabrese* ready for takeoff. He was discussing the maintenance schedule and the aircraft rotation with Ray when Abdi drove in.

"Here we go," said Ray and greeted the old man courteously.

"Is this the plane we are taking?" he asked, pointing at the *Calabrese.*

"Yes, sir," Laura said and directed Abdi to the plane. She opened the door and turned to him: "Permit me to board first, sir, and show you the way."

"By all means."

She guided Abdi to the copilot's seat, fixed his belt, and took her place.

"With your permission, sir, the captain suggested I take a left turn after takeoff, fly south along the beach, and give you a bird's eye view of Mogadishu. Would that be satisfactory?"

"Yes, it would."

With Deria cranking, Laura started the engine and taxied to the end of the runway. She turned the plane into the wind and opened the throttle. She had the confidence of a professional, since she had about a dozen takeoffs under her belt. She wanted to impress Ray and Abdi with her prowess.

All was well until the *Calabrese* lifted off the runway. At the altitude of about ten meters, the engine coughed, let out a mighty boom, and quit. Laura had no more than a hundred meters of runway left. She closed and opened the throttle, as one does on a motorcycle. Suddenly, the engine started, and she felt the pull of the propeller again.

I must gain altitude, Laura thought and leaving the throttle fully open, lifted the nose of the plane. In a steep climb, the *Calabrese* cleared the dune at the end of the runway by inches. She kept her eye on the airspeed indicator to make sure she would not stall the plane, but the *Calabrese* had other ideas.

The engine quit again, and the plane dropped its nose heading for the hard sand on the other side of the dune in a steep left turn.

Laura kicked the right rudder and leveled the wing. Pumping the throttle, she got a few seconds of life out of the dying engine, lifting the plane over the crest of the dune again. Staring ahead, she realized the plane had made a full 180-degree turn above the runway, and was headed for the hangar.

Laura chopped the throttle keeping the plane's nose up, and dropped it on the runway. Almost instantly she deployed the emergency-breaking device, a spade-shaped piece of metal mounted behind the tail wheel. The spade dug into the soft sand slowing the *Calabrese's* run. The aircraft came to a halt by the apron.

For a moment Laura was speechless, her hands trembled, her body bathing in cold sweat.

She looked at Abdi. The old man apparently did not realize the danger they were in. He smiled at Laura, and asked: "Can we do it again? But please, take it a little slower."

Laura could have strangled the fellow, but remarked with a forced smile: "I think we ought to take another plane. This one is too fast."

"Okay," said Abdi and started getting out of his seat.

Ray and Deria were standing by the door. Laura got out first and said to the mechanic, "With *Calabrese*, we do not like each other. Can we have another plane?"

Ray and Deria looked at each other, shrugged, and proceeded to drag the *York* out of the hangar.

Laura's second attempt at the flight test started without a hitch. As they reached five hundred meters, she leveled the plane and let Abdi enjoy the scenery. For a while, he looked at the city below and then turned to Laura: "This is the best time to tell you something, Missy. Do you know that you are supposed to be dead?"

"No. I wasn't aware of it."

"A white man paid ten pounds to one of the local thugs to kill you. You are lucky he chose that one, because the other guy, Noor, charges twenty pounds and guarantees his work."

The shocking news did not get into the way of Laura's flying the aircraft perfectly.

"Why didn't the fellow kill me?"

"He got greedy. After the *Oleandris* departed, your cut-rate assassin figured he would sell you to one of the chieftains in the Ogaden for a couple of camels. No woman has ever escaped from the desert."

Cold sweat kept running down Laura's back, but she held the plane level. Reaching the southern limits of the city, she made a right turn heading toward the field.

"If I were you, I would keep this news under my hat, Missy, because if I had to testify in court, I would deny having this conversation with you. Nevertheless, in your place I would always carry a dagger or a gun, because Tamar is very angry at you."

"Why?"

"You broke his foot."

"He should not have kidnapped me."

"Correction, Missy," he interrupted. "If he had done his work properly, you would not have had a chance to stomp on his toes. You'd be dead."

"Thank you for telling me, Mr. Abdi."

"I owe that much to the captain. Now, I'd better concentrate on your flight test."

Laura decided not to pry into the matter or question Abdi's connection to Tamar. She concentrated on flying the aircraft.

Abdi was very happy to see the harbor and the ships. He managed to identify his own house.

After landing, he took out a driver's license from his pocket, which he decorated with a blue diagonal stripe. It stated: "*The bearer was tested and found competent to operate any commercial aircraft, carrying passengers or cargo.*"

"Congratulations, Missy, you are the first person in the Colony to earn a pilot's license," Abdi said, and with his head held high he retreated to his car, and drove away.

When he disappeared, Ray asked: "What the hell happened?"

"I had a rough time. First, the *Calabrese* quit on me. I was trying to gain some altitude when she stalled, went into a spin, and I was lucky to take her out of it in time."

"It was scary," Ray said shaking his head. "I knew a mad Russian named Chalov or something like that. He regularly put his plane into a spin and took it out a few meters above the surface. Seeing you do it, I almost had a heart attack."

"Thank God, I am not flying today and tomorrow. It is great fun, but if I had to take off after this fiasco, it would be too much of a good thing. I still haven't recovered from the panic," Laura said.

"You never will. Airline flying is hours of boredom punctuated by seconds of sheer terror," Ray said. "Let's go home."

Although Laura had no reason to worry, her self-confidence had taken a beating by the misbehavior of the aircraft.

The Calabrese is a cantankerous female, Laura thought. *She's jealous of me and Ray.*

Laura enjoyed having nothing to do, just sunbathe in the garden, occasionally getting up and going into the house, touching Ray, and having a glass of mineral water, the famous *Aqua di Brava,* produced right there in Somalia.

After lunch, Laura realized she had survived two events when she could have easily died.

I am lucky, or perhaps my guardian angel was working overtime, she thought.

She debated telling Ray about her stepfather hiring someone to kill her. For a moment, she thought of Ray's weakened condition and that likely stress caused by Abdi's revelation might have serious consequences.

I must tell him, she thought, and in the afternoon, she told him about Edward hiring an assassin.

"I knew about it," said Ray.

"Who told you?"

"Mr. Abdi and I go back a long way. We are good friends. He told me when I asked him to make you a passport."

Ray took Laura's hand and drew her close to him.

"I do not know what I'd do without you," Laura said.

They sat on the patio holding each other's arms for perhaps an hour when Laura stood.

"It is time for your medicine, darling."

"Which one?" asked Ray. "Are you going to give me pills for my body or treat my soul?"

"I give you the tablets the doctor prescribed you and I am going to hold you in my arms to treat my soul and yours."

"I could do without the first one, but the second is essential."

~ * ~

Next morning, shortly after breakfast, the doctor came, examined Ray, and nixed his request to fly again.

"Forget about flying for at least a few weeks," he said. "I do not have proper diagnostic tools and no laboratory to establish exactly what is wrong with you. As I do not want you passing out at the controls of an aircraft, I must keep you grounded for a while."

"Reluctantly, I agree," Ray replied. "Although I would like to relieve Laura occasionally."

"She is young and tough, she can take it," the doctor said.

After Doctor Bertoli left, Laura sat down with Ray to learn a little more about meteorology, but she did not get too far.

"First, I must tell you about the facts of life," Ray started.

"Don't you think I know enough?" Laura said with a coquettish smile.

"I was not referring to your mastery of the art of love, although it puzzles me how you could learn that much from a Sandhurst cadet in one summer."

"In addition to Bert and you, I had another instructor...a French lawyer visiting Dacca."

"He taught you well. Anyway, I had something else in mind."

"Namely?"

"You are a fully licensed pilot, and your wages are going to be five pounds a week plus one third of all moneys collected from the passengers on your mail routes."

"I am going to be rich."

"This is the amount we pay ourselves when we are flying," Ray explained. "In addition, I set up a logbook for you to keep track of your flying hours. You have twenty-two hours of dual instructions and fifteen hours of solo. This is almost enough for someone in England to take the private pilot's test. For a license like yours, one needs many more hours."

"I see."

"Okay, now let's talk a little about meteorology," Ray said.

~ * ~

It became routine that Laura flew all the mail routes, with Ray occasionally going with her as a copilot. He did that contrary to the strict orders of Doctor Bertoli, but Ray defended breaking the rules by saying, "She is still young, and I am trying to teach her the tricks of the trade."

"No matter how well you train her, if something goes wrong with your heart between Mogadishu and Kismayo, it will take hours to get you here. By the time I could do something, it would be too late," the doctor said, and reiterated his objections to Ray's flying as a copilot.

"You are right, Doctor. Regardless, I am going to fly with her occasionally."

A month later, when the first signs of the rainy season appeared, Laura still had not heard from her grandmother.

"I must have misspelled the address, and the letter went astray," she told Ray one evening sitting on the patio.

"You should have more faith in the Royal Mail, darling. Isn't it possible that she died?"

"Granny is bulletproof. She will outlive me by at least ten years."

"Nevertheless, it is a possibility."

"Okay, okay, I give up. Let us compromise. I'll write her again," said Laura.

"Do that, my dear. I am worried about your future."

She edged closer to Ray and put her head on his shoulder.

"I love you when you say that."

Ray turned his face toward Laura and lifting her chin, he looked deep into her eyes.

"I assume you know that I love you, and you'll agree I have plenty of reasons to worry about you."

"Rubbish, my dear, I know how to handle the planes, I know the routes, and you turned me into an expert at meteorology. You have nothing to worry about," Laura replied and gently kissed Ray on the lips. "Nevertheless, I love you for worrying about me."

"You misunderstand me, Laura. I am not worried about your flying. You are an excellent pilot. Your status is my reason for concern.

You are living and working under an assumed name, and you have only a forged passport."

"Nobody is going to bother about that," Laura interrupted.

"I am not so sure. If the authorities found out, they would throw you in jail."

"You worry about nothing."

"Nevertheless, I'd like to see you get your identity back."

"Let us wait another month," Laura suggested. "By that time the pilots from England should arrive, and I can board a banana boat to Naples and take the train from there."

"I have another worry," Ray started, but Laura put her hand on his mouth and remarked: "I know what you are going to say. Let me tell you the way I see it: we don't know what tomorrow might bring; let us live for the moment."

She stood up, took Ray by the hand, and started toward the bedroom.

~ * ~

A few weeks later, Laura had a rather hairy flight returning from Obbia as several thunderheads spread out between the seaside village and Mogadishu. The weather forced her to change the route several times, getting in late, landing at the airstrip in the twilight, and having had her problems complicated by blinding rain. Soaked to the skin Laura arrived at the house.

Ray sat on the couch, his feet up, but stood to greet her saying, "Although I was sure you would manage, darling, the weather frightened me."

He took her in his arms and kissed her.

"Let me go and dry my hair," she said and peeled off Ray's arms.

"Just put on a robe and come out. Hurry, I have good news."

Laura dried her hair, toweled, put on her bathrobe, and returned to the patio.

Amina had already prepared her Campari. She took her customary place next to Ray on the couch.

"I am ready for the good news," she announced.

"Well, I got a letter from the Junkers Factories in Dessau. The Germans are going to ship our new engines as soon as they find a ship to Mogadishu leaving from a German port. They want to supervise the loading of the sensitive shipment."

"That's good. We need those engines badly. I told Abdullahi to pull the *Calabrese* off the line. The engine quit soon after takeoff, and I had a hard time turning around and landing safely," said Laura. "My day did not start well."

"I have another item of good news. I found a pilot."

"That is really encouraging."

"Don't get your hopes too high, my dear. Although he is a pilot, I've no idea about his skills."

"Who is the guy?" Laura asked.

"An Italian, a former fighter pilot called Pietro. He is visiting his fiancée, the daughter of a banana planter. I checked him out this morning. He knows how to handle the aircraft."

~ * ~

The next day they met Pietro. Laura took him up and he impressed her with his competence. Ray went up with him to make sure he could handle the F13.

Starting Friday, Laura showed Pietro the route, and on the following week, they covered both the Kismayo run and the inland routes. The Italian performed like a professional. Laura thought the time might have come for her to visit England.

They divided the workload. On the first day the Italian went on the first solo to deliver the mail to Kismayo, both Laura and Ray waited for him at the airfield.

"There he comes," Laura said and pointed at the *Calabrese* appearing from the south.

"He should line up the runway now," Ray said.

However, instead of easing on the throttle, blue smoke came out of the exhaust, and the plane accelerated.

"What is that idiot trying to do?" Ray grunted.

"I don't know. Perhaps he misjudged the runway," Laura suggested.

The *Calabrese* roared over the field low at full power. The pilot took it into a steep climbing turn, came back, and did a victory roll over the field before landing the F13 perfectly. As he got out of the plane, Ray was practically at his throat.

"What the hell were you doing? These planes are old, little airliners, not hotrods. They are not aerobatic planes. You could have torn off a wing."

"Did I?" interrupted Pietro.

"No, because you are too goddamn lucky," roared Ray. "If I see you pulling a crazy stunt like that again, I am going to fire you."

"Okay, I won't do it again," Pietro promised.

~ * ~

As the letter from Granny did not arrive, Laura did not wish to leave until Pietro learned all the routes and Ray had confidence in the fellow's flying. Pietro split the flying duties with Laura. She took the southern route and the Bossasso run every second week, but the expected relief never materialized.

On the second Tuesday, Pietro had to visit Mr. Abdi about his pilot's license, and he switched routes with Laura. The Italian flew the southern route, and she took the inland run.

When she arrived in Galcaio, a large crowd waited at the strip. She stopped the engine to refuel and got out of the plane.

"What are these people doing here?" she asked the postmaster.

"They came for the show."

"What show?"

"Last week Mr. Pietro showed us what flying is all about. He did this," and he indicated a loop, "and that," and he showed a spinning motion, "but the best was when he flew the plane upside down."

"Did he do all those tricks?"

"Yes, Missy, he did, and he promised an even better show for this week."

Laura did not say anything. She thanked the postmaster, assured him there would be no more shows, filled up the tank, and continued her route.

On Friday, before Pietro took off for Bossasso, Laura and Ray went to the airfield. This time Laura took the lead.

"The people in Galcaio were disappointed on Tuesday," she said.

"Why?"

"You promised them a show."

"Oh, that was only a little innocent fun. Flying straight and level bores me. I have to let some steam off."

"You mean you did some aerobatics with my plane?" Ray asked.

"It did not hurt anything, or did it?" Pietro said calmly.

"I hope it did not hurt the plane, but you are fired," Ray said, calmly handing an envelope with the last pay to the Italian. He left Pietro standing in the middle of the apron.

"Abdullahi," Ray turned to the mechanics. "Take the *Calabrese* into the shop and check every bolt, every strut on it. We are taking the *York* for the Bossasso run."

Pietro tried talking to Ray, but he completely disregarded him. Finally, they took off for Bossasso.

"The idiot," grunted Ray, "he could have damaged the *Calabrese* beyond repair. I do not want you flying the damn plane until the guys go over it with a fine tooth comb."

"I agree," Laura said. "Now we are back to square one."

"I am very sorry, darling. I wish the doctor would let me fly alone," Ray said.

~ * ~

Sitting on the patio on Sunday evening, Laura complained about not receiving a reply from Granny, when Ray remarked again, "Your grandmother may have died."

"I thought of the possibility," Laura said.

"In that case you should hurry to England and collect your inheritance."

"I don't think so," Laura replied.

"Why?"

"Look at it this way, Ray. If she died, Edward would have learned about it. In that case, his lawyer already has taken possession of Stanton Manor, and laid claim to the trust by my maternal grandfather. By the time I reached England, he'd have sold the estate, paid the death duties, and stashed the money in a safe place."

"That requires thorough organization."

"Edward is good at it. Besides, I barely have enough money to pay for a one way passage on a banana boat to Naples, and a third class railway fare to Folkestone. When I got there, I might have five pounds in my pocket. That is not enough to hire a lawyer to help recover my name, and it is not enough to buy a ticket back to my job here. Furthermore, what would happen to you and Air Mogadishu while I was away?"

"You shouldn't worry about it, darling. I could take a Somali nurse with me on the routes to give me the pill if I started to faint. I could manage without you for a while."

"You would endanger the life of your nurse."

"It is better than risk losing you to the Somali justice system. Look, Laura, I have an emergency stash. I could give you a hundred pounds."

"Forget it, Ray, just forget it. It is ridiculous. What happens if you collapse as you did a couple of months ago? Nurse or no nurse, you couldn't fly, and Panetta would lift your contract. The bank would foreclose, you'd be out of a job, the house, and they'd even take the Norton. In addition, if you gave me the money from the secret stash, you couldn't return to England. You'd starve to death. No, Ray, just forget about the whole thing. I am going to England when I can finance my return trip, when I have some money for the lawyer, and in the end, I could come back to you and keep flying for Air Mogadishu."

"How about recovering your identity?"

"I am quite happy being Laura Madison, thank you very much. I must go to England before my forged passport expires, but until that time, we'd better drop the subject," said Laura in a firm tone.

"God save your husband."

~ * ~

By the end of the skimpy rainy season in Somalia, Laura could deal with all the weather-related problems.

"I wish I could teach you instrument flying," Ray said, "but I didn't have proper training in it either."

"Are you suggesting we should try learning from the books?"

"Well, our planes don't have all the necessary instruments, but we can try," said Ray.

They worked out a system of installing curtains on the windows of the right seat, and drawing them shortly after the takeoff to create the appropriate conditions for the pilot. Laura had to navigate using the available instruments, while Ray was looking out on the window making sure he knew where they were. As far as radio navigation was concerned, they just learned the theory from the books because the old F13-s did not have radio.

"You are becoming very good, Laura," Ray said, returning from an instrument flying exercise. "God created you to be an airline pilot."

"Last night you said that I was created to make love," Laura said with a smile.

"The two are not incompatible," mused Ray.

"Based on my limited experience, pilots are the best lovers. You would make an excellent husband for me."

"I am sorry, Laura. You are dead wrong. Look at it this way. I am over fifty, have a bum ticker, and could drop dead any minute. How could I marry you?"

"After I come back from England, we should go to the City Hall."

"No, Laura, forget it. It would be crazy," Ray interrupted.

"But I am so happy with you."

"That, my dear, is due to one thing. Let us face it. The sex drive of a female is just as strong as a male's. Frustrated people do not make good pilots. If you had the slightest psychological baggage, you wouldn't be able to make life or death decisions within a fraction of a second. As you are not sexually deprived, you are an outstanding pilot," Ray explained.

"Are you telling me that I am a good pilot because we sleep together occasionally?"

"In addition to your God-given talents, it helps a great deal. If you were stressed, you would have died on the day of your flight test, or you could not have nailed the runway in the twilight during a blinding rainstorm the other day."

"In the interest of maintaining my professional standing, remind me to seduce you after landing," Laura said with a coquettish smile.

~ * ~

Ray wrote to several friends asking them to find pilots because he knew Laura could not stand the strain of flying nearly thirty hours a week very much longer, but nothing turned up.

Laura was gathering strength for the grueling Bossasso run, sitting on the patio, and sipping her Campari.

"I think it is time for you to learn bridge," Ray said.

"I am game," she said.

"Okay. I'll get the cards," said Ray, but he never got around to it.

A big car drove into the compound, and General AlessandroPonti appeared.

"Captain Madison, forgive my intrusion, but I have an emergency. I need your help."

"Come on in, General, have a drink with us," said Ray, inviting the man to the patio.

"Don't mind if I do."

"What can I do for you?"

"I must charter one of your planes with Laura at the controls."

"Where do you want to go, sir?" asked Ray.

"I must reach Aden by Saturday morning."

"You could take the regular mail flight tomorrow, the one we call the northern route," Ray said. "It starts in Mogadishu, ending in Bossasso. Usually our pilot sleeps there, and comes back next day. However, if we can persuade Laura to fly the extra two and a half hours to Aden..."

"I can do it with pleasure," Laura interrupted.

"Thank you," said the general. "It's settled. I am flying with you. Now we have to take care of the mundane financial details."

"Why do you have to go to Aden, sir?" Laura asked.

"I am taking Imperial Airways to Rome."

"I didn't know Imperial landed in Aden," Ray said.

"The flights started two weeks ago. From now on, they fly east every Saturday morning. Another plane comes from the west and heads for Karachi the same day. If you had additional aircraft, you could connect Imperial Airways to Mogadishu, Nairobi, and a few other centers of East Africa. It would be a good move," the general replied.

"I have a hard time finding pilots."

"I am not surprised. To live and work in Somalia is not a pleasant experience. My officers dislike it as well. However, if you moved your headquarters to Nairobi and rotated your pilots, you could do it."

"If I were ten years younger and fifty thousand pounds richer, I would try it," Ray concluded.

"Nevertheless, if you decided to take the plunge, let me know. I would gladly invest a few thousand pounds in such a venture. I believe the future is in air transportation. You should see the size of those huge Handley Page four-engine monsters."

"I've seen them," Ray replied. "I just cannot believe they can fly."

Laura just listened to the conversation. Suddenly, the picture of Bob flashed in her mind, but she quickly put it back in the hidden corners of her brain.

For all intents and purposes I am married to Ray, she thought. *Besides, we met a long time ago. Bob might have married or transferred out of Aden. Nevertheless, our meeting would be different this time, because I have become a professional pilot.*

"What time do we take off?" the general asked.

"At sunrise," blurted Laura.

"Actually, it is six-thirty," Ray corrected.

"Okay, let me settle the finances with you, Captain," said Ponti, taking out his checkbook.

After Ponti departed, Laura felt lucky to have the chance to fly to Aden, carrying a passenger, and receiving a lot of extra money for the trip. However, she would gladly have foregone the additional pay for the chance of meeting Bob and showing off with her pilot's license and new professional standing.

Ray gave Laura a long look.

"I think something is missing from your flight suit," he said.

She quickly checked over her attire.

"I do not see anything missing."

"I do," he said and pinned a pair of golden wings onto Laura's flight suit. "Now your attire is almost complete."

She blushed and did not know what to say.

"The nametag saying *Captain Laura Madison, Air Mogadishu* is still missing."

"I am not a captain."

"All pilots in charge of an aircraft are called captain. May the machine be a two-seater or a huge monster like Imperial's Hanno, your proper title is captain."

"I see."

"Okay, Captain," said Ray. "I wanted to teach you the game of bridge, but I must change the topic. I am going to tell you about the dangers of flying long distances over water."

~ * ~

To Laura's relief, she was flying her favorite plane, the *York*. The general turned out to be a pleasant traveling companion. Apparently, flying with Laura did not scare him anymore. He entertained her with the recent gossips in the Colony and tried to recruit Laura to join the local theatrical group, the Mogadishu Amateur Dramatic Society.

"They could use a good-looking diva, I am sure," he said.

"I was never the acting type," she replied. "I preferred athletics."

"What did you do?"

"I was the captain of the field hockey team and county fencing champion."

"Actually, we tried a fencing club here a few years ago, but in the heat nobody could take it very long. We gave it up eventually."

The general being an inquisitive person made Laura talk about her family, which she did not really appreciate, because she had to lie, changing the name of her father, although she kept the gist of her story true. There was very little chance of General Ponti reading the roster of the Indian Civil service looking for the Madisons.

In Bossasso, Ahmed's donkey cart and fuel waited for the plane by the landing strip. When Ahmed saw Laura, he asked, "Did you come alone again, Missy?"

"Yes, I did. The captain is very busy nowadays."

"I see," Ahmed said. "Are you going to sleep at the Mission?"

"No, I have a passenger to Aden."

"Very well," Ahmed said. "I will be here with two barrels expecting you from ten o'clock onward."

"Thank you, my friend. I appreciate it."

Following the refueling, Laura had all the mailbags off the plane and stored in the post office until the next day.

"I'll have them out here for you by ten tomorrow," the postmaster said.

"Thank you, sir," she said and signaled to Ahmed to start cranking the engine to life.

The flight to Aden was fortunately uneventful. The general did not object to landing at the military airstrip, because he knew the R.A.F. officers were hospitable when Italians came through their base.

Bob parked Laura in the mess with Flight Lieutenant Fred Hanley, and took the General in the squadron's car to his hotel. In fifteen minutes he came back, sat down and asked Laura, "Where did you stash the old man?"

"What old man?"

"I meant Ray."

"I flew the plane today," Laura said. "Ray is sick, he has malaria."

"Are you qualified?" asked Bob.

"Sure I am. For more than two months," replied Laura and she put her elegant Somali pilot's license on the table.

"This calls for a drink," said Bob and ordered a bottle of champagne.

After the pilots got their drinks, Bob stood and proposed a toast. "Here is to the most beautiful pilot in the whole world."

"Hear, hear," said the others and drained their glasses.

"You must tell me all about qualifying in Somalia," he said.

"If you take me for a walk after sunset, I will," said Laura.

Her reaction to Bob surprised her.

Now, I've done it. I am going to open myself to his advances. It is unfair to Ray, she thought.

"It's a deal," said Bob quickly.

Later he escorted Laura to her quarters and waited until she changed for dinner. The sun was just setting when Laura came out of her room.

"It is going to be dark in five minutes," Bob said. "We can take a little walk before dinner."

"May as well go," Laura agreed. *You are playing with fire, old girl*, she thought and accepted Bob's arm as they stepped out onto the desert airfield.

"You promised to tell me how you obtained your pilot's license," Bob asked.

"It is a long story, Bob, and I am not going to lie to you anymore. I am not the niece of Ray, my name is not Laura Madison."

When she finished her saga, carefully hiding her relationship with Ray, Bob just stood there gaping. He took Laura's hand and pulled her closer to him: "I don't care if your name is not Madison or whom you are related to. As far as I am concerned, you are the most wonderful woman I have ever met."

"Do you really mean it, Bob?"

"Come on, you are beautiful, intelligent, gentle and have accomplished the impossible in less than ten days. You learned to pilot that monster from scratch. To check out on your airliner would take a few weeks even for an experienced pilot. That is incredible," he said and pulled her closer.

Laura put her arms around Bob. She did not have to say a word… their lips touched, and the world dissolved into something pink, something neither of them had ever experienced.

"I love you," said Bob.

His sudden revelation surprised Laura. She did not know what to say or do. With a sudden decision, she hugged Bob and offered him her lips. The magic continued for a few minutes.

After the long kiss, Bob released her and remarked, "I am hosting a small gathering for the captain and crew of the Imperial Airways Handley Page."

"I know. My passenger is flying to Rome with them tomorrow."

"It is quite something. They fly to London via Cairo, Rome, and Munich. Captain Wills and his pilots are coming over for a drink."

"I loved to meet them," said Laura, hoping to get to the mess, a place where she had to control her animal instincts.

"Let's go."

The Imperial crew arrived in a short while. Their elegant navy blue uniforms were impressive.

Bob took Laura to meet them.

"Captain Wills, this is Captain Laura Madison of Air Mogadishu. She flies the little Junkers out there."

"Captain Madison, the pleasure is mine," said Wills. "I'd be glad to show you our aircraft if you could come over to the civilian field in the morning."

"I am afraid, Captain, I must leave by sunrise."

"Are you connecting to our flights?"

"We are not, but we have a mail run to Bossasso every Friday. To extend it to Aden is not too difficult."

"I am going to tell my boss, and they might contact your manager. Can you give us his address?"

"I can," she replied and wrote the postal and the telegraphic addresses of Air Mogadishu on a piece of paper from her notebook. "I am afraid I just joined the company, and have no business card."

"This is good enough. By the way, how long is the flight to Mogadishu?"

"I guess it would take seven or eight hours with a refueling stop."

"When did you arrive?"

"Yesterday. Actually I brought you a passenger from Mogadishu, General Ponti."

"Are you telling me you are flying eight hours a day, two days running?"

"Yes," Laura replied. "Since the chief pilot is sick, I have to fly almost thirty hours a week."

"Amazing." Wills shook his head. "We are not allowed to fly that much. You must be very tough."

"I am," replied Laura, "and I am also crazy about flying. It is the greatest fun I can imagine."

"Well, if you want to fly with us, we can arrange an airline service/ courtesy ticket for you."

"What does that mean?"

"As a captain of another airline, space permitting, we can fly you to London for ten pounds."

"I may take you up on that, Captain, but not right now."

"Whenever you want to do it, just show me your license and a statement from Air Mogadishu affirming your status as captain. In fact, just send a telegram to Bob; he can let our crew know."

"Thank you, Captain Wills. I am sure Air Mogadishu would reciprocate," Laura said.

In a couple of hours, the Imperial crew departed, and Bob walked Laura to her room.

At the door, he took her into his arms and kissed her. Laura felt his muscular arms around her, the swelling desire, and kissed him back passionately. Bob's hand found its way to Laura's breast. She did not object, in fact, she opened the top button on her blouse.

"This is no good, darling," Laura said.

"I tend to agree with you," said Bob in trembling voice.

"Why don't you come in?"

As they entered, Laura started shedding her clothes at the door. By the time they reached the bed, she was completely naked. Bob had also managed to get rid of most of his clothes.

They made love with passion hitherto unknown to Laura. Ray did not exist during the most exciting ten minutes of Laura's life.

She felt safe resting comfortably in Bob's strong arms. Although Ray holding her gave Laura a feeling of security, this was different. This man could give her long-term support, while Ray could vanish in one minute. She thought about exploring her relationship with the Squadron Leader further, even though she felt she was cheating on Ray.

Bob woke and kissed Laura's breasts, wakening the sleeping tigress in her. She started exploring the man's body and found what she was looking for.

An hour later Laura propped her head on a pillow and turned to Bob.

"Although I loved every second of it, I think it would be a good idea if you left. I am bushed."

"Was I too aggressive?"

"No darling, I met you after a grueling eight hour flight. It is a miracle I had the strength to fall in love with you."

"It is a miracle indeed. However, I would like to have you here for a week. When Ray recovers."

"Let's face it, Robert," Laura interrupted. "Ray is not going to recover. He may live for many years, but I am sure his days of flying solo are over."

"What do you mean?"

"He has fainting spells, and it has nothing to do with his malaria. Some time ago, while landing at Bossasso, he overshot the field and had to abort the landing. The last time we were here, on the way home he passed out, and I had to land the plane in Mogadishu with less than a week of flying experience. When we fly together, he is giving me training, moral support, but the plane is always in my hands," Laura explained. "We need pilots desperately."

"I'll see what I can do for you," replied Bob. "Can you delay your departure tomorrow an hour?"

"Why?"

"I want to take you up in my bomber."

"Why don't I take you up for a spin in my airliner?"

"Aren't you interested in my bomber?"

"To be honest, Robert, your planes are open cockpit. I would have to wear one of those heavy leather flying suits."

"Say no more, we are going up in your machine."

"Thank you, Robert."

"Don't call me Robert, please. Everybody calls me Bob."

"Look, Bob is a name for a boy, but you are every inch a man. Therefore, I would like to call you Robert if you don't mind."

"No objection."

After a fifteen-minute kiss, Bob left, and Laura happily stretched out on her bed.

Thank you, my Lord, for giving me Robert. I may just get somewhere with him. Although I feel a little bit guilty about cheating on Ray, I am sure he would forgive me, and I hope you would too, and she happily fell asleep.

~ * ~

The sun rose over the desert early. Laura and Bob walked hand in hand to the Junkers.

"I am going to crank," said Bob.

"Wait for my signal," Laura replied and ran through the pre-flight check before she gave Bob the signal.

The engine started easily, and Bob took his place in the copilot's seat.

"I never flew in a closed cockpit aircraft," he said. "The engine is so quiet."

"Wait until I give the *York* her head," said Laura, pushing the throttle forward and beginning to taxi.

As soon as she turned into the wind and started the takeoff, to her the engine was loud.

"How is it now?"

"Too quiet," replied Bob. "Have you got full power?'

"Oh yes," Laura replied, lifting the plane off the runway. "How does it feel?"

"Weird, but pleasant. I think I could get used to flying one of these things."

"Ray says monoplanes are the future."

"He may be right. One of these days, I should visit you and check out on the Junkers."

"I am sure Ray would gladly check you out."

By this time they were at five hundred meters, making the traditional left turn after takeoff.

"Look, Laura, there is the Hanno," Bob said, pointing at the giant airliner on the civilian field.

The people moving around her looked like ants.

"It is huge," remarked Laura. "It must be fun flying it."

"Would you try?"

"If they gave me a chance, I would, but I am a woman, and Imperial would never consider an application from a female pilot. They need men without military training and a few war medals. I am afraid I must stick to these little airliners. By the way, do you want to take over?"

"Sure," replied Bob and took over the controls.

"Take the left turn," said Laura.

Bob executed the turn perfectly, and they flew parallel to the runway.

"Apparently, you fly as well as you kiss and make love," said Laura with a coquettish smile.

"You ain't seen nothing, young lady. Wait till we land."

Bob took another left turn and lined up the runway.

"I'll take it," said Laura and took over the controls. She concentrated on the speed and touched down with a barely perceptible bump.

"I can't say which is better: your flying or your kissing," Bob said.

"As I have very little experience in both, I must be a natural," Laura said.

Laura cut the ignition, and the propeller stopped. The empty field, the distant line of the biplanes and the rising sun made Laura feel like she was on a desert island. The quiet was deafening. Suddenly, she wanted Bob more than anything else. As she looked at him, she saw the desire on his face as well.

"I must get off," said Bob and stood up.

"Wait, I'll escort you," Laura said and got out of her seat.

She squeezed by Bob into the cabin of the F13. The nearness of him almost drove her crazy, but before she could do anything about her strange desire, Bob took her in his arms and kissed Laura passionately.

Her knees buckled, and she sat on the passenger's seat in the cabin.

"This is no good, darling," the man said. "You must go, and we can't return to your room."

"Have you lost your sense of adventure? What is wrong with the isle between the seats?" Laura asked.

Bob just stood there looking at the woman he desired so much, but when Laura pulled the zipper of her flight suit all the way down exposing her breasts, he lost his common sense too.

Making love in the isle had its redeeming features, but when it was over, Laura remarked, "This was exactly what the doctor ordered, even though I'd prefer the bed in your guest room."

"So would I," replied Bob. "When are you coming again?"

"As soon as I can find a good reason to come to Aden."

He tightened his belt and kissed Laura passionately saying, "I wish you'd never leave."

"That would be nice," Laura agreed.

"This is it, darling," said Bob. "See you next week if you can come. Practice the flying, but let me do the instructing when it comes to making love."

"I love you, Robert."

"It is so nice to hear you say that. Take care of yourself, darling, and come next week if you can. It is better to be with you when you are tired than being without you."

He quickly got out of the plane and waved to Laura.

"My sentiments exactly," she said and closed the door after Bob left.

He cranked the engine to life. Laura turned the *York* into the wind and opened the throttle. As she set the course to Bossasso, she looked back and saw Bob standing at the apron waving.

Seven

During the long flight over the sea, Laura tried to figure out what to do about Bob.

I'd marry him, but it is too early to think of that. I should get to know him better. I read the secrets of love and good marriage in Doctor Lewiston's book at Wyndham Academy. Unfortunately, Miss Hampton confiscated the copy before I could finish it. She claimed the book was pornographic. According to the doctor, the most important things in a marriage are good sex and understanding. If these two were there, mutual respect came next, leading to true, lasting love and a happy marriage. I got to the first stage with Robert, but how can I reach the second and the third? My weekly visits to Aden are uncertain and infrequent. I always arrive tired and leave next morning. Perhaps before I return to England, I should spend some time in Aden. However, that is far, far away. Meanwhile, I must make the most of my visits to Aden, she thought when Bossasso appeared on the horizon.

Ahmed waited with the fuel by the runway, and the postmaster had the mailbags loaded while Laura sat in the shade. Suddenly, the thought of Ray hit her. Shaking her head, she boarded the *York.*

"What am I going to tell him?" she asked herself while tightening her seatbelt. The thought of cheating on Ray weighed heavily on her mind. However, she remembered talking about marriage with him, but he always turned her down. Granted, his arguments were solid, and she agreed with him: marrying Ray verged on the ridiculous. However, she slept with him at least twice if not three times a week, and enjoyed every minute of it.

"Would going to bed with Ray constitute cheating on Bob?" she asked herself.

The reply was obvious. It did not, as Laura needed to relieve the stress because according to her mentor only a relaxed pilot could make the life and death decisions within fractions of a second.

My priorities are my passengers, the aircraft, and the cargo, she thought as the plane touched down on the dusty runway of Mogadishu. The landing was smooth, and the mechanics greeted her with respect. Doctor Bertoli was waiting for her in the shade, next to the hangar.

"Hello," Laura said cheerfully.

"Hi. I came to ask you a favor," he started.

"Just name it."

"I am going to tell the captain that he has recovered fully, but please do not let him fly alone."

"Why not?"

"Look, his fainting spells are still a mystery, but otherwise he is healthy as a horse."

"I think you'd better tell him that yourself," Laura replied. "He is the boss, and if he wants to fly one of the routes solo, there is nothing I can do about it."

"I don't dare tell him. I understand Doctor Swanson actually grounded him and the captain threatened to shoot him," Bertoli replied.

"Tell you what: when you explain to him why he should not fly solo, do it in my presence. I'm sure I can calm him down."

"You might just do it. However, if he decided to shoot someone, it would be me."

"Have no fear," she interrupted. "Nowadays, I carry his bag with the papers and the gun. He may want to shoot you, but he won't have the weapon. Trust me, you do what you have to, and I will make sure he takes it in stride."

"You are very sure of yourself."

"In my profession self-confidence is the first prerequisite."

Arriving at the house, she found Ray feeling much better. When Doctor Bertoli gave him a clean bill of health and permitted his return to the cockpit as a copilot, he was elated. Nevertheless, he extracted a promise from the doctor to let him fly solo again following a period of observation.

After the doctor left, Laura took a long bath and changed for dinner. As soon as they sat down, and she reported on her trip, Ray remarked, "We are going to have a little bit of excitement around here. Our new engines arrived... the boys are picking them up Monday morning."

"That's good news. Every time I get into the *Calabrese*, I break out in cold sweat."

"It is the plane with the most number of hours, and the fuel pump never functioned properly. We are going to install the first new engine into the Calabrese."

"A good idea."

"I have some more good news," Ray said. "You have two passengers to Aden on Friday."

"Great."

"Apparently, General Ponti's wife gave some other travelers the idea of flying with us to Aden and taking Imperial to Rome. Now, if we could get some return passengers..."

"I met Captain Wills of Imperial. He asked for your address. They may ask you to connect to their flight."

"Without pilots, we cannot do it," Ray said.

"The shortage may not last. Squadron Leader Carstairs promised to try finding a few pilot for us."

"Let's hope he'll have some constructive ideas. Anyway, after I recover completely, you should go to London, and straighten out the mess with your identity. While you are there, I'd appreciate if you found me a few pilots."

"May I come back?"

"You are always welcome at Air Mogadishu."

"And you can always count on me. I am not going to let you down, Ray. I owe you."

"You do not owe me anything, Laura. You saved my life twice, and saved the company. Let me assure you, my dear, you are not indebted to me."

"I hate arguing with you, Ray, but you saved me from a fate perhaps worse than death, gave me a passport, and turned me into a professional pilot. At best it is a tie, you being ahead on points," Laura declared.

"I give up," said Ray. "There is no sense arguing with you."

He took Laura in his arms and kissed her on the lips. Although the events of the last day and the long flight from Bossasso had taken their toll on Laura's body, she did not have the heart to say no to Ray. Surprisingly, she enjoyed the main event as much as if she had rested all day.

Back in her room, Laura contemplated the ceiling thinking about her relationship with the two men, and thought of talking about them to the Almighty hoping to get a hint to help her out of the quagmire.

~ * ~

During the next week, everybody was very busy. Ray started the Herculean task of replacing the old engines, working side by side with Deria and Abdullahi, while Laura flew the mail routes alone. Although she took to the air on Monday and Tuesday and she rested on Wednesday, on Thursday she went to the airfield to see if she could help. She did not have the physical strength to do much work, but she learned a great deal about aero engines and the flight controls.

Just before closing up shop in the evening, they received a telegram from Aden asking Air Mogadishu to fly three arriving passengers of Imperial to Djibuti on Saturday. Ray cabled back immediately confirming the reservations and letting them know the fare.

In the evening, Laura studied the charts, and they worked out a flight plan to the French colony.

"It won't be difficult," Laura said. "I doubt I have to refuel in Aden, but I will check when I get there."

"You might do it on one tank, but it would be cutting it too fine. You should refuel in Aden as well as in Bossasso," Ray said.

"I will," Laura replied.

"In order to become respectable, we must do a few things."

"What do you mean?"

"First, I am going to send a telegram to the French authorities asking them for landing permission at their military airfield."

"What if they deny permission?"

"In that case, I am going to send a cable to Imperial in Aden canceling the reservations. You should apologize to the passengers and return to Mogadishu."

"Okay. What else?"

"In Aden land at the civilian field, pay the landing fee, and refuel. I'll give you the cash to pay the expenses."

"How am I going over to the military field?"

"Take a taxi. I am sure they have one, but you could sleep in a good hotel, if you wanted to. The airfare we charge is quite high."

"I am going to the military field in a taxi and sleep in the BOQ guest room there. I must talk to Squadron Leader Carstairs about the pilots and a personal matter that has nothing to do with Air Mogadishu," said Laura. Ray did not pursue the matter. This was as much as Laura wanted to tell him about her relationship with the handsome Squadron Leader.

This is my insurance against Ray becoming jealous of Robert. He cannot say I did not tell him anything. But to describe the sensitivity points of Bob's body would be carrying truthfulness to an extreme, she thought.

For a while, they were quiet.

"Well, I am going to the airfield tomorrow morning to see you and your passengers off," Ray remarked.

"I'll appreciate your support helping to calm them, Ray. Some passengers might be scared to fly with a woman pilot," she said.

"I do not think you need any support. I am sure you would charm the passengers while making them feel safe."

"Can you ask Amina to make a few sandwiches, fill the large thermos flask with coffee, and a bottle of water? The flight is long, and I believe we should feed the passengers," Laura said.

"That is a very good idea."

"I have another matter to discuss," said Laura, feeling a little bit guilty about hinting to Ray that she might have something going on with Bob.

Ray looked at Laura anxiously. "What is it?"

"I am thinking of a large double bed in your room with dark silk sheets."

"In spite of the successes in the hangars and the passengers, this is the best proposition of the day," Ray said and stepped to Laura.

She looked up to him, smiled, and offered her lips.

In the morning, Laura found the Cornwall ready for the trip to Bossasso and Aden. Panetta arrived with the mailbags, and Abdullahi loaded them together with the bags of the passengers, a very pleasant Italian couple. They were banana planters on the way to Rome.

Ray guided the passengers on board, gave Laura the last minute instructions, and said, "Break a leg."

She kissed Ray on the cheek, and boarded the plane.

The takeoff was smooth. The *Cornwall* pointed its nose to the north, and they were on their way. Laura noticed that the passengers were scared stiff, fear written all over their faces. She turned around and said, "One of you should come up to the copilot's seat. The view is magnificent."

The couple looked at each other, and the man released his safety belt.

"I am coming if you don't mind."

"Come on, sit down, and fix your safety belt. This is a very pleasant route without turbulence, and absolutely no danger," Laura explained. The man looked out the window and seemed to relax a little.

"You have nothing to worry about. This plane is well maintained. There is only an infinitesimally small chance of something going wrong."

"But if it would..."

Laura interrupted with a smile. "Don't worry. The land is flat as a billiard table. If the engine conked out, which is most unlikely, I would just land somewhere and wait for the other pilot to come here with the spare aircraft and fly you to Aden."

"How about the flight over the water?"

"Don't worry. I always fly higher than now, and if the engine stopped, I could glide to the nearest land," lied Laura. "Just relax and have a cup of coffee."

The man helped himself to a drink. He seemed to settle down and began enjoying the flight.

"Take the wheel," Laura said and pointed at the yoke. The man reluctantly put his hands on the controls, while Laura let them go. If something happened, she was ready to grab it.

"How does it feel?" she asked.

"Great."

She let the man hold on to the controls for a few minutes, then she said seriously, "I'd better take it, because if you hold it much longer, I will have to pay you copilot's wages."

They flew in silence until the first stop. The postmaster removed the mailbags and placed one on board addressed to Mogadishu.

"See you next week," Laura said and opened the throttle.

When they reached cruising altitude, Laura invited the woman to sit with her for a while in the cockpit. After landing in Bossasso, the postmaster already knew he would have to store the mail, and Ahmed brought up the barrels to refuel the *Cornwall*.

"I think one barrel will be enough tomorrow," Laura said. "I must come back via Djibuti. Therefore, I will refuel in Aden."

"As you wish, Captain Missy," Ahmed said politely and started cranking to start the engine.

In two and a half hours, Aden appeared on the horizon. The civilian airfield called airport was much better developed than the strip the air force used. To land on asphalt was pleasant. The passengers had no reason to complain.

The Imperial Airways agent, a pleasant young Englishman took care of the Italians and offered to take Laura to a hotel.

"By the way, the French gave you permission to land at the military field. They do not have an airport like ours," he said.

"Great, I'll take over your passengers at seven o'clock in the morning. Have them and their baggage here," Laura said.

"All right, Captain. I'll look after them. Which hotel are you going to take?"

"Can you drop me at the R.A.F. base?" Laura asked. "They have a guest room at the BOQ. Usually I sleep there."

"Of course, Captain. It is on our way."

At the gate of the base, she asked to see Squadron Leader Carstairs. The duty sergeant recognized her, assigned an airman to carry her bag and told her to look for Bob at the Officers' Mess. Half way to the building, Bob appeared, walking briskly toward them.

"A pleasure to see you, Captain. I'll take your bag. Airman, you may return to the gate," Bob said.

The soldier handed over the bag, saluted, and headed for the entrance to the airfield.

"I saw you landing, darling. Why did you go to the civilian field?" Bob asked.

"I had passengers for Imperial. Tomorrow, I am taking three people to Djibouti," Laura replied.

"I envy you. You can fly so much," said Bob as they reached the BOQ and the door of the guest room. As there was nobody on the corridor, Bob took Laura in his arms.

"I missed you terribly," he said.

"I was so happy when Ray told me about the passengers. I longed to see you," she said and standing on tiptoes, she gently kissed Bob again. "I did not practice, sir. So forgive me if my kissing is not up to par."

"Are you sure?"

"No, sir," she said, but thought, *a little white lie won't hurt anybody*. Bob took her in his strong arms and held her lithe body close to his.

"I was waiting for this for a whole week," he said planting his lips on Laura's, while his hand found the zipper of her flight suit. He pulled it down a few inches and caressed her breast. She responded, and before they realized, they were involved in an active foreplay right there in the corridor.

"I think we should stop," she said after they came up for air. "We have no time for anything creative. I must go, put on a ladylike dress, let you take me to the mess, and buy me a Campari with soda. Just wait here because if you come in, we'll never make it for dinner in time."

"You're right, of course, but being without you for a whole week was too long," he said.

"A week is a week, whether you are in Aden or in Mogadishu," Laura said cryptically and slipped in through the door.

Following the dinner, they sat on the patio of the Officers' Mess, and Bob declared, "I believe I solved your pilot problems for a few weeks."

"How?"

"I have four sergeant pilots. Actually, they are fully licensed. Each has about one hundred-fifty flying hours. My officers barely let them fly an hour a week, and the sergeants are frustrated. I asked the Wing Commander if I could loan them to you."

"What did he say?"

"He said it was okay as long as you paid their board and room in addition to training them to fly low wing monoplanes. If Ray certifies them, you could take two guys with you tomorrow."

"Robert, you just saved my life, and perhaps assured the success of Air Mogadishu. Ray will be grateful."

"If he gives you a week off, I can let him have the other guys after he finished checking out the first batch," said Bob.

"How long can we have the sergeants?"

"I think the training would take about three weeks. At least this is what the boss said."

"This is great news. Can I see them?"

"Sergeants Lee and Walters are eagerly awaiting the chance to meet you. Let's go."

They left the patio and walked to the Sergeants' Mess. As Bob could not enter, he asked the attendant to call the men. The two fresh-faced youngsters came and stood in stiff attention.

"Fellows, this is Miss Madison, the chief pilot of Air Mogadishu. She graciously agreed to take you to Somalia and give you some training in flying low wing monoplanes. If you wish, you could leave tomorrow."

"Yes, sir," they roared in unison.

"Okay, Laura, they are all yours."

"Thank you, gentlemen. We are leaving with a full load tomorrow at seven from the civilian air field."

"I'll drive them over," said Bob.

"Thanks," Laura replied. "Just one thing, gentlemen. You won't need your leather flying suit, because all our aircraft have closed cockpits. They are proper airliners."

"If I may, ma'am," said one of the sergeants. "How many hours do you expect us to fly?"

"I don't really know. It is up to Captain Madison, your instructor, but I guess it won't be less than twenty hours in the first week. It will consist of dual instructions, of course, but in the second week, you should expect ten hours solo and perhaps ten hours dual. Does this answer your question, Sergeant?"

The young man's face lit up like a Christmas tree. He said in a trembling voice, "That will be just wonderful, ma'am, Thank you very much."

"Okay, fellows. I'll pick you up at the main gate by oh-six-thirty hours. Have a good breakfast, because it will be a long flight to Mogadishu. Dismissed!" Bob said.

The men saluted and returned to the club.

"You just made two guys very happy. They will be the envy of the squadron. Let's go back to the patio and talk about something more exciting, like you and me."

Sitting on the patio hand in hand, they did not have to talk much. They just looked at the sky, and the stars spoke to them.

"I need a rest," said Laura. "I had two passengers, and they were scared stiff of having to fly with a female pilot."

"This is the conservative attitude. One does not need big muscles to fly an aircraft," he replied as he stood up. "I'll walk you home."

He took Laura's arm, and they started out toward the guesthouse.

"I hope you are not going to chase me away when we reach our destination," Bob said.

"What do you mean? Our destination is that horrid narrow iron framed bed with the skimpy mattress in the guest room. I wish we would have a proper bed in there," Laura said.

"Tell you what: I am going to take the mattress from my bed and take it over to your room. If we put both of them on the floor, it would give us a larger bed," Bob suggested.

"You are brilliant, Robert. You are going to build a proper playground for me. Am I worth the trouble?"

"Darling, there aren't many things I wouldn't do for a tiny little kiss of yours," Bob said

"Let me give you something on account," Laura said and kissed Bob hard on the lips. He started putting his arms around her, but Laura pulled away.

"I was talking about a small advance," she said.

"Okay," he said.

Bob's invention worked out all right, and they slept in each other's arms until reveille. He got up first and sheepishly remarked, "Now you see what you did to me? I must sneak to my room, shave and come back for my half of the playground later."

"Now you're discovering the dangers of associating with promiscuous lady pilots," Laura said with a smile. They went to the mess for breakfast separately. Laura half finished her bacon and eggs by the time the freshly shaved Bob arrived. He did not seem tired at all, but the lack of sleep showed around his eyes, while Laura looked fresh as a daisy. They left the mess after breakfast and found the sergeants wearing regulation summer flying suits sitting on a bench at the gate. They snapped into attention when Bob and Laura arrived. They got into the squadron's car, and set out to the civilian airport.

The agent of Imperial Airways waited for them. The passengers turned out to be officers of the French Foreign Legion stationed in Djibouti.

Laura paid the landing fees and the fuel before sending the passengers onboard.

"Mr. Lee, I want you to be my copilot on the first leg of our trip. Kindly take your seat. Mr. Walters, you'll be the loadmaster. Please tie down all freight securely and make sure our valued passengers wear their seatbelts properly," Laura issued her orders.

As they closed the door and the attendant started cranking, she heard one of the passengers saying to the other in French, "I thought she'd be the cabin attendant, not the captain. She is too pretty to waste in the cockpit."

Laura turned back, she gave the fellow her million-dollar smile and in her limited French replied, "Times are changing, gentlemen. Nevertheless, I appreciate the compliment," and pushed the throttle forward.

The Frenchmen were pleasant passengers. They came up and stood in the cockpit door entertaining Laura with stories from the Legion. Sergeant Lee turned out a competent pilot holding the *Cornwall* on course to Djibouti. Laura had a rough time putting the Frenchmen back to their seats before landing.

"You should come to see us in Djibouti," said one of the officers. "We have excellent restaurants with proper French cuisine."

Laura promised to visit them if they had more passengers.

The *Cornwall* thundered off the Djibouti strip with Sergeant Walters in the copilot's seat.

In Bossasso, Sergeant Lee supervised the refueling, while Laura paid Ahmed for the fuel.

"You are flying to Aden almost every week, Captain Missy. It is very good for my business, but I may run short of fuel in a month or so," said Ahmed.

"Tell you what," Laura replied. "From now on, I am going to refuel in Aden. Until the coastal boat comes, I'll buy only two barrels from you every week."

"That would be a help," he said and started cranking.

The sergeants were good pilots. Laura only took the landing in Mogadishu, and she arrived fresh as a daisy. Ray was delirious with joy, and immediately arranged for the sergeants to stay at the Lido Hotel.

"If I were you, I would go to England next week," he suggested. "I can train these guys."

"Remember, Ray, you are not supposed to fly too much this week."

"Okay. When the sergeants can fly the northern route solo, you should go."

Laura knew that it would be futile to argue with Ray. He was going to fly with these young men, whatever the doctor might say.

"Okay, I will go. These fellows might stay with you for three weeks. I'll try to be back before they return to Aden," Laura agreed.

That evening Ray was more passionate than last time, keeping Laura up until the wee hours of the morning.

"I am terrified of losing you," Ray said.

"Don't worry, darling. You cannot get rid of me," she replied sleepily, snuggling up to him.

In Arden, Bob, but in Mogadishu, Ray took precedence.

Back in her own room, Laura discussed her state of mind with the Almighty.

"Thank you for bringing me home safely, my Lord. I have a problem. I am at a loss when it comes to the men in my life. I love Robert with my brain first. He is young, pleasant, understanding, and an excellent lover. He makes me feel wanted. Being with him I always think he is the guy I want to marry. However, when I am back to Mogadishu, my body thirsts for Ray's touch. I love him with all my heart, but my brain tells me that we cannot get married ever. Sooner or later, I am going to lose him. I will have to make a choice, but please do not hurry the time of the decision, my Lord. I am quite happy as I am."

Even though the Lord did not give her an assurance about the deferment of the crunch time, Laura fell asleep.

On Sunday, Laura woke up late. After lunch, she took off with the *York* having Lee and Walters practice landing under her supervision. Both were fast learners, and they managed the routine takeoff and landing very well.

Later Laura took two palm fronds and laid them across the runway simulating the short runway at Kismayo. First, she showed them how to do it, then let them try landing on the short field. Lee managed it at the first try, but Walters could not. However, the sergeant had enough presence of mind to abort the landing in time and to try it again. The second time he nailed it.

"You think like an airline pilot, Mr. Walters," Laura said. "With an airline, safety is the most important consideration. While flying for the military, you might take chances, but in the airline business you may not."

Although the sergeants were about the same age as Laura, they listened to her wise remarks, which were actually not hers, but had come from Ray.

Taking off from the shortened field was another task the sergeants had to practice.

"Unfortunately, you do not have a second chance, and you cannot abort the takeoff. You must have the procedure down pat. Let me show you," she said and demonstrated the hairy takeoff.

Again, the two young pilots had no difficulty learning the procedure. After their fifth successful takeoff, Laura stopped for the day and took them to their hotel.

"I'll pick you up at six in the morning," she said as she started the Norton to return to the house.

She found Ray in an ebullient mood. They sat on the patio, and Laura had her Campari while after so many days Ray had his whisky.

"I see the doctor gave you permission to drink," Laura remarked.

"He did much more than that. The little bastard wanted to ground me again."

"Then why are you so happy?"

"Because I managed talking him out of it. In fact, he gave me permission to fly as a copilot six hours a day. This means I can go with the sergeants and teach them."

"I'm glad to hear you didn't try to shoot the doctor."

"I could not because you took both guns. Anyway, we had a drink, and he explained what the problem was with my ticker. It is not very serious, but he gave me some medicine to take every day. He thinks it will cure the fainting spells. However, he is not one hundred percent sure. Therefore, I realized it's obvious that solo could be dangerous," Ray said.

"How are the engines?"

"We are finishing the *Calabrese*. On Wednesday you can test fly it, and if it is all right, we can take the next one."

"That is great news," Laura said. She was genuinely happy to see the affairs of Air Mogadishu starting to straighten out.

After dinner Laura went to bed early, and before falling asleep, she remarked, *"Thank you, my Lord. I do not think I deserve so much help, but I believe Ray does. So please keep helping him."*

~ * ~

The next week was rather hectic. Laura had a rough time sitting in the command pilot's seat, having nothing to do except observing the sergeants doing the flying. When the plane hit the Merca wind shear, Walters was at the controls. He tamed the wildly bucking aircraft with ease. Nevertheless, Laura was scared stiff at each landing and takeoff. She could not justify the fear, since Lee and Walters were fast learners and handled the F13 like pros.

Returning from a successful flight to Kismayo, Laura sat with Ray on the patio enjoying the magnificent sunset. They held hands and did not need to talk. Their hearts were beating at the same rhythm, and their bodies building up desire for the other.

"I was scared stiff when the sergeants flew the plane," said Laura.

Ray just laughed at her: "Every pilot is scared when someone else is at the controls."

"Are you?"

"Always, even when I am in control. Flying is a scary business, and if you are not afraid, you become bold, and bold pilots usually die young. By the way, I have some more news for you. On Friday, you have five passengers for Aden. Therefore, you cannot take a copilot."

"It doesn't matter. Won't we overload the plane with five people, their baggage, and the mailbags?"

"Yes, just a little, but you can take less fuel to compensate."

"Ahmed is running short of gas. I told him I was going to take only one barrel from each time I land in Bossasso."

"One barrel would take you to Aden easily. Fly a tight course, and make your first approach perfect."

"I would gladly do it every week if we had five passengers."

"You are going to be rich."

"I'll need the money in England."

"On the way back from Aden you will have your favorite passenger, General Ponti and two of his officers flying with you."

"It will be nice seeing him again," said Laura. They sat side by side quietly for a while.

Suddenly, Ray broke the silence. "I am worried about your trip tomorrow. The plane will be overloaded, and you will have less than the normal quantity of fuel. If you get some headwinds, you may have problems."

"We never get significant winds on this route. I'll be all right," Laura replied.

"If you crashed, I'd..."

"Hush," Laura said putting her hand over Ray's mouth. "I am not going to crash. I'll be back safe and sound in one piece."

"I cannot help worrying," Ray said.

"Well, if you cannot help it, I might try giving you some reason for anxiety," she said as she put her legs across Ray's lap and leaned back away from him.

"What do you mean?"

"I am not letting you sleep tonight."

"You are a little sex maniac, but thank God for it."

"I keep thanking him every night before falling asleep. He wisely arranged our lives in such a marvelous manner that I doubt he would break up the harmony," said Laura.

"I hope you are right," he said, kissed her leg, and stood.

She was aroused too, stood and hugged Ray, thrusting her breasts against his chest. As she wore no bra under the flight suit, their bodies touched, and the flame of desire began to consume them. Ray picked Laura up and started toward the bedroom.

~ * ~

Contrary to her promise, Laura did not keep Ray up all night. She was back in her own bed by midnight.

On the inland route, the two sergeants were handling their flying chores like professionals. Lee managed the tough crosswind landing in Obbia with ease.

On Wednesday, the sergeants had the day off, but on Thursday, Ray gave them theoretical instructions.

"I am sorry, fellows, tomorrow Laura takes the Aden run without copilot as she has too many passengers."

"Does it mean we cannot fly until Monday?" asked Walters.

"Don't worry, my friend. You are going to practice takeoffs and landings solo all day tomorrow. You are going to fly until you drop. On Saturday, you are going to take a test with Mr. Abdi and get your Somali pilot's license. After that you can take one of the routes on your own."

"Is the test going to be difficult?" asked Lee.

"Not really," Laura replied. "Just make a smooth takeoff, give the old fellow a nice, slow aerial tour of the city, and land softly. I was the first one he tested."

The sergeants quizzed Laura about the test, but she tried not to tell them anything.

"It is a good idea to keep them guessing," she said to Ray before retiring for the night.

Friday morning the airfield was a beehive of activities. The passengers arrived, Panetta came with his mailbags, and Ray supervised the loading of the aircraft. He calculated the amount of fuel and established a point of no return saying, "Listen, Laura. If you have less than one hundred twenty liters of fuel in the tank, at this point, turn around," he said marking the point of no return on the map.

"I will. Don't worry, Ray. I am a professional."

"Okay, Laura. Break a leg," said Ray and left.

She was stepping to the door of the aircraft when Panetta stopped her saying, "May I have a word with you, Captain, in private? It is important post office business."

"By all means, sir. Let us go into the office."

As they entered, the Italian stopped at the door and leaned against it. Keeping his voice low, he said: "I know you are in possession of a forged passport, and your name is not Miss Madison. I know everything there is to know about you."

Laura just stared at him. She did not have a prompt reply.

"Anyway, my dear, you have nothing to fear as long as you do precisely as I say."

"Are you trying to blackmail me?"

"You could say that, but rest assured I am going to deny it in court, and you couldn't prove a thing."

"As you know everything about me, you must know that I am poor as a church mouse."

"I am not going to ask you for money."

"Then what do you want?"

"I want you to pay me with the best international currency there is: your body."

The calm statement stunned Laura, and the concept did not reach her conscious mind immediately.

"Well, if you do not wish to visit the inside of the Somali prison, I'll pick you up at the field on Saturday when you land. Then we take my automobile, drive to my beach house just south of the harbor, and we spend the night there. In the morning, you may go back to Captain Madison's house. As long as you spend Saturday nights with me, I'll keep quiet. Miss just one weekend, and you are heading for the prison. *Capisce?* Have a nice flight, Captain Madison," he said, turned, and left Laura gaping.

It took a few minutes for Panetta's ultimatum to sink in.

He is a pig. I'd rather die than sleep with him, she thought.

As she left the shack racking her brain about what to do, she saw the Italian standing at the plane. She had an idea and decided to test it. Walking by Panetta, she whispered to him, "No garlic between now and tomorrow, *capisce?*"

Then she climbed into the crowded cabin, got into the cockpit, and started the pre-flight check.

Panetta's demand weighed heavily on Laura's mind, but she had to concentrate on flying an airliner with passengers, and could not afford to think about the Italian.

The overloaded aircraft used almost the entire runway before leaving the ground. Upon reaching cruising altitude, Laura leaned the mixture as much as she dared, and settled down for the long flight.

The passengers were terrified seeing a young woman flying the plane, but later warmed up to Laura. She let them rotate in the copilot's seat and explained the controls to them. Eventually, the passengers relaxed and began enjoying the flight. When they reached the point of no return, Laura checked the fuel gauge and found 140 liters in the tank.

We are fat, she thought.

When Garoe appeared on the horizon, Laura pulled the throttle back, and the *York* started sinking like a gluttonous duck. The landing with the heavy plane was not easy, but she managed. Fortunately, after unloading five bags, the postmaster gave them only a small one for Mogadishu, and actually, the plane became much lighter. The takeoff run was long, but not as tough as the one at Mogadishu. The passengers were in good spirits, ate all the sandwiches, and drank the coffee before landing in Bossasso.

As Laura had nothing to eat, she ordered a beef sandwich at the Bossasso restaurant. While sitting at the rickety little table, her thoughts wandered, and the weasel face of Panetta popped up in her mind.

The bastard! He wants to take me to bed! Granted, it is a compliment, but he is so repulsive. What am I going to do? Sure, I could tell Ray, but he would immediately grab one of the guns and shoot the Italian. They hate each other's guts. I could stay in Aden, but if I did, what about the passengers and the mail? How would the plane get back to Mogadishu? If I did not come back, Panetta would terminate the mail contract for missing one of the routes. It would ruin Ray and Air Mogadishu. I bet the bastard would do it with a smile on his weasel face. No matter what, I must return to Mogadishu, but if I do, the weasel is going to wait for me. If I do not give in, he'd arrange for my arrest. Ray could bail me out, but I could not fly anymore, and Air Mogadishu would be in jeopardy. Do I have any alternative? she thought while munching on the very pleasantly spiced sandwich. *I am going to solve this problem somehow,* she thought and shook off the depressing thoughts.

Ahmed refueled the *Cornwall.* Laura herded the passengers on board, ran through the pre-flight, and started the engine.

Eight

Laura flew a tight course to Aden, continuously checking the plane's position on the map. She knew how long the flight should take, but it seemed they were bucking headwinds. Therefore, they fell behind schedule. It did not bother her, since both tanks were three quarters full at takeoff.

Under normal circumstances, the fuel on board should have sufficed for the return trip from Bossasso. She calmly increased the power to compensate for the lost speed and relaxed.

As the shoreline appeared, the engine coughed and stopped. Laura knew she could not glide to the beach, but did not panic. As she played with the throttle, the windmilling propeller restarted the engine. To be on the safe side, she immediately began climbing, but after a few minutes, the engine quit again. Looking at the fuel gauge, she saw the right tank three quarters full and the left empty. Laura checked the cross-feed valve and found it fully open.

The cross-feed line is blocked, she thought and tried working the valve, but to no avail. The engine remained quiet. Suddenly, the wind lifted the left wing, and she was a few seconds late to correct. The engine caught and gave Laura a little power to climb, but it stopped again. She remembered the fuel tanks being cylindrical and the suction pipe coming in from the top as not to pick up the sediment from the bottom.

The gas is swishing in the bottom of the tank, she thought and turned to the passengers.

"Hang on, the winds are picking up. We may have a few minutes of rough air."

She violently moved the aileron from left to right to move the fuel in the bottom of the tank. Apparently, the pump sucked up a few precious drops of fuel, and the engine started again, giving Laura a few seconds of power. When she repeated the maneuver a few times, the *York* gained altitude, but after the third try, the engine remained quiet, and the plane kept sinking.

We are going into the drink, Laura thought, but she had no fear in her heart. The beach kept coming closer, and she clearly saw the end of the runway. *So near yet too far*, she thought. The *York* hovered perhaps a hundred meters above the sea, over the fishermen in their small boats. They stopped working, and stared at the low flying iron bird. *Panetta is out of luck*, thought Laura bitterly, and allowed herself a wry little smile. Laura knew they would not make it to the runway, and had just about decided to warn her passengers to brace for impact. She remembered the F13 had a small tank of fuel behind and above the pilot. When starting the engine, the fuel pump could not pick up the gas from the tank to the carburetor. Thus, it had to come from the starter tank by gravity.

She threw the switch, hoping for a few liters of fuel remaining in the overhead tank. The engine came alive, and she gently pulled the plane up. Although the *York* did not gain much altitude, when the engine quit again, they cleared the beach, the chain link fence of the military airfield by inches, and touched down on the runway. With no power, the plane rolled to a gentle halt near the end of the concrete apron.

"Welcome to Aden," said Laura just to relieve her tension, and the passengers clapped.

She unbuckled her safety belt and with trembling knees, covered in cold sweat, she started going through the passenger cabin to open the door and let the people out of the plane.

In the second row sat an elderly Italian man. He rose and extended his hand saying, "Thank you for the wonderful sightseeing tour, Captain. It was most considerate of you to fly low, allowing us to look at the fishermen and their quaint little boats. Thank you again."

Laura really wanted to slug the fellow, but thought better of it.

"I always do that for special passengers," she said and opened the door.

In a few minutes, Bob arrived with the squadron's car. Laura wanted to rush to him and bury herself in his arms, but an airline captain has to behave according to a certain code. She told Bob about having a spot of trouble on the way, force-landed at the airbase, and asked him to call the Imperial's agent to get the passengers off her hands. Bob said okay, took two of the people with him, and left in the direction of the mess.

In a few minutes, the Imperial's agent arrived to collect the passengers.

"Welcome to Aden," the agent greeted Laura. "One of the returning passengers was asking about you. General Alessandro Ponti wanted to know who would captain the flight to Mogadishu. Now I can tell him it is you. Where are you staying?"

"In the guest room of the BOQ right here at the R.A.F. base," replied Laura. "Why?"

"I don't think they can give you a room. Two of the general's officers are billeted there by order of Wing Commander Thurston. I can drive you to the Excelsior."

Laura had just seen Bob's car coming back.

"Thank you, sir, but I'll ask Squadron Leader Carstairs to take me to the hotel. Here he comes."

Laura regretted that she could not kiss and hug Bob in public, but when they got into the car, she snuggled up to him.

"You must stay in the hotel tonight, darling. The boss gave your room to two Italian officers," Bob said.

"I know. I am taking them to Mogadishu tomorrow."

"Okay, I'll take you to the Excelsior."

"That's the place the Imperial's agent suggested," Laura replied.

In those days, the Excelsior was one of the better hotels in the city, and even though Laura had no reservation, she got a room. Bob carried her flight bag upstairs.

"Come on in, Robert," Laura said as they arrived at the door. "We have an important matter to talk about."

As they entered the room, Bob took Laura's hand and pulled her close to him.

"I missed you, Laura, you are becoming a part of me. I cannot live without you," he said and their lips touched.

As Laura entered into the pink world of happiness, she suddenly realized that a black cloud began to spread over her field of perception. It was Panetta. Nevertheless, she did not want to spoil her arrival and the meeting with Bob by thinking or talking about the weasel. She felt dead tired, but mustered enough energy to thrust her body against Bob's muscular frame.

"You had some trouble on the way, didn't you?" he asked.

"Nothing to worry about, really," she replied. Strangely, the events of the afternoon did not have any aftereffects.

This must be a professional hazard. I was ready to die any minute, and the fact of coming close to crashing did not bother me in any way, Laura thought.

"What happened?"

"Bagatelle, darling, I ran out of fuel because of a blocked cross-feed line. Hitting the beach seemed inevitable," she replied.

"Holy mother of God. How did you manage?"

"The F13 glides well."

"What are you going to do?"

"I am going to find one of the mechanics of Imperial and ask him to fix it."

"Nonsense," responded Bob. "I am going to take you to the base, park you at the mess, and have one of my mechanics look at it."

"Thanks, Robert, but I must be with him. He might not find the cross-feed line."

After they returned to the base, the air force mechanic quickly located the problem under Laura's supervision, found the cracked valve, and replaced it within half an hour.

If I had a mechanic on board, he could have fixed it in flight, Laura thought when she saw the precise location of the valve.

Bob took her back to the Excelsior near sunset.

"I am going to wait for you downstairs," Bob said. "We have a gala dinner at seven-thirty to honor General Ponti. The wing commander will be there, and they all want to see you."

"You'd better come up to my room because if I were left alone with a bed, I might fall asleep," Laura said.

"As you wish, darling," said Bob with a flash in his eyes. Both knew what would happen if they entered the room together as they still had an hour before the expected events started taking place.

Laura felt tired so she let Bob take off her sweat-soaked clothes, and did not bother to shower before embracing Bob's naked body. However, when they were in each other's arms, Laura's tiredness vanished, and she became the tigress Bob loved so much. They almost forgot about the dinner, but Bob somehow managed to disrupt the most entertaining activities.

"We are going to be late, darling."

"I don't care," Laura said.

"Why?"

She slowly peeled Bob's arms off her, but took his hands and turned to face him.

"I have a problem, Robert."

"Can I help?"

"I am afraid not."

"What is it?"Laura reiterated the demands of Panetta.

"I am going back with you and shoot the bastard."

"You are not. If I mentioned it to Ray, he would break Panetta's scrawny neck."

"Does he know?"

"No, I did not have time to tell him."

"If you do not let me go in your plane, I am going to take one of the bombers, fly to Mogadishu, and shoot the bastard," Bob declared calmly.

"Nonsense, you'd be AWOL, and it would end your life as a career officer."

"I could become a civilian, go to Mogadishu, and fly for Ray," he interrupted.

"You are mad, darling. They would throw you in prison for shooting the weasel. He is not worth it."

"What are you suggesting?"

"He has me over a barrel. If I do not give in to him, I am going to jail," Laura said. "Perhaps I should just refuse him and accept the consequences. I could last one day in prison because I am sure Ray would bail me out promptly. Then I could steal a plane, take one of the sergeants, and fly to Aden. Perhaps I could get on board Imperial and take my chances with the British authorities," Laura explained.

"It may work," Bob said, "but if you could get a week respite from Panetta, next Friday you could take a copilot with you, and stay in Aden."

Laura thought hard how to dissuade Panetta from going to the authorities, but she had nothing coming to her mind.

Suddenly, there was a knock on the door.

Laura wrapped a large towel around her, ushered Bob into the bathroom, and went to see who interrupted them. One of the uniformed bellboys stood there with a note.

"This is for Captain Laura Madison," he said.

"I am Captain Laura Madison of Air Mogadishu," she said.

The man gave her the note saying, "I need a reply."

Laura took the paper and read it.

Dear Captain Madison,
Would you consider joining me for a sundowner on the patio?
General Alessandro Ponti

The note suddenly gave Laura an idea.

"Wait," she said to the bellboy and rushed to the bathroom door.

"Robert, your wing commander is not going to start the gala dinner without the guest of honor. I am going to have a drink with Ponti. I believe he is the solution to my problem. Go back to the base and tell the wing commander that I am arriving with the general."

"Very well, darling," he said and started dressing.

"Can you survive without me for an hour?" Laura asked.

"Perhaps," Bob replied.

She returned to the door and said to the bellboy, "Please tell the general I'll be on my way in a few minutes."

"Yes, ma'am," said the young man and left.

"What do you have in your devious little mind?" Bob asked taking Laura in his arms.

"I'll tell you after dinner. Now go," she said and planted a kiss on Bob's lips. He held her strong, and the pink clouds again appeared in Laura's field of perception. There was no dark lining to them.

During the dinner, Laura was sparkling, witty, and the center of attention. After the excellent meal, the general thanked Wing Commander Thurston for the R.A.F.'s hospitality and returned to the hotel.

After the party broke up, Bob and Laura sat at the patio having a nightcap.

"Where do you get the energy?" Bob asked.

"I got it from you in the early evening. Do you remember?"

"Oh yes, how could I possibly forget. By the way, do you need any more energy?"

"If you have some to spare, darling."

"Let's go, I'll drive you to the hotel," said Bob, as he stood and downed his drink.

"You have brilliant ideas, Robert," replied Laura and she too finished her Campari.

After arriving at the Excelsior, a vigorous transfer of energy followed, and they were lying side-by-side naked, feeling exhausted.

"By the way, did you solve the problem?" he asked.

"Oh, yes, the general promised to help. It will be a great charade."

"How did you manage to persuade Ponti? His officers are saying the old guy is a straight- laced infantryman."

"I promised to become his personal pilot if or when he gets his own plane. He said it might happen in a year or two."

"Are you serious about it?"

"No, I am not and neither is he. You see, if they give him a plane, it comes with an Italian military pilot."

"So, what are you going to do?"

"I'll tell you," said Laura and acquainted Bob with the scheme she and the general concocted. When she finished, Bob burst out laughing.

"You are certainly going to look like the *femme fatale* of Mogadishu."

"Don't you think I am that?" Laura asked with a mocking smile.

"You are a *femme fatale* no matter where you are, darling," Bob said.

"I thought so."

They sat on the terrace of Laura's hotel room until midnight holding hands and talking about many interesting topics. Before driving back to the base, Bob gave her a long kiss and remarked, "I'll see you next week, I hope."

"You bet. I'll be here for sure, because I am going to England with Imperial. I may stay there for two weeks unless they decide to throw me in jail for using a forged passport."

"No, they won't. The British sense of justice and fair play would not allow it."

"I hope you're right. Good night, darling."

"Good night, Laura, and have a good flight tomorrow. Don't forget I love you."

When she finally got to her bed, she stared at the ceiling and turned to the Almighty.

"Thanks, my Lord, for saving me from crashing into the sea and for the wonderful time I had with Robert," Laura prayed. *"I have a problem. Should I tell Ray about him? I know it would hurt him, and I do not want to cause pain to the man to whom I owe so much. What am I going to do? Help me, my Lord."*

Even though the Lord did not reply, she was sure he knew about the problem and in due course, he would do what was necessary to fit Laura into his grand design.

~ * ~

In the morning, the Imperial's agent picked up Laura and her passengers and drove them to the airport. Before leaving Aden for

Bossasso, she arranged for her service/courtesy ticket to London and back to Aden with Imperial Airways for next week.

"You have to confirm the return reservation in London, Captain," the agent said. "Thank you for flying Imperial."

"The pleasure is mine," she said. She strolled to her Junkers, and started loading the passengers.

Since the *York* did not carry a heavy load this time, the little F13 took off from the paved runway of Aden like a racehorse out of the gate.

The flight to Mogadishu following the refueling in Bossasso was very pleasant. The general traveling in the copilot's seat helped to refine their strategy upon arrival.

When Mogadishu appeared on the horizon, Laura took a deep breath and chopped the throttle. Before the actual touchdown, she saw three automobiles near the apron.

"It is like they expected the Hanno or some other major aircraft landing," remarked Laura.

"Air Mogadishu is the national airline of Somalia. As such, it is most important," said General Ponti.

When they landed, Laura taxied to the apron and stopped the engine. She was the first off the plane, helping her passengers. The general left the plane last. As he stepped off, he put his arm around Laura's waist and started walking toward the large car with an army driver. Panetta stood there dumbfounded. As they got near to him, Ponti stopped and offered his hand to the postmaster.

"My dear Mr. Panetta, Captain Madison tells me how well you two manage to cooperate in handling the mail. Believe me, we both appreciate it," and turning to Laura he continued, "Don't we, darling?"

"Yes, Alessandro. Mr. Panetta is the nicest guy in the colonial administration."

"Let us go, my dear, we do not have much time. I hope you will fly me to Kismayo on Monday."

"I will, darling," replied Laura and with a coquettish smile turned to the postmaster.

"I am going to see you next Saturday, Mr. Panetta."

"Of course, Captain," the weasel-faced man replied. "It was a pleasure meeting you again, General."

Laura boarded the general's car and they took off in a great cloud of dust.

"I could kiss you, General. You got me out of a rather unpleasant date," Laura said.

"Come and meet my wife, she is waiting for us at the Croce."

Mrs. Ponti laughed very hard when they told her about the way they had hoodwinked Panetta. Apparently, she did not like the postmaster very much either. The dinner with General and Mrs. Ponti was very pleasant and entertaining. At ten, the general ordered his driver to take Laura home.

"We are going to meet you on Monday," said Ponti. "Both of us are flying with you to Kismayo."

"I am going to take good care of you," Laura promised.

She fell asleep in the car on the way to the house. Ray actually carried Laura to her own room, but she woke up, and snuggled up to him.

"Please, stay with me, darling, for a few moments," Laura said, sensing the desire in Ray.

"You are dead tired."

"There are things which revitalize me," she said and kissed Ray on the lips.

As Ray was always a gentleman, she did not have to ask again. This was the first time they had made love in Laura's bed.

"You are marvelous, Laura. No matter how tired you are, you never refuse me," he said.

"It is not a matter of me refusing you. Love is actually the transfer of energy and I am on the receiving end," she said just before Ray returned to his room.

Although fatigue overtook Laura, she did not forget her report to the Lord.

"Thanks for looking after me on this difficult day. Thanks for General Ponti, Robert, and Ray. Good night, my Lord."

~ * ~

On Monday, out of deference to the general and his wife, Laura sat in the captain's seat, but Lee did all the flying. At one point, she went back to the cabin to have a little chat with the passengers.

In Kismayo, Lee managed the difficult landing and taxied the plane to the terminal building. They stopped the engine and General Ponti invited both pilots to have lunch with them.

"Sometimes I wonder how you did master flying so well. I flew with several military pilots, but I never saw anybody handling an aircraft better than you do," the general said after lunch when they all sat on the patio having their coffee.

"I guess I have the talent. Nevertheless, I owe you a confession, General," Laura replied and took a sip of her espresso. "You were my very first passenger on my first professional solo flight. Believe me I was scared stiff."

"Flying with a woman scared me too. Nevertheless, you handled the plane precisely," said the general.

"Perhaps you should visit us for a few days, Laura. It is much nicer here than in Mogadishu," Mrs. Ponti said "I see a lot of greenery."

"We'd take you hunting, if you were interested," the general interrupted.

"I've never hunted, but my father taught me to handle firearms and shoot straight. I'd love to go hunting with you," Laura replied, finishing her coffee.

"We'll arrange it when the turmoil around you clears a little," said Mrs. Ponti, "won't we, Alessandro?"

They were late taking off from Kismayo and arrived in Mogadishu just before sunset. Panetta waited at the airfield sitting on a camping chair in the shadow of the mail truck.

As they landed, Laura immediately hurried to the Italian.

"I am very sorry, Mr. Panetta, I got bogged down with the general. After all, he is the commander of the colonial army. I couldn't possibly say no to him."

"I understand, Captain, believe me I do. Nevertheless, I expect you to deliver the goods on Saturday."

"Do you think I would go back on my word, Mr. Panetta? A promise is a promise. If I can, I will take a copilot with me to Aden, and come back fresh as a daisy. You will have the time of your life, I'm sure," Laura said in a convincing tone.

"I am very much looking forward to it," the postmaster said. "See you on Saturday, Captain."

"*Arrivederci, Signor* Panetta."

~ * ~

Tuesday the sergeants took the inland route, and Laura stayed home with Ray. They had lunch at the club, and in the afternoon, sat on the patio. Ray took his black satchel and checked some of the documents before turning to Laura.

"I reviewed our financial status last week. Because of the number of passengers flying to Aden, we are doing very well. I'd like you to do a few things for me in England, my dear," Ray started.

"If they do not throw me in jail, you can count on me."

"They won't, I am sure of that."

"I hope you are right. Whom do you want me to visit?"

"Phone Jim Thorpe in Canterbury. He is supposed to manage Herron Motors, an automobile dealership. I asked him to find us pilots."

"It is not far from our place. I may stop over there on my way to the Old Bailey."

"I am worried about Jim. He did not reply to my letters. It is strange, as he was always reliable."

"I'll check on him," Laura promised.

"I also want you to visit the Bristol Aircraft Company on the west coast, and look up my old buddy, George Stone."

"Why?"

"We are getting more and more passengers to Aden, and lately I had several inquiries to fly people from Mombasa and Nairobi to Cairo, hooking up with KLM, Lufthansa, and Imperial."

"Wow!"

"Therefore, I decided to take the plunge. I want to buy two or three long-range aircraft, each with at least eighteen or twenty seats."

"Do you think Mr. Stone can help us find the proper aircraft?"

"I hope he can."

"What is his position?"

"I've no idea. Although George flew in my squadron during the war, since I came to Africa, we lost touch. I remember him having a mechanical engineering degree. The last I heard he had a job at Bristol. Most likely he could put you in touch with the right people."

"I see. Do you think I should visit Junkers in Dessau?"

"Of course. That would be the third favor. Look for Mr. Werth. He is our contact man in international sales."

"Should I ask these firms for a written offer?"

"Of course. They should include spare parts, training for our maintenance staff, and a few pilots. I'll need the information for the bank."

"Very well, Ray. I will bring you the proposals."

"Ask them to seal their tenders and do not tell you how much their price is."

"Why?"

Ray gave Laura a long look. "I want to be fair to both companies. You may inadvertently betray the price of one to the other."

"It may give you a better price."

"Money is not the most important criteria," Ray interrupted. "Insist on test flying the machine they propose to sell us."

"Why does it matter?"

"As you are going to fly them, I want you to be happy. Your opinion will be the deciding factor," said Ray and handed Laura four envelopes.

"I prepared several letters of introduction for you to each of those guys. As I don't know which identity you are going to use, I introduced you as Laura Madison in the first two letters, and as Laura Blake-Stanton in the other two, identifying you as the chief pilot of Air Mogadishu. The letters will lend credibility to your negotiations."

"I am sure it will be all right. However, I worry about you. You have one more week with Lee and Walters. Next week you'll get two more people for another two or three weeks. As it is, I must be back before those guys return to Aden."

"I'll send you a cable if I have to return the sergeants earlier."

"Where are you going to send it?"

"Let's think about it. I might send it to Jim Thorpe, or to any address you specify."

They had lunch on the patio, another one of Amina's Italian specials. Up to this point, Ray had behaved like a proper airline executive talking to the chief pilot. However, when he pushed Laura's chair under her, he touched her shoulder. It was like an electric shock. Laura did not think about the meal, the incident over the bay, or Bob. She wanted Ray more than anything else. She wanted to hold him and be one with the man.

During the meal, Laura kicked off her shoes and pressed her bare feet against Ray's leg. Obviously, he noticed it, and smiled at Laura.

"Just have a little patience, darling," he said with a smile.

"I am not the most patient person, you've ever seen."

"I am not going to put your staying power to a test," Ray said with a smile.

As soon as Amina cleared the table, Laura stood and gave Ray her all-knowing, seductive smile. He stood, took Laura by the hand, and started for the bedroom. Upon entering, Laura started shedding her clothes, and when she reached the bed, she remarked, "I left my shoes under the table."

"So what?" Ray asked removing his shirt.

"Amina might get the wrong idea."

"I have news for you, darling. She knows what is going on between us. The servants always know."

"You're right," replied Laura and pushed Ray onto the bed, covering the man's body with hers.

"I want to be in control," she said to herself.

"I know you are a control freak, my dear, and I love it," he said.

~ * ~

Thursday evening Laura packed up her meager belongings. Apart from the dress she had worn on leaving the *Oleandris*, Laura took only a spare flight suit and a pair of sneakers, but wore the gold wings Ray had given her. The farewell night with Ray was something to remember.

In the morning, as Laura was leaving his bedroom, Ray remarked, "I hope this was not our last night together."

"I don't think so, unless I find a handsome airline executive willing to promote me to chief pilot," she replied and kissed him on the lips.

Panetta did not come to the field to see the mailbags depart. With three passengers and Lee in the copilot's seat, the *Calabrese* roared off the dusty Mogadishu strip.

Following the uneventful journey, the agent of Imperial Airways picked up Laura and her passengers. They all drove to the Excelsior and checked into their comfortable rooms. Laura just dumped her bag and with Sergeant Lee took a taxi to the base.

Earlier Bob had taken his squadron out for an exercise, but the officers in the club welcomed her. Laura sat on the patio of the mess waiting for the planes to return. The bombers' landing was a magnificent sight. Bob flying the lead plane with a red streamer reminded Laura of the stories Ray told her about the colors of the leaders.

At four o'clock, Bob, wearing his summer flight suit, entered the mess. A long handshake had to suffice instead of the kiss.

"How was your exercise, darling?" Laura asked.

"Tiring, very tiring," Bob replied. "Using concrete bombs we were aiming at circles in the desert. We did all right."

"I am glad the targets did not shoot back."

"In these old planes we would not have had a chance," said Bob with a deep sigh. "I heard of new medium bombers being designed for the R.A.F. I hope I will get a chance to fly them."

"You'll get it, I am sure."

"Are you going to England this time?"

"Yes, I am."

"Are you coming back?"

"Unless they throw me in jail for using a forged passport I am coming back in two, perhaps three weeks."

"You should try looking for pilots in England, because three weeks from today, we must have all the sergeants back. Next month we are going to get additional aircraft."

"In other words, I have maximum three weeks in England," Laura remarked.

"It should be enough to retake your identity," Bob suggested. They chatted about flying in general, but Laura did not mention Ray's intention of buying long-range aircraft.

They went for a walk on the runway, and a long kiss in the shadow of the bomber's wing were the starting points of the evening's main event. In the heat of the late afternoon, Bob drove Laura to the hotel. As they entered Laura's room, a simple kiss from Bob woke up the sleeping tigress in her, and despite the long night with Ray and the exhausting flight, she took him in her arms. Off came the flight suits, and in a matter of seconds, they became one body and soul. As far as Laura was concerned, Ray did not exist anymore.

By dinnertime, Bob was spent. They were lying side by side naked when he remarked, "I am not as tough as you are, darling. Flying six hours took a lot out of me."

"I flew eight hours. I hope you believe me that the female is the stronger of the sexes," Laura said, gently kissing Bob.

"I am afraid you are right."

"Come on," Laura said jumping off the bed. "Let's have something to eat."

"Okay," said Bob and stood up slowly. He took Laura's hands, looked her in the eyes, and said, "I will have to make some major decisions soon, darling."

"What about?"

"Very serious matters, Laura. Please, don't ask."

"I have no intentions of prying."

"Have a good time in England, darling, and stay away from the dashing Air Force officers."

"Oh, Robert," she said.

~ * ~

Saturday morning, with all the Imperial passengers, Laura took the airline's elegant bus to the airport. Her service/courtesy ticket was in order, and the agent ushered her into the comfortable cabin. The stewardess assisted the passengers in finding their seats and tightening their seat belts. She gave Laura a jump seat in the back of the aircraft next to the galley.

"I am Celeste," she said. "Here you will have a little bit of peace and quiet. If anybody found out you were an airline captain, they would overwhelm you with stupid questions. I know, it happens all the time."

"I am sure I couldn't answer any of the questions. My plane is too small. I couldn't fit your galley in it."

The huge, four-engine biplane started rolling and to Laura the takeoff run seemed very long. In the end, she worried if they were going to leave terra firma. Contrary to her expectation, the huge aircraft lifted off, gained altitude rapidly, and soon leveled off.

"I must look after my passengers," Celeste said, got off her seat, and went forward to talk to the travelers, giving them comfort, blankets, and whoever wanted it, a cup of tea.

They had just reached the Red Sea when Celeste came to Laura saying, "Captain Wills' compliments. He would like to invite you to the flight deck."

"Thank you."

"Just follow me," said Celeste. Laura got out of her seat and full of anticipation followed the stewardess.

At first, the flight deck completely awed her. The multitude of the instruments, dials, and controls were frightening.

"Welcome to my domain," said Wills and turned to his first officer.

"I trust you won't mind letting Captain Madison take your seat for a little while, Gary."

"Of course not."

"Thank you, sir," Laura said. Looking at the panel, she immediately found the instruments she had in her little Junkers. The wheel and the rudder controls were the same, and as Laura leaned forward to check some of the dials, she concluded the Hanno was not that much different from her aircraft. Although there were several instruments she did not know, she felt she could fly the monster with very little instructions.

"Believe it or not, this plane flies like a fighter," said Wills. "It could use a little more power if we wanted to do aerobatics, but I am sure the passengers would not appreciate it."

Laura didn't answer. She was too engrossed with the cockpit. Wills' voice disrupted her preoccupation.

"Would you like to fly her a little?"

"Yes," she said meekly and put her hands on the controls.

"You've got it," said Wills.

"I have it," Laura gave the standard reply.

The controls of the aircraft were rather light. When a slight wind rocked the plane, Laura counteracted with ease. The feeling of being in control of the gigantic Hanno gave her a sense of victory. In a way, the feeling was sensual, but since she did not have full, unrestricted control, the sensation of flying the monster did not invoke special emotions in her.

"She is light on the controls," Laura remarked.

"She is a very well designed, stabile aircraft," Wills replied. He let Laura fly the Hanno for a few minutes. Then he restored the normal operation of the flight deck, asking Laura to return to her seat.

This time Celeste did not take Laura to the jump seat, but gave her a comfortable, leather upholstered aisle seat. A young man sat next to her.

"Let me introduce your traveling companion, Captain Madison. This is Mr. Paul Lafere."

"Nice meeting you, Mr. Lafere."

"The pleasure is mine." They got into a conversation. Paul was a civil engineer returning from French Indo-China to London.

"I am from Quebec City, but since my father moved his lumber business to England, I took the job of chief engineer with his company and followed him to London," he said.

"Are you going on to Canada?"

"No, the company needs me in England. You see I examine the raw material and make sure we get the right quality. This trip was an exception. I built a wooden railway bridge in French Indo-China."

"It must be satisfying to see your ideas on paper becoming a real structure."

"It is. Celeste told me you are an airline pilot. That must be fun."

"Yes, I love flying. It is actually an addiction, worse than alcohol."

They talked about their professions and the time passed quickly. The passengers spent the night in Rome. In the morning, under the guidance of another cockpit crew the Hanno took off.

During the next leg of the journey, Laura learned a great deal about Paul. He never married, had a house on Belgravia Square, and drove a Triumph sports car. He turned out a pleasant person, although as a man he did not excite Laura.

"I will show you around. The place is absolutely wild," Paul said after the landing in Corydon.

"I'll call you if I make it to London," Laura promised. The bus took the passengers into town, and Laura checked into the hotel. In the dining room, among the memorabilia of the early flying machines, she felt like she was walking on hallowed grounds.

Following the early dinner, she checked the train schedules and sent a telegram to her grandmother announcing her arrival.

I wonder if she's still alive, Laura thought after going to bed. *Thanks for getting me home, my Lord. Please let Granny be alive,* she sighed before falling asleep.

~ * ~

The precise departure and arrival of the British trains were a little strange after the relaxed schedule of the Bengl Railways and the liberal timing of the flights at Air Mogadishu.

As the train pulled into Folkestone station, Laura immediately recognized James, the major domo of her grandmother standing on the platform wearing his bowler hat.

"Welcome, Miss Laura," the aging butler said and took her small bag. "You seem to be traveling light this time. Is the rest of your baggage following?"

"No, James, this is all. How is Granny?"

"Dame Edith is very well indeed," he replied. "Although on the doctor's orders she had to give up riding."

"Did she fall?"

"Oh no, she did not. Dame Edith is the best horsewoman in Britain, but the doctor thought her bones were too brittle, and even the smallest mishap could kill her."

"I see."

Laura got into the old black Bentley. James cranked the engine to life, and headed for Stanton Manor some ten miles distant. Laura had ridden the Bentley along these roads several times. When she stayed in the boarding school, she always spent the Christmas holidays with her grandmother. As it was summer, the countryside was green, as green as only England could be.

The sun was still high when they drove into the garden, stopping in front of the old stone building.

James took Laura's small suitcase and carried it into the house. In the middle of the parlor her grandmother, Dame Edith Stanton waited. Although Granny was very old, the wiry, five feet six inches tall woman stood ramrod straight with her long gray hair tied in a neat bun at the nape of her neck.

She always looked the same without apparently aging. She wore sensible shoes in addition to the tweed clothes an English noblewoman should wear while at her estate.

"Laura darling, how in the name of God did you get here so fast? How is Edward?" she asked, after hugging her granddaughter.

"I flew in with Imperial Airways from Aden yesterday."

"Wait. How did you get to Aden? I got a letter from you yesterday telling me you were going to visit the new Mikumi game park with Edward this weekend," she said after they sat down on the couch.

"I did not write that letter, Granny."

"Then who wrote it?"

"I have no idea. Didn't you see it was not my handwriting?"

"My eyesight is getting weak, therefore, James reads all the letters. Besides, he said the letter was typed."

"Hold it, Granny," Laura interrupted. "I wrote you two letters in the last few months from Mogadishu after some thugs kidnapped me. I asked you to help me."

"My God, it was you, after all. I am very sorry, darling. The story sounded unbelievable, and I had James throw out the letters. I thought the writer was a swindler wanting to chisel money out of me. Tell me what happened."

Laura reiterated the story of the kidnapping. In the end, her grandmother was gaping.

"It is hard to believe Edward would want to have you kidnapped."

"Much worse, Granny, an old friend of mine, Mr. Abdi, found out about the kidnapper's plans. Although he had been contracted to kill me, the fellow thought of making extra money by selling me to a nomad for a couple of camels. Due to his greed I survived, and managed to escape."

"How terrible. I just do not understand why Edward wanted you dead. Sure, when I die, Stanton Manor would be yours, but this is not very valuable. He would most likely have to sell it just to pay the death duties. To kill you for say ten thousand pounds would not be worth his while."

"I don't know, Granny. According to Mr. Abdi, the going rate of a proper professional assassination in Mogadishu was twenty pounds. Fortunately, miserly Edward hired a cut-rate killer who, because of sheer incompetence, let me escape."

"Regardless, Edward must have a young female accomplice."

"Having my passport, arriving at a new duty station would be the best time to introduce someone else as me," Laura concluded.

"How did you get the money to pay the fare?"

"I worked for it very hard," Laura replied.

"Doing what?" Granny asked suspiciously.

"First, I worked as a loadmaster for Mr. Madison, but after he got sick, I flew his aircraft. Now I am a fully qualified airline pilot."

Granny was completely stupefied. "That is beyond me, Laura. If God wanted us to fly, he would have given us wings. You are tempting fate."

"Come on, Granny, it is a science."

"Could be a science or black magic, I don't care, but right now I cannot think of anything else than how to make Edward pay for what he did to you."

"What can we do?"

"We are going to look into the matter presently," the old lady said. "James," she shouted.

"Yes, madame," the butler materialized.

"Delay the tea. Call Mr. Biggles on the telephone and tell him we are going to be in his office tomorrow after three o'clock. Also ask him to reserve two rooms for us in the Cumberland Hotel."

"Yes, Dame Edith," said the butler and disappeared.

"He has to go to the telephone exchange in the village, but it is not too far."

"What are you planning, Granny?"

"I don't know. Mr. Biggles is our solicitor. For the money I pay him, he should be able to tell us what we can do. Regardless, I'd prefer to take my dagger and disembowel Edward. Anything else would be too good for him. If your mother were alive..."

They talked about the chicanery of Laura's stepfather until dinner, but after the meal, Granny started quizzing Laura about her new profession, and they went to bed well after midnight.

Nine

The well-organized transport system, the red double-decker buses, and the calm demeanor of the people in London always amazed Laura.

After checking into the Cumberland Hotel, they had lunch, and Granny called for a taxi to take them to the lawyer's office. They drove to an old building off the Strand on Dover Street. The spotless polished brass plaque by the entrance said: Marmaduke M. Biggles Q.C.Barrister and Solicitor. The inside of the building matched its exterior: old but in pristine condition.

Mr. Biggles' secretary, a tall, skinny woman, had the manners of a sergeant major when it came to the employees of the firm, but she treated the clients as visiting royals.

"Dame Edith, Miss Laura, what a pleasure to see you. Please take a seat. Mr. Biggles is going to be with you in a moment. May I offer you a cup of tea?"

"No, Miss Pritchard, thank you very much," Granny replied and sat down.

"You've grown, Miss Laura. The last time we met you were still a little girl in school."

"It was a long time ago," mused Laura.

"She is a fully qualified airline pilot now," Granny bragged. "Would you have believed it just two years ago?"

"Most certainly not," the secretary said and looked at Laura with undisguised admiration. "You must be very brave, Miss Laura."

She returned to her desk shaking her head, and in a few minutes came back saying, "Mr. Biggles is ready for you, Dame Edith."

In the elegant office, the lawyer had the women sit at a coffee table on comfortable leather upholstered armchairs. Although Laura's presence seemed to surprise Biggles, he did not say anything about it.

"Dame Edith, Miss Laura, what can I do for you today?" he asked after the formalities.

"We have several problems, Marmaduke," Granny started. "First of all, Laura did something she should not have done. She entered the country with a forged passport under an assumed name. However, she had proper justification to do so, but it is better if she tells you her whole saga. Believe me, it has the makings of a penny thriller."

"I am listening, Miss Laura."

By this time, Laura had her story properly organized. She left Ray out of it as much as it was possible, claiming that having the passport forged her own idea. The rest was the truth.

When she finished, the lawyer gave them a long look and said, "You were right, Dame Edith. It is quite a story, but I do not see any problems. I am going to arrange a hearing with one of the judges for tomorrow following the regularly scheduled trials in the Old Bailey, and let him decide."

"What are they going to do to me?" Laura asked, frightened.

"It depends on the judge. I believe the worst-case scenario is a five or ten pound fine. My problem is only the verification of your true identity. Miss Pritchard and I can vouch for it, and of course, Dame Edith's word will weigh heavily in your favor. However, we would like to have some more physical evidence."

"I have her birth certificate, her high school diploma, and the yearbook of the graduating class from Wyndham Academy. Her picture as a valedictorian and county fencing champion are there, and only a blind man would deny she is not the same person," Granny said with conviction.

"If it were necessary, we could ask the Principal of Wyndham Academy to identify me," Laura said.

"That should be enough," said Biggles. "The timely recognition of her pilot's license would also help. My nephew, Wing Commander Chadwick Brannigan is the chief instructor at the Corydon Flying School. If he gave Miss Laura a flight test with passing marks, it would also weigh heavily in her favor."

"When can I take the test?" Laura asked eagerly.

"I will call him presently, and let you know tonight."

"Can you and your good wife have dinner with us at the Epee D'Or tonight?" Granny asked.

"I am afraid, Dame Edith, we have a previous commitment. However, let me assure you I will visit you in the hotel before six o'clock and let you know where we stand."

"I appreciate it, Mr. Biggles," said Granny.

"By the way, ladies, are you aware of the provisions of the Brett Trust?"

"Is it the trust Gramps Brett set up for me?" Laura asked.

"Yes."

"I knew about it, but as he was not rich, I thought it insignificant. In fact mother received five hundred pounds for his schooner and the cottage after he died," Laura said.

"Well, it was like that for quite some time. The fund was about a thousand pounds set aside for your education. However, your grandfather bought some land in Canada, and since a prospector discovered oil on the property, the trustees sold it for a lot of money. At the age of twenty-four, you will be a rich woman, Miss Laura. Until such time you could draw an annuity of a few thousand pounds a year. I just had a request from Barclay's Bank to verify the location and identity of Miss Laura Blake-Stanton. I meant to ask you, Dame Edith, for her whereabouts," Biggles said.

"What are you suggesting?" Granny asked.

"Well, after we have established Miss Laura's identity, I will introduce her to the trustee at Barclays."

"Have you any idea, Mr. Biggles, how much money is in the trust?" Laura asked.

"Not off hand, but I know the man looking after the account. He does not touch anything less than a hundred thousand pounds," the lawyer said.

Laura and Granny looked at each other. They instantly knew what motivated Edward to try to do away with Laura.

"I think you just realized why those nasty things happened to Miss Laura," the lawyer said. "Although we do not have any proof of the chicanery, I have my suspicions."

"Can we do anything to Edward?" Granny asked.

"I doubt it. If we confronted him, he could claim the telegrams sent by the captain of the *Oleandris* were mistakes. He would say he hired a private detective to search for Miss Laura."

"What about the woman masquerading as me?" Laura asked.

"As soon as the real Miss Laura Blake-Stanton turns up in England, the other woman will vanish," Biggles said. "Edward is safe as the Church of England."

"The bastard," growled Granny.

True to his word, Biggles dropped in at the Cumberland and he had good news. The flight test was to take place in Corydon at eight o'clock in the morning, leaving Laura and Granny plenty of time to return to the city for their hearing at the Old Bailey after two in the afternoon.

~ * ~

Seeing the number and variety of aircraft at the flying club dazzled Laura. Before entering the office of the chief flight instructor, she just stared at the planes the same way as a starved puppy eyes the window of a butcher.

Wing Commander Chad Brannigan, a pleasant individual and Ray's commanding officer during the war, greeted Laura as an old friend.

"Since a pal of mine taught you to fly, I must give you a tougher than usual test," he explained on the way to the little trainer, the type Laura had never seen.

Brannigan took ten minutes to explain the flying characteristics of the plane. He put Laura in the left seat and directed her to take off.

She remembered Ray's instructions to submit a flight plan to the control tower before taking off, therefore, she asked the Wing Commander about it.

"I already filed the flight plan," he said. "It is the standard commercial pilot's testing course."

Laura took the pre-flight checklist, cleared her takeoff with the tower on the radio, and opened the throttle. The test was easy, as the Wing Commander did not ask Laura to do any fancy aerobatics, only a few things that she already knew how to do well.

"You are quite a professional, Miss Laura," he said. "You're the type the airline industry needs. I am sure you could get an instructor's ticket quite easily. Many ladies want to learn piloting these days, and they would appreciate being taught by a woman."

"I'm afraid I could not do it. You see Ray needs me, because we are losing two pilots in three weeks, and I will have to fly some of the mail routes again. That is roughly thirty hours a week."

"It is quite a load."

"By the way, Wing Commander, where can I find a couple of pilots willing to come out to Somalia and fly for us?"

"It is not easy, Miss Laura. There are plenty of people with licenses, but most of them are old guys like me with wartime experience. They would not be happy flying the small Junkers F13 airliners. These guys want to do aerobatics, chasing the Hun all over the sky. The young yahoos with the proper qualifications want to barnstorm, and they would not enjoy the serious airline type flying you do. Perhaps you should advertise in the *Manchester Guardian*."

"Thanks for the tip, sir," said Laura.

"Let me drive you and your grandmother into town and attend your hearing. Perhaps my testimony would help."

~ * ~

The hearing at Old Bailey was shorter than expected. After Biggles delivered his summation and the Crown Prosecutor accepted Laura's guilty plea, the judge fined her a guinea for using a forged passport, taking into consideration the extenuating circumstances. He ordered to change the name changed on her commercial pilot's license and logbook to Laura Blake-Stanton, and her application for a passport.

After the hearing, Biggles told Laura about the judge being a wartime pilot himself, twice shot down, and had the same D.F.C. as Ray did.

"You rigged the trial," Granny said.

"I am not ashamed of it," Biggles said smiling. "I am going to send one of my associates to look after your passport, Miss Laura."

"Could you call me Miss Stanton, please," Laura interrupted. "I do not want to bear the name of that bastard a minute longer than I have to."

"We can have your license and passport issued to Miss Stanton, but it would take some time to have the adoption annulled."

"Can you take care of it, Mr. Biggles?"

"I'll prepare the papers for your signature. You could come to my office and sign them the day after tomorrow."

With all the official business taken care of, Laura and Granny had a couple of days for themselves in London waiting for Laura's passport.

"I am sure my company would not be enough entertainment for you, Laura," Granny said after they returned to the Cumberland. "I tire easily and could not take you to a theatre or to a concert."

"I have a friend here, a Canadian engineer. We sat next to each other on the plane from Aden to London. He is quite an entertaining individual."

"I would like to meet him," Granny said.

Laura phoned Paul and invited him for dinner at the Epee D'Or. Despite the short notice, Paul arrived carrying a bouquet of roses for Granny. The conversation around the dinner table was proper upper class, the topics well chosen, and the language highly civilized.

Paul invited Laura for a Brahms concert at Albert Hall the next day, and she accepted. All considered, it was a boring, conventional evening. Nevertheless, it was in strict accordance with the code of conduct prescribing the way a young man of good breeding should start the conquest of the heart of a young lady having proper upbringing.

After the dinner, Granny invited Laura for a nightcap in her room. As soon as Laura got her Campari, Granny asked, "Did you think of getting married, darling?"

"Oh, yes. I have a perfect candidate."

"Is he someone like Paul?"

"No, Granny. He is much more exciting: a squadron leader with the R.A.F. stationed in Aden."

"Don't marry a soldier, Laura. They are here today, but tomorrow you may get a telegram from the War Office and a couple of medals."

"That is in wartime, Granny."

"Do you think we would not get into a war during your lifetime?"

"I have no idea."

"We will, I guarantee that. Then your husband will be among the first ones to ship out. Just like your father's two brothers, Andy and Ronny. Both professional soldiers, both killed in the Great War. Your father, the engineer had all the luck. He came back after three years in the trenches without a scratch."

"I love Robert very much."

"I loved your grandfather too. The stupid old goat died on me during the war. Had a heart attack when the War Office told him that he was too old to fight," Granny said. "Take someone like this fellow, Paul. He is an engineer, like your father, he is well-off, and if we got into a war, they would not call him up."

"That may be, Granny, but as a man he is not too attractive."

"You'd get used to him, I am sure. However, you are old enough to decide what you want. I just thought to warn you against soldiers. They are the best lovers, but make lousy husbands. Have a good time with Paul tomorrow, think about what I told you, but do as you see fit."

Granny's understanding was surprising. Following the enjoyable discussions, Laura returned to her room. She took a long bath, and as she stood in front of the mirror naked, she cupped her breasts and sighed.

"I need you, Robert very much."

As a proper lady, she put on her nightgown and went to bed. Looking up at the ceiling she spoke to the Almighty.

Thanks for your help with the flight test and finding an understanding judge to hear the case, my Lord. I need Robert very much now, but I'd gladly compromise with Ray. Would it be right if I got involved with Paul? Although the answer did not come directly, she felt it would be negative.

I thought so, my Lord, she said with a deep sigh, pulled up the blanket and fell asleep.

~ * ~

Granny and Laura went shopping, and by the end of the day, Laura had all the clothes a fashionable young lady should have. Laura picked every outfit in a style which permitted her to wear the gold pilot's wings on her breast. In the evening, Laura enjoyed the concert. It took her back to the time she was in high school. The students of Wyndham Academy had traveled to London once every month to attend either a concert or one of the theatrical productions.

Paul behaved like a proper gentleman, as prescribed in the code of etiquette applicable to the British upper middle class.

"Actually, we should have had a chaperone," said Paul.

"Nonsense. We are fully qualified professionals. At times, we hold the fate of many people in our hands. Society should overlook the lack of a chaperone," Laura replied.

Following the concert, before starting the car, Paul asked, "Where do you want to go for the nightcap? Should we find a nice place, or perhaps my humble residence would suffice."

"Thank you, Paul, but I am developing a nasty headache. We could have our nightcap at the Cumberland if you don't mind," Laura replied, not wishing to visit Paul's apartment because she knew what might happen.

"Could I change your mind?"

"Not today, Paul. Although I am very much interested in the decor of your house, I think this is not the right time for me to see it. I am sure I will come to London a few times in the near future."

"In other words it is a rain-check."

"It is," she replied.

Despite her alleged headache, they spent an hour in the hotel's bar discussing subjects of interest to both of them. After Paul left,

Laura thought that if she had not been quasi-betrothed to Bob and/or Ray, Paul might be an acceptable third choice.

Perhaps Granny is right, she said starting her conversation with the Almighty.

Should I consider Paul as an alternate to Bob or Ray? I have a problem with men, my Lord, help me to sort them out, please."

As the Almighty was not in a communicative mood, he left her questions without answer. Laura had no other alternative than to go to sleep.

~ * ~

In a couple of days, Laura's passport arrived and she went to see the trustee at Barclay's. The plush, all marble interior of the bank located in the heart of the city did not surprise her. It was what she expected from one of the premier financial institutions of the Empire.

The uniformed tellers, the well-laid-out main hall created the impression of riches and good organization. The pleasant, fifty-ish trustee of the account, Mr. Eagles, wore a small, black beard, reminding Laura of a pirate. *Perhaps the descendants of the pirates went into banking*, she thought.

"It is nice meeting you, Miss Stanton," said the man as he offered to shake hands.

"The pleasure is mine, Mr. Eagles."

"Please sit down, Miss Stanton, we have a lot to discuss."

"I am sure we have," she replied and sat in the comfortable armchair. "You must excuse my insistence on meeting you as soon as possible, sir, but I am worried about someone impersonating me and claiming ownership of the trust."

"I am sure you have nothing to worry about, Miss Stanton. Mr. Biggles has already drawn my attention to this possibility. Indeed someone approached us by mail claiming she was you, and inquired about the conditions of the trust. Although we sent her a generalized reply, we managed to maintain the confidential nature of the account. Should something like that happen again, you can rest assured: we will take the appropriate steps to safeguard your rights and property."

"Thank you, sir. I appreciate it."

"It is our duty, Miss Stanton. Anyway, let us get on with our business. Mr. Biggles submitted several court papers to support your identity. Nevertheless, I must make sure you are the rightful heir to the Brett Trust. May I see your passport and your commercial pilot's license?"

"Of course," Laura replied, handing over the documents. The man checked them thoroughly.

"May I check the validity of these documents?"

"By all means, Mr. Eagles."

The man left Laura alone for twenty minutes. When he came back, his manners had changed. He warmed up to Laura as much as a banker can warm up to anybody.

"In order to avoid future complications about your identity, Miss Stanton, can you give me a signature and suggest a password?"

"Of course," replied Laura and signed her name on the form the banker gave her.

"Can you give me a password?"

"Air Mogadishu," Laura said quickly.

"Everything is in order, Miss Stanton. If you wish, we can record your fingerprints for added security."

"Thank you, sir, but I do not believe that is necessary."

"As you wish. According to my instructions, I have to reiterate the terms of your grandfather's will governing the management of the trust account."

"I'd appreciate that because I thought I only had a small, insignificant trust," Laura replied.

"Your stepfather should have told you about it. A few years ago, I gave him all the information I was permitted to divulge."

Laura swallowed hard. *That had to be the time when Edward married my mother. The bastard knew. This is why he adopted me. He may have killed Mother too. Now I am beginning to understand why Granny wants to slit the belly of Edward. I am going to buy a dagger and do it myself*, she thought, then smiled at the banker saying, "I was too young at the time, sir, and would not have understood."

"Very well, the heir of the Brett Trust would never gain control of the initial cash principal, as it is in perpetual trust."

"I see."

"According to your grandfather's will, Commander Steven Brett, you only get the returns from the investments. However, in addition to the interest, you are entitled to the capital gains. These monies have been accumulating since the opening of the account. We opened an account for you some five years ago, deposited the accrued income there and reinvested the money," Eagles explained.

"I see. How much is on that account?"

"I am afraid it is confidential, and I cannot give you any information until your twenty-fourth birthday, but rest assured it is well in excess of a hundred thousand pounds. The income varies. It is a few thousand pounds each year."

"Not bad."

"Actually, according to the rules of the trust, we should start paying you an annuity, regardless of age, provided you graduated from high school and acquired trade certification or a professional license. As you have fulfilled those requirements, I propose to open an account for you and deposit your first year's annuity."

"Thank you, sir," replied Laura. "How much is my annuity?"

"It varies with the yield of the securities. However, you may reasonably expect two thousand pounds annually after taxes."

The amount stunned Laura, but she quickly recovered.

"What kind of account are you suggesting?"

"Since you live abroad, you have limited options. You may wish to open an investment account, which we can maintain for you in sterling. You could have shares, bonds, gold, and cash deposited on this account."

"Can I buy and sell shares from this account?"

"Of course. We have agents at all the major stock exchanges. Our fees are standard. When you buy, we charge point seven-five percent of the value of the purchase, plus cable costs if applicable. When you are selling, our fee is point two five percent. However, if you wish to withdraw funds, you must give us two working days' notice."

"Two thousand pounds per annum is a considerable amount," remarked Laura. "Nevertheless, why are you suggesting such a sophisticated account?"

"You live and work overseas, Miss Stanton. In less than two years, considerable amounts may accrue on this account. I recommend investing it."

"I see. As I might not be here, would you invest the money for me?"

"Of course, but you have to authorize the bank to manage your account."

"I have no problem with that, Mr. Eagles. However, can you find a way for me to withdraw money from the account if I need it?" Laura asked.

"We can give you a line of credit, secured by your account and the expected accrual. After we issue an international letter of credit, you can visit any of our tellers, or for that matter any corresponding banks, and draw up to the limit we establish. Telegraph and other charges will apply, of course."

"Can you arrange it right now?"

"Of course. I can have a four-thousand-pound letter of credit issued to you, but I hope you understand there are some service charges in connection with every transaction."

"That's all right."

"Just fill out these forms, Miss Stanton. Meanwhile, let me have your passport again for a few minutes and I will open the accounts for you," said Eagles.

Leaving the bank, Laura felt rich. As she walked by the elegant stores and looked in their windows, she knew she could buy almost anything taking her fancy. The thought gave her a sense of security, something she had sorely lacked in the last few months. Granny was waiting for her in the hotel

"How did it go?" she asked.

"Very well, Granny. I am rich."

"What do you mean?"

"I have a letter of credit for four thousand pounds, and I can expect more than a hundred thousand pounds on my account in three years."

"Stay out of the way of the fortune hunters."

"Have no fear, Granny. The guy I have lined up thinks I am poor, and he still loves me."

"I'd like to see him."

"I am afraid he is in Aden with his bombers."

"You know how I feel about soldiers, Laura. Nevertheless, it is your decision, but I'd like to see him to make sure he is on the level," said Granny.

"All right, I am going to give you a chance to look him over before I marry him," said Laura.

"That's my girl. Now all we have to do is find you a dagger like mine."

"I carry a gun in Mogadishu, Granny."

"In the tropics, the damn things might misfire. It cost my father his life when his revolver misfired during the rebellion. A dagger is the best for the last line of defense," she explained.

Laura did not want to argue and just nodded.

"Well," Granny continued, "now we have everything arranged. You can come back to Stanton Manor, and finally I can teach you riding the way I always wanted to."

"I am afraid, Granny, I do not have the time. I must go back to Mogadishu."

"I thought you were having your home leave."

"Air Mogadishu is a business, not the Indian Civil Service, Granny. I came to England to retrieve my name, see you, recruit a few pilots, and check out an aircraft manufacturer."

"Hold it," Granny interrupted. "Some of these are things an airline executive should do. You are not trained for that."

"You are absolutely right. I am not. However, the owner of Air Mogadishu told me exactly what I must do, how to handle the aircraft manufacturers, what kind of planes he wanted, and so on. I even have a crib sheet I study every evening."

"I see you are taking this flying business very seriously."

"Yes, Granny, I do. I believe I found my calling. I want to be an airline pilot flying large aircraft like the Hanno of Imperial Airways. It won't be easy to break in because I am a woman. However, with Air Mogadishu I am the number one pilot. If I stick with Ray, eventually I will fly the large multi-engine planes," said Laura.

"I don't know what could be so great about flying."

"I have an idea, Granny. Do you have an airstrip in Folkestone?"

"Yes, I believe so."

"Okay. Today is Friday. I must make a phone call to Bristol and to Canterbury before lunch to make sure I can meet the right people next week. Then I will call Wing Commander Brannigan, rent the little trainer we used at my test, and I fly you to Folkestone tomorrow. Have James pick you up at the airstrip."

"That is a great idea," she said. "However, I think you are in danger all the time. You are not armed."

"What dangers are lurking in the shadows for me?"

"You never know," Granny said. "However, I do not like you going around defenseless. Take my dagger, the one I have carried since the sepoy rebellion." She pulled up her skirt and removed the finely crafted weapon from her thigh.

"You'll get used to it," she said.

"Honestly, I do not need it, Granny. In Mogadishu I carry a gun."

"Nonsense, take it!"

The ornate sheath made of thin gold plate held the six-inch, slender, pointed, razor-sharp blade. The dagger would fit either the arm or the leg of the wearer, fastened by an adjustable garter belt-like rubberized material.

"Do me a favor, darling. Just wear this weapon all the time. It will give me peace of mind."

"I do not want to take your dagger, Granny. Obviously, you have sentimental ties to it."

"Don't worry. I have a couple of spares," Granny interrupted with a smile. "Take it."

"Okay. I will," said Laura seriously.

"Promise me you'll wear it, darling, please."

"I give you my word, Granny," said Laura and meant it, "but with my flight suit I cannot wear it."

"Why?"

"I could not draw it if needed."

"I see, but you'll wear it with any other outfit, will you?"

"I promise."

~ * ~

Laura first called Herron Motors in Canterbury. The phone rang for a while, and a feminine voice replied: "Herron Motors, Mrs. Thorpe speaking. How may I help you?"

"My name is Laura Stanton. I am the chief pilot of Air Mogadishu. Our managing director asked me to contact Mr. Thorpe. Is he available?"

The line was silent for a few seconds, then Mrs. Thorpe replied in a trembling voice, "I am afraid Jim passed away in January. He had a car accident."

"I am terribly sorry, Mrs. Thorpe. Please accept our condolences. Is there anything Ray or I could do for you?"

"Thank you very much. I have everything I need. I am learning to run the automobile dealership, but it is not easy. It was better being a housewife in Mogadishu. Do you still have his plane flying?"

"It was the *York*, wasn't it?"

"Yes."

"It is my plane now."

"Look after it for Jim. The picture of the airplane is still on the wall of his, I mean my office," said Mrs. Thorpe.

"Do you want me to tell Ray anything?"

"Yes. Tell him to come to England and help me with this godforsaken business."

"I will. Rest assured, ma'am."

"Thanks for calling, Miss Stanton. Take care of *York*," she said and broke the connection.

~ * ~

Laura's second call was not as depressing as the first.

A pleasant voice answered the phone at the Bristol Aircraft Company and put Laura through to George Stone's secretary.

"I am Laura Stanton, the chief pilot of Air Mogadishu. I would like to speak to Mr. Stone."

"One moment, please."

"Stone speaking," came a man's voice.

"I am Laura Stanton, the chief pilot of Air Mogadishu. Our managing director, Ray Madison, instructed me to call you."

"How is the ancient pelican?" Stone interrupted.

"As well as he can be."

"What can I do for you, Miss Stanton?"

"Well, sir, Ray told me to call you because we would like to purchase some long-range aircraft."

"You called the right person, Miss Stanton. When can you come to Bristol?"

"I expect to be free Saturday afternoon."

"Where are you calling from?"

"I am in London."

"If you have nothing better to do, spend the weekend with us. I can show you some of our experimental aircraft."

"That is a great idea, Mr. Stone. You see, I am rather pressed for time."

"Fine," thundered Stone. "Send me a telegram with the time of your arrival, and I will have someone pick you up at the station. Do you need a hotel room?"

"I would appreciate it if you could reserve one for me," said Laura. "I will try to reach Bristol on Saturday evening."

"That would be very nice. Have dinner with us. My wife will be thrilled to meet a female pilot. She is toying with the idea of learning to fly."

"I hope I won't be too much trouble."

"Nonsense. At Bristol, we look after potential customers. Especially if they are associates of old friends like Ray. Just send me the telegram and all will be well."

"I'll do that, Mr. Stone, Thank you very much."

"Don't mention it, Miss Stanton. I'll see you soon."

"Bye, Mr. Stone," said Laura and hung up. *That was lucky*, she thought.

Granny and Laura had a good lunch at the Epee D'Or, went for an afternoon concert at Albert Hall, and turned in rather early.

I had a good day, my Lord, Laura thought before falling asleep. *Please look after Jim Thorpe.*

Ten

The instructor on duty gladly rented one of the Flying Club's trainers to Laura. However, it was rather difficult to get Granny up on the wing and into the copilot's seat. Nevertheless, with the assistance of a flight instructor and a mechanic, they managed.

Before starting the engine, Laura pointed out the barf bag to Granny, but the old lady refused to even look at it.

"If I did not throw up on the Ferris wheel and the roller coaster, why would I throw up in an airplane?"

"Just to be on the safe side, Granny. I have to draw the attention of all my passengers to the bag. It is part of the duties of an airline pilot," Laura said.

"I see."

Granny did not need the bag. In fact, she enjoyed the flight very much, especially the part when Laura circled Stanton Manor a few times.

"It is exhilarating. If I were seventy years younger, I would also want to be an airline pilot. In comparison, horses are no fun at all."

Laura lined up the grass runway and landed the little trainer as smoothly as silk.

With James' help, they got Granny out of the plane.

They said farewell to each other. Laura promised to come to Stanton Manor as soon as she could get away from her duties, got back into the plane, and started the engine. She had tears in her eyes when the plane circled the airfield and saw Granny waving.

~ * ~

In London, Laura did not have time for anything. However, since Granny thought the world of Paul, she decided to maintain loose links with him. She telephoned Paul, telling him she was in transit and could not meet him, but next time she made it to London, she suggested having a meal together.

"It is a brilliant idea, Laura," he said. "Call me either at my house or in the office, and I'll meet you at the station."

"Very nice of you, Paul," she said.

Laura arrived at Bristol in the evening. A middle-aged, uniformed man carrying a sign with her name stood at the platform.

"I am Miss Stanton," she addressed the man.

"Welcome to Bristol, ma'am. I am Mr. Stone's chauffeur. I am to take you to the Red Lion Hotel, wait for you, and drive you to Mr. Stone's residence."

"Thank you, I appreciate it. Mr. Stone must be a very important man in the company."

"He is the Chief Engineer and Director of Operations, second only to the general manager."

"I see."

After freshening up and changing, Laura arrived at the Stones' residence. The man was about Ray's age, well built and in good shape, although he wore glasses. His wife, Sarah was a plump, little blonde. The modest house was situated in an upscale residential area, having a magnificent view of the sea.

"Welcome to our home, Miss Stanton," said Stone.

"Thanks for having me," Laura replied.

Another middle-aged couple, the Marstons, were present. The approximately thirty-five year old man looked like a pilot, and his statuesque wife, an elegant brunette, seemed only a few years younger.

"Ted is our chief test pilot. I thought it would be a good idea for the two of you to meet. I've asked Ted to show you around tomorrow," said Stone.

"I appreciate it, sir."

"Anyway, how is Ray?"

"He is working hard, running a successful, little airline."

"Is he still flying?"

"Occasionally he takes one of the postal routes," Laura said, thinking that Ray's state of health was not Stone's business.

"He's a tough old pelican. How come you became his chief pilot at such a young age?" Stone asked.

"It is rather difficult to find good, reliable airline pilots in Somalia. Actually, Ray trained me."

"What kind of pilots do you have?" asked Marston.

"The turnover rate is rather high. We have our trainees staying with us after completing their course, or we get stuck with the ex-fighter jocks, but they rarely work out," Laura explained, according to her crib sheet. "The secondary purpose of my trip is the recruitment of pilots. I am placing an ad in the *Guardian*."

"You will have a hard time finding the airline pilot types," said Marston. "We have problems keeping good test pilots on our staff."

"Why?"

"Most people are looking for the glamour in flying, barnstorming, the air force, or perhaps flying those monsters of Imperial. Being a test pilot is dangerous, and there is no glamour in it," Marston explained.

They sat at the table, but the conversation still centered on business. The other women were content with being beautiful and silent participants.

~ * ~

Sunday after lunch, Ted invited Laura to the factory's airfield to show her the experimental aircraft. Stone came along too, just in case Laura wanted to talk about the design features of a plane. The number and type of airplanes awed her.

"Actually, what type of aircraft would you need?" Stone asked.

"I will let you help me with the selection. We want a plane to carry about twenty passengers in comfort, with their luggage and a limited quantity of mail. The service ceiling could be less than ten thousand feet, and the range should be five hundred miles," Laura recited Ray's instruction.

"Well, that isn't easy," Stone said scratching his head. "We have a twin-engine aircraft, which would fit your requirements, but we are building them for the R.A.F., a troop carrier. If we fixed up the seats a little, you could perhaps use it."

"Are you referring to the Bombay?" Ted asked.

"Yes," said Stone.

"That would fit the requirements, although it is a stripped-down, basic aircraft designed for the military. That is the one standing there," said Ted, pointing at a large plane.

Laura looked at the aircraft. In comparison with the little Junkers, it was huge. The angular body and the engines hanging on the high wings created the impression of strength rather than beauty.

"How does it handle?" Laura asked.

"You can try it tomorrow," said Marston.

"How many planes did you have in mind?" asked Stone.

"We are planning to acquire three aircraft," said Laura.

"How about your maintenance facilities?"

"I am afraid they are not too hot. If we added three new twin-engine aircraft, we would be overwhelmed. At the moment we have three small Junkers F13s."

"Are they still flying?" Ted asked. "They are ancient."

"The airframes are old, but we have the latest engines in them. Actually, it is the third time Ray had new engines installed. He is planning to phase them out in a couple of years or so and find a much faster aircraft for the mail routes," Laura explained.

"I believe you will want a couple of technicians for about six months to train your people in maintaining the Bombay. I will include the training, the complete tool kits and spare parts in my proposal," said Stone.

"How about qualified pilots with each plane for a period of say, a few months to train our pilots?" Laura said.

"Yes, we could do that," said Stone. "By the way, do you have the multi-engine endorsement on your license?"

"I am afraid not," Laura replied.

"How many hours do you have all together?" Ted asked suspiciously.

"I have British and Somali commercial tickets and nearly five hundred hours of flying time," Laura replied.

"Look," Ted started. "I can give you a demo on the Bombay. It would be three hours. In addition, as you are a potential customer, you could fly six hours free with one of our instructors. That would take you half way to the multi-engine endorsement."

"Can I rent your plane and hire your instructor to complete the course?" Laura interrupted.

"How long are you staying?"

"Why?"

"I do not think you could take any more than three or four hours a day."

Laura laughed.

"I fly nearly eight hours a day, four times a week. You are talking about eighteen hours. I can do it in two or three days easily," she said.

"You may, but our instructor couldn't. They are not made of chrome-vanadium steel," said Ted.

"Perhaps I should pay extra for wearing out your instructors," Laura said with a smile.

"If you are really willing to pay for ten hours of aircraft rental and the instructions, we could arrange to have you certified on multi-engine aircraft, and check you out on the Bombay at the same time," said Ted.

"You've got a deal," Laura said and turned to Stone.

"Can you have the proposal ready for me in three days?"

"Yes," the man replied. "I can even guarantee swift delivery of the aircraft, a couple of months, no more."

"How are you going to do that?" Ted asked.

"We have two planes ready for delivery. They are only due in August. If we can build three more until then and juggle the delivery dates, we will be all right. I owe that much to Ray. He saved my bacon a few times. If we make a deal, you could have the three planes by mid-September," Stone said.

"I'll tell him, but you'd better put the delivery date in the proposal," Laura said.

"Do you want to see the details?"

"No, Mr. Stone. Ray expressly forbade me to learn the details of your proposal. You see, I must go to Dessau and get a quote from Junkers. If I knew the amount, I could subconsciously manipulate the process," explained Laura.

"That sounds like Ray," said Stone. "The guy always has to be fair to everybody. This is what made him great. He shot down a German in France, practically over our airfield. We captured the enemy pilot who somehow survived the crash, but he had broken both his legs. Ray went to the hospital and visited him regularly until the war ended. They became friends."

"I did not know about this side of him," Laura said quietly, thinking how fair a person Ray was.

Ted let Laura go inside the Bombay and check the interior. It was spacious. Adding comfortable seats would not present any problems.

"We could place either a bulkhead or a net separating the passengers from the cargo," Ted explained.

"A net would be enough," Laura mused.

"I'd prefer the bulkhead," Ted said. "It would permit the installation of a proper toilet."

"Bulkheads it is," Laura declared, blushing.

She had studied the operation of multi-engine aircraft from Ray's books and knew the theory, but nothing prepared her for the exhilarating experience of flying the Bombay. The huge aircraft was very responsive, and after the sixth hour, she felt as if she had flown the aircraft for years.

The instructor was surprised at her aptitude at handling the twin-engine plane.

"You are a born pilot," said Ted, when he took Laura out for certain exercises necessary for her certification. After the eighth hour,

Ted had Laura land the Bombay on a shortened field. Following the successful exercise, he unbuckled his safety belt, got out of his seat and turned to Laura: "Take her out over the sea, do a few stalls and tell me how she recovers," and left her in the cockpit alone.

Laura slowly got up, took the left hand seat, tightened the belt, and began the pre-flight checks. She ran up both engines, found everything in order, and started for the end of the runway to turn the plane into the wind. Suddenly, she had the same feeling she experienced in Mogadishu the first time she took off alone. The bra was choking her. Stopping at the end of the runway, before releasing the brakes, she removed the useless garment.

Flying the Bombay turned out a sensual experience. Actually, the contact with the plane became a strange feeling...something Laura had never felt. Flying aroused her sexually. Although leaving the ground was similar to a climax, she did not allow her emotions to influence her flying. From that moment on, she felt as though she were an integral part of the plane, or that the aircraft had become an extension of her body. The exercises were easy and a lot of fun. She loved being one with the plane.

Following the required number of hours, Marston subjected Laura to the certification test. They went out over the sea, and Ted gave her many exercises to conduct. In the middle of the tests, he asked her how to deal with the setting sun over the sea.

"With this aircraft it is a breeze. According to Ray, one could easily become completely disoriented. It happened to me once in my little Junkers. I had to stop looking out on the window and rely on my meager instruments. With the Bombay I'd just watch the artificial horizon."

"How do you like this aircraft?"

"The Bombay and I understand each other," she replied. "According to Ray, every aircraft has a soul and a personality. This one gives me good vibes. She would not let me down, I am sure of that."

"Let's see," said Ted and cut the left engine.

Laura immediately increased power to the remaining engine and started looking for a potential emergency landing spot in case the other engine quit.

Ted suddenly cut the right engine.

"Do you see the old abandoned highway there?" Laura asked. "I will try landing there."

"Do you think it is wide enough?"

"It is if I hit it precisely," she replied confidently.

"Let us see," said Ted. "Start the engines and make a low pass over the road."

"As you wish," Laura replied and began the process, but the engines did not start.

Ted desperately tried to start the engines, but they stubbornly remained silent. Laura concentrated on keeping the Bombay on the straight line, watching the speed, heading for the old road.

"We are going to see if you're right. I cannot see another emergency landing site. We just ran out of alternatives," said Ted bitterly.

"Come on, baby," Laura said, pulling on the starter without result.

However, no more than twenty feet above the surface the left engine caught. Now they had limited power. Contrary to Ted's expectations, Laura did not feed full power to the remaining engine. She checked the road, found it just wide enough, and set the plane down.

"If I held back your certification, I would be a fool," remarked Ted. "Nine out of ten pilots would have attempted climbing and returning to the airport. Why didn't you try it?"

"First, you told me the Bombay does not climb well on one engine even if it is empty. Second, if the engines already quit once, there was no guarantee of them running reliably. Since the road was wide enough, I chose the safest alternative as far as the aircraft and the passengers were concerned. Mind you, if the road were too narrow, I would have chanced climbing and trying to find an alternate spot for a forced landing."

"Congratulations! Only a seasoned airline pilot could have gone through so many alternatives in such a short time. Would you mind staying with the plane until I get a mechanic here to see what went wrong?"

"If he fixes the plane, can I fly her back to base?"

"I don't see why not. You are fully qualified and checked out on the Bombay."

In a couple of hours, the mechanic arrived, repaired the engines, and made some adjustments. Just before sunset, Laura flew the plane back to the field of the factory.

Taking off from the shortened runway was the ultimate in sensual experience. When she landed at the factory field, put her hand on the instrument panel: "If my men would be as pleasant and understanding as you are, I would not have any problems with them," she said to the plane.

Stone arranged a small cocktail party at his house to say farewell to Laura and congratulated her on acquiring her multi-engine certification.

Dead tired, she returned to her hotel with a thick sealed envelope from Bristol Aircraft in her briefcase.

Before going to bed, Laura sent a telegram to Mr. Werth at the Dessau Junkers factory advising him about her arrival.

Thanks for the feelings you let me have while flying the Bombay. Thank you for my talent of uniting with my aircraft, and the help at the forced landing, my Lord, she prayed before falling asleep.

Eleven

In the morning, she had a reply from Werth. He promised to meet Laura at the railway station, and escort her to a good hotel.

The trip to the heart of Germany took a long time. In Dover, Laura boarded the midday ferry to Calais. From the French harbor, she took a sleeping car to Berlin. From the station, she phoned Werth to let him know her time of arrival at Dessau.

Werth, a tall, straight-backed man wearing a monocle and limping slightly met Laura at the station.

"Miss Stanton, it is a pleasure to meet you."

"The pleasure is mine," she said, shaking hands with Werth.

They took a taxi to the hotel. On the way he said, "Ray asked me in his telegram to make arrangements for your return by next Saturday."

"Do I have to go back to London to get on Imperial?"

"No. I already called them. They said you could join their flight in Cairo on Friday."

"How am I getting to Cairo?"

"With a service/courtesy ticket on Lufthansa, of course. It would be an excellent opportunity to see our 52s in action," Werth said.

"Is that the aircraft you are suggesting to sell us?"

"Yes. It is the best commercial aircraft built in Europe these days. I have a test pilot ready to show it to you first thing tomorrow morning."

"Can you check me out on the Fifty-two?"

"If you have multi-engine endorsement, it will take only a few hours. I'd gladly arrange it for you."

"I have the certification. Let's do it."

"You are all business, Miss Stanton."

"What do you mean?"

"We have an excellent cabaret in town. I would gladly escort you there."

"Thank you very much, Mr. Werth, but not tonight. I am bushed."

"Manfred von Altman, our senior test pilot, is going to pick you up at nine o'clock in the morning. Mr. Hoffer, the man in charge of sales, and I would like to meet you for tea at the Edelweiss. It is a little café but the best in town. Can I pick you up at your hotel?"

"I am sure Mr. Altman will deliver me there. I intend to keep flying until late in the afternoon to decide if I like your plane."

"You are as tough as a fighter pilot. I am going to instruct Manfred to drive you to the Edelweiss," replied Werth.

"Very well. I will see you tomorrow."

"May I ask you a favor, Miss Stanton?"

"Of course."

"I am sure you will want some technical support, mechanics, and pilots. Could you write down those conditions for us?"

"I already prepared the document for you," Laura replied and handed over the sheet listing Bristol's suggestions.

"Thank you very much. Have a good time in Dessau, Miss Stanton."

Laura rested until eight in the evening, and decided to have dinner in the hotel's restaurant. In the impressive grand hall, the *maitre'd* led her to a table just under the boxes.

She ordered a Campari with soda and enjoyed the scenery. A large band appeared and started playing very pleasant dinner music. After finishing the meal, she stayed at her table relaxing and listening to the songs. A few couples appeared on the dance floor doing the waltz.

Suddenly, a young man wearing a brown uniform with an armband bearing the swastika stepped to her table. He clicked his heels, bowed from the waist, and said something in German.

"I am sorry, I don't speak German," she replied in English.

To her surprise, the man switched to English and said, "I did not know you were British. I speak your language quite well. Would you care to dance with me?"

"Why not?" she asked. "My name is Laura."

"I am Lieutenant Helmut Klein, at your service. May I?" he said and gallantly offered his arm.

Lieutenant Klein turned out an excellent dancer.

"I think the rumors of English women being excellent dancers is true. You are as good as a professional," Klein said.

"Thanks for the compliment, sir, but I am out of practice."

"Nonsense. If you were better, I should take lessons from you."

"You are too kind, sir."

"By the way, what are you doing here in Dessau? This is a godforsaken industrial city. There is nothing to see here."

"Except the Junkers factory and their aircraft."

"Do you know anything about airplanes?"

"Yes. I am a licensed airline pilot."

"You are joking."

"I am not. If you want, I can show you my pilot's license."

"You are a beautiful, intriguing woman, Laura," he said. As the music stopped, he escorted Laura back to her table. "Thanks for the dance."

"The pleasure was mine."

At her table, she thought of Bob.

"I am sure he is also an excellent dancer," she mused. *It would be wonderful to do the waltz with him.*

Laura closed her eyes and imagined being in Bob's arms. The pink clouds started gathering, and she actually felt his body touching hers. She was aroused sexually when the music started again.

Where are you, Robert? I need you so desperately, she thought and imagined Bob holding and caressing her when a voice speaking accented English brought her back to Earth: "May I have the pleasure?"

She looked up expecting Helmut, but instead an elderly, slightly overweight man wearing the same uniform stood at the table.

"Forgive me, sir, but I am a little tired. I'll have a long day tomorrow, and believe me, I do not feel like dancing right now."

"To be honest, I did not want to dance with you. I had something entirely different in mind," the man said and sat at her table.

Laura gave him a devastating look and signaled the waiter, but he hesitated.

"I want to go to bed with you," the man announced.

"Really!"

"I am willing to pay top price."

"I beg your pardon," Laura said angrily, stood, and went to the *maitre'd's* station, while the uniformed man remained at her table grinning from ear to ear.

"That man over there propositioned me."

The headwaiter looked at the man first, then Laura. He shrugged and remarked: "So what? It happens all the time."

"Let me have my bill," she said brusquely. When the waiter handed her the slip, Laura added her room number and signed it.

"Didn't you forget something, miss?" the waiter asked.

Laura looked at the bill she just signed. Apparently, she had forgotten the tip. She looked the headwaiter in the eye and declared, "So what? It happens all the time," and marched out of the restaurant.

In the safety of her room, she sat down. She thought of the elderly, brown-uniformed man, and his crude manners.

Even a prostitute deserves a more civilized approach, she thought kicking off her shoes, when someone knocked on her door.

"Who is it?"

"Housekeeping," came the reply.

Opening the door, Laura was surprised finding herself face to face with the elderly brown-uniformed man. He stood there grinning.

"I am sure you'll see things my way," he said, starting to push inside, but Laura stood her ground. Quickly drawing Granny's dagger and pressing the point to the throat of the unsuspecting man, she hissed, "Get out of here before I cut your throat."

Suddenly, fear flared up in the man's eyes and he retreated out of the room. When he reached the corridor, he stopped and gave Laura a dirty look.

"You bitch, you'll be sorry," he grunted, turned on his heel, and walked away.

Thanks, Granny, Laura thought after slamming the door and putting the weapon back into its sheath.

She threw herself on the bed and contemplated calling the house detective, but changed her mind.

This fellow might be someone high in the army or the police organization, and my report of his behavior would be swept under the table anyway, she thought.

Wedging the door with one of the chairs, Laura sent her daily report to the Almighty. "*Granny was right, my Lord. Women are often the targets of men or robbers, thus we should always carry some kind of a weapon to balance the scales. Thanks for looking after me today. Please help me when I discuss the business with those people tomorrow. Good night, my Lord.*"

~ * ~

Laura dressed carefully for the morning's test flight. She did not wear her bra, which might have given her the feeling she had flying the Bombay. In fact, she wore one of Mrs. Madison's flight suits, with the white socks and the tennis shoes. Precisely at nine o'clock, Manfred von Altman, a younger version of Werth, arrived in a little sports car. Discounting his Prussian manners, he was as attractive as Bob.

In the cockpit of the Junkers 52, Manfred proved himself a thorough professional. He explained the characteristics of the aircraft. After the takeoff, he put the plane through the same exercises as she already had with the Bristol Bombay.

When Laura took over, at first she concluded that the 52 was a stable, well-made aircraft, handling very much like its smaller cousin, the F13. Despite sitting in the right-hand seat, Laura began having the same sensual experience she had in the Bristol Bombay. The huge, ungainly tri-motor aircraft became an extension of her slender, elegant body. It was like intercourse, with the climax. The strange sensation did not take long, but apparently, Manfred noticed her reaction to the plane.

"Do you always become one with your aircraft, Laura?"

"Yes, I do," she replied. "That is the only way to dominate these monsters completely."

"Strange," said Manfred, "to me every aircraft is a female, a person I must make my own. With some of them it works immediately, while with others I never get the love connection."

"This proves my theory of every plane having a soul and individual disposition. There are no two of them exactly alike. We have the small F13-s. One of them actually dislikes me and wants to kill me. She tried it twice, but I turned out the stronger of the two of us," Laura explained.

"How do you feel about this particular 52?"

"He is something like you... strong, and would not let me down under any circumstances."

"I thought you and the Fifty-two are very much alike. Both of you are beautiful, determined, and have a mind of your own," said the pilot.

He wants me and I want him, but under the circumstances, it is not feasible. I wonder how I am going to feel after landing, Laura thought.

She gave Manfred a long look. Their eyes locked, and as the man touched the controls, he became one with the plane and Laura. She felt the same way as she had when she first touched the wheel of the *York* with Ray at the controls.

They read each other's mind, just as if they were flight instruments.

They did not talk for a while, but after landing in Berlin and having lunch at the brand new Tempelhof Airport, Manfred gave up the left-hand seat to Laura.

"It seems you have a better rapport with this particular aircraft than I do," he said, helping Laura into her seat. As their shoulders touched, she felt the electric shock of desire running through her body.

They flew a few more hours carrying out some more tests with the Junkers 52. The plane performed admirably well. The differences between the 52 and the Bombay were insignificant, although the Junkers flew happily with only two engines and could even take off. This meant added safety in comparison with the Bombay. In the end, Laura thought she would be happy flying either of the two.

Returning to Dessau, they landed on the factory field, and Manfred taxied the plane to the end of the runway onto the grass, parking it.

"We have arrived," he announced and started getting out of the plane, accidentally again touching Laura's shoulder. They both froze and stared at each other.

Laura undid her safety belt and slowly rose from the seat. As Manfred did not move, their bodies touched and that was enough. Manfred took her into his arms and kissed her passionately.

"That was something," he remarked. "There is no aircraft as exciting as you are."

"I won't complain either," she said and pressed her body against Manfred.

"Sadly, we cannot do anything here," he said.

"Have you any spirit of adventure?" Laura asked with a coquettish smile, and pulled the zipper of her flight suit, looking at the comfortable passenger cabin.

Manfred drew her closer and put his hand on Laura's breast. The zipper of the flight suit went all the way down, and they lay down on the carpeted floor of the cabin, Laura pressing her body against Manfred.

"The angle of the fuselage is just perfect," she remarked, while Manfred buried himself in Laura.

In half an hour, they stood. Laura got into her flight suit, pulling the zipper up to her chin and smiled at Manfred saying, "I hope you have no wife."

"You just seduced her up there," he replied. "The way you treated this aircraft actually made me jealous. You see I consider myself married to the Junkers Fifty-twos. I love them all."

Before they headed for the Edelweiss, Manfred signed the necessary papers qualifying Laura to fly the Junkers 52.

"It normally takes much longer to check someone out on this plane, but your performance should satisfy anybody."

"In more ways than one," Laura said smiling.

"Yes," he said seriously. "I would gladly have you as a test pilot."

"Would you really?"

"Yes."

"Wouldn't the fact of my being a woman bother you?"

"No, not at all," he said, kissing Laura's hand and helping her into the car.

They drove to the Edelweiss, a pleasant little café with comfortable boxes. Werth and his colleague, Mr. Hoffer were already sitting in one of them, having a beer.

"Come on in, Manfred. Join us," Werth said after seating Laura and introducing her to Hoffer.

"I am working on your proposal, Miss Stanton," Hoffer said. "We could send you a pilot with each of the planes, but in addition we would like to have your staff here for a short while to train on the Fifty-two. Would this be possible?"

Laura was prepared for the question. She smiled at Hoffer and replied, "Our current operation is very small, sir. Consequently, we have rapid turnover in pilots. I am now advertising in Britain for properly trained pilots. It is not going to be easy. I would appreciate any help you could give me in recruitment."

The three men looked at each other, and almost simultaneously, they said: "Hannah!"

Werth recovered first and turned to Laura: "Could you use a pilot right now?"

"Yes, of course. Why?"

"Would Ray mind another lady pilot?"

"Of course not. As long as she is qualified and can follow the rules, he wouldn't object."

"We have a lady, an excellent pilot, fully qualified, and checked out on the Fifty-two. She is pestering us for a job. If you hired her, we would be most grateful."

"If she is so good, why don't you take her?" Laura asked.

"Politics, Miss Stanton, politics," Hoffer remarked.

"What do you mean?"

"Well, it is a long story, but I'll give it to you in a nutshell. Hannah Bartosch's father was killed during the war flying in the squadron of Mr. Goering, the right-hand man of Hitler, our new chancellor. Goering is his advisor on matters of aeronautics. He is pushing for Hannah to become a test pilot with us. So far we managed to resist," Hoffer stated.

Laura looked at von Altman and slowly remarked, "I don't think you should discriminate against women."

"It is not that, Laura," Manfred interrupted. "There is absolutely nothing wrong with her flying or qualifications. Test pilots are a close-knit group. We would be nervous having someone among us with close ties to the National Socialist Party."

"What has one's politics got to do with her job?" Laura asked in a hostile tone.

"Apparently, you are not aware of the realities in the new Germany. Mr. Hitler has a few brown-uniformed goons ruthlessly eliminating his perceived enemies. Most of our test pilots are Prussians, apolitical with strong military traditions. We wouldn't like someone in our team who might be too committed to the new regime. Such a person might think we are the enemies of Mr. Hitler and his party," explained von Altman.

"I see. If Miss Bartosch is willing to come to Somalia, I'd take her gladly, irrespective of her politics."

"Manfred, please introduce Hannah to Miss Stanton as soon as possible."

"How about dinner tonight?" Laura asked. "You could join me at the hotel's restaurant. The food is excellent, and the music is good. However the company may leave a lot to be desired."

"What do you mean?"

"I had a rather unpleasant encounter with one of those brown-shirted fellows last night."

"With Hannah and Manfred around, you should not worry. They only approach lone women," Werth remarked.

"Very well, Manfred. Could you pick up Hannah and bring her to the hotel? I'd like to talk to her in private, and later all three of us should have dinner together," said Laura.

"I will get your proposal ready by tomorrow, and on Wednesday, you can take Lufthansa for Rome."

"You had me flying to Cairo with Lufthansa," Laura said.

"That was the original idea, but I realized you would have very little time for the transfer. It is better this way. You'll have to spend almost a full day in Rome and take Imperial on Friday to Athens, Cairo and Aden," Hoffer said.

"I much appreciate your looking after my travel arrangements," Laura said.

"I believe we do not have much else to discuss," said Werth.

"You're right, sir," Laura agreed. "Perhaps I could impose on Manfred to drive me to my hotel."

"It will be a pleasure," said von Altman.

Manfred escorted Laura to the reception and gave her a questioning look.

"You should come with me, Manfred, and see that I don't have an unpleasant visitor hiding in my quarters," she said.

As they entered the sumptuous hotel room, Manfred touched Laura's arm, initiating the much-desired contact. Although there was no electric shock as on the plane, she responded like a thoroughbred to the spur.

"We have some unfinished business," she said with a smile and put her arms around Manfred.

He kissed her passionately and began fumbling with the buttons of her blouse.

"I am much better with them," said Laura and started shedding her clothes.

Manfred left an hour later, and the happy, satisfied Laura took a long bath. She dressed and took her crib sheet to prepare for the encounter with a fellow woman pilot, but finding nothing in the notes to cover the situation, she grunted, "Hell, I have to play it by ear."

Hannah arrived to the hotel at seven o'clock sharp. Manfred introduced the two pilots to each other. Hannah was not a bad looking woman, had an excellent figure, was not too tall, blonde, with a scarred, hard chiseled face, a little bit like a man's, but she had deep blue eyes like most Germans. Her English was okay, although she had the typical Teutonic accent.

"I think we'd better go to my room," suggested Laura.

"By all means," Hannah replied.

As they entered the room and sat down, Hannah produced her pilot's license and logbook. Since Laura did not know what to ask, she looked at the logbook. There were plenty of hours on the Junkers F13 and its improved, upgraded versions.

"I see you flew the F13 quite a bit," Laura started.

"Yes, I like it. I did not fly the older models, but I am sure they cannot be much different."

"We have three ancient F13s with brand new engines, but the boss is contemplating buying three multi-engine planes."

"Manfred told me that you might buy the Fifty-two."

"I don't know. It is up to Ray. He could decide on the Bristol Bombay."

"I don't know the type, but if you touch them the right way, they'll perform for you. Every aircraft has a soul."

Laura suddenly took a liking to Hannah.

"Would you mind living in Mogadishu for a while, Hannah?"

"As long as I could fly at least ten hours a week, I could make peace with the darkest African jungle. Why, I'd even live in a tree house."

"I am glad, because you are not too far off the tree house in Somalia."

"It doesn't bother me."

"Well, Hannah, Air Mogadishu works like this: As long as it is going to be the two of us flying the mail routes, we fly minimum eight, maximum twenty-four hours a week."

"That's very good. How about housing?"

"Temporarily we'd put you into the Lido Hotel and try to work out something later. Normally, the pilots get five pounds a week in addition to full room and board."

"As long as I have my own shower, I'll be happy," Hannah said.

"I can guarantee that," said Laura, since Ray had briefed her about the layout of the rooms in the Lido.

"How about a contract?"

"Ray will send you one, just like this," Laura said and from her briefcase, she extracted a blank form.

Hannah read it carefully and in the end remarked, "It is all right, but I would like to include the minimum of eight hours of flying per week guaranteed."

"I am sure we could arrange it. How soon can you travel?"

"I do not need more than a week after I get the contract. I can have a service/courtesy ticket to Cairo on Lufthansa, but from there on, I must pay full fare on Imperial to Aden."

"I am sure we can get you the same service/courtesy ticket on Imperial from Cairo to Aden. I'll pick you up personally, and you could even fly the F13 on the way back to Mogadishu."

"We agree," said Hannah.

"Well, I am going to send a telegram to Ray this evening, reporting what we have discussed. I will ask him to get in touch with you through telegram and confirm the acceptance of the conditions."

"Wonderful," Hannah replied. "This will be my first paying job as a pilot."

After dinner Laura returned to her room, wrote the message to Ray, called a bellboy and had it sent. Later she again wedged the door with a chair and went to bed early.

Thank you for the wonderful day, my Lord. Thank you for Manfred, Hannah, and the Junkers Fifty-two. I love them all. Do you think I betrayed Robert and Ray by going to bed with Manfred? I do not think so. This is the way I am. The way you created me, my Lord. If I was wrong, please, tell me.

Without her conscience bothering her, Laura fell asleep.

~ * ~

Laura left Dessau with the Junkers' proposal in her briefcase. On Wednesday at sunrise, Hannah flew her to Berlin using a borrowed F13 to catch the morning Lufthansa flight to Zurich and Rome.

Shortly after takeoff, the captain invited her to the flight deck.

"I am Captain Koenig, Miss Stanton. A friend of mine, Manfred von Altman, suggested I invite you here. I understand you recently checked out on the Junkers Fifty-two."

"I did," Laura replied.

"Manfred felt you should try flying a fully loaded Fifty-two. I am sure you will find it somewhat different from the earlier test flights. If you wish, you may take the copilot's seat. I am sure Hans wouldn't mind giving it up for you."

"Thank you very much, Captain," said Laura and took the right seat.

Koenig permitted her to fly the plane between Berlin and Munich for more than an hour. The fully loaded aircraft handled well, and Laura enjoyed flying it. Although she had a brief sensual experience, she managed to control her emotions.

Laura spent a lazy day in Rome, did not go out to see the city because she began feeling tired. It was not the physical, but the mental strain getting to her. She became rather impatient, wanting to see Bob and rest in his strong arms for a while. She needed him, needed his touch, his soothing voice, and his exciting lips on hers. She completely forgot Manfred.

When she boarded Imperial on Friday morning, Celeste was again the stewardess on duty.

"Hi, Captain Laura," the girl greeted her cordially. "Do you mind the jump seat next to my galley?"

"Not at all, Celeste."

"How was London?"

"Exciting, but I am just a simple country girl. I wish to be back to my planes and my home. It is so nice being on the way."

"By the way, Captain Thornton is in charge of the plane today. He is going to invite you to the flight deck after we leave Cairo."

"That's all right, I am going to sleep until then," Laura said.

As promised, after leaving Cairo, Laura visited the flight deck. By then, she almost understood all the instruments. The captain invited her into the copilot's seat and asked, "I understand you fly for an old friend of mine, Ray Madison."

"Yes, I do."

"His airline is using single engine machines. How do you like this one? It is rather complex, isn't it?"

"I like large planes," Laura replied. "I have my multi-engine endorsement, and I checked out on the Junkers Fifty-two as well as the Bristol Bombay. Your plane is gorgeous. I envy you the chance to fly it."

"Perhaps you'll be flying one of these monsters one day," said Thornton and let Laura do the flying for almost an hour.

When they had Aden on the horizon, the copilot returned to his seat, and Laura took her jump seat by the galley.

Twelve

When the giant Handley Page airliner touched down on Aden's paved runway, Laura felt she had arrived home. As it was only three o'clock in the afternoon, she did not expect Ray to be there, but after the bus discharged the passengers at the terminal building, she saw him standing in the crowd waving. However, for one reason or another, Bob had not come to the airport.

Ray's presence surprised Laura. For a moment she did not know what would happen if Bob showed up at the terminal.

I'll cross that bridge when I come to it, she thought.

"Hi, Laura," he said as soon as she passed the passport control. "I missed you. How was London?"

She hugged Ray and said, "London was fantastic. I got my name back, my proper commercial license, and got the multi-engine endorsement too. The trip to Dessau was also interesting."

"I just cabled my acceptance of Miss Bartosch's contract to Werth. I hope she's going to come soon, because I had to return the last of the sergeants today," Ray said.

"I am back now. There is nothing to worry about."

"Have you ever seen me worried?"

"Not really."

"I got rooms for us in the Excelsior. There are all kinds of military brass here and the BOQ guest room is occupied. Tonight, they will have a gala dinner at the Officers' Mess."

"Have you seen Robert?"

"Yes. I told him about your arrival and staying in the hotel. He should be around presently to take you to the gala dinner. I am going with the Imperial crew," he said nonchalantly.

"By the way, how did you get here so early?"

"We took off while it was dark. I had the boys build a fire at the end of the runway. I aimed at it, and here we are."

"How did the postmasters react to your early arrival?"

"They were pleasantly surprised, because then they could return to doing nothing much earlier."

They took a taxi to the hotel. Shortly, Laura occupied her comfortable room, while Ray went to see the local manager of Imperial Airways.

She had barely dropped her suitcase when someone discreetly knocked on the door. Opening it, she found herself facing Bob.

"Oh, Robert, I missed you so much," Laura said, took Bob by the hand and led him inside.

He took her in his arm, and their lips touched. Finally, they disengaged, but Bob did not let go of Laura's hands.

"Do you remember me telling you about having to make some serious decisions?"

"Yes, I do. It was before I left for England."

"I made my decision. Will you marry me?"

The question was completely unexpected, and for a moment, Laura lost her voice. She just stared at Bob.

"You heard me right, darling. I want to marry you."

"Are you sure, Robert? We don't know each other very well."

"I know enough," he interrupted. "Besides, marriage is a matter of luck, and I am willing to bet on you."

"Be serious, Robert. As far as I am concerned, marriage is for keeps, until death do us part. I do not believe in divorce."

"Are you getting cold feet, darling? You know we make excellent music on the playground. You come from a good family, and know how to behave in any social setting. You graduated from Wyndham like my mother. They trained you how to be the wife of a high-ranking officer. I love you, and I believe we will be very happy together," Bob explained.

"I thought we should spend some more time together before taking the plunge."

"Come on, darling, the Air Marshall is visiting Aden. He can give me permission to marry you, and the chaplain is ready. In addition, I was just promoted to Wing Commander and transferred to the Air Ministry with immediate effect. We should be able to take Imperial next week."

"Slow down, darling," said Laura.

"No," he interrupted.

Laura panicked. Sure, she wanted to marry Bob, but she could not see their future working out after the whirlwind wedding. She had too many loose ends.

"I couldn't go to London next week with you, Robert. I have certain obligations to Ray."

"Don't worry about him," interrupted Bob. "He's a big boy and can look after himself. Ray doesn't need anybody."

"I am afraid you're wrong. He is not supposed to fly solo."

"That is a load of crap."

"I know it is a fact. He has a medical condition."

"In other words his well-being is more important to you than our life together."

"You are being selfish, Robert. Let us understand each other once and for all. I have an obligation to Ray. He saved me from a fate worse than death, taught me to fly and gave me a profession, a purpose in life."

"I am afraid you won't be able to fly too much after we get married."

It was Laura's turn to interrupt. "Why not? Because I am a woman? I am just as good a pilot as any man having the same qualifications and experience."

"It is the man's job to support his wife and family. Granted, I am not rich, but as an R.A.F. Wing Commander, I can support you in style."

"It is not the matter of who can support whom," Laura said firmly. "You are asking me to give up my profession for you. What would you say if I suggested you resign your commission and come to fly for Air Mogadishu?"

"I am afraid I couldn't do that. I worked very long and hard to get where I am now. If I resigned my commission, my family would disown me."

Laura thought her heart would break, but she raised her head and in a firm voice she said, "Although I love you, Robert, very much, I believe it is premature for us to get married. We do not know each other well enough to make a lifetime commitment. However, if that were the only problem, I wouldn't mind taking a chance on you. Unfortunately, you want to turn me into a housewife and stop my professional career. This is a major difference in the vision of our life together. As we did not have the time to discuss it and work out a compromise, I am afraid I cannot marry you on such a short notice."

Bob looked at her with his eyes wide open. He did not say anything, stood, and went to the door. He turned around and said, "Now or never, darling. I am thirty-five years old. If I want to see my children through their higher education, I should get married now. I have been putting it off until I met you. Is that your last word?"

Laura steeled herself and declared, "As I said, unless we took some time and ironed out our differences, I am afraid it is."

"Have a nice life, Captain Laura," said Bob and stormed out of the room, slamming the door.

Laura threw herself on the bed and started crying. She knew she loved Bob more than anything else, needed his touch, and wanted to bear his children, but there were too many unresolved conflicts between them.

She calmed down a little, washed her face, and started to rationalize.

I would marry Bob if we had a little more time together, and I could find out more about him, his likes and dislikes. I know he is an excellent lover and an over-all nice guy, but I do not know his everyday routine behavior. We have had good sex, but we did not reach the level of understanding to develop intellectual ties. It was rather selfish of him to want me to give up my job and profession spontaneously. I would be a housewife with an airline pilot's qualifications. The Wyndham Academy prepared me to be a wife and a mother, but I want more out of life. Is it wrong for a woman to expect a career?

"Help me my Lord," she prayed. *"What should I do? I do not wish to hurt Robert, and at the same time, I want to fulfill my obligations to Ray. What do you want me to do? What is my purpose in your grand design?"*

Although he did not answer, the mere thought of connecting with her God placated Laura.

"He knows what is best for me."

She took a shower and dressed for dinner.

As Bob did not take her to the gala, she went downstairs and had a late dinner in the hotel's restaurant.

~ * ~

In the morning, she put on her faithful flight suit and waited for Ray in the lobby. By six thirty he appeared.

"Morning, Laura," he said. "Where were you last night? I figured you'd attend with Bob."

"I felt too tired," she lied.

Ray gave her a strange look. Laura knew immediately she did not fool the wise old pelican. However, Ray did not pry. He switched the subject.

"We have three passengers to Mogadishu, Captain. Imperial took them to the airport together with their passengers. I have a taxi standing by for us."

"Let's go home," said Laura quietly and stood, grabbing her suitcase.

The routine flight to Mogadishu made her feel at home, but like her passengers, she was tired when they landed.

Surprisingly, Panetta was not at the field. Two of his assistants unloaded the mailbags.

Following their arrival at the house, they sat on the patio the same way as they used to a few weeks earlier. Ray sipped his whisky, and Laura drank her Campari.

"Which aircraft did you like better: the Junkers or the Bristol?" Ray asked.

"I cannot really tell you. I did a forced landing in the Bristol Bombay. It is a safe aircraft, glides well, and has strong undercarriage. The Junkers, on the other hand, feels very much like the F13 with three engines. It doesn't matter which one you decide. Take the better offer."

"They are too damn close. The costs are a little higher than I expected, but well within my means."

"May I ask you a favor, Ray?"

"Sure."

"I would like to invest in Air Mogadishu. Mind you, I do not have too much money, but since I might have something to do with the success or failure of the enterprise, I would like to own a small piece of the company," Laura explained.

"You are already a shareholder," Ray replied. "I had five percent of the voting shares transferred to your name. I did it while you were in London, just to express my gratitude. All it needs is your signature. Without you there would be no Air Mogadishu."

"Come on."

"By the way, General Ponti bought another five percent."

"Could I increase my share if I gave you some cash?"

"Not a chance, my dear," Ray said firmly. "At least not now. The expansion of the airline is risky. If I failed, I would not want you or the general losing too much money. However, if the operation works out, I am going to give both of you an option to buy another five percent for two thousand pounds, which is the current value of five percent of the Air Mogadishu shares."

"Thank you."

"Now tell me, how did it go in London?"

They forgot to change for dinner, talked about England and the proposals of the two aircraft manufacturers until midnight.

"It is late," said Ray. "We'll talk about everything tomorrow. Good night, Laura."

He gently kissed her on the cheek, but she could not restrain herself. Her hungry lips searched out his. They held each other tight. In the end, Ray broke the silence.

"I thought I was going to lose you."

"You cannot get rid of me so easily," she replied and opened her blouse, offering her breasts. At this point, Laura completely forgot Bob.

"Not here, darling. Let's go inside," he said.

"Okay, but promise me we will do it out here one of these days."

"Why?"

"I don't know. It feels adventurous and exciting," Laura said and started toward the bedroom door. As soon as they were inside, she looked up at Ray and remarked, "I think I can make our time adventurous here too," and started shedding her clothes.

At three in the morning, Laura got to her own bed. She did not have the strength to take a bath, just flopped on her bed naked, looked up at the ceiling, and turned to God.

"I thank you for bringing me home, my Lord, and thank you for Ray. Your taking of Robert from me hurts, and I'll suffer every time I land in Aden. However, you decided to give him to someone else. Nevertheless, would you reconsider the matter?"

The conversation with the Almighty calmed her down and put her into a deep restful sleep.

~ * ~

The next two weeks were harrowing. The number of passengers kept increasing. On a particular occasion, Laura had to fly an extra section to Aden in the middle of the week on her days of rest. It was particularly difficult because she had to take a full load both ways, therefore Ray could not come along as a copilot, giving her a little rest during the long flight.

A cable arrived from Hannah, stating her date of arrival. It was cause for celebration, even though Laura had a hard day coming up. She had five passengers to Aden, but on the way back, she had only two.

Hannah arrived to the airport in Aden wearing her silver wings on a pink silk flight suit decorated with the Junkers emblem and the distinctive four stripes of a captain. She looked impressive.

On the way to Mogadishu, Laura abandoned the captain's seat on the left and let Hannah do most of the flying.

"I like these little planes," Hannah remarked. "They fly like the Fifty-two."

"I think so too," Laura replied, taking control at Mogadishu just before the landing.

Ray waited at the airport to welcome Hannah on behalf of the company. In spite of her flashy outfit, he immediately took a liking to her.

Panetta stood in the shadow of the mail truck, and while Ray was busy with the new pilot, he stepped up to Laura.

"Are you coming with me tonight?" the weasel-faced man asked.

"Why?" Laura asked innocently.

"I could expose you, Miss Madison."

"Go right ahead. By the way, I am Laura Stanton, not Miss Madison. I have my passport and my pilot's license to prove my identity."

"I am sure they are forgeries," he said.

"Prove it," Laura snapped. "However, if you cannot, I am going to sue you for everything you own."

"We'll see, Miss Madison."

At this point, Ray came to them, introducing Hannah: "Mr. Panetta, this is Captain Bartosch, the third pilot of Air Mogadishu. She just arrived from Germany."

"*Enchante*, Captain," said Panetta, and in the proper European way kissed Hannah's hand.

"How nice to find cultured people in the heart of Africa," she said. "I hope to see you often, Mr. Panetta."

They got into Air Mogadishu's recently acquired automobile and drove to the Hotel Lido.

"After you are settled in, I'll come over with the Norton and take you to our home for a drink," Laura said.

Just before dark, Laura picked up Hannah and took her to Ray's house. They had a few drinks and a long discussion about the flight schedules and the proposals of the aircraft manufacturers.

Laura drove Hannah home by ten o'clock.

After returning, she found the house quiet. Apparently, Ray had gone to bed, and only a single yellow bulb shone over the patio. Amina came up from the direction of the kitchen.

"Do you want a drink, Missy?" she asked.

"I might as well have a Campari," replied Laura and took her usual place on the couch.

She looked up on the cloudless African sky with its crooked moon and let out a big sigh.

Why did you take Robert from me, my Lord? Was I wrong going to bed with Manfred? Did I sin carrying on with Ray and Robert at the same time? If I sinned, my human nature, love, and my desires made me do it. Can anyone blame me for giving in to my God-given instincts?

Amina came back with her drink and lumbered back toward her room. Laura sat at the patio arguing with God about human nature, instincts, and desires.

~ * ~

Life at Air Mogadishu became a little easier. Ray took Hannah on a familiarization tour of all mail routes, with Laura occasionally tagging along. In the following week, Hannah flew the inland route alone. On the first Friday, she took the northern route and delivered three passengers to Aden. From there on, they split the flying duties, Laura taking the southern route weekly and the trip to Aden every second week.

The first time Laura entered Aden's Hotel Excelsior, her heart stopped for a moment because she noticed an R.A.F. officer with a heavily veiled woman. First, she thought it was Bob, but it turned out to be someone else.

After returning to Mogadishu, she found Hannah at Ray's house sipping a whisky with him. When Laura arrived, Amina brought her the Campari without asking.

"How was the trip?" Ray inquired.

"Routine, nothing exciting happened. Ahmed told me he had plenty of fuel because the boat came last week."

"Well, I've decided to go to Europe in a couple of weeks," Ray said.

"Are you going to finalize the deal with one of the factories?" Hannah asked.

"I think so. We have too many inquiries from Mombasa and Nairobi. Many passengers want to connect to Lufthansa, Imperial, KLM, and Air France in Cairo. It seems we could fill an aircraft every week," Ray explained.

"Things are looking up," Laura added. "Why do you have to wait two weeks?"

"Because I can't leave Hannah here alone. She can fly, but she doesn't yet know the mechanics, the fuel suppliers, and the postmasters," Ray replied.

"What is going to happen to me?" Laura asked suspiciously.

"General Ponti chartered one of our planes for next week. He is going to Nairobi for a parade of the King's African Rifles. He wants to fly with his wife and two of his officers, and insists on you being the captain," Ray explained.

"I've never been to Nairobi," Laura mused.

"Obviously, they will invite you for a number of social gatherings. You should represent Air Mogadishu properly," said Hannah. "Why don't you have a sky blue flight suit made to measure like mine? That would create the impression of a respectable airline captain."

Laura looked at Ray, but he just sat there like the Sphinx.

e talked about it with Ray," Hannah continued. "I designed a new Air Mogadishu emblem, and Amina found a fellow to embroider it for us. It looks really impressive."

"Am I supposed to wear it?"

"You should," Ray agreed. "As you are a beautiful woman, every man turning his head to look at you would see our airline's crest. You would be a walking advertising poster."

"Thanks," Laura said with a wry little smile.

"I am not half as good looking as you are," Hannah said, "Therefore, I would need to wear two of them. I'll even have one stitched on my swimsuit."

As Hannah had a superb, sporty figure, Laura smiled and remarked, "You are the company's bathing beauty, your figure is much better than mine."

"Yeah," Hannah replied. "I can conquer any man with my figure as long as I keep my face turned in the other direction."

~ * ~

Laura picked up the two Italian officers on Monday after lunch and flew them to Kismayo. The Pontis were happy to see her and insisted on Laura staying in their house for the night.

The following morning, they took off for Mombasa. Laura enjoyed the trip because the general and his wife were entertaining her while they kept alternating in the copilot's seat.

"What is this gathering all about?" Laura asked the general.

"It is the parade of the King's African Rifles, an anniversary of their establishment. Actually, it is an even birthday of the Regiment."

"How come they invited you?"

"I am their tame Italian. Actually, I was liaison officer of the British troops in the war at the Battle of the Isonzo. In fact, I was wounded, and in the end, the Brits hung some gongs on me. The new commander of the K.A.R. stood next to me when one of the Hungarian infantrymen bayoneted me. He saved my life and we became friends. They occasionally come to Kismayo when their Navy gives them a ride."

"I see. Is this parade going to be a big do?"

"Most certainly. The governors of all the neighboring colonies will be there. I am sure a few high ranking South African officers will also attend."

As Edward Blake's appearing at the parade seemed a distinct possibility, Laura tensed and tapped Ellen Madison's revolver in the pocket of her flight suit.

I may have a chance to shoot the bastard's balls off, she thought.

"Are any of the guests coming by plane?" she asked.

"I am sure some of them will. In fact, they reserved a room for you in a small hotel called the Equator Inn with the other aircrew."

"It should be interesting," Laura mused.

"If I were you, I would pass on the actual trooping of the colors at Fort Kahaua, but I would not miss the dinner in the Avenue Hotel. We stayed there a couple of times and found the restaurant outstanding."

"I'll think about it," said Laura slowly as she switched to the reserve tank.

Mombasa was coming up, and they landed on the dusty runway. The local garrison sent an honor guard to receive General Ponti. Their spectacular performance impressed the visitors. As it was very late, they did not fly on to Nairobi, even though it would have taken only a couple of hours.

The garrison commander gave them a gala dinner in the club. The ambience and the chicken curry awakened pleasant memories in Laura. It used to be Sunday's standard fare at the Chittagong Club, as the Stanton family usually ate lunch there after church.

When Laura went to bed, the tension kept her up. The chance of meeting Edward Blake made her blood boil. When she thought of Bob, the stress increased and forced tears into her eyes.

"Thank you, Lord, for delivering Edward to me. I don't know what I am going to do to him, but I believe I have the right to some form of revenge."

The idea of settling the score with Edward did not let her sleep. Out of sheer desperation, her mind strayed to Bob, and she turned to God again.

I need him, my Lord. Why did you take Robert from me? I am beginning to realize I did not deserve him. However, could you give me another chance?

Although Laura did not receive a reply, she calmed down and fell asleep.

~ * ~

The flight to Nairobi was a relatively simple affair. Laura just followed the railway from Mombasa, and two hours later, she landed at Nairobi Airport. Again, an honor guard received the general. The discipline and the marching of the soldiers were just as impressive as in Mombasa.

"We are the first of the visiting dignitaries," Ponti said when they got into the car for the drive to their hotel. "As you will be alone all day tomorrow, my friends made arrangements for a white hunter to take you to one of the parks to see some game. We went once, and you just cannot imagine the spectacle."

"Thank you, General, I appreciate it," said Laura.

The Equator Inn, a pleasant little hotel with lush vegetation and breezy rooms, appealed to Laura. After the heat of Mogadishu, the cool night and the ambience made her feel like she was in Europe. Regardless, the idea of meeting Edward weighed heavily on her mind.

In the morning, a handsome young man wearing a sleeveless safari suit came to take her to the Nairobi game park.

"I am Geoff Gordon," the fellow introduced himself. "Just call me Geoff."

"I am Laura," she said.

"We are going to take the new Morris Commercial, a four-wheel drive vehicle especially designed for Africa," Geoff said, taking her to a sturdy, impressive looking vehicle, something Laura had never seen.

"It looks interesting," she remarked.

Geoff helped Laura into the vehicle, and they took off.

The white-clad, Pitt-helmeted policemen directed the sparse traffic expertly with their batons. The vehicles moved at a sedate speed. The odd Masai appeared on the sidewalk wearing the colorful garb of his tribe carrying a spear, which was strictly illegal, but nobody dared to remind the Masai of the law. Geoff, like a cat among the pigeons, waded into these serene surroundings at breakneck speed, startling every traffic cop in sight.

The drivers forced off the road shot disapproving glances at the Morris. They narrowly missed two trucks and a Fiat Topolino with two nuns in it. The sister at the wheel stuck her arm out, and gave Geoff the unmistakable, international sign of her disapproval. Judging from the vehemence of her signals, she was obviously Italian.

Geoff smiled and challenged a beat-up old Ford for a few inches of road space. He won, but the driver turned out to be more vocal then the nuns; shouting aloud the sister's thoughts.

The young man's driving made Laura apprehensive about her safety, but did not say anything. When they left the city, on the country roads, Geoff slowed down considerably.

"For a while we are going to stay on the smooth asphalt road. There is not much game here, only the herds of the scrawny cattle stirring up the peace of the landscape," said Geoff.

"How far is the park?" Laura asked.

"About five boring miles. Until then, there is hardly anything to see. The vegetation consists of sparse grass, flame trees, thorn bush, and the odd baobab tree. Once you've seen this, you will know what the East-African Plateau looks like all the way to Lake Nyassa."

Looking at the scenery, Laura found it unusual in comparison to the arid, semi-desert of Somalia.

"It does not change much," Geoff continued. "The vegetation varies little, but the red dust is ever present. It gets into your clothes and your hair. Your skin turns reddish even though you never leave the asphalt road. On the dirt tracks, the discoloration process is much faster, and in a matter of minutes, all passengers in a car turn into red Indians."

"Are we going to leave the asphalt?"

"Yes, madame, right now," said Geoff and he turned off the road. "Do you see the gate over there? That is the entrance to the park."

"I see."

"The drive through the park normally takes two hours, but when one is in a hurry, it takes half as much. Do you want the fast trip or the slow waltz?"

"I have nothing to do this morning. As long as you get me back to the hotel by lunch, it is all right," Laura said.

"I'll take it medium speed, and show you everything worth seeing."

"As long as you do not try to pass every car on the road."

"I thought you being a pilot wanted a fast drive through Nairobi. I am sorry."

"It is okay. I am not a barnstormer. I fly an airliner and always try to keep a reasonable distance between my passengers and other aircraft," Laura remarked.

After thirty minutes, Laura tired of viewing the arses of zebras, the giraffes galloping in slow motion, and she thought the time to return to the safety of the Equator Inn had arrived.

Suddenly, they came up to few elephants.

Geoff stopped the car and turned to Laura: "Isn't she beautiful?"

The elephant was something just off the pages of a picture book. Although Laura had seen the pachyderms in India, the size of their African cousin frightened her. She remembered reading somewhere about the African elephants being untrainable.

"They are huge," she said. "Are they dangerous?"

"Not really, but one must be careful."

Suddenly, one of the elephants started flapping her ears and made short fast runs for their car.

Geoff put the car in reverse and started slowly backing away.

"What is the problem?"

"She is trying to scare us away. Her calf must be somewhere near in the bush. I do not want to be stuck between Mommy and her baby. She could trample us into the ground."

They drove away and did not see the baby elephant. Geoff kept on roaming in the game park for another hour looking at the variety of animals. He named each of the gazelles, but by the time the next appeared, Laura had forgotten the name of the last one. In the distance, they saw a cheetah trying unsuccessfully to chase down some Grant's antelopes.

Geoff behaved respectfully and did not flirt with Laura. It was curious, but the reason for his behavior became evident when they returned to the hotel. A cute little blonde, his wife, was waiting for Geoff. He held her just as Bob had held Laura.

Some people have all the luck, she thought enviously.

Laura invited Geoff and his wife for lunch. They were a pleasant young couple; just married a month ago, and their infatuation with each other was evident.

At three o'clock, the hunter and his wife departed. As they left the lobby, three boisterous people wearing leather jackets and riding boots entered.

Judging from their accents, clothing, and manners Laura realized they were South African pilots.

The *maitre'd* introduced Laura to the flyers at dinner. By that time, the crew of the Ford Tri motor had slowed down a lot. Their long flight and the amount of whiskey they consumed before dinner had worn them out. They talked about their aircraft and all of them went to bed early.

Thirteen

The chance of meeting Edward upset Laura and the mental strain kept her up most of the night. At breakfast, she sat with the South Africans and the Rhodesian crew that had arrived late last night. Since she was the only woman in the group, the men treated her as one of their tribe.

"How did you become an airline pilot?" asked Teddy, the captain of the Rhodesians' plane.

"I had a choice between a banana boat and an F13 and picked the latter," replied Laura.

"You're lucky," said Teddy. "You picked a good one. We are stuck with a crummy Bristol Bombay."

"Why? That is a fine aircraft."

"Did you ever fly one?" interrupted Teddy.

"Sure, I checked out on the Bombay. I even force-landed one. I like it."

"If it were possible, I'd trade my Bombay for your little F13. It is a monster with two minds, both vicious."

"Obviously, you do not treat him right. The Bombay has a nice personality."

They talked about their planes a lot. Strangely, every pilot complained about his aircraft for one reason or another.

Apparently, they treat their planes as machines. *They do not realize that every aircraft has a soul*, Laura thought.

"I heard we are going to have a special table at the gala dinner," said the South African copilot.

"The big cheese don't like us," remarked Teddy. "We are the only people who can tell them they cannot go somewhere. They are all control freaks."

"Yeah," grunted the South African captain. "Imagine we picked up the Chief Administrator of Tanganyika in Dar es Salaam. Actually, the boss agreed to take him as a favor, but our freeloader passenger had the gall to ask me to fly close to Mount Kilimanjaro to show it to his daughter."

"Was she good looking?" Laura asked.

"Not too bad," the fellow replied, looked at Laura, and refrained from further comments.

It is like Edward, Laura thought. *I'd better find out about the girl masquerading as me.*

She turned to the South African: "Don't be shy. Do tell us what she was really like."

The man looked around like someone in a desperate situation with no way out.

"Well," he scratched his head. "She had the face of an angel, the body of a courtesan, and the manners of a drill-sergeant. She was a foul-mouthed little witch. I am sure if I were alone in the cockpit, she would have raped me. You'll see her at the gala, I am sure."

"I'll make a point of checking her out," Laura said. "By the way, what are you fellows wearing for dinner?"

"I'll wear my air force uniform," said Teddy. "How about you?"

"I'll wear my Sunday best flying suit," replied Laura. "I do not wish to create the impression of being one of the floozies you picked up in the lobby of your hotel."

"I bet your flying suit will be something to look at," remarked Teddy.

~ * ~

Laura spent the afternoon in her room. The book she bought could not keep her mind off Edward.

"I have no idea what I am going to do to him," she said to herself. "Should I call him a murderer? Should I declare the woman masquerading as me an impostor? Perhaps I just ought to walk up and shoot the bastard. That's the best. I'll aim for his balls or perhaps his knees."

By sunset, Laura's tension had risen to a crescendo.

In the evening, a car came to pick up the pilots. They all squeezed into the Morris, and since they were too many, Laura had to sit on Teddy's lap.

"I am glad to have a small car pick us up," the Rhodesian remarked.

Laura felt comfortable. Teddy wore pleasant cologne and he put his arms around her to make sure she would not lose her balance. She forgot Edward for a moment. Turning her head, she saw the desire in Teddy's eyes, and she gave him a seductive smile.

"You should not look at me like that," the Rhodesian whispered.

Instead of reply, Laura wiggled her arse a little and immediately felt the desire welling in Teddy. The tall, handsome air force officer aroused Laura, and she decided to carry on flirting with him.

"Now I know where I'll sit on the way back," she remarked.

"You should give the other guys a chance, Laura," the South African captain remarked.

"It is only one of me and six of you," she replied with a smile. "How am I supposed to choose?"

Before the pilots could come up with a logical way to choose, they arrived at the Avenue Hotel.

The aircrews' table was in one of the corners quite a distance from the head table. However, when they marched in, Laura's blue silk flight suit with the new Air Mogadishu badge, her golden wings, and a flaming red cravat created a stir among the guests.

They sat and waited for the introduction of the guests of honor. The list was long, but at about halfway through Laura heard: "Representing the Governor of Tanganyika and Zanzibar, His Excellency Edward

Blake O.B.E., Chief Administrator of the colony, and his daughter Miss Laura Blake."

Laura saw Edward stand and take a bow. The woman next to him curtsied, and sat. Laura tapped Ellen Madison's gun in her pocket. Contrary to protocol, she marched to the head table, straight to Edward. The surprised man suddenly lost his voice, turned pale, and grabbed the edge of the table. Laura had her left hand on the gun, but released her grip. She smiled at Edward saying, "It is a pleasure to meet you again, Mr. Blake. If you don't remember me, I am Miss Stanton, a close relative of your late wife. I came over to express my gratitude. Without you I would never have become an airline pilot. I am eternally grateful, sir."

She offered to shake hands. The man, apparently in a stupor, accepted it.

"I forgive you," Laura whispered when she let go of Edward's hand. She spun around and returned to her table.

Seeing Edward and settling the outstanding account with him did not relieve the tension in Laura, although she felt as though she had dumped a heavy load off her shoulders.

~ * ~

After the dinner, the aircrews returned to Hotel Equator. Some of them stayed at the bar to do some serious drinking. Laura sat with them sipping her Campari and trying to release the tension, but she did not succeed. She simply could not remove Edward's surprised face from her mind.

"What did you say to the governor of Tanganyika?" Teddy asked.

"We are acquaintances from way back in India. Actually, without him I would never have become an airline pilot. I just thanked him and showed off with my elegant uniform," she replied.

"How did it happen? Please tell us," Teddy asked. Under the table, he put his hand on Laura's thigh.

She did not object...in fact, the man's touch relaxed her a little. However, she was still tense following the events of the day.

"There is nothing to it. I bet you it is less interesting than your professional history," she said, and let her left hand drop under the table. Her hand found its way to the pilot's muscular thigh. He gave Laura a strange look.

I am committed now, she thought.

"Let's hear Teddy's story," the South African captain suggested.

"You can listen to his story, fellows, but I am bushed. I am going to bed," Laura said and with the fingernail of her index finger carved her room number into Teddy's thigh before standing up and saying good night to the pilots.

She threw off her flight suit and stood in the middle of the room naked when someone knocked discreetly. She wrapped a large towel around herself and opened the door. Teddy stood there with an ice bucket and a bottle of champagne.

"May I come in?"

"I'll make an exception," Laura said with a smile.

Teddy came in, put the ice bucket down, and looked at Laura saying, "I hope you like champagne."

"As long as it is French and cold," she replied.

"The drink is cold, but you are…"

"Hot, hot, hot."

Teddy stepped up to her and took her in his arms as Laura's towel dropped to the floor.

By midnight, the champagne had disappeared, and they lay in each other's arms dead tired.

"It is time for you to go," Laura said. "We both have to fly tomorrow."

Teddy slid off the bed, and looked at Laura.

"You are the most."

"I can't complain either," she said.

"I am worn out. How I am going to fly all the way to Salisbury tomorrow I do not know," Teddy said while he dressed.

Laura raised herself onto her elbow and smiled at him. "You have a copilot, don't you?"

"Yeah. Aren't you too tired to fly tomorrow?"

"I am not leaving yet, but if I had to, I wouldn't worry. I got plenty of energy from you. I'll be in the pink tomorrow."

Teddy shook his head, kissed Laura passionately, and slipped out of the room.

She stretched luxuriously, got up, took a shower, and returned to her bed.

When she was lying safely under the mosquito net, her thoughts wandered, the tension dissolved, and before falling asleep she touched base with the Almighty.

"Thank you, my Lord, for stopping me from shooting Edward. For a while, I considered killing him, but in the end, I realized you wanted me to forgive him. Thank you for giving me Teddy to relieve the stress. Please, do not penalize me for having such a good time with him. I hope he is not married."

~ * ~

The South Africans left, Teddy moved out of the Equator Inn with his crew, and did not leave a forwarding address to Laura. His lack of interest did not bother her. The Pontis stayed two more days in Nairobi, and on the first evening, they took Laura to a dinner and dance with the local dignitaries. It was nice to socialize with people of her own kind, the hard working British Colonial civil servants. The company was familiar, and the feeling of belonging uniquely pleasing. Although she had lived an active social life before boarding the *Oleandris*, she hadn't felt the pleasure being part of a group since she began her new life in Mogadishu.

These people are just like my parents, she thought during the party.

It was nostalgic talking the same language and hearing about the same problems her father and mother had in the good old days when the Stanton family lived in Chittagong.

"Man is a social animal," she concluded when the general's car dropped her at the Equator Inn.

Next morning, Laura went to the airport to make sure her plane was ready for the trip home. She noticed the Bristol Bombay and the Rhodesian crew moving around the plane. As the local mechanics serviced the *York*, she decided to take it for a test flight, but before she took off, Teddy came over.

"Hi, Laura," he said. "Sorry for disappearing, but the boss wanted to move us suddenly. Did you get my message?"

"No, I didn't."

"I'll murder the goddamned bellboy," he grunted.

Based on his reaction, Laura concluded that Teddy had not left any message. Although it turned out to be a good excuse, she saw through the man's defense. At this point, she did not mind the lack of contact.

"That's all right, Teddy, I had a very busy day. We could not have gotten together anyway. Perhaps I will visit you in Salisbury."

Teddy's face changed somewhat, and he quickly changed the subject.

"Your F13 is a compact little plane. It is hard to believe this particular bird being more than ten years old."

"It is, but this one has the third motor in it."

"Do you have Italian or British mechanics in Somalia?"

"Neither, they are Somalis. The boss trained them himself."

"I wish he could come over to Salisbury and train our guys. I have many problems with them."

"Perhaps that is why your Bombay is misbehaving."

"Could be," mused Teddy.

There was no tearful farewell, just a brief handshake.

Laura watched the Bombay take off and promptly forgot Teddy.

~ * ~

Next day, the return flight to Somalia was tiring. As Laura wanted to fly all the way to Mogadishu, she had to start early. She took off while it was still dark, enjoying the luxury of having lights by the runway. Although she stopped in Kismayo for a quick lunch with the Pontis, she made it back by the evening. The Italian officers gave her a ride to Ray's house.

When she arrived, she found Ray and Hannah on the patio having drinks and chatting about the theories of instrument flying.

"How was Nairobi?" Hannah asked.

"It is a very nice place. I liked it very much."

"After we get our new aircraft, I am going to transfer our center of operation to Nairobi, and perhaps sell Air Mogadishu with the F13s and the postal routes to some young fellows. I want you two to come with me to fly the big planes to Cairo," Ray said.

"Would you trust us with the Fifty-twos or the Bombay?" Hannah asked.

"Why not? You are as good as any man I've ever flown with. I doubt you would be very good fighter pilots, though, but that is not your vocation. You are airline pilots, a special breed, a bunch of people to whom training is never enough. You have to have the proper temperament, and I could not find better captains for my planes anywhere."

"I am glad you are satisfied with us," said Hannah.

"I am bushed," Laura declared. "I am going to bed."

~ * ~

Next week, Hannah took the Friday flight to Aden with four passengers. Laura spent the day with Ray. They went to the airfield, but by lunch, they ended up in his bedroom.

"I missed you terribly," Laura said in the first intermission.

"I was rather lonesome, too, despite Hannah hanging around. She is a strange person. She has already acquired a couple of boyfriends. One is an Italian lawyer, allegedly the richest man in the colony."

"She can pick her men right," mused Laura and suddenly thought of Manfred. She thought of the two of them in the passenger cabin of the Junkers 52. The thought aroused her, and she kissed Ray hard on the lips.

"You are insatiable, my dear," he said, pulling Laura on top of him.

"And you are a mind reader."

~ * ~

In a few days, Ray left for Europe. Together with three passengers, Hannah flew him to Aden.

The week after, all hell broke loose. Several people wanted to fly from Nairobi and Mombasa to Aden or Cairo to hook up with Imperial. Laura had to fly two extra sections to Aden. Even on the way back, the little plane was full.

Hannah had fun flying all the postal routes and entertaining her Italian boyfriends.

Laura had the mechanics put two additional seats in the *York* restoring the original passenger configuration. It was a good move since they had plenty of passengers. Laura did not fly people to Cairo, solely because she had no idea about the refueling stations and the technical services en route, but she took a couple of loads from Nairobi to Mogadishu and onward to Aden on the next day.

Three weeks later, on a bright Monday morning, a telegram came from Ray asking Laura to reserve rooms for five people in the Hotel Lido for Sunday.

"I wonder who those people are," Hannah said before taking off for Kismayo.

"I guess Ray made a deal with someone, and he is bringing in an aircraft," said Laura. "He is a fast worker and a decisive individual."

Sunday afternoon a Junkers 52 appeared and landed on the dusty runway.

Manfred von Altman, the pilot, had Ray in the copilot's seat. They had two mechanics, a radioman, and a flight engineer with them. They loaded the plane with spare parts and tools.

After dropping the newcomers, Ray went home, inviting Hannah and Laura for a drink.

"I think it is time to fill you in about the deal I made with Junkers," he started.

"I am most curious," Laura said.

"Well, it is really simple. They bought part of the company. After delivering all three planes, they'll own all of Air Mogadishu."

The two women looked at each other, but did not say anything.

"I looked after you two," Ray continued. "The Germans agreed to the introduction of the pilots' seniority numbers to the airline. Laura has the first, and Hannah has the second lowest number. At the large airlines, the captains with the lowest seniority numbers usually pick their itinerary, aircraft, and co-pilot. I wanted to make sure you could fly the routes and the planes you wanted."

"Thank you," said Laura.

"I am grateful," Hannah added. "This way we are both going to become bona fide airline pilots. How is it going to work?"

"The guys I brought will fly with you because the Fifty-two needs a flight engineer and a radio operator. Each subsequent aircraft will have a pilot and the crew. The two technicians are going to set up a maintenance facility in Nairobi. One of you will have to keep flying the mail routes, while the other takes the right-hand seat with Manfred. However, you'll rotate every week."

"How long is it going to take before one of us can captain a ship to Cairo?" Hannah asked.

"I assume after you did two return trips with Manfred, you'd be ready to take a flight on your own."

"I'll take the postal routes tomorrow," Hannah said.

"Well, I am going to be a passenger on the flight to Nairobi," Ray said. "We will have a lot of arrangements to make there."

After Hannah left for the Hotel Lido, Laura sat next to Ray on the patio.

"What are you going to do after the Germans buy you out?" she asked.

"I'll return to England," he said quietly.

"How about me?"

"Let's be honest, Laura. We were not meant for each other."

"You told me that often enough. What do you expect me to do?"

Ray kissed Laura's hand and said, "You are going to move to Nairobi with the new airline, become the star pilot and find yourself a nice young man to marry. Somebody like Bob Carstairs."

"I hope not."

"Why? What's wrong with Bob?" Ray queried.

"He is a self-centered egomaniac, who does not consider women as human beings."

"I see. He evidently proposed and insisted on you becoming a housewife with a pilot's license."

Laura sat up and looked at Ray suspiciously.

"How did you find out?"

"It was obvious, darling. You had a red-hot love affair with him, and the idiot did not realize the rare gem in you. He proposed too soon without discussing the details, and when you refused him, he took offence."

"Did he tell you?"

"No, I figured it out myself. I even know the date of your first going to bed with him."

Ray's revelation shocked Laura.

"Why didn't you say something? Why did you not call me a whore or a slut?" she demanded.

"Because you are not. You need men as a fish needs water. Anyway, what could I have said? It was better to keep quiet, have you part-time than losing you," Ray said with a smile. "In case you didn't know, I love you very much with all your faults and human weaknesses."

"Then why don't you marry me?"

"We have been through that several times, Laura. I don't wish to curtail your freedom. When I die, you will inherit my Air Mogadishu shares anyway. We slept together, making wonderful love just as if we were man and wife. I did not see any advantage of you marrying me," Ray said.

Laura listened quietly. As Ray finished, she kissed him on the lips and said, "You are one hundred percent correct, darling. Let's see about the wonderful love you just mentioned."

~ * ~

Laura's first trip to Cairo with Manfred turned out to be a successful flight, although he behaved in a strange formal manner. On the return flight to Nairobi, with Laura in the captain's seat, she decided to find out what was eating him.

"How come you are avoiding me, Manfred? Did I offend you in any way?"

"No, but I am afraid our relationship must be revised."

"Why?" Laura asked innocently.

"I am afraid I have two very good reasons. The first one is my marriage. We had the wedding before I came to fly for Air Mogadishu. As soon as I am settled in, my wife will come to Nairobi."

"I am not interested in your second reason," Laura said. "Please accept my congratulations. Tell your wife that I believe she is a lucky girl."

From there on, Manfred did not try to avoid Laura.

A month later Air Mogadishu settled into a groove. Although they had only one Junkers 52, it sufficed to handle the initial traffic. They made one round trip every week from Nairobi to Mogadishu, and to Aden, crossed the Red Sea to Port Sudan and on to Cairo.

A young pilot, Billy Gray from England, arrived to help fly the postal routes, relieving Laura and Hannah, as the two women became seriously involved with the long-haul flights.

"We are getting another fellow from Germany to fly the postal routes. As soon as the second aircraft arrives, you'll be able to leave the F13s for the new guys," Ray declared.

In another month, the face of Air Mogadishu changed a great deal. Two young men were flying the postal routes. Laura, Manfred, and Hannah took turns as captains on the long-haul flights.

After the third 52 arrived, Ray handed over the management of the company to a German called Rudolf Weinberger, and returned to England. The new director was supposed to move the operating center to Nairobi.

It was hard to say farewell to Ray.

Laura spent Ray's last night in Mogadishu in his bedroom. The emphasis was not on the sex, but on the fact that Ray was leaving for good. Laura understood losing her mentor, lover, but above all her best friend.

"I will never forget you, Ray," she said with the tears streaming down her face. The sun had just begun to rise, and the thin orange line appeared on the edge of the horizon.

"Do not cry, darling. Think of my departure this way: you have a career, you are a professional, and you are taking your life into your own hands. I leave you strong enough to stand on your own feet. Do not disappoint me, darling. I love you and will never forget you."

Ray's words calmed Laura the same way her evening prayers did. It was strange.

There were no tears when they boarded the brand new Junkers for Cairo. Laura and Hannah as co-captains took Ray to a date with Imperial Airways. Both cried when the ancient pelican left them to board Imperial on the next leg of his journey.

"Look after my airline, girls," Ray said as he walked toward the towering Hanno.

On the way back, they flew silently. Hannah sat in the captain's seat. After landing in Mogadishu, they handed the plane over to the German crew to take it to Nairobi and pick up the next batch of passengers.

"We will have to move to Nairobi eventually, but I am moving into Ray's room tonight." Hannah broke the silence when they drove toward the house.

"Aren't you getting tired of moving?" Laura asked.

"No. With my one suitcase, I could move to Nairobi tomorrow if I had to."

"I am sure we will, but the timing is up to Mr. Weinberger. I would prefer to live in Nairobi, but for the time being I don't mind good old Mogadishu," Laura said.

"As long as I can fly those gorgeous Fifty-twos, I am happy," Hannah remarked.

"Me too."

That evening Laura couldn't get to sleep. Even though she had her evening prayer asking the Almighty to take care of Ray, the thought of getting in touch with God did not calm her. She tossed and turned until the morning.

As they were off next day, they got up late, planning to go to the club for a game of tennis, and possibly a swim later. However, shortly after breakfast, Weinberger arrived.

"I am glad I caught both of you at home. I came to discuss the company's move to Nairobi with you," he said.

"Come on in, Mr. Weinberger. Have a cup of tea," said Laura.

Amina brought the kettle, and they settled on the patio.

"Well, I am finished with the reorganization plans," he announced.

"Are we moving to Nairobi?" Hannah asked eagerly.

"No. The two of you are staying in Mogadishu. We are raising your pay."

"That helps," Hannah interrupted.

"I will give you a third pilot to help take care of the Somali postal routes in addition to the charter flights."

"How about flying the Fifty-twos to Cairo?" Laura challenged. "My seniority number is one. I don't want to fly the little F13s."

"I have the number two, and I don't want to fly the single engine jobs either," Hannah joined the fray.

"As far as I am concerned, your seniority numbers do not mean a thing," said Weinberger quietly. "The passengers want to see men in the cockpit. We will split the company into two parts. The postal flights remain with Air Mogadishu, while the group flying the long-haul routes, will be called Kilimanjaro Airline, a subsidiary of Lufthansa. You do not have any seniority in that firm. However, we recognize your standing at Air Mogadishu."

"Shit," grunted Hannah. "This is crooked. The only reason I hung on to this miserable job was the chance of flying the Junkers Fifty-two. If you want to play it this way, I quit."

"I agree with Hannah. If she quits, so do I. In addition, I swear to make your life as miserable as I can. I am a shareholder of Air Mogadishu. I understand that under Somali law I can hold up your splitting off the postal routes. Until you buy my shares and General Ponti's, you cannot split the company," Laura said.

Weinberger looked at Laura in surprise: "What the hell are you talking about?"

"I'll tell you," Hannah got into the act. "She is going to call an emergency shareholders' meeting. As her shares and the general's will be the only ones voting legally, they can have you fired, and Laura will take over your post herself. As Air Mogadishu is a Somali corporation, the local law applies. The Fifty-twos are the property of Air Mogadishu, and you have no jurisdiction because you are only an employee. We spoke to Mr. Cagliari, a lawyer and specialist in corporate affairs. The transfer of Mr. Madison's shares to you might take a few weeks, perhaps a few months if we pay a few pounds baksheesh to the right person. Your majority shareholding is not worth a pinch of shit until it is in your name."

"Would you do that, Miss Stanton?"

"Damn right I would. Therefore, Mr. Weinberger, based on seniority we take the next flight to Cairo. And there is nothing you can do about it."

"This is ridiculous," the man said. "I must check with my superiors. Good day, ladies."

After he left, Laura turned to Hannah. "Did you really talk to a lawyer?"

"Of course I did. Ernesto Cagliari is my current boyfriend. I told him I expected my worthy countrymen to pull a fast one like this."

"What else did he say?"

"He said you could delay the inevitable, but could not stop it."

Laura's world collapsed. Since she had tasted being the captain of a serious airliner, she had no desire to return to the postal routes flying the little F13s.

"I guess we can take a few trips to Cairo before the axe falls," Laura remarked. "What are you going to do?"

"I am going back to Germany. Now I have serious credentials, sufficient long-haul airline experience, and I am sure Uncle Hermann could find me a flying job. I may even become his personal pilot. How about you?"

"I am going to England. Perhaps I'll get an instructor's ticket and start teaching bored housewives to fly, or I might try hooking up with one of the factories and become a test pilot."

"That was the job I really wanted with Junkers," said Hannah with a heavy sigh.

"Do you know why you didn't get it?"

"No, I don't."

"Well, I can tell you. They were afraid of your politics."

"Idiots. I am a completely apolitical animal."

"Nevertheless, that's what they told me," Laura said.

"To hell with them. They can stick to their precious politics. Is it a sin to want to fly?"

"No, it is not. If it were, I would be a sinner too."

"Why don't you come to Germany? Junkers would gladly have you as a test pilot."

"I do not speak German. Besides, I do not like your new regime."

"I also detest those macho, brown-shirted idiots, but I have to put up with them."

"Even though I have plenty of experience, and an unblemished record, nobody would consider me for a serious flying job. I do not have high powered connections, like your Uncle Hermann."

"I tell you what the problem is," interrupted Hannah. "We are females and not supposed to have brains or guts. We should be beautiful, brainless sex machines producing babies for the men, the crowns of creation. We should have been equal from the first moment in the Garden of Eden. However, Adam only had brawn and no brains. If he had, he should have told Eve to stay away from the goddamned apple tree."

"I believe you are right."

"I know I am right. Consider this: God is supposed to be a male. As such, he messed up the creation completely by constructing man, the most important component, on the sixth day. Nobody works very well on Saturdays."

Hannah's sudden attack on the Almighty shocked Laura, but she had to agree. Hannah made sense.

"He gave us instincts, built-in desires, and other qualities he doesn't like. He punishes us when we follow our instincts," Hannah continued.

"There is nothing wrong with the creation," Laura remarked. "The only trouble is that he created the male of the species first."

"Damn right. Look at my country. Those stupid men are going to get us into a war if we do not stop them. They talk about revenge and other dumb things."

"The hell of it is that we are girls. We cannot do anything on our own. If we want the respect of society, we must become the property of a man."

"I wouldn't mind the right guy," said Hannah.

"I had the right one on the line, but I lost him. Now I am not sure if he was the right guy," Laura said.

~ * ~

Three weeks after their fateful interview with Weinberger, Ray formally transferred his shares, and the new owners immediately offered to buy out Laura.

She held out for a while, but in the end, sold her shares for four thousand pounds, like General Ponti.

After the negotiations, Laura and Hannah took a week off, borrowed the *York*, flew to Kismayo, and spent a few days with General Ponti and his wife.

They had a wonderful time with them. After a couple of days in town, the general decided to take them for a hunt, which became the high point of their visit.

"You cannot leave Africa without hunting. You need trophies," the general said after he took the two women to the firing range. Laura used the general's Remington to the satisfaction of the old soldier.

"You are pretty good, Laura," he said. "How about you?" he asked Hannah.

"I have never fired a gun in my life," she said.

"We'll teach you," the general said, and they returned to the house for dinner.

Next morning, a huge Somali sergeant major came for Hannah and invited her to the firing range.

Meanwhile Laura went out to the hunting grounds with the general and a few of his soldiers riding in a four-wheel drive military vehicle.

"I am going to have you shoot a lion," the general said.

"A lion?" Laura asked with her eyes opening wide. "Isn't it dangerous?"

"Not at all, my dear. I am afraid you have grave misconceptions about lion hunting. One only hunts lion in the movies on the narrow trails in a rain forest, walking until a huge, black- maned lion appears from the nowhere and charges. The hunter shooting from the hip kills the beast with one bullet through the heart is hunting Hollywood-style."

"How is it done?"

"Well, we are going to the south where a local tribe is raising cattle. Where cattle are raised in East Africa, the lions will eventually appear. Then I go out, shoot a zebra, gut it, and leave it at a strategic place, quasi inviting the pride of lions for lunch. Next day, we'll go there, and from a distance of about a hundred meters, you'll shoot the lion. That is all there is to it," the general explained.

"I understand a pride of lions means a large family of the beasts. Won't they charge if I shoot one of them?"

The general burst out laughing. "If the lady lions had the habit of attacking the hunters after culling their aging lover, very few trophies would be hanging on the walls of the stately homes in Italy, Britain and America. The noise of the shot usually stampedes the pride in the opposite direction. Don't worry, Laura. We'll be all right."

For lunch Hannah came back beaming, and she very proudly declared, "The sergeant said I could go hunting, but he did not recommend going after the big five. He said I should try to shoot an oryx or a kudu. What do they look like?"

"They are antelopes with large antlers," said Mrs. Ponti.

"Great," Hannah said. "A pair of African antlers would look great in the parlor of our farmhouse in Bavaria. The largest antlers we have are about fifty centimeters long. Allegedly, it was a suicidal buck, and my dad shot it."

"The antlers you'll get here will be much larger," the general said. "I asked my adjutant to take you out tomorrow. While you shoot an oryx or a kudu, I'll go lion hunting with Laura."

"I knew she was brave, but I did not think she had the courage to go after a lion," Hannah remarked.

"She is all guts," the general said and winked at Laura.

~ * ~

They headed for the rendezvous with the lions. The hunting party took two vehicles with soldiers and a few civilians to look after the preservation of the trophy. When they reached the appointed place, the general, with his binoculars hanging on his neck, climbed on the hood of the car.

"I know exactly where the lions are supposed to be," he said. "I just want to check."

"Do you see anything?" Laura asked.

"We are very lucky today."

"Lions!" Laura interrupted with her voice trembling.

"Yes," the general said. "He seems to be an old gent, very good trophy quality. Come and have a look."

He held out his hand to Laura, helping her onto the hood.

"Where are they?" she asked.

"Over there," he replied and pointed in the general direction. "They are not too far. We should get within shooting distance in fifteen minutes."

"Beautiful, they are very beautiful."

"Do you see the big one with the black mane? The one a little closer to us than the rest."

"Yes. He is absolutely marvelous."

"Well," Ponti declared, "that is the one you are going to shoot."

He helped Laura off the hood; they grabbed the rifles and started out on foot. Passing through a little rough patch in the bush, a thorn scratched Laura's leg a little.

Never mind, she thought. *It is an honorable battle scar, which I could point at on poolside to my friends and say: I got this in Africa, when I shot my lion.*

They approached the pride. When they reached a large baobab tree, no more than a hundred feet from the old gent, the lion stood up and stretched just like a big kitten.

"Okay, Laura," the general said. "I hope you remember the spot to hit. Rest the barrel of your rifle on that knob, aim, and fire when I give you the signal."

"Okay," she whispered.

The general knelt, wrapping the strap of the rifle around his shoulder, and he was ready to intervene in case Laura missed.

He flipped the safety on his rifle, raised his left hand, and whispered, "Fire!"

Laura had the lion in her sights, and at the general's command, she gently squeezed the trigger. As the heavy slug of the .45 Magnum hit, the lion jumped, twisted in the air, and fell to the ground. He slowly staggered on his feet, let out another mighty roar, and collapsed at the same time when the second slug of Laura's rifle hit. The lion's body jerked, acknowledging the second hit. He was stone dead.

"Hold your fire," the general said. "You do not want to damage the trophy any more than you must."

They trotted to the lion. The first shot took him straight through the heart. The second hit below the rib cage of the already dead lion, breaking his spine. Both shots were fatal.

"Congratulations," Ponti grunted.

In a few minutes, the crew arrived with the car. The general dug out his Leica, and took several pictures of Laura with the dead lion.

"He is going to be the star of your family photo collection," he said.

The general issued instructions to the civilians. Taking Laura into one of the vehicles, he started the drive back to his residence.

"Can I have the skin?" she asked.

"Most certainly! The civilians were the boys working for my taxidermist. They are going to tan the skin and mount the head properly. You will have a very nice lion skin rug. Just tell me where you want it delivered, and I'll see to the shipping."

"It is going to cost a lot of money. You see, I am going back to England. Whom should I pay?"

"It is my treat. After all, your hard-nosed bargaining with the Germans made me two thousand pounds quick profit. Just as a token of my appreciation, let me pay for the tanning and the shipping of your lion skin."

"I shouldn't."

"Why not? Why do you always want to be so independent? Why don't you let anyone close to you?"

"I did it once, and it was a catastrophe."

"I suspected that," Ponti said. "Ray told me your story. In fact, we talked about you a great deal. When he sold his shares to the Germans, I knew they would try easing us out."

"Why?"

"The Krauts are conservative people. They believe a woman's place is in the kitchen, barefooted and pregnant, which is utterly ridiculous."

"Many people think like that," mused Laura.

"They do, and when it comes to the average woman, that idea is going to be tenable for a few decades longer. However, when more and more women like you became high achievers, they will force the establishment to change its tune."

"I'll be about a hundred years old by then."

"Nevertheless, it is going to happen."

"What am I going to do in the meanwhile?"

"You will marry someone who will accept you as an equal, like we are with my wife."

"What do you mean?"

"When we got married, she was a budding scientist, a biologist. For a while, she taught at the university, but when the Army promoted me to general and asked where I wanted to serve, I sat down with my wife and we discussed the possibilities. We knew she needed spectacular achievements to get a chair at one of the universities. Therefore, instead of asking for a Bersaglieri Regiment, I applied for posting in the Colonies, the job nobody wanted. Now it is her turn. She has a laboratory in the house, and she is working on the flora of East Africa. She has already published a well-regarded book on the subject. The second one is almost completed."

"In actual fact, you took a less prestigious assignment just to accommodate her career. Did you?"

"Yes, I did. She is an equal partner. It is her turn to make a name for herself. After the second book, one of the universities will offer her a chair for sure. At that point, I am going to retire and perhaps enter politics."

"There are very few people like you around."

"You'll find one, I am sure. If your husband cannot accommodate your career plans, he doesn't deserve you," said the general. "This is why I wanted you to shoot a lion. In a man's eyes, the trophy of a lion skin will elevate you to a macho man's level. The guys will have to look at you as an equal or better."

Suddenly, she thought about Bob and his demand of giving up her career.

If the fool would have had a talk with Ponti before proposing to me, everything would have been all right, she thought.

When they reached the general's house, Hannah was already there. She had shot two very nice oryx bulls. She had the taxidermist pack the large antlers for shipment to Germany.

They spent a very pleasant evening, and Laura had tears in her eyes when they said farewell to the general and his wife.

~ * ~

Laura landed the *York* in Mogadishu, and since the director was at the airfield, she marched straight to Mr. Weinberger and said: "I quit."

Then she turned and went to the car. She could not help overhearing Hannah saying something to him in German. She was sure of the volatile Hannah giving Herr Director a piece of her mind.

Fourteen

According to their contracts, Laura and Hannah received return transportation to their home station. Weinberger issued them tickets on Air Kilimanjaro to Cairo, connect Lufthansa to London and Berlin respectively.

Laura immediately sent a cable to Granny about her arrival. Weinberger did not rush the arrangements. It took more than two weeks for Laura and Hannah to depart Mogadishu.

It was painful seeing the aircraft landing and taking off from the runway they used to rule between them. When they finally boarded the flight to Cairo, the captain, von Altman, offered the right hand seat to Laura as far as Aden, and let Hannah fly the 52 to Port Sudan.

"I think Weinberger is an asshole for letting you two go," von Altman declared. "He is not going to get two captains with better qualifications and attitude than you have. I am ashamed for him."

"Don't worry about us, Manfred," said Hannah. "If we don't get a flying job in Germany or Britain, we are going to buy a small aircraft, go to Kenya and start a safari business. The last time we went hunting, Laura shot a lion, and I bagged two oryx bulls. We did well as pilots, and we would do well as big game hunters. Wouldn't we?"

"We could sure do it," Laura agreed.

~ * ~

When Laura and Hannah parted, they were both sobbing. The two young women had forged strong bonds of friendship. They were both flyers, overachievers, and determined not to play second fiddle to anybody.

"I am going to get a flying job even if I have to go to the North Pole flying Eskimos and beaver pelts to the market. I am going to make my living as a pilot, no ifs and buts about it," Hannah said.

"I won't change profession either. I will get an instructor's ticket, and if worse comes to worse, I'll work for the Corydon flying club."

"You should try the aircraft manufacturers. They always need test pilots. You would do very well with them."

"I might," said Laura as she hugged Hannah. "Look after yourself, girl, and don't let the bastards grind you down."

All the way to London, Laura kept thinking about Hannah.

"I am going to miss her," she said with a heavy sigh just before the captain told the passengers to fasten their seat belts.

In London, Laura checked into the Cumberland Hotel. She planned to see her banker, spend a day shopping, and travel to Stanton Manor the day after. She thought of Paul. *I wonder if he is in London or off to the boondocks somewhere.*

On the spur of the moment, she dialed Paul's number and got an immediate response.

"This is Laura Stanton."

"Hi, when did you arrive?" came Paul's baritone.

"Today."

"How long are you staying?"

"I have returned to England for good," she replied.

"Great! We should celebrate. Are you free for dinner tomorrow?"

The invitation came rather unexpectedly, and Laura automatically replied, "Yes, I am free, but the day after tomorrow I'll leave for Stanton Manor."

"It is a date. I'll pick you up at seven if it is all right with you."

"I am looking forward to it," she replied and hung up.

Next day, she visited Barclay's. Mr. Eagles greeted her like an old acquaintance.

"It is an unexpected pleasure to see you, Miss Stanton. Did you come to discuss your account?"

"Yes, Mr. Eagles, that is the purpose of my visit. I have a check for four thousand pounds drawn on the Dresdner Bank issued by the Junkers Aircraft Factory. I want to deposit it on my account."

"Have you had the income cleared by your accountant?"

"What do you mean?"

"Taxes, Miss Stanton. The government will want to take their cut from this money," Eagles said.

"I am not sure if it is taxable in Britain," said Laura.

"Why?"

"It is the price I received for my shares in Air Mogadishu, a corporation registered in Somalia, an Italian colony. The buyer is a German firm."

"I am not sure about it, Miss Stanton. I believe it is a complex transaction. I am going to discuss it with the expert on the matter."

"Thank you, sir. I expect to stay with my grandmother for a while. You could send me a letter about the taxes. Here is my address."

~ * ~

After the meeting with Eagles, Laura had a quick lunch in the hotel, and went to do some shopping. By five, she was back at the Cumberland. At seven o'clock, Paul arrived in his sports car. "Where are we going?" Laura asked as they took off.

"I took the liberty of hiring a French chef for the night. He is preparing a fabulous meal for us in my house. I hope you have no objections."

Laura remembered the last time they met. Paul invited her, and she expressed interest in the decor of the engineer's residence.

"It is all right. I am curious to see your house," she said.

They arrived at Paul's residence on Belgravia Square, the most prestigious location in the city. The houses all looked alike, but the interior of Paul's residence did not reflect the taste of the British upper class. To start with, he had central heat, and modern furniture. The abstract paintings on the wall fit into the surroundings.

"Very interesting decor," Laura remarked as they entered the parlor.

"Please have a seat," Paul replied and pointed to one of the comfortable armchairs.

The moment she took her place, the butler appeared asking what they wanted for aperitifs.

"I am going to have a Campari with soda and ice," she said.

"I'll have Cardhue neat, Chadwick, please," Paul said.

The butler bowed and withdrew.

"You mentioned coming home for good. What happened? Last time we spoke, you were determined to return to Africa and fly some new aircraft. What made you change your mind?"

"The circumstances changed. A German group bought Air Mogadishu, and they did not want women in the cockpit. Therefore, I quit."

"To be honest, Laura, flying an aircraft is a rather masculine profession. I understand the airline's preference for male pilots."

Laura did not wish to go into the details of Paul's beliefs and perhaps trigger an argument. She simply remarked, "Although it was painful, I understood them too. However, let's not talk about my career. What is your French chef going to dazzle us with?"

"Oh, yes. I instructed him to prepare a four-course meal, maximum twelve hundred calories."

"What is he going to cook?"

"He suggested a menu: trout fillet with a sharp cheese sauce. Actually, the French call it Orly-style, but he says this is his own recipe."

"It sounds exciting. What's the next course?"

"He is going to make French onion soup with whole wheat croutons and Swiss cheese. The main course will be grilled tenderloin in red wine and mushroom sauce. For dessert he will serve us flamed crepes filled with chestnut mash."

"Wow, this meal is fit for a king."

"He said the same thing. We had a slight argument when it came to the wine. For starters, he suggested a rose with the fish, which was okay. Since you do not like dry wines, I wanted to overrule his choice for the main course. We argued, but in the end, we managed to compromise. Alain suggested a Medina, a rare, demi-sec red wine from the vicinity of Naples."

"Who told you I don't like dry wines?"

"I am not at liberty to talk about it."

"Granny, I suppose," mused Laura.

"Yes," replied Paul. "We talked quite a lot about you. I found her an amazing person, and you the most exciting woman."

"Thank you for the undeserved compliment, but how did you talk to my grandmother?"

"I visited her a few times. She is very proud of you."

"It is better if we don't talk about me. I am very hungry and very much looking forward to the meal."

As she finished the sentence, the butler entered saying that dinner was ready.

Laura enjoyed the excellent food thoroughly. Alain occasionally appeared. He was not what she expected. Master chefs are supposed to be fat, but this guy was not. Built like a circus strongman, he did not carry an ounce of excess fat.

After dinner, they retired to the parlor, and the butler served them the best Martell cognac in large snifters.

"This is the perfect conclusion to a meal fit for kings," Laura said, warming the snifter in her hands.

"Do you like light classical music? I just bought a new record player...it changes the records automatically."

"I like classical music," said Laura.

"Your wish is my command," said Paul and stepped over to the large polished box, stacked the records and manipulated the switches. It was magic. The tempo of the Habanera followed by the love-filled aria of Turiddu, and the temperamental choir of the blacksmiths had an effect on Laura. The music aroused her sexually.

The melody and the meal somehow stimulated her to climb into Paul's large bed covered with red silk sheets. A few hours later, in Paul's arms, Laura suddenly realized where she was and what they were doing.

This is all wrong, she thought.

"I'd better return to my hotel," she said, got up and started looking for her clothes, finding them neatly laid out on the chair next to the dresser.

"I'll drive you," said Paul and got up.

"Don't bother, Paul," Laura said. "Just call me a cab."

"As you wish, darling," he replied and picked up the receiver on the nightstand.

On her way back to the Cumberland, Laura contemplated her recent encounter with Paul.

Something is not right, she thought. *I had no desire, no love, just a little bit of physical attraction and convenience. I never put my clothes down as neatly as I found them. I start shedding them at the door. Something strange happened, and I don't know what it was. Is it possible Paul drugged or got me drunk?*

Back in her own room, she checked the time. It was not yet midnight. After a long hiatus she turned to God again.

I do not know if I should thank you for Paul or not, my Lord. There was no love between us and I did not want him. Is he going to be a part of my future?

Strangely, the idea of touching Paul again did not appeal to Laura, but the contact with the Almighty calmed her enough to fall into a deep exhausted sleep.

~ * ~

Laura arrived at Stanton Manor in the middle of the week. James picked her up at the railway station, and Granny greeted her in the parlor.

"I am glad you are home again," the old lady said.

"I can't say I am not happy to see you, Granny, but unfortunately I lost my job and I have to find other employment."

"Whatever you do, Laura, never give up your dreams. Last time we spoke you said you are going to train as a flight instructor."

"I will," she replied, "but first, I am going to find a friend and ask his advice."

"Are you thinking of Ray Madison?"

"How did you know?"

"He visited me a few weeks ago. Ever since, he comes each Saturday for lunch. Occasionally he brings Mrs. Thorpe from Canterbury. Ray is helping her to manage an automobile dealership. They are very nice people," Granny said.

They talked for hours, but Granny soon tired and retired to her room, leaving Laura to her thoughts.

Based on what Paul had told her, apparently Granny had tried to play Cupid, inviting the man to Stanton Manor.

Although he was not the first man in Laura's life, sleeping with him left deep scars on her soul. This was the first time she kissed a man and held him in her arms without a burning, all-consuming desire.

"Perhaps my long period of celibacy had something to do with it," she reasoned to herself, but immediately every ounce of her objected to sleeping with a man for strictly health reasons. This turned into a major problem.

As she had a lot of thinking to do, Laura needed solitude, and went on exploring the property surrounding Stanton Manor. Only Sparky, the family dog, accompanied her. For one reason or another, the mutt took a liking to Laura. The two covered a lot of territory. Sparky occasionally decided to chase a bird or a rabbit, but when it turned out to be a lost cause, he came back to Laura.

Her thinking did not help much, as after the second day she started talking to the dog.

"Apart from Granny, you are the only friend I have around here, Sparky. It is a good thing you cannot talk, because if you could, I am sure you would tell me what I am doing wrong. As criticism hurts me more than it should, we wouldn't be friends very long. Nevertheless, it seems I cannot find peace anymore."

Sparky barked and took off after another rabbit. Laura sat on a big rock by a little brook. The dog went to the water, took a long drink, came back, and sat next to her quietly looking at her.

"Yeah, I am sure you understand me," she said.

~ * ~

It took Laura a few days to fit into her surroundings. However, the inactivity bothered her a great deal. After the heavy schedule of flying, suddenly she had nothing to do.

At breakfast, she thought about finding something to occupy her, and she had an idea.

"Next week I may visit Ray in Canterbury," she said.

"Are you planning to buy a car by any chance?"

"How did you know?"

"It is what I would do in your place. Anyway, I ordered a little sports car. You can have it if you wish. Ray is delivering it on Saturday. It is a Triumph roadster."

"Granny, you always read my mind. We must be very much alike."

"We are from the same stock, and our minds work the same way, Laura. Sometimes I wish I were as young as you are. I'd be your first student learning to fly. Perhaps I could eventually become your copilot."

"How did you find Ray?"

"Actually, he found me. He came first to tell me about your ordeal in Somalia. From there on, I invited him for lunch almost every Saturday," Granny said.

The thought of Ray developing ties to another woman first unnerved Laura, but she quickly realized that he had to have his freedom, just like her. *I am going to take him back*, she thought defiantly.

In the afternoon, Laura had a long walk with Granny along the same paths she had used many years ago. Every stone, every tree, had a place in Laura's heart. *This is what home means*, she thought.

Before dinner, they settled down in the parlor. James came in asking what they wanted to drink before dinner.

"I will have a drop of sherry and Miss Laura will have a Campari with soda and ice, won't you, dear?"

"You are a mind reader."

"I am not. Ray told me about your taste in liquor. I had a hard time getting hold of this horrid Italian concoction. In the end, Ray sent me five bottles. He said you are going to need it."

They had a nice roast for dinner, and chatted about the business of Stanton House. Laura never knew about Granny's strawberry business and her training of horses.

"You are quite a businesswoman," she said.

"I have to make enough for you to pay the death taxes after I am gone. I do not want you to sell Stanton Manor. Your children will love it."

"My children," mused Laura. "Where am I going to find a father for them?"

"He will come. Don't worry."

After Laura went to bed, she chatted with the Almighty.

"Thanks for getting me home, my Lord. I am going to Corydon one of these days, and ask the Wing Commander about the instructor's license. Please help me to get it because I feel I cannot live without flying."

~ * ~

Saturday morning Laura was on edge, as she wanted to see Ray very much. He always managed to soothe her when something upset her. Of course, in those days, his touch in the bedroom on the large bed came in handy, and the combination greatly enhanced his diplomacy. *This time, he must relax me with his iron logic only*, Laura thought.

She was in the kitchen with Granny, learning the art of making Yorkshire pudding when James entered.

"Dame Edith, your guests have arrived. Captain Madison and Mrs. Thorpe are in the parlor."

"Laura dear," Granny said. "Please take over as the lady of the house. I have a lot to do here."

"Yes, Granny," she replied and headed for the parlor.

Ray stood and hugged Laura before introducing Mrs. Thorpe. James appeared with the aperitifs, and Laura gave Ray a long look.

"How can you manage without flying?"

"Not very well, but the long drought is coming to an end. I just signed up with Hawker as a test pilot."

Without saying a word, Laura just pointed at her heart.

"Have no fear. I passed all the damned medicals. Nevertheless, if my ticker acted up again, the worst I could do is crash a plane. It would be a fitting death for a fighter pilot."

"You said this once, Ray," Laura replied.

"In those days I had you for a guardian angel."

"I want him to come to Canterbury as often as he can," Mrs. Thorpe said.

Laura instantly realized Louise Thorpe was after Ray's affections. *Something is going on between them*, thought Laura, but did not let on.

"What are your plans?" Ray asked.

"I am still thinking."

"Don't mess around too much, darling. Get your instructor's license. It is not the best flying job with your temperament, but let's you get off the ground," Ray said.

"Great idea. Next week I am going to London and visit Wing Commander Brannigan at Corydon."

"Give him my regards. He is a great guy."

"You should give my new car a test run today," Granny said after lunch, pointing at the car standing outside the window.

The discreet little Triumph sports car, British racing green of course, had the look of power and elegance.

"On a good road she can do the ton easily," said Ray. "Let me show you."

Laura looked at Granny, and she nodded.

They went outside, and Ray showed the car to Laura. She enjoyed driving it, because it handled much better than the old Fiat they had in Mogadishu.

"I am going to talk to George Stone one of these days. He might have a few ideas about finding a job for you," said Ray while they tested the Triumph.

"Isn't he mad at you for buying the planes from Junkers?"

"Actually he thanked me for it. They had a big, urgent order from the South African Air Force, and he would not have been able to deliver the planes to us. Actually, he asked me to take the German plane."

Even though Ray's nearness aroused Laura, she knew he would not be susceptible to making love in the tight little car on a country road, and she did not attempt anything. She realized Ray had the same feelings, but this was neither the time nor the place.

After testing Granny's new car for an hour, they returned to Stanton Manor.

In the late afternoon Ray got into Mrs. Thorpe's elegant Rover and returned to Canterbury, while Laura drove the new roadster to the Folkestone telephone exchange, called the Corydon Flying Club, and made an appointment to see Wing Commander Brannigan on Tuesday morning.

~ * ~

Even though Granny tried to talk Laura into driving the roadster to London, on Monday she took the train. After checking into the Cumberland Hotel, she thought of calling Paul, but changed her mind.

Although I need a man, he is not it, she thought.

Wing Commander Brannigan was happy to see Laura.

"When did you come back to England?" he asked.

"I arrived two weeks ago."

"You must have something very urgent on your mind if you came to see me so soon. What can I do for you?"

"I would like to obtain a flight instructor's license. I came to ask for your help."

"I don't think it would be very difficult. I can sign you up for the course right now."

"Do I have to stay here?"

"No, you can live wherever you wish, but you have to take a few hours of instruction in aerobatics, then write your paper and pass the flight test to get your license."

"How long do I have to prepare?"

"Take your time. I am going to be your examiner. I will give you a book, and assign an aerobatics instructor for you. When you feel ready for the tests, let me know, and we'll schedule them."

"Thank you, Wing Commander."

"Don't mention it. We are woefully short of instructors because everybody with a pilot's license wants to join the R.A.F. Some people even went to Canada and joined their Air Force. We will be able to use you, when you got your ticket."

In the afternoon, Laura had her first introduction to aerobatics. Wing Commander Brannigan assigned an elderly fighter pilot, Squadron Leader Ross, to give her a taste of aerobatics.

"How did you like it?" he asked after a series of loops and rolls.

"It was flying, but no fun. You were torturing your plane."

"Come on. This is what they were designed for."

"Look at it this way, Squadron Leader. I believe I could do most of the tricks you just did, but I would not enjoy them. It is like being a strong man and made to carry heavy weights all the time. An aircraft is designed to take people or freight from A to B. I do not see the sense in throwing the poor plane all over the sky," Laura explained.

"You are one of those airline jocks, I presume. Nevertheless, if you want to teach people to fly, you must know aerobatics. You said you could do most of the tricks. How about a number eight?"

"As you wish," Laura replied and took over.

She chose the more difficult configuration and executed the maneuver perfectly. "Sorry, my dear," she said, and touched the instrument panel.

Ross shook his head, but challenged Laura to do a couple of other exercises, which she executed perfectly.

"You will make a fine instructor, I am sure of it," he said after landing.

~ * ~

As she returned to the Cumberland, a message awaited her from Paul.

How in hell did he know I was here? she thought, but immediately realized it had to be Granny playing Cupid again. With a deep sigh, she returned Paul's call. At first, they chatted about inconsequential things, but Paul managed to spring a dinner invitation on Laura. She accepted, but made up her mind not to go to bed with him.

"Okay, darling. I am going to pick you up at seven, and I hope Alain is free tonight. Bye, Laura," he said and hung up, not leaving her time to object to the location.

The dinner at Paul's house was just as luxurious as last time, and Laura again ended up unwittingly in his bed. *I wonder how he managed to get me into his bed,* she thought, picking up her neatly folded clothes from the chair.

After returning to the Cumberland, she kept thinking about the main event of the evening.

I am sure the bastard drugged me, she concluded. *I had only one Campari and a small glass of wine with the meal. That is not enough to make anybody drunk. I will confront him next time we meet. However, I must tell Granny to stop playing Cupid.*

~ * ~

Back in Stanton Manor, Laura diligently studied the textbook for flight instructors. In three days, she got to the end, and started memorizing the paragraphs, when a telegram arrived from George Stone of Bristol Aircraft Company asking her to telephone him urgently about a possible job.

Laura slammed the book on her desk, borrowed Granny's car, and drove to the telephone exchange.

She got through in a matter of minutes.

The vice president of Bristol aircraft answered the call in person.

"How are you, Miss Stanton?" Stone started.

"Very well, thank you."

"Ray suggested you might be interested in returning to flying professionally. Is that so?"

"Of course. Piloting is my passion and my profession. I am planning to take an instructor's exam and teach people to fly at the Corydon Flying Club. It is not really the type of work I want to do, but it is flying."

"I have an urgent, alas temporary, assignment for you in case you are interested."

Laura's heart started pounding faster.

"What kind of assignment?" she asked.

"Why don't you visit me in Bristol? It is rather complex, and you might not wish to take the job."

"When do you want to see me?"

"As soon as possible. Can you make it tomorrow?"

"I am sure I can. I will telegraph my time of arrival."

"There is no need for that," said Stone. "I have the train schedule in front of me. We should agree on a time, and I will personally pick you up at the station."

"All right."

They selected the trains Laura should take, and she said farewell.

"It was a pleasure talking to you, Mr. Stone. See you tomorrow," she said and hung up.

Back in Stanton Manor, Granny was elated hearing about Laura's possible job with Bristol aircraft, even though she had to hurry to pack and get to the station.

"Stay at the Cumberland tonight, darling," Granny said. "James will make the reservations for you."

"Thanks, Granny, but this time do not tell Paul about my being in London."

"Why not? He is such a nice boy, exactly the type you should marry."

"He is a ruthless son of a bitch," Laura declared.

At first, Laura's outburst stunned Granny, and she remarked, "You should watch your language, my dear. It is not polite talking about people in such crude terms. By the way, what did he do to invoke your wrath?"

"I had dinner with him twice. On both occasions he drugged me and made me sleep with him."

"He took your virginity, darling, Paul must marry you."

"I am not a virgin, Granny. I lost it to Bert many years ago. Nevertheless, I would not marry that bastard Paul if he were the last man on Earth. I would like to slit his belly with your dagger. No, worse: I'd cut his testicles off."

"I understand your anger, Laura. Forget him. Think of this job you are going to take with Bristol. Perhaps they could make it permanent, and you might not have to become a flying schoolmarm. You are not the teacher type."

"What happens if the Bristol job is going to be only temporary? I do not wish to become a strawberry farmer."

"I know exactly what you want, Laura," Granny said. "You and I are too much alike. I know what I would want in your place."

Laura stood up and kissed Granny saying, "You're right. You read my mind with the sports car and you are reading it again."

She went to her room and started packing. On the spur of the moment, she threw two of her old Air Mogadishu flight suits and the blue silk outfit, the gift of Hannah, into the suitcase.

"Who knows?" she mused.

Before she left the house, Granny stopped her and gave her a beautiful brooch studded with rubies.

"I got it as the last gift from your grandfather," she said. "It always brought me good luck. Wear it."

Laura kissed the old lady and pinned the brooch on the lapel of her blazer.

"It actually complements my wings," she said, getting into the Bentley with James at the wheel.

The trip to Bristol took a long time, but Laura did not mind the journey. Brimming with nervous energy and anticipation, she stepped off the train.

Stone drove her straight to the factory and resisted all of Laura's efforts to try to pump him. In the conference room, Laura found two stern-faced R.A.F. officers and Ted Marston, the chief test pilot waiting. The R.A.F. uniforms reminded her of Bob.

I wonder where he is now, she thought. Stone introduced her.

"Gentlemen, this is Captain Stanton, the best female airline pilot in the British Empire," and turned to Laura: "You already know Ted. These gentlemen are Wing Commanders Carter and Brant."

"It is a pleasure to meet you, gentlemen."

"Please sit down," suggested Stone. "As time is pressing, I want you to get into the meat of our discussions."

"Indeed we are in a hurry," Carter added.

Although perplexed about the presence of the Air Force officers, Laura did not say anything.

"As you may know, we built two aircraft for the Shah of Iran. They are both Bombay freighters fitted with special facilities, like a bedroom with a double bed, an audience chamber, a ladies parlor, and a comfortable travel compartment for His Majesty. We are to deliver them to Tehran. Ted is going to fly one of the planes with a full complement of crew. If we can persuade Miss Stanton to fly the second plane with a radio operator only, we are going to be all set."

"There is very little question about my taking the assignment," Laura said. "To fly a Bombay half way across the world would be a dream job."

"There is a catch to it, Miss Stanton. In the interest of our national security, we want you to undertake a rather dangerous maneuver. Are you willing to risk your life?"

"I don't know what you want me to do."

"We want you to fake a forced landing in Germany, repair the plane, and take off in a few minutes again."

"Why?"

"We want you to pick up a British secret agent, and take him with you as a member of your crew."

Laura thought for a moment, and looked at Carter: "Why do I have to take this man?"

"His cover is blown. He is in hiding, with the Gestapo trying to arrest him. The man is actually a British Air Force officer in deep cover for many years, masquerading as an engineer for Junkers. We don't even know what he looks like, but you do."

"How is that possible?"

"It is a long story, Miss Stanton. Let it suffice that someone killed his contact man in MI5. We have had radio contact with him, and found his codes correct. After we told him about the death of his handler, he wanted to be taken out of Germany as soon as possible."

"Why didn't he take a train?"

"He figured the Gestapo knew about his spying, and if he tried to leave the country, they would arrest him. Therefore, he took a vacation inside Germany at a place far from the border in an area which cannot be approached by air without attracting attention. In fact there is only one unlikely place where an aircraft could land."

"Besides, you are the only living pilot who ever made a forced landing with a Bombay," added Ted.

"I see. Who is this super spy, and where did I meet him?"

"I will tell you his name and fill you in with the details after you have accepted the assignment and taken the oath of secrecy," Carter said seriously.

Laura thought about the job. There were certain aspects of it she did not like: namely the involvement with the secret service, and the possibility of being caught and shot as a spy. However, to do something for her country, and in the process get a chance to fly the Bristol Bombay outweighed the associated risks.

Suddenly, she had an idea.

"Don't get me wrong, gentlemen. I would like to take the assignment, but I want something in return."

"We will pay you the regular delivery fee and your return air transportation costs," interrupted Carter. "However, if it is not enough, we may..."

"It is not the money," Laura interrupted shaking her head.

"As far as the return transportation is concerned, I would not mind riding a camel all the way to Bristol. What I want is a chance to fly large modern aircraft professionally. If you can help me with that, I'll do what you want."

"We can give you the job you desire," said Carter. "Do your thing, Joe."

Wing Commander Brant took a form and a Bible from his briefcase.

"I am going to administer the oath of secrecy and afterwards we can discuss the details. Are you ready, Miss Stanton?"

The ceremony was short and to the point.

Afterwards, Carter took over again.

"The man you are going to pick up calls himself Heinrich Werth. He works for Junkers."

"I remember him."

"I already selected a remote place for your forced landing in Bavaria," Marston got into the act. "I am going to mark it on your map and actually lead you to the point."

"Do you want me to instruct my radio operator to send out an S.O.S., land, pick up Mr. Werth, and take off again?" Laura interrupted.

"That's about the size of it," said Carter.

"What do I do with him for the rest of the trip?"

"He is going to be your flight engineer. We will hide his papers on board your aircraft. The moment you take off, head for the Austrian border, land at Schwechat, that is the international airport of Vienna, and spend the night there. The Bristol mechanics who are already there will check and service your plane."

"Do I keep Mr. Werth on board all the way?"

"No. Fly to Budapest in Hungary, let him get off, continue to Bucharest immediately, and stick to the original flight plan. From Tehran take KLM via Amsterdam to London."

"How is Mr. Werth getting back to Britain?"

"That is classified."

"I see. Now I have only one more question. How about my flying assignment following this junket?" Laura asked.

"I will have a contract ready for you," said Stone. "We are going to hire you as a ferry pilot. We still have quite a few Bristol Bombays to build, and you are going to deliver them. Some of them go to Scotland, Northern Ireland, and we have a large order from South Africa. I suppose we will keep you on the road for about ten days to two weeks each month. When we run out of the Bombays, you can deliver the new Blenheim bombers to the R.A.F. bases and a few of them again to the South African Air Force."

"That is acceptable," Laura said, thinking of a chance meeting with Bob.

"It is not going to be easy, Miss Stanton," Stone continued. "Instrumentation is improving in leaps and bounds. You might have to study all the time you are on the ground, and take tests often. It is not going to be a picnic, I assure you."

"Actually, picnics bore me," said Laura with a smile.

"Alright," Wing Commander Carter got into the conversation. "I suggest Mr. Marston and Miss Stanton get together, prepare their flight plan to leave at sunrise tomorrow. Ted has already selected the landing site. Please estimate the timing of the pickup and we'll let Werth know."

"We will do just that," Ted replied.

"Before you take Miss Stanton to her hotel and start the planning, I have some special instructions for her, which I must do in private. Follow me, please."

Carter led Laura out of the conference room into the corridor and, through the emergency exit, he stepped outside the building. When they were a few yards from the walls, the Wing Commander turned and faced Laura:

"Your radio operator is a soldier from our most secret and very special detachment. His primary assignment is to kill anyone trying to masquerade as Werth. As only you or Captain Ray Madison could positively identify Werth, we had to get one of you to do this job."

"Did you offer it to Ray?"

"We did, but he said he had no multi-engine ticket. We solved the problem, and had him fly as a copilot, but he did not take our offer. He suggested that you could do the job better than he," Carter said.

"Why did he refuse the mission?"

"I do not know. Anyway, Miss Stanton, when you get Werth on the plane, you must tell your radioman if he is genuine or not. He'll know what to do. If he were the guy you knew as Werth, you should tell the radio operator to get the signal to a ground station to determine your position," Carter explained.

The thought of having to order someone's execution frightened Laura.

"I am not very enthusiastic about having someone killed aboard my plane."

"If he has to eliminate the German agent, it is not going to happen on the plane. This is why you must land in Schwechat."

"I see," Laura replied with a heavy heart.

~ * ~

Later, in the engineering office of the Bristol aircraft company, Laura and Ted prepared their flight plan from Bristol to Amsterdam, Munich, and Schwechat.

"The Bristol mechanics will be waiting for us at the Austrian stopover to check our aircraft overnight, before setting out to Budapest on the next day. From there, we go to Bucharest and Istanbul. George told me about a crew of mechanics who left for Istanbul a week ago. We will spend the night there, and if the aircraft is okay, we would fly to Baghdad and on to Tehran," Ted explained.

"Have we got the met?"

"We do. It is going to be all clear and sunny tomorrow, but we might have some marginal weather between Budapest and Istanbul. I am sure we can climb over it."

"Very well," Laura said. "Let me have a good meal and a good night's rest before we take off."

"Okay, I'll pick you up at five o'clock. Now let me drive you to your hotel," said Marston.

Laura took it easy in the afternoon, composing a long letter to Granny, telling her about ferrying an aircraft to Tehran. She promised to cable the time of her arrival to Folkestone after her return.

In the evening, she had a light meal, finishing the day with a Campari and soda. Going to bed, she felt stressed, and as always, she turned to the Almighty.

Thanks for the job, my Lord. Please let the man I pick up be the real Mr. Werth.

She fell asleep almost instantly.

The next thing she heard was the shrill of the telephone and the voice of the operator announcing it was four o'clock.

Fifteen

Laura got out of bed, ordered breakfast, showered, and put on her sky blue silk flight suit. Finishing the morning meal, she grabbed her small suitcase and headed for reception. She had just paid her bill, when Ted Marston arrived.

"Morning, Laura," he said. "I like your outfit."

"It always brought me luck," she said.

"In the aviation business, despite the best professional approach, you always need a little bit of luck," he remarked. "Let's go."

At the airfield of the factory, two gold-colored Bristol Bombays, named *Flying Lion One* and *Two*, stood bearing the elaborate crests befitting the ruler of Iran.

"Each of these planes looks like a work of art," remarked Laura.

They entered the briefing room where several people were waiting. Each wore a flight suit and had small overnight bags next to them.

"This is Alan Hargrove, your radio operator," Ted introduced a big fellow to Laura. He was about forty years of age, built like a prizefighter, but had a mischievous smile lurking on his lips.

"Pleasure meeting you, Captain," the man said and shook hands with Laura.

Following the introductions, all crewmembers sat down. An employee brought them tea or coffee, while Marston stood up to address the group.

"Except Captain Stanton, Alan Hargrove, and myself you have a one-year contract to serve in Iran. I am going to remain in Iran for two weeks to start the training of the Iranian pilots before heading home. I will have everybody traveling on my plane with the exception of Alan. He is flying with Captain Stanton. Any questions?"

"How about our personal effects?"

"Your suitcases are all loaded on Lion One."

"Are we carrying spare parts?" a technician asked.

"Yes, we do. I had most of it loaded on Lion Two, but we have some on Lion One as well."

"Did you file a flight plan, sir?" asked a young man wearing a pair of pilots' wings.

"I did. We are flying visual all the way to Vienna keeping loose contact. In case of radio failure, we can use the backup Aldis lamp to communicate. Is that clear?"

Laura and the other pilot nodded silently.

"Our first stop is Amsterdam. It is going to be a long haul, but the weather is good, and the Dutch are expecting us. We'll have a meal and proceed to Munich. That will be shorter. However, the German authorities did not permit us to leave the aircraft. They will look after the refueling, checking the oil levels, and a few other things."

"Begging your pardon, sir," the grizzled old flight engineer interrupted. "I don't trust anybody messing with my aircraft. I want to see what the Krauts are doing."

"One person is permitted to get off for the purpose of checking the planes and supervise the refueling. It has to be you. Do you speak German?"

"Not very much, but enough," the man replied.

"Okay. Let's move, fellows. The best of luck to you."

The takeoff was uneventful. The two golden aircraft heading east rose majestically over the countryside. Even though Ted did the navigation in Lion One, Laura also kept track of their position. She looked at Ted's plane occasionally and maintained a loose formation.

She was alone in the cockpit. Alan was in the back sitting next to his radio wearing the headset. The hours slipped by, and eventually Amsterdam airport appeared on the horizon. They received permission to land. The Lions touched down one after the other.

During the meal, Ted drew Laura aside and explained her in detail where she would have to land.

"I understand," Laura said after memorizing the location.

After lunch, the two Lions roared off the Amsterdam runways. Alan came to the cockpit and sat in the copilot's seat, while Laura gave him the instructions. Apparently, Alan also knew what to do.

"This is the message you must send when we get to the landing site. Can you do it?" Laura said and handed Alan a sheet of paper with the codes and the message.

"Yes."

"After you send the message, burn this piece of paper," she said.

"Okay, I will. Just make sure you tell me to get a QDM if the guy is genuine."

"I won't forget."

They climbed to the altitude of two thousand meters and headed to the southeast, the sun shining directly into their eyes. In the early afternoon, with the majestic Alps in the background, Munich crept up on the horizon.

It was a busy airport. Most of the planes were either Junkers 52s or American Douglas DC 2s, with a few smaller aircraft, and the odd four-engine Italian Capronis standing on the apron.

Each plane had to ask permission to land independently. The tower issued the appropriate clearances with typical German precision, directing each plane to a predetermined position. Armed, uniformed people stood guard to make sure no one left the planes. Laura could not make out if these Germans were the regular border police, the customs, or some other agency.

The flight engineer from *Lion One* got off, and conferred with the white-uniformed technicians as the refueling process began. Within an hour, the *Lions* were ready to take off.

Again following the precise instructions of the air traffic controller, the two Bristol Bombays took off.

Staying away from the Alps, following the Danube, they proceeded eastward. After the first forty-five minutes, Alan came to the cockpit.

"Captain, I just received a QQL from Marston."

"Very well, Alan. Go back, send the message I gave you earlier, and tighten your safety belt."

As soon as Alan started sending, Laura pulled the throttles back, and the *Lion Two* started losing altitude.

"There is the funny church steeple," Laura reminded herself, and started the steep turn to the south, rapidly losing altitude. When the plane's nose pointed due west, she identified the landing zone, a large pasture rising toward the edge of a forest. Although the approach was scary, the *Lion Two* landed with only a slight bump on the firm Bavarian turf. Laura taxied as close to the forest as she dared and turned the plane facing east. Looking out of the window, she saw Alan getting off and marching toward the tail of the plane. From the north, a man wearing green hunting clothes ran toward the plane, and with Alan, climbed aboard. As the aircraft was facing downhill, Laura had to stand on the brakes until Alan appeared and stuck his head into the cockpit.

"The cargo is on board, Captain," he announced.

"Okay," Laura said, opened the throttles, and took her feet off the brake. *Lion Two*, befitting her name, roared off the peaceful hillside, lifting off just over the little brook separating the pasture from the village. Laura could read the name of the place: Ulbering.

They continued eastward at almost treetop level for a few minutes until the River Inn, the border between Germany and Austria, appeared.

She started climbing to two thousand meters and set the rough course to Vienna on the gyrocompass.

"Okay, Alan. Bring our passenger up," Laura said. With her heart thumping, she leaned back on her seat, when a familiar face appeared. It was Werth all right.

"Miss Stanton, what a surprise," he said.

She instantly recognized the Junkers executive.

"Nice meeting you again, Mr. Werth," Laura said. "Alan, get me a QDM, if you please."

"Right away, Captain," the radioman replied and withdrew.

"You were running pretty fast," Laura said to Werth. "Have you had your leg cured by a German miracle doctor?"

"No, I just put proper shoes on. You see, according to my cover, I had to limp. As one can do that consciously only for a short while, I raised the heel of my left shoe three centimeters. Whether I liked it or not, I was limping. It was very hard on my back, though."

"Ingenious," replied Laura.

Werth stayed in the copilot's seat and stared forward

"By the way, do you know anything about Hannah?" Laura asked the new passenger.

"No. I believe she is still in Africa unless she quit Air Mogadishu."

"We left together. She was very determined to keep on flying, figuring her Uncle Hermann would find her a job."

"It won't be easy, unless she becomes one of the Chancellor's staff pilots. We built two special Junkers Fifty-twos for Mr. Hitler. They are just as luxurious as your plane. Allegedly, he asked Goering to find the best pilots in Germany to fly him around."

"It wouldn't surprise me if he picked Hannah. She is very good."

"But she is a woman."

"Don't you start it, Mr. Werth. I am also a woman. Not too many pilots could have done what I just did. Landing and taking off practically from the side of a mountain without cracking up. It doesn't make any difference if the pilot is a man or a woman. Hannah could have done it. I am sure. Just because we are females, we are as good in the cockpit as any man."

"I apologize," replied Werth. "I am sure you are as good as any man, but according to the perception of the conservative establishment, you could not be as reliable pilots as your male counterparts."

"Unfortunately, you are right," Laura said with a sigh. "This is why I will be only a ferry pilot instead of flying a proper airliner."

Werth had no answer.

~ * ~

In Vienna, Laura reported to the air traffic control that she had made a forced landing in Austria, repaired the elevator, and took off almost immediately. The duty controller accepted the report.

Laura, with the rest of the crew, took a small bus and drove to the Wandl Hotel, while Alan and Werth disappeared in a taxi.

Although Laura was tired, she joined Ted Marston and two of his men to take a sightseeing tour of the city. They had *Wiener Schnitzel* and *Dobos Torte* in the famous Hotel Sacher in the heart of the downtown area before returning to the Wandl.

"The bus will leave at five thirty," said Ted before they parted company at the reception.

Laura arranged with the management to have breakfast in her room by five o'clock and retired. She did not fall asleep until making her daily report to the Lord.

"Thanks for guiding the real Werth to my plane, my Lord, and I did not have to pass the death sentence on another human being."

~ * ~

In the morning, the ride to the airport was uneventful. Ted went to check out the meteorological reports. When he came back, he seemed to be in a hurry.

"We must leave at once," he stated. "There are low clouds rolling in from the southwest. I don't want to have any problems. We must hit Budapest before the weather."

"I am ready," Laura said shrugging, "but I don't see my crew."

"Tell you what," Ted replied. "I'll take off with *Lion One* and you follow as soon as you can."

"It's okay. They should be here any minute."

The wait turned into three quarters of an hour.

"Where in hell were you?" Laura demanded when the men arrived.

"We had to lose a couple of Gestapo goons," replied Alan. "I am afraid someone made Michael. We must leave as soon as possible."

"I am not sure we can reach Budapest," Laura said. "Te meteorological officer told me to expect poor visibility at Budapest, but conditions were appropriate for an instrument landing. Although I am not very happy about it, we are going," she said and herded them onto the plane.

They took off, and headed for the east.

"Alan," Laura called the radioman. "Check with Budapest every five minutes. In between, try to find alternates for us."

"Yes, Captain," Alan replied and took his place in the radio cubicle, while Werth sat in the copilot's seat. Although he was not a licensed airline pilot, he had flown fighters during the war. He occasionally relieved Laura, allowing her to navigate.

"I am going to fly visual as long as I can," Laura declared.

"Follow the Danube," suggested Werth.

"Good idea."

The good visibility did last only for twenty minutes out of Vienna. Alan came forward saying, "Captain, Budapest and Vienna are both closed."

"We are not very fortunate," Laura replied. "Did they suggest an alternate?"

"They said a military airport southwest of Budapest has basic instrument landing facilities, and their visibility is still good."

"Let's find it on the map."

"Its name is a tongue twister. Sek and something.

"Szekesfehervar," Werth interrupted.

"Okay," Laura said. "Get me a QDM, Alan."

She established their position and put the course into the gyrocompass with ease.

"It is going to be less than an hour to our destination," Laura announced.

However, the tranquility did not last long. In half an hour, they were advised about worsening weather, and the field was declared closed.

"Shit," grunted Laura angrily. "Did they suggest an alternate?"

"Yes, in fact they gave me several."

"Let me see," Laura said.

There was one in Debrecen, far to the east. There were no mountains in their way. Szombathely was due south of their position, but they had some hills near the field. Farther south, Zagreb had instrument landing facilities, but according to Laura's calculations, the place lay at the extreme limit of their fuel reserves.

"They gave me another alternate much closer," said Alan. "It is called Ketschemet."

"Kecskemet," Werth interrupted. "Further south you should have another field near the city of Szeged. It is only a short hop to Belgrade."

"Let me calculate," Laura said, and after a few minutes she looked up saying, "We are going to Kecskemet and try Szeged if we have to. If worse comes to worse, we can reach Belgrade."

"Okay," said Alan. "I'll keep checking."

They headed for Kecskemet.

"You seem to know Hungary well, Mr. Werth," Laura remarked. "Did you visit the place once?"

"Yes, I was the intelligence officer with the Entente Military Mission just after the war in Hungary. I know the place as well as a native. I even speak their language after a fashion."

"I see."

They sat quietly for a while.

"I have bad news," Alan stuck his head into the cockpit.

"I am sure I know," Laura said. "Kecskemet is closed."

"It is, Captain."

"Okay, we are heading for Szeged and keep our fingers crossed."

For a long time Alan did not come forward.

"We might be lucky," Werth said. "If we land in Szeged, I will treat you to the best fish chowder you ever tasted."

Laura was banking the plane to line up the runway, even though she did not see it, when Alan appeared.

"Bad news again?" Laura asked.

"Yes. Ground fog rolled in at Szeged. Visibility is zero."

"Not really," said Werth, pointing downward. "Look, the end of the runway is there."

"It is not the best, but beggars can't be choosers," Laura said and forced the Bombay into a tight spiral.

"This is strictly for suckers," Laura remarked. "This hole might close at any moment, and then we are screwed." She kept the protesting plane in a tight spiral, as if it were a small aerobatic aircraft. Although inside the cockpit the thermostat maintained twenty-two degrees centigrade, Laura began sweating and felt her bra strangling her, but she could not do anything about it.

Forcing the plane to do something it was not designed for gave Laura a feeling of sensual domination. Her sexuality aroused, but she had to concentrate on keeping the plane in the spiral as long as she could.

I feel as though I am raping him, she thought, and in her mind apologized to the *Lion Two*.

"I don't like it any better than you do, darling, but it must be done."

The engine temperature kept dropping. The left engine backfired, stopped, and started again, but she kept the plane going down. "Don't quit on me, darling," she said to the plane.

Lining up the little tip of the runway, Laura side slipped the huge plane to lose altitude, and dropped the *Lion Two* onto the runway of Szeged military airport. When they rolled to the makeshift terminal, an air force officer stepped to the plane and asked where they came from.

Werth took over, pointed to the gray sky, and in Hungarian explained their situation.

"I am Major Vasady," the officer said in passable English. "I want to congratulate your pilot. It is impossible to land in this weather. How did he do it?"

He was most surprised when Werth introduced Laura as their captain.

That evening, they were the guests of the Royal Hungarian Air Force in the Officers' Mess. The fish chowder was exquisite, just as hot as the Bengal curry Laura liked so much. The Hungarian Air Force officers drank to Laura's health often.

She went to bed with a huge headache, but had time to thank the Almighty for the fortunate sighting of the end of the runway.

~ * ~

In the morning, the weather had cleared. Laura managed to talk to Ted on the telephone.

"Although the airport was closed, I declared an emergency, returned to Vienna, and managed a hairy instrument landing," Ted said. "I am taking off for Budapest again and hope this time the weather will cooperate."

"Do you want me to head for Budapest, or carry on to Bucharest?"

"Leave it up to your passenger. If he can manage from the place you are at, head for Bucharest and wait for me."

~ * ~

Werth said he could take the train to Budapest. Therefore, Laura headed for the Romanian capital. The weather was clear, no sign of yesterday's miserable conditions. They flew over the majestic Carpathian Mountains. Skirting the castle of Dracula, they reached Bucharest.

Shortly after lunch, Marston arrived. In the afternoon, the two planes headed for Turkey.

Istanbul airport was chaotic. Nevertheless, Laura felt at home because it resembled the African landing fields.

The city appeared European, but the people behaved in a manner similar to the Somalis and the Bengalis she knew so well. Feeling practically at home, Laura checked into the hotel with the rest of the crew, but later she went to the market and bought some Turkish rose oil in a small vial inserted into a beautifully carved wooden container. Although she bargained hard and paid only half of the first asking price, she had the feeling that the smiling Turk had cheated her.

"Just use a drop of it in your closet, Mademoiselle," the dealer said when he packed Laura's purchase. "It will keep your clothes smelling like roses for weeks. When you run out, come back and I will give you a special price."

She carefully placed a drop into her suitcase. In the morning, she realized the Turkish vendor had not lied. When she got into the cockpit next morning, Alan remarked, "You smell like roses, Captain. Did you buy rose oil at the market by any chance?"

"Of course I did," Laura replied. "It was expensive, though."

"How expensive, if you don't mind?"

"About one pound for the ten cc vial."

"Holy mackerel," Alan exclaimed. "It cost me more than twice as much for the same thing. The fellow threw in a carved wooden container free."

"You were taken, Alan," Laura remarked and opened the throttle.

The two *Lions* landed at Tehran late in the afternoon. The Iranians did not handle the formalities related to the delivery of the planes efficiently. In fact, they ran around like chickens with their heads cut off. In the end, a huge, handlebar mustachioed colonel appeared and created some semblance of law and order. He assigned an Iranian crew to take possession of the machines and taxi them away from the public terminal to the military controlled part of the airport.

"Your pilots are not supposed to fly these planes until they have had proper training," Ted told the colonel signing for the aircraft.

"It is consistent with His Majesty's orders," the man replied. "I am Colonel Musa, His Majesty's first adjutant."

"I am Ted Marston. Allow me to introduce my crew."

"It is not necessary, I'll meet them at the gala demo tomorrow anyway. I just came to make sure your accommodation is going to be properly arranged."

"I appreciate it, sir."

"We are going to take the training crew to the barracks, to staff officers' quarters. You and your co-captain are going to stay in the palace. Where is he?"

"Meet the other captain, Miss Laura Stanton," Ted said pointing at her.

The officer's face changed. It went through all the colors of the rainbow.

"A woman," he muttered. "This is no good. How am I going to explain this to the high-ranking officers of our air force? A woman could not possibly fly such an expensive, sophisticated aircraft. Most of our men cannot."

"Have no fear, sir," Ted replied, obviously enjoying the situation. "In fact, she is better than I am. If you want a demonstration of how to fly the royal aircraft, I suggest Captain Stanton should take charge."

"You expect me to place the life of the shah in the hands of a woman?"

"His Majesty would not be safer with anybody and that includes me," Ted said.

The officer seemed to have a major problem. He thought for a while, then turned to Ted.

"If you want her to captain the demo flight, it is all right with me. However, we must hide her from public view. Put her on the plane before the news reporters arrive."

"Okay," said Ted. "The crew will board *Lion Two* inside the hanger."

"Why can't you use *Lion One* for the demo?"

"It has a slight problem, which must be taken care of. Besides, *Lion Two* is Captain Stanton's aircraft."

"It seems I cannot win," the officer said with a deep sigh. "However, I am afraid Captain Stanton cannot stay in the palace. The quarters are set up for men only."

"No problems, sir," Laura interrupted before Ted gallantly refused the shah's hospitality. "I can stay in a hotel, incognito if you prefer."

"Thank you, Captain," the Iranian replied with obvious relief. "I will have the most comfortable apartment at the best hotel made available to you. They will serve your dinner and breakfast in your room. I will personally pick you up tomorrow at eight in the morning."

"Thank you, General," replied Laura with a twinkle in her eye.

"I am only a colonel," the officer replied.

"My mistake, I am sorry," Laura replied. "You may not be a general, but based on your diplomacy and chivalry, I think you should be one."

"Thank you, Captain Stanton."

~ * ~

The Iranians assigned the suite called the imperial apartment to Laura. Persian rugs covered every square inch of the floor. Priceless brass work and original paintings adorned the spacious rooms. As a woman, Laura could not attend the gala reception at the palace, but it did not bother her because she was thinking about having a good sleep in a comfortable bed. After a long bath, she discovered that while she sat in the tub, someone had started burning incense in her room. The pleasant scent put her in nostalgic mood.

"I wonder if they serve alcoholic drinks," she asked herself and rang for service. Surprisingly a young woman came to attend to her needs.

"Can I have a Campari with ice and soda?" she asked.

"Most certainly, madame," the woman answered and disappeared.

In a few minutes, she returned with a full bottle of Campari, a bucket of ice and a large soda siphon.

"I do not know the proportions, ma'am," she said.

"Please leave everything. I don't mind mixing my own," Laura replied. The young woman bowed leaving Laura alone with her thoughts and the Campari.

"I could use Robert now," she said to herself with a deep sigh. As the room was warm, she did not put on anything and lay down on the bed. Outside, the sun was setting, and the sky began to change color. *It is just like in Africa,* she thought.

Suddenly, the memories overwhelmed her. She remembered Bob's kisses, Ray's firm loving embrace, and Teddy's urgent, breathless lovemaking. She felt abandoned, alone, and in desperate need of tenderness.

I had three men leave me in the past year. I wonder if I'll ever find someone who understands my need for love, flying, and a career.

She ran her hands over her smooth thigh, her waist, and cupped her breasts, wondering how she might have felt if Ted Marston or Alan had caressed her, but she chased away the thoughts.

"Is it possible I will get stuck with Paul?" she asked herself. "I hope not. Although I can do much worse than marrying him, I am going to reconsider this possibility after I returned to England and have had a good rest." She put on a robe and ordered dinner. The same young woman brought her food, a tray of cold cuts that included a few of slices of ham.

"When it comes to visiting Christian royalty, ma'am, we compromise our laws a little," she said, placing the food on the table.

"If you wish wine, I can bring it to you."

"Thank you. I can do without it," Laura replied.

Much later, when she retired, she looked at the ceiling, as she talked to the Almighty.

Thanks for the good weather en route, my Lord. Please help me with the demo flight tomorrow, and look after Robert and Ray until I find them again.

~ * ~

In the morning, there was a lot of hullabaloo at the airport before the Shah and the members of the royal family boarded the aircraft. In the audience chamber, the crew waited patiently. Ted, Bristol's representative, wore a tuxedo. Laura had her blue silk flight suit with a red scarf worn in the Islamic fashion, covering her head fully.

"The Captain of the Imperial Flight, Miss Stanton," Ted announced. The shah nodded slightly and said, "A pleasure meeting you, Captain," and turned to his entourage.

"Take your places. Kindly take off, Captain."

"As you wish, Your Majesty." Laura took Ted's young copilot into the cockpit and they started the pre-flight check.

In a few minutes, the *Lion Two* turned into the wind. Laura opened the throttle. When they safely reached cruising altitude, she invited the Shah to the flight deck. He came and took the copilot's seat for a while. Laura could see the fear in his eyes. He wasn't comfortable.

"Perhaps the Crown Prince would be interested in seeing the cockpit," Laura suggested, wanting to give the Shah a chance to return to the safety of the passenger cabin without losing face.

"You are right, Captain. Prince Mohamed is very much interested in flying machines," he said and quickly returned to the cabin.

In a few minutes, Ted conducted the prince to the cockpit. He was about eleven years old, dark haired, slim, tall for his age, and behaved like the future ruler of a country. His eyes betrayed his interest, while he took the copilot's seat with obvious gusto.

Ted returned to the cabin to entertain the royal party, leaving Laura alone with the prince.

"If Your Highness is interested, I would gladly explain how the controls work," Laura said.

"Would you really?" he asked with his eyes opening wide.

"It is not very difficult. However, if you ever wanted to pilot an aircraft, you must always strap yourself in. Unexpected turbulence may bounce you all over the cockpit, and you can lose control of the plane," she said before starting the explanation.

Prince Mohamed quickly buckled up and listened intently. When Laura finished, she asked him a few questions to find out if he had understood it. She had no reason to worry. The prince was an intelligent boy and had the right answers.

"All right, Your Highness. As you know the theory, you might as well drive for a little while," said Laura and pointed at the yoke.

"You mean I should fly the plane?"

"Why not? You know how it is done."

The Prince took the controls even though his feet barely reached the rudder pedals.

Laura could see the delight on his face, while he held the wheel. After about ten minutes, she turned to the prince.

"Now, I am taking over, but keep your hands on the wheel, your feet on the rudder, and follow my movements. We are going to make a turn."

Prince Mohamed nodded. She made the slow ninety-degree turn. As she was one with the *Lion Two*, she sensed the boy's tremendous energy and desire to fly the plane.

"You take it for a while," said Laura, following the turn, and leaned back in her seat.

"This is the greatest thing I've ever done," the prince said. "Would you teach me flying?"

"I am sure you have many well-qualified instructors in your country, Your Highness. They can teach you as well as I could."

"But I want to learn from you!"

"To start with, Your Highness, you are a little too young. You should wait a couple of years until you have grown taller. Then you can start your flying lessons in earnest."

"We'll see."

They flew in silence until they reached the point where Laura wanted to make another turn.

"Lesson number two," she announced. "You are going to make a ninety-degree turn, Your Highness. Just remember how I did it, and keep your eyes on the needle and the ball. I will also hold the controls. If you make a mistake, I will correct it instantly."

The boy nodded.

"Start your turn now," Laura ordered.

The prince began the turn just as she had taught him. Laura did not have to intervene. When the plane flew straight again on course, she remarked, "Eventually, you'll make a good pilot."

"I am sure it would be more fun flying an airliner than running a country," he replied with a sad smile.

Perhaps you'd live longer, Laura thought, but did not say anything. That the boy already knew what his responsibilities would be surprised her. *He would become a great leader someday*, she thought, and turned to the boy.

"I believe it is time to relinquish the controls, Your Highness, and return to your seat."

"Can I stay just a little longer?"

"All right, five more minutes."

"You are the greatest," the boy said.

In precisely five minutes, Prince Mohamed handed the control back to Laura and said, "I am most grateful, Captain," and he left the cockpit.

For the remainder of the flight, Laura flew with Ted's copilot. The young man was supposed to stay in Tehran and check out the Shah's pilots on the Bombay.

After landing, the official party left the aircraft, but the crew remained on board until the royals had left the field. During this period, Laura helped herself to a Campari and soda from the well-stocked bar of the *Lion Two*. As she left the plane following the others, she could not resist walking around the *Lion Two*. At the tail, she stopped, put her hand on the elevator, and said, "Thanks for bringing me to Tehran. We got along famously. Please be gentle with Prince Mohamed. The kid wants to fly, and you are going to be his plane. Look after the poor little shah."

Next morning, Laura and Alan boarded the KLM flight to Berlin and onward to London.

Sixteen

"Last night I witnessed a very interesting confrontation between the Shah and the Crown Prince," Alan said after the airliner took off.

"I bet the old man behaved like a dictator," Laura remarked.

"Curiously, he did not. He treated Prince Mohamed as an adult."

"How so?"

"Anyway, you were the main topic of the conversation. The prince wanted to marry you."

"Are you talking about Crown Prince Mohamed? He isn't a day older than twelve."

"That's right. The Shah explained to him patiently that he was too young to marry and you are too old for him."

"What did the prince say?"

"He said he did not care."

"What about the father?"

"It did not faze him. He smiled and reminded the boy of his traditional responsibilities of having several children and maintaining the good name of the family. He also decreed that as soon as Prince Mohamed reached the legal age to marry, the Shah would accept his son's choice of a wife as long the traditional conditions were satisfied."

"What did the boy say?"

"Surprisingly, the prince was very mature about it. He promised to write you and formally ask for your hand in marriage a few years hence."

"At least I won't be an old maid. I have a prince waiting for me," Laura said with a sad smile.

They landed in Istanbul, Bucharest, and Warsaw before the captain put the plane down gently on the lighted, concrete runway of Berlin's Templehof airport. As transcontinental flights were long and tiring, the airlines occasionally gave their passengers a rest and paid for their hotel accommodation. With the outrageous ticket prices, they could afford it easily.

Laura and Alan were installed in a comfortable hotel on the Unter den Linden in the heart of Berlin. After supper, Laura wanted to go to her room and have a rest, but the headwaiter came to the table with a message. An officer of the SA, having the proper credentials, wanted to speak to her about a serious matter.

Suddenly, she tensed, but before she could say anything, Alan remarked, "I would not be surprised if it were about our forced landing near Ulbering. I'd better stay here with you."

"Thank you, Alan," Laura replied and turned to the headwaiter. "Please, invite the gentleman to our table."

"As you wish, ma'am."

"Keep calm and stick to the truth," Alan said and winked at Laura. "You have nothing to fear."

A couple of brown-uniformed officers wearing red armbands with the swastika came to their table and politely introduced themselves.

"I am Major Hart and this is my adjutant, Lieutenant Brankoff," the older of the two said. "We are from state security."

"I am Laura Stanton and this is my radio operator, Mr. Hargrove. Please sit down, gentlemen, and have a drink with us."

"I am afraid this is not exactly a social call, Captain Stanton," the major stated in an official tone and sat down.

"What is it all about, sir?"

"We heard about you making an unscheduled landing in Bavaria and taking off without notifying the authorities," Hart said.

"To start with, Major, it happened to be an emergency landing. Judging from the jerky behavior of the elevator, I thought we had lost a hinge bolt. If that should happen, a dangerous process called unporting could develop. I had no time. I used the trim-tabs and landed on a pasture. I asked Alan to check the elevator. He went to the tail of the plane realizing the hinge bolt was loose, and the elevator stuck. He tightened it, and we took off for Vienna. If you check with the Austrian authorities, I reported the emergency landing. You see, I thought we were already in Austria."

"Unfortunately, you cannot substantiate your story. A witness claims you took a passenger on board."

"That is ridiculous. My crew consisted of two people apart from me, but my flight engineer became ill, and left the plane after another emergency landing at the Szeged air base of the Hungarian air force. If you had checked our manifest, you'd realize he was on board *Lion Two* when we landed in Munich."

"We have no record of him."

"Listen, Major," Alan intervened. "You did not let us open the goddamned doors in Munich to get a whiff of fresh air. You couldn't possibly know how many of us were aboard. I assure you, Fred was with us all the way from Bristol to Hungary. You can check with the Dutch customs and immigration people. In addition, the medical officer of the Royal Hungarian Air Force in Szeged arranged his evacuation."

"We are going to check your claims. However, until we get the results, you are not permitted to leave Germany," declared the major. "In fact, consider yourself under house arrest."

"What is the charge?" Laura asked.

"It is spying. When you landed in Bavaria, you picked up a British agent and flew him out of the country."

"This is ridiculous," replied Alan. "As you are charging us with espionage, we are entitled to legal representation, and you must permit us to contact our embassy."

"Go ahead, you may call anybody you wish, as long as you do not leave the hotel. Please, have a good time in Germany. Heil Hitler," the major said and with the lieutenant in tow, he departed.

"What are we going to do?" Laura asked after the two Germans left.

"We have two alternatives," Alan said calmly. "We can try brazening it, or run."

"You are the expert in the cloak and dagger business, you should decide."

"I'd suggest staying and toughing it out. If we cut and run, it will be an admission of guilt. If the SA caught us, they'd take us to their headquarters and beat everything out of us. In the end, they would shoot us as spies. However, if we sit tight and stick to our story, they cannot do anything without some ironclad proof."

"Okay, let us play it your way."

Alan called the embassy. An official came over to lend moral support, but he could not help them much.

"They did not charge you formally with anything," the consular officer said. "Officially, you are free to go, but if I were in your place, I would not try it. I am sure the SA is watching you."

"What do you suggest?"

"I cannot do anything until they arrest you and take you to one of their interrogation centers."

"Dreary prospects," said Laura.

"I know a few guys in the so-called Gestapo, their state security organization. I am going to ask them to watch out for you, and let me know if they arrest you."

"What good will that do?" Laura asked.

"The consul could intervene before they beat us up too much," Alan said.

"Well, if you wish, I am going to have one of my junior officers stay with you during the day," the consul said, "but that is the best I can do."

"I do not think it is really necessary. I can ask the manager to call you if we leave the hotel," said Laura.

"Regardless, my office will send someone to keep you company most of the time. We do not want you disappearing in the German prison system," the embassy staffer said.

"We appreciate it," Laura said.

The consular officer departed, promising he would call the next day.

Laura tried phoning Hannah, but there was no answer.

Despite working out in the hotel's gym, getting a massage, a hot bath, a good dinner, and several glasses of wine, Laura could not sleep. She was tossing and turning in her bed. Even the customary one-sided conversation with God did not calm her down.

I need someone to hold me, encourage me, and tell me everything will be all right, she thought, realizing that in spite of her flashy airline pilot's qualifications and her skill in flying an aircraft, deep down she was just a frightened, little girl.

She got out of bed, put on a robe, and stepped out onto the corridor. Alan's room was next to hers. Although she knew that a sexual relationship with the radio operator might develop, she went to his door and knocked.

In a few seconds, Alan came.

"Yes," he said sticking his head out.

"May I come in?"

"I am afraid not," replied Alan sheepishly. "I have a lady visitor."

"I am very sorry," said Laura and returned to her room.

At breakfast, Alan apologized: "You see, if I am stressed, I need feminine companionship," he said. "This girl was at the bar, and I had…"

"No need to explain, Alan," Laura interrupted.

"I don't know how long I am going to be free. The situation is getting me down. Normally, I would not worry about putting my life on the line, but if there is a chance of being shot as a spy, it scares the hell out of me," he explained.

"How do you think I feel?"

"Worse, much worse," he replied.

After breakfast, Laura's luck changed. Hannah's phone answered.

She was genuinely happy to hear from Laura.

"I just came back from Austria," Hannah said. "Where are you?"

Laura gave her the name of the hotel. Within half an hour, Hannah came. They sat in the lobby, while Alan kept the embassy official entertained not too far away from the two women.

At first, Laura did not mention the pending espionage charges, but after Hannah invited her to stay with her, she broke down. "I am being charged with espionage."

"That is ridiculous. Tell me more."

Laura outlined the gist of what Major Hart had told her. Hannah listened intently.

"I don't care whether you picked up a passenger or not," Hannah said after hearing the story. "You are my best and possibly only friend. I am going to talk to Uncle Hermann. He is a very powerful man. Hitler calls him Reich Marshall. I am his personal pilot. We talk to each other every day. I am sure he would help you."

As the matter of spying was quickly off the agenda, they talked about the good old days when they both flew for Air Mogadishu.

"That was the only time in my life when I was completely happy. I had a hot-blooded Italian lover, a good friend in you, and I could fly many hours. Those were the days my friend," Hannah said with a deep sigh.

"What's wrong with your current job?"

"I do not fly enough. Uncle Hermann doesn't travel too much. However, he loans his plane to other officials, and I get a few chances to take them to interesting places in Germany, Austria, Italy, and Hungary. Unfortunately, these trips are rare. On the average, I fly perhaps three or four hours a week, sometimes less."

"It is more than nothing," Laura mused.

"How about you?"

"I am a ferry pilot for Bristol Aircraft Corporation. We just took two large planes to Iran."

"I would love to be your copilot."

"We could have had a lot of fun."

"My co-captain, von Werner, is a nice old man. We split the flying right down the middle. That is why I am the captain of Uncle Hermann's plane only half the time I spend aboard."

"How about your private life? Did you find a substitute for your Italian?" Laura asked.

"No, Germans are not very entertaining lovers. However, von Werner got me into a new hobby: flying fast overpowered aircraft," said Hannah.

"How do you like it?"

"It is fun, but I really prefer flying the new four-engine plane, the Condor, which is still on the drawing board."

"How about those fast, small planes?

"They are designed to be fighters, good for aerobatics, but nothing else. I love racing with them, but deep down, I am an airline pilot like you. For us, air racing and aerobatics are just fun and games."

They talked about their jobs and many other things as they had in Mogadishu on Ray's patio. After lunch, Hannah promised to call in the evening and left, but she did not phone.

~ * ~

Next morning, Alan and Laura were nervous.

"I am surprised the SA didn't pick us up yet," Laura said after breakfast.

"Perhaps they expect us to run," mused Alan.

"I don't think Major Hart is clever enough to do that."

"Speak of the devil," said Alan. "Here he is."

Laura turned around and saw the major coming alone.

This must be good news, she thought. *If he wanted to arrest us, he would have had a few goons with him.*

"Captain Stanton," Hart started. "I am now permitted to have a drink with you. You and your radio operator are free to leave."

"Thank you, Major."

"Both the Austrians and the Hungarians confirmed your claims. If you wish, you could stay in Germany for a few days, or take KLM to Amsterdam and London this afternoon."

"I think my nerves are a little frayed. I have no intention of staying in Germany longer than I have to. We'll take the afternoon flight," said Laura.

"I regret your leaving very much," Hart replied. "This is a wonderful country with many things to see."

"Perhaps I'll come back some day," mused Laura, and even though she did not feel like it, shook hands with the major.

After the departure of the brown-shirted officer, Laura called Hannah.

"Hi, Laura," she said. "I believe you are leaving this afternoon. I'll see you at the airport, in the KLM departure lounge," she said and hung up.

Hannah's abrupt breaking of the contact surprised Laura, but she did not say anything to Alan.

In the luxurious departure lounge, Hannah showed up at the last minute, just before the loudspeaker invited the passengers for Amsterdam to board.

The two women hugged, and while they held each other, Hannah whispered into Laura's ear, "Don't visit Germany for a while."

Laura looked her friend in the eye and said, "Thank you very much, Hannah. Whenever you can come to England, my house is your house."

"I know," she said with a sad smile. "Good luck, Laura."

"May God fly with you," she replied, and with tears in her eyes, headed for the gate. The farewell greeting to Hannah surprised her. She had never said anything like it to anyone.

Laura did not dare talk about the events in Germany until they had landed safely in Amsterdam.

"We survived," she said to Alan when they were boarding the bus to a hotel for the night.

"Hart's claim of having a witness bothered me, but I soon realized he was a figment of his imagination. They lost Werth somewhere in Bavaria, and he considered our emergency landing suspicious. That was all he had."

"You mean they did not have a witness?"

"Someone might have seen the plane land and take off, but that's all. Without a couple of witnesses seeing Werth boarding the plane, Hart could not make his charges stick."

After she went to bed, Laura thanked the Lord for getting her out of the tight spot.

~ * ~

Landing in Corydon relaxed Laura's frayed nerves. However, before going to the hotel, she visited Brannigan.

"I heard you became a ferry pilot, Miss Stanton," the Wing Commander said after inviting her into his office. "I assume you are not interested in the instructor's ticket."

"Quite the contrary, sir. As I am going to deliver new aircraft to Bristol's customers, I would like to have the instructor's qualification. This way, I can teach the buyer's pilots to fly their new planes."

"It's an interesting idea. When are you going to take your first aerobatics exercise?"

"I am in no hurry to go home," Laura replied. "Whenever you can find an instructor to take me up, please call."

"Say no more. I am free in the afternoon and tomorrow morning."

"Wonderful. How many hours do you think I need to practice?"

"I'll tell you after we take the first flight. Let us meet here at three in the afternoon."

Laura checked in to the Corydon Hotel, had lunch, put on a flight suit, and took a taxi to the flying club.

"Now we'll see what you are made of," said the Wing Commander when they boarded the little trainer.

The loops, the rolls, and the spins were interesting, but they bored Laura. She learned to execute them, but her heart was not in it.

"You'll need a couple of hours of practice, and you could perhaps pass the test," Brannigan said after they landed.

"I would like to practice a little tomorrow morning," Laura replied.

"How about the test?"

"As I just came back from Iran, I would like to go home, have a rest, come to Corydon next week and practice a few hours before tackling the test."

"As you wish," shrugged the Wing Commander. "I noticed you did not enjoy aerobatics. Why?"

"I do not see the point of it. Why have a plane turning and twisting and doing wild flips like a trout on the line?"

"Those twists and flips won us the air war over France. A good fighter pilot must be good at aerobatics. It is the pinnacle of flying."

"Well, sir, you may be right, but as a woman I would never get near a fighter aircraft. Fortunately, that is not the style of flying I am interested in. You see, aerobatics seems to me a form of art, and I have no artistic talents whatsoever. I am rather the scientific type. I'd like to fly an aircraft the size of Imperial's Hanno on instruments across the oceans and continents. That is science and my kind of flying."

"You are strange, Laura," said the Wing Commander. "I appreciate your point of view. I will make the aircraft available for you tomorrow morning."

"Thank you, sir."

As soon as she returned to the hotel, Laura immediately sent a telegram to Granny about the time of her arrival.

Spending a lazy afternoon in her hotel room was pleasant. The stress gone, she did not have to worry about the brown-uniformed SA officer or the British agent they had picked up in Germany. Laura relaxed. For a moment, she considered calling Paul, but discarded the idea.

"I am beginning to come out of my depression. I do not need to be drugged, even though I thirst for a man. He should not be anybody like Paul. I'd rather have Robert or Ray."

The ring of the telephone interrupted her relaxation.

"This is Laura Stanton," she said.

"Ray Madison speaking. I just spoke to Granny on the phone."

"A week ago she did not have a telephone."

"She got it the day before yesterday. I was the first one she called. She said you were arriving in Folkestone day after tomorrow in the afternoon."

"I am glad to hear your voice, Ray. I missed you. How did you know where to find me?"

"Chad Brannigan called to tell me about your aerobatics lesson. He mentioned that you were staying in the Corydon Hotel. How was the flight to Iran?"

"It was very interesting. I'll tell you all about it when we meet. Where are you?"

"I am at Farnborough, but I am leaving for the south tomorrow."

"What are you doing there?"

"Testing the latest fighters. I love them. You should try doing aerobatics with the new Hurricanes. They are superb and very fast. It is a joy to fly them."

"How is your heart?"

"Still ticking, touch wood."

"When am I going to see you again?"

"I'll visit Granny day after tomorrow. I'll be there before you."

"Great! You might give me some pointers on aerobatics. As you know, I took my first serious lesson today and I am going up tomorrow to practice," said Laura.

"You don't sound very enthusiastic about it."

"I am not. I think it is boring, and it is torturing the aircraft. I do not like causing pain. Anyway, I'd rather fly something big."

"*Vive la difference*," said Ray. "Thank God for pilots like you wanting to fly those monsters with wings. I prefer the little hotrods."

"It is understandable. You were always a fighter pilot at heart," Laura interrupted.

"We'll discuss it day after tomorrow."

"Very well. I'll ask Granny to have a nice tender roast with Yorkshire pudding ready for you."

"Thanks, Laura. See you soon."

"I am going to phone Granny presently."

"Do that. She will be thrilled."

After Ray hung up, Laura immediately asked the telephone operator to ring Stanton Manor.

Granny was happy to hear from Laura. They talked for twenty minutes. She promised to lay on the roast for Ray.

"He is going to bring someone else with him. I bet it is Mrs. Thorpe. I think they are involved."

"It is none of our business."

"I agree, but somehow I would like to see you involved with someone."

"I am not yet ready, Granny," she replied. The thought of Bob still hurt, and she did not want to talk about the subject.

~ * ~

The aerobatics exercises were okay. Laura managed to do all the required maneuvers, but she did not have her heart in it.

"It is flying, but not the type I want to do," she said to herself while boarding the train to Folkestone.

As the train pulled in, she did not see James. However, she saw several civilians and men in R.A.F. uniform.

Standing at the platform, Laura spotted two men walking toward her. It was Bob wearing his R.A.F. uniform, and Ray in flannels and a blazer displaying the Hawker Siddley emblem.

They both smiled and waved.

Fear overtook Laura. She stopped, put down her bag, and felt the taste of brass in her mouth, the sure sign of a panic attack. However, as an airline pilot she defeated the fear within a fraction of a second.

"This is it, old girl, the moment of truth. Whether you like it or not, you must choose between these guys," she said to herself.

With a deep sigh, Laura picked up her suitcase and walked toward the men. Even though her mind shifted to overdrive, the decision seemed to escape her. About five paces from the two men, the solution flashed through her mind. *I am going to keep them both.*

Meet Gabriel Timar

Born in Hungary in 1932, a cadet at the elite military school of Nagykaroly during World War II, Gabriel Timar studied civil engineering at Budapest University. Taking active part in the 1956 revolution, he decided to defect to the West.

In the United Kingdom he worked as a structural designer. Ten months later he immigrated to Canada and worked as an engineer. After seven years, he got his first contract in Asia.

For the next twenty-odd years he worked in Africa, Asia and the South Pacific as a consulting engineer, chief executive officer, United Nations environmental engineering advisor and finally as a professor. In 1982 he married, returned to Canada with his Hungarian wife and taught environmental engineering at Seneca College in Toronto. In 1994 he retired as the Chair of the School of Civil and Resources Engineering Technology. Following his retirement he began writing. To date, he has published sixteen novels in English and Hungarian, ten English language novels to his credit as shown on the home page. He also wrote several manuals and college textbooks published by the Province of Ontario, Seneca College, United Nations and the University of Malawi.

Works From The Pen Of Gabriel Timar

Aura of War - The story of Arthur DeVendt, born in 1927, proves that even though war, political and economic turmoil. adversely impacted his future, by maintaining his honor, dogged persistence, and ability to adjust to changing conditions he manages to succeed. Seventeen-year-old Arthur, the son of a Hungarian army officer of French extraction, finds himself orphaned in a refugee camp of postwar Germany.

Lucifer's Project - George Pike, a lawyer dies. His soul, delivered to the Third Dimension, decides to work for Hades Inc. Getting a new body, he is given an assignment to go back to the First Dimension and promote the interests of Hades by preventing Armageddon.

Addiction - Starting in the early nineteen thirties, accompany Max in the cockpit while he flies the mail through the storms over the Carpathians. His love for life, adventure, and his burning desire to fly see him through the antiaircraft fire, or the encounters with enemy fighters in the Second World War.

My Jungle - The world is a jungle! To find happiness one must find his/her own patch. Gabriel's adventurous life (actually, a fictionalized autobiography) is the search for a culture which would accept him.

As he travels five continents, his accounts reflect the true picture of society in the late twentieth century. The presentation of the world girdling corruption, violence, oppression, and prejudice are featured in the story.

The Khartoum Project - The Khartoum project takes the reader for a ride in the netherworld of the intelligence community. On this highway to hell, one must win or die...No matter how brave, ruthless, and inventive. Monica Brett is on the mission to Khartoum as it pushes to the limit and beyond.

The Falcon Project - This is a hard science fiction exposé of corporate ruthlessness. Lives and the truth are acceptable losses on the altar of performance and political expediency. Aficionados of science fiction will find this novel intriguing. In particular, those of you who thrive on the intricacies of engineering solutions to tricky unearthly problems will have a field day.

Air Mogadishu - Set in the nineteen thirties over the hot, arid desert of the Horn of Africa, Air Mogadishu depicts the saga of an Englishwoman, an ailing airline, an aging war hero, and a dashing RAF officer. She struggles to succeed in a man's profession, while trying to choose between two men.

Lions, Kisses and Petrodollars - A lighthearted, romantic adventure. The tumultuous love affair of Geoff and Michelle in the late 1960s and a questionable real estate transaction in Canada are the backdrops to an accurate, though irreverent, humorous, and politically incorrect still photograph of the post-independence Africa.

Stop the War - Environmental catastrophe threatens the survival of Earth. It's too far gone! Technology won't help. Perhaps time travel is the solution.

Letter to Our Readers

Enjoy this book?

You can make a difference.

As an independent publisher, Wings ePress, Inc. does not have the financial clout of the large New York publishers. We can't afford large magazine spreads or subway posters to tell people about our quality books.

But we do have something much more effective and powerful than ads. We have a large base of loyal readers.

Honest reviews help bring the attention of new readers to our books.

If you enjoyed this book, we would appreciate it if you would spend a few minutes posting a review on the site where you purchased this book or on the Wings ePress, Inc. webpages at: https://wingsepress. com/

Thank You

Visit Our Website

For The Full Inventory
Of Quality Books:

Wings ePress, Inc

Quality trade paperbacks and downloads
in multiple formats,
in genres ranging from light romantic comedy
to general fiction and horror.
Wings has something for every reader's taste.
Visit the website, then bookmark it.
We add new titles each month!

Wings ePress Inc.
3000 N. Rock Road
Newton, KS 67114